the redgum river retreat

ALSO BY SANDIE DOCKER

The Kookaburra Creek Café
The Cottage at Rosella Cove
The Banksia Bay Beach Shack
The Wattle Island Book Club

sandie docker

the redgum river retreat

MICHAEL JOSEPH
an imprint of
PENGUIN BOOKS

MICHAEL JOSEPH

UK | USA | Canada | Ireland | Australia
India | New Zealand | South Africa | China

Michael Joseph is part of the Penguin Random House group of companies whose addresses can be found at global.penguinrandomhouse.com

First published by Michael Joseph in 2023

Cover illustrations courtesy of Shutterstock
Cover design by Laura Thomas © Penguin Random House Australia Pty Ltd
Internal design by Midland Typesetters, Australia
Typeset in 11/17.5 Sabon by Midland Typesetters, Australia

Printed and bound in Australia by Griffin Press, an accredited
ISO AS/NZS 14001 Environmental Management Systems printer

A catalogue record for this book is available from the National Library of Australia

ISBN 978 1 76104 601 8

penguin.com.au

We at Penguin Random House Australia acknowledge that Aboriginal and Torres Strait Islander peoples are the Traditional Custodians and the first storytellers of the lands on which we live and work. We honour Aboriginal and Torres Strait Islander peoples' continuous connection to Country, waters, skies and communities. We celebrate Aboriginal and Torres Strait Islander stories, traditions and living cultures; and we pay our respects to Elders past and present.

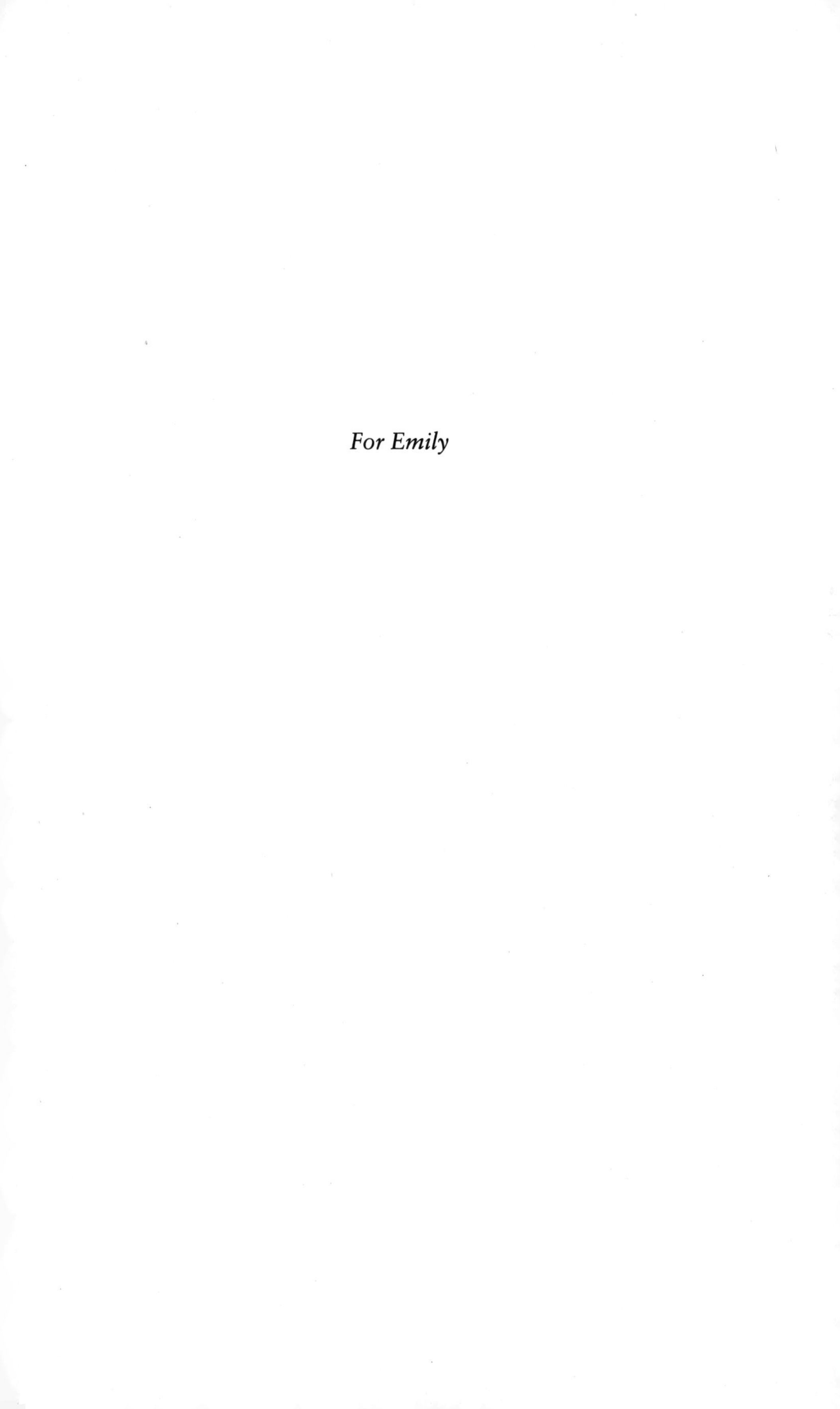

For Emily

Prologue

March 2017

Sarah stood and took a bow, allowing the swelling sound of rhythmic clapping from the audience to wash over her. Goosebumps pricked her skin as shouts of 'Encore!' filled the concert hall of the Sydney Opera House. She'd dreamed of this moment since she'd first touched her father's cello when she was five years old, and drawn his bow across the strings, coaxing a deep, melancholy groan out of the dark wooden beast that stood taller than she did.

'You are a prodigy, my little minim,' her father, Pierre, had said, and she'd blushed, even though she hadn't known at the time what a prodigy was. He was wrong, of course, she wasn't a prodigy at all; the sound she'd coaxed out of the cello that first try was more of a fluke than anything else. But the thrill that had washed over her that day had set her on a melodic path that had led to this moment, twenty-five years later, playing on arguably the biggest stage in Australia as the most recent addition to the acclaimed Five Bows Quintet.

The members of the string ensemble bowed once more then retook their seats and raised their bows, poised ready to play their arrangement of 'Bohemian Rhapsody'. Tabitha, the first violin, drew in a breath and lifted her shoulders to signal the upbeat as the other members of the ensemble followed her lead. The vibrant notes of the piece danced on the expectant air, building to a crescendo that filled the great space around them.

Waiting backstage after the concert, Sarah's family greeted her with broad grins. Granny Rose, dressed in a black sequined dress that clearly took inspiration from the 1920s, clapped and gave her granddaughter an approving nod. Sarah's cousin, Ryan, hugged her, handing her a bouquet of red roses, before her daughter launched herself into Sarah's arms.

'Mama, you were so totally, completely, *ah-ma-zing*,' Melody shouted in Sarah's ear, squashing the bouquet between them in a tight hug. 'Oops.' She looked down at the mashed flowers. 'Sorry.' The six-year-old's face fell.

'That's okay, my little minim. We can put the petals in the floating candle bowl on the dining table. They will look so pretty there.'

Melody's smile returned. 'Good plan, Mama.'

'She's right. You were amazing,' Ryan said, his blue eyes a pool of warmth and caring.

'Really?' Sarah knew she was a competent musician; indeed, if she could believe the critics of the Five Bows, she was 'a fresh, exciting addition to the ensemble, playing with a depth and soul rarely seen'. But her mum, Lynne, also a talented musician, had taught her long ago not to pay much heed to critics. 'They will love you one moment, tear you down the next, though nothing you've done will have changed. And you'll be forever chasing the accolades,' she'd often said, a far-off look in her eye. From a very young age Sarah understood how her mother had given up thoughts of a career in music having realised that Pierre's relentless pursuit of his own was to the detriment of the family unit. A professional musician all his adult life, Pierre had seen the highs and lows from every angle and was away more often than home. Despite this, Sarah worshipped him and, desperate to follow in his footsteps, rode every crest and fall with him, from close up and afar. She was ten when her mother died, and after that she sought her father's approval even more, hoping he would notice her talent and stay at home with her more. But he hadn't, and it left her scarred with doubt about her ability.

So now here she was, having just played in front of a sell-out Opera House crowd to a standing ovation and encore, yet still thinking she didn't belong.

'Of course. Did you hear that applause?' Ryan, her biggest fan, kissed her on her forehead. 'You were brilliant.'

'Mama is the best cellist in the whole wide world. And the best mama.' Okay, maybe Ryan was her second-biggest fan.

'*Brava*, my darling.' Granny Rose smiled. 'I'm very proud of you.'

Sarah swallowed. This was high praise coming from her grandmother.

'Come back to our place to celebrate.'

Melody wriggled out of Sarah's arms and twirled so her white chiffon and silk skirt swirled and rustled, the tiny rainbow butterflies dotted all over it dancing with the movement. 'We can have a par-tee,' she sang.

'I should probably get Granny Rose home.' Ryan ruffled Melody's tight black curls.

'Oh fiddlesticks.' Granny Rose shook her head. 'A party is most definitely called for and I haven't been to a good one in far too long.'

Ryan smiled. 'Meet you back at ours, then?'

'We'll be right behind you.' Sarah nodded.

Sarah and Melody made their way towards the car park, humming random movements from the evening's repertoire of classic and modern pieces. Melody had inherited Sarah's ear and was showing great promise, often not needing to rely on sheet music when she was playing the piano or cello.

They jumped into the car and joined the queue of vehicles trying to leave the car park. Melody sat in the back, Sarah's cello, in its hard white case, propped up next to her, wedged behind the passenger seat. With Sarah's bow in her hand, Melody slid it across imaginary strings, mimicking Sarah's technique perfectly. She often sat opposite Sarah when her mother practised and always watched intently. Her own lessons were going well, exceptionally well, and Sarah was convinced her daughter had more natural talent than she and Pierre combined. And she was fairly certain her assessment wasn't skewed by maternal bias.

'Will Grandpa Pierre come to the next concert, Mama?' Melody asked, her arms moving slowly.

Sarah sighed. Her dad was supposed to be there tonight – the European leg of his latest tour was over – but his flight from Paris had been delayed. He would arrive in the morning and catch tomorrow's performance instead.

'Yes, my little minim.' Sarah gave her a half-smile. Her whole life had been a parade of missed moments when it came to her father – he was always travelling, always performing, and now lived on the other side of the world.

Eventually they spilled out of the congestion of cars leaving Circular Quay, and streetlights flashed past them as they left the city, the bridge behind them as they headed into the suburbs.

In the back seat, Melody was approaching the crescendo of her rendition of 'Bohemian Rhapsody', belting out the words 'bubblegum has a devil for a son, that's me'. Despite the mondegreen – it always made Sarah laugh when Melody mis-sang that line – her voice was angelic.

'A little quieter, please, Melody. Mama can't concentrate if you sing that loudly.'

Melody lowered her voice. Slightly. But she moved the bow back and forth with increasing vigour.

'Be careful with Mama's bow, minim.' Sarah took her eyes off the road for a moment. It was an expensive bow, and usually she wouldn't let Melody touch it. Especially at home, where Melody often ran around the house with her own, much cheaper, beginner's bow, pretending she was conducting an orchestra made up of dining chairs and teddy bears and the clotheshorse. Sarah had lost count of the number of training bows Melody had broken.

But tonight, filled with the warm glow of the evening's success, Sarah couldn't bear to tell her off and make her put the bow down. Melody's voice rose again. 'Got a moose, got a moose, will you do the fan dance-o.' Perhaps she might be a singer one day, Sarah thought.

Melody launched into the thunderbolts and lightning.

'*Pianissimo*,' Sarah whispered, but Melody simply grinned and sang even louder.

As Sarah turned her head to look at her daughter, a flash flew past the corner of her eye. She looked up into the rear-view mirror, her hands turning the wheel ever so slightly.

A clatter. A crack.

A scream. Melody unclipped her seatbelt and clambered along the back seat.

'Sorry!' she cried out, picking up the broken bow.

'What did you do? Get back into your seat!' Sarah yelled louder than she'd meant to.

'I'm sorry, Mama.' Melody started to cry. 'I didn't mean to.' Her cries became wails.

'Hush, now. It's okay.' Sarah righted her steering, her eyes darting from the road to the mirror.

'I'm sorry, Mama.' Melody sobbed and the despair in her voice made Sarah turn around again.

'It's okay . . .'

'Mama!' Melody screamed and pointed. 'Truck.'

Sarah snapped around but it was too late. The truck had clipped them and they spun, the car flipping onto its roof, Melody sailing across the back seat, Sarah lurching forward, stretching out her arm to catch her baby girl.

'No!' Sarah screamed, the crunch, shatter, screech filling her ears before the world went dark.

One

February 2018

Sarah sat at the back of the room in the soft suede armchair that was far too familiar to her. She wanted to punch the lime-green cushion that pushed into her back, punch it until it burst, spilling its stuffing out into the overly cheerful room, but she simply adjusted her weight in the hot-pink chair as she watched Melody's session go nowhere.

With pastel chalk, Melody drew a family of animals on the far wall, which was painted with blackboard paint. Always animals. Just like at home. Beside her, Judy, the therapist, sat on the same orange stool she always sat on, the one that looked like a mushroom, and spoke quietly as Melody continued to draw.

'That's a lovely elephant. Can you tell me what she's been up to?'

Melody drew a balloon.

'A party?'

Melody smiled.

'Now, Melody, I'm going to close my eyes and I wonder if you can describe the party for me?'

Sarah pushed down the sticky black guilt that always rippled just below the surface and picked at the multi-coloured foam puzzle flooring with the toe of her shoe. Eight months now. The same thing. Sarah knew routine and repetition were important when dealing with children in a developmental setting, but surely if a method wasn't working, it was time to try something different. Anything. Eight months with Judy since they left the hospital, and still no progress. Eleven months since the moment Sarah allowed distraction in and shattered Melody's life. Her own life.

She closed her eyes and the flashing lights, the wailing sirens forced their way into her mind. Not that the images and sounds were ever far from her consciousness. Melody's cries for help, the last words her daughter had spoken. The blood pouring down Sarah's face, soaking her shirt. Pinned beneath the steering wheel, she couldn't reach her daughter, couldn't comfort her, couldn't save her.

Eleven months of hoping for improvement, change. Eleven months of futile hope.

When she'd asked Judy for her assessment after the last session, Sarah was met with a sympathetic look and a condescending reminder to be patient. And when she'd asked her GP about changing Melody's therapists, she'd been told Judy was the best in the business. Perhaps that was true. But being the best didn't necessarily mean she was the best fit for Melody, did it?

Sarah's therapists hadn't been a good fit. Not the first, or the second, or the third. They'd kept wanting her to put into words her pain, her guilt. But how could anyone find words for what she'd done to her baby girl?

Sarah desperately wanted to find another way forward, but what if Judy was only one or two sessions away from a breakthrough? What if all this time she'd been building trust and a connection that would mean any week now they'd turn a corner?

If Sarah changed therapists, would they miss that breakthrough and be right back at the beginning, starting from scratch?

All she wanted was what was best for Melody. Trouble was, she didn't trust herself to know what that looked like anymore. It had been easier in the hospital, although it certainly hadn't felt like it at the time.

In the fog that had surrounded her the first few days in ICU, the pain of her throbbing head wound and the lack of mobility and feeling in her hand had felt like weights too heavy to bear. Then, as the daze lifted and the extent of Melody's injuries sank in, Sarah had descended into a deeper low.

Melody's T12 was fractured and she would never walk again. Melody had endured three months of physical therapy and, while it hadn't been the progress Sarah had hoped for, at least they had something to show for the arduous sessions. Melody had learned to use her arms again and to use the wheelchair so she didn't need as much help now getting around. Every week of that three months in the hospital was hard, but, throughout, there had been tiny markers of improvement. When Melody had fed herself for the first time once the swelling on her spine had gone down; when she'd been able to get into her wheelchair without assistance.

This psychological therapy, though . . . Sarah let out a silent sigh. She'd poured all her energy into this therapy for Melody, forgoing her own therapy and physio, knowing she'd never play her cello again, and it was going nowhere.

Melody continued to draw in silence, Judy with her eyes closed.

In the far corner of the room was a bookshelf of puzzles and toys and books. In about twenty minutes, Judy would pull out Connect Four and challenge Melody to take her on. Melody would agree and would roll her eyes when Judy let her win.

When Melody grew tired of scrawling chalk on the wall, she wheeled over to the books and thumbed through the pages of whatever title was sitting on top of the low round coffee table.

'Would you like to read that one to me today?' Judy asked.

Melody shrugged and put the book down. Like always.

'Why don't we try something different?'

Sarah nearly fell out of the chair at Judy's words. She sat forwards, watching, waiting, holding her breath, running her finger over the scar that ran along the edge of her face.

From a small plastic tub, Judy pulled three containers of Play-Doh and placed them on the table. 'I was thinking we could maybe make something with these.'

Melody put her hands on her hips, lifted her chin and opened her eyes wide. *Like what?*

'Why don't we make some instruments? For the toys.' She placed a stuffed rabbit and turtle on the table. 'What do you think they would like to play?'

Melody put her index finger to her chin, her thinking pose. Then she smiled. *Got it.* But she looked over at Sarah and frowned. Neither of them had touched an instrument since the accident.

'Sarah, there's fresh coffee out in the kitchen, if you'd like get some.'

Sarah had never been dismissed from a session before.

'She'll be fine,' Judy reassured her.

Standing slowly, Sarah looked at Melody, who refused to lift her eyes from the Play-Doh in her hand.

'I'll be back in a minute.' Sarah mustered as much nonchalance as she could.

Out in the hallway, she paced back and forth, no interest at all in whether there was any coffee in the kitchen or not. She could hear Judy talking – something about it not being important if it was exact – but there was no other sound.

Passing minutes felt like forever, and eventually Sarah gave up trying to hear what was unfolding in the therapy room and headed into the kitchen, not that she felt like drinking anything. She sat on the white plastic chair and leafed through a *House & Garden* magazine on the small table, not taking in any of the pictures or words. She flexed her left hand: the stiffness she still had from the accident was always worse when she was tired. She really ought to book another physio appointment. But when was there time?

A *thwack* broke the deafening silence and she jumped up and strode back towards the therapy room. Her shoulders dropped when she re-entered to see Melody pouting with her arms folded across her chest.

On the table, the rabbit looked like she was playing a . . . possibly a flute, though it looked more like a stick. The turtle sat with a gloop of clay in front of him that looked like it had been thoroughly thumped.

At the end of yet another seemingly fruitless session, Sarah walked beside Melody as they made their way out of the office. Right on time, Ryan was there to pick them up and Melody wheeled straight over to him.

'Ms Blakely?' Judy called after Sarah.

'Yes.' She turned around.

'I know it may not seem like it, but that was progress today.'

'Really?'

'The flute was mine, which you may have guessed given its rudimentary form . . .'

'And the sound I heard?'

'Melody was trying, I believe, to make a piano. She was determined to replicate it so perfectly that she got a little frustrated when it didn't quite work out.' Judy shrugged.

'And how is this good?'

'Because she was trying. She may not be ready to talk just yet, but she is expressing herself, and that isn't a small thing. Your daughter's trauma is deep and complicated, and the fact she tried to make a piano today is a big step forward. We just need to have . . .'

'Patience.' Sarah nodded. She was so worn out by the last eleven months, so scared for her daughter's future. And just about out of patience. But perhaps this was it. The breakthrough she was desperate for, within reach. Perhaps in the next session it would come.

A thought she'd had far too many times these last few months.

In the van, Ryan peppered Melody with questions, and she answered with nods and shakes and facial expressions. And one tongue poked out with happy squinty eyes. When they pulled up to the grand old house in Wahroonga, Sarah let herself out, flexing her hand by her side so Melody wouldn't see.

Ryan helped Melody and her wheelchair out of the back of the van and Melody raced forward to Granny Rose's guesthouse.

Living in the guesthouse was an interim measure until Sarah got her life back on track. After the accident, she'd sold her tiny apartment in Milsons Point, which was not at all wheelchair friendly, and moved in here. Granny Rose had offered rooms in the main house, but Sarah didn't want to be in the way. Besides, there were far too many stairs in the grand old place. No. The guesthouse would do for now, until the tune of Sarah's life was less dissonant.

She drew in a deep breath, drinking in the lavender that bordered the paved path to her temporary accommodation.

'I take it today didn't go well?' Ryan asked.

Sarah shrugged. 'I don't know. And that's the thing. Judy seems to think she's making progress, but I don't see it. Do you?'

He raised his hands in the air. 'I'm no psychologist. Isn't this where we're supposed to trust the experts?'

He was right. Trust the experts. Her mind knew that. But her gut wasn't so sure.

'A dog, Sar-bear. I keep telling you, you should get her a dog,' Ryan said, wrapping a strong arm around her shoulder.

'I think I've got enough on my plate as it is, thank you very much, without having to worry about picking up poo.'

'You will get through this. Eventually. Sometimes we just have to surrender to the universe and trust it will find a way to help us heal.'

'Is that what you tell your clients when a build isn't going well?' She lay her head on his shoulder. 'Trust in the universe.'

'Hell, no. I tell them I know exactly what I'm doing, that it's all under control and that's why they pay me the big bucks.' He forced a laugh.

'Tell me,' Sarah said. 'Are the big bucks worth the stress?'

Ryan's smile fell, just for a moment. Only ever for a moment. 'Don't you worry about *my* stress. I'll be fine.'

She'd never believed him less. He'd been miserable at work for so long now and Sarah suspected it was even worse than he was letting on. But, bless him, he wouldn't confide in her. He was protecting her from his worries.

'So, about that dog . . .' he changed the subject.

'You're incorrigible.'

'But you love me anyway.'

She did. And she had no idea where she'd be without him this past year.

'Hang in there, Sar-bear.' He kissed the top of her head and headed towards the main house.

Hang in there.

She could do that.

If she could only figure out what it was she could hang on to.

*

The following day, Sarah made her way to the Forgotten Pasts Museum, tucked away in an old terrace house down in The Rocks between a vegan café and an Indigenous art studio. Quitting the Five Bows after the accident had been the right decision – the only decision given her physical limitations – but at Ryan's urging she'd taken a job with an ex-client of his.

'It will do you good to have something other than Melody to focus on,' he'd said.

She'd never admit it out loud, but working at the museum had indeed been a welcome distraction.

She settled herself in for the day, and worked out what needed to be done. She decided her first task was to rearrange the vintage suitcase display, making sure each piece of the 'Travel Through the Ages' exhibit was in exactly the right spot. Herman would be checking in in just a few minutes and, while he was always polite and professional, the museum's curator had very specific ideas about how each new exhibit should be set up. Sarah didn't blame him. The museum was Herman's realisation of a life-long vision to bring to life those stories often overlooked by the bigger, more traditional museums.

The clip-clop of Herman's lopsided gait echoed along the wooden floorboards of the hall and Sarah moved the gentleman's leather top-hat box a quarter of an inch to the left and stepped away from the display. She ran her hand along the red scar that trailed down the left edge of her face and neck and down onto her shoulder – an unwelcome reminder that stood out against her tanned skin. Her pain had mostly subsided over the year, leaving just a slight tinge in her right hip when the weather was cold. And her hand. Not that it was painful. It just didn't function like it used to. Like she needed it to.

'Well, well, Ms Blakely.' Herman limped up beside her and stopped, adjusting his monocle with a weathered hand. He stroked his grey handlebar moustache and gave a slight nod.

Sarah was relieved. A moustache stroke was high praise indeed.

'Coffee, Ms Blakely?' He headed towards the small back room they used as their staff room.

Sarah followed behind along the narrow hallway that ran down the middle of the building. On each side were two rooms – spacious considering the age of the terrace house – that had been stripped right back to the original hardwood floors and white-panelled walls to form the four mini halls of the museum. Every month they changed one room's exhibit, to ensure there was always something new for repeat patrons.

'Sit.' Herman took off his maroon blazer and hung it over one of two chairs in the cramped room, stuffed full of files and boxes. A small Formica table was pushed up against the side wall, sitting below a shelf bowing under the weight of dusty books and archive boxes. Under the window on the back wall was a tiny sink, an old microwave and a cupboard where they kept the coffee and biscuits.

Sarah manoeuvred her orange vinyl and metal 1960s chair carefully so it didn't bump the table and knock over the stack of files balancing precariously on one corner. That pile had been there since Sarah had started working for Herman and she was fairly certain it hadn't increased or decreased in size since her first day on the job.

Herman handed her a coffee – he made a mean expresso using the only modern appliance in the staff room.

'You did a great job of our new display, Ms Blakely. I just hope it's enough to bring in the punters.' His shoulders slumped ever so slightly.

'Well, it's a wonderful theme, and we've had some good coverage in the press.'

He nodded. 'Yes. Thank you for that.' He drew a slow sip from his coffee cup and pulled on the right side of his moustache.

'Is everything okay, Herman?' Sarah asked, his tell-tale sign giving him away.

Folding his hands in front of him on the table, he looked Sarah in the eyes. His faded blue gaze held none of the spark she was used to seeing.

'I'll be honest with you.' His fingers drummed out a beat. 'We're in trouble.'

'I take it the lead you were chasing down last week didn't pay off?' She shifted in her seat.

'The problem is, these days anyone with a collection or artefact worthy of display in a museum wants to see their precious belongings in the hands of one of the bigger players. I blame social media, Ms Blakely.'

He usually did.

'Everyone these days thinks they are a star. People with the least significant treasures want to be treated like they're bloomin' Lara Croft.' He shook his head. 'They have a false sense of importance and they don't want to deal with small players like us. Influencers and brand ambassadors, my hiney.'

'But the bigger museums won't take the sorts of collections we love here.'

'I told a recent Mr Too-Big-for-His-Britches exactly that, but he seems to think the Australian Museum or the Powerhouse are going to knock on his door any day now and beg him for his collection of tiny figurines. Over-inflated numbskull, he was.'

Sarah choked on the sip of coffee she'd just taken. 'Surely it isn't that bad? I know numbers are down, but . . .'

Herman raised his hand. 'I've been keeping this place afloat for so long now with my personal savings.' He stood and stared out the small window. 'I don't know how long I can keep it up. What we need, Ms Blakely, is a scoop of a collection. Something unique.' He tapped his chin.

'We'll think of something, Herman.'

'I hope so,' he said. 'Right. Back to work.' He looked at her and smiled. 'A new day brings new hope.'

Yet his smile didn't reach his eyes.

'Hey, Sar-bear.' Ryan stood at the doorway to the small guesthouse tucked away at the back of the large yard when she arrived home.

'Oh no. How bad?' Sarah's shoulders dropped.

'Can't I just greet my favourite cousin at the door because I'm happy to see you?' He smiled.

'I'm your only cousin and not usually.' She punched him playfully on the shoulder.

'Ouch.' He rubbed his arm, the dimples in his cheeks deepening as he pursed his lips together.

Cousins through her father, Pierre, Ryan was more like a brother to Sarah. They'd spent much of their childhood together, neither with a sibling. And when Ryan's parents had disowned him just after his eighteenth birthday – the day he came out to them – Granny Rose took him in and he became the grandson Rosalie had never had. After Melody was born, the bond between Sarah and he had grown even stronger. Melody's father had taken off when Sarah fell pregnant, and often Ryan had stepped into that void to be there for Melody and Sarah. He was there for Melody's birth, waving her off with Sarah on her first day of school, and there every day when they were in hospital and since.

'What happened?' Sarah asked Ryan now. Though she wasn't sure she wanted to know the answer.

He kept his voice low. 'We read and did craft and had mini frankfurts for lunch . . .'

'And?'

He put his arm around Sarah as they stepped inside. 'And then we watched *The Saddle Club*. And there was a car accident in the episode.'

Sarah pushed her cousin out of the way, but he caught her arm. 'Wait, Sar-bear. She's fine. She had a wobbly moment, but she's okay.'

'A wobbly moment?'

'She kind of froze. Just for a second. Then she was fine. Really. I just wanted to tell you, in case you have trouble tonight.'

Sarah wasn't the only one who had nightmares.

'Thank you.' She rushed into the loungeroom and found Melody colouring in. 'Hey, minim.'

Melody looked up and smiled as Sarah wrapped her arms around her neck and smoothed back the dark brown ringlets that fell around her daughter's face. 'What did you two get up to today?'

Wheeling over to the coffee table, Melody picked up the pictures of walruses they'd painted with paper plates and drinking straws.

'Aren't these fabulous?' Sarah blew out a whistle, and Melody sat taller. 'What else did you do?'

Melody showed her the castle made of paper cups, her Barbie doll wrapped in a pink serviette.

'Is that her princess cape?' Sarah asked. Melody's princesses always wore capes.

Melody nodded. With nimble manoeuvring of her wheelchair, Melody raced into the kitchen and returned with a Polaroid Ryan had taken of the two of them eating frankfurts. Well, eating was a stretch. Ryan had two long frankfurts stuffed into his upper lip, hanging out like tusks. Sarah shot him a look and he winked.

Melody picked up the painting of the walrus and held it up next to the photo.

Sarah smiled. 'Well, I'd say that is a pretty accurate likeness. In fact, this one,' she pointed to the purple painted walrus, 'is actually more handsome.'

Melody's shoulders shook. A silent giggle.

'I'll leave you to it.' Ryan squeezed Melody tightly, tickling the back of her neck, and she batted his hands away, her shoulders shaking with soundless giggles. She poked her tongue out at him when he stepped away. He returned in kind. 'See ya.' He kissed Sarah on the forehead. 'The Denner-Little blueprints await,' he groaned.

She walked him to the door. 'Thank you. Again.' Ryan was a godsend helping her out on the Sundays she had to work. Especially when his own work was so consuming.

'Any time.' He jumped from the small veranda to the ground, skipping the ramp altogether.

Watching him leave, Sarah closed the door, shutting her eyes to brace herself for the night ahead. Granny Rose and Ryan were, technically, only a few steps away in the main house but at night it was as if an ocean was between them; Sarah alone, adrift.

As evening darkened, Sarah stood at the kitchen bench chopping up onions, the *clop-clop-clop* of the knife against the wooden board resonating around her. From behind her, the whirring of Melody's wheels broke the staccato rhythm.

'Hey, minim. Dinner's nearly ready.'

Melody positioned her chair by the dining table, and raised her eyebrow.

'Yes, psketti Sunday, like always,' Sarah answered the unasked question.

Melody smiled.

Sarah served up dinner, giving Melody extra shavings of parmesan until she raised her tiny scarred hand telling Sarah to stop.

'So, did you have a good day with Ryan?'

A nod and the right side of her mouth turned slightly up.

Sarah imagined the cascade of tiny little details spilling from Melody's mouth like they used to do. Each thought spoken as it came to her, often unconnected to the last, colour and movement filling the room like a symphony.

We sure did, Ryan didn't know how to make purple so I showed him how, with the blue and the pink, the pink was just like the insides of the frankfurts we ate for lunch, I found the straws in the back of the cupboard, did you know that walruses eat clams? Ryan told me that, paper plates get soggy if you paint them, I can't wait to go to school tomorrow, did you know Tommy Small has lost his front teeth too . . .

But the room echoed with silence and Sarah berated herself. She knew to use open questions, not yes-no questions, to try to encourage Melody to communicate with words, not just a nod or shake of her head.

'How long did you spend painting those very gorgeous walruses?'

Melody raised her hand, holding up three fingers.

'Three days?' She pulled a funny face, hoping the ridiculous might do the trick.

Melody shook her head with a smile and pointed to Sarah's watch, circling it once with her finger.

'Ah, three hours.'

An emphatic nod.

'And how did you make the brown of the tusks?' She knew they had no brown paint in the house.

Now, that was a better question. Melody tilted her head to the left and squished up the right side of her face, just like she used to when she was about to explain something very complicated to her mother, like the life cycle of a butterfly, or how to divide big numbers like ten. This was it. Sarah held her breath.

Come on, darling. You can do it.

Spinning her chair around the room, Melody pointed to the red tea towel, the blue spatula and the yellow parmesan in the bowl on the table.

Damn it.

'Ah.' She forced a smile. 'That's very clever.' *Too clever*. Sarah wondered if they would ever get the breakthrough they needed to free Melody from her voiceless cage.

After dinner and the usual bath-time routine, Sarah opened the cupboard in Melody's room with a flourish of forced excitement. 'So, what do you want to wear tomorrow for the school trip to the zoo?' She pulled out Melody's favourite rainbow skirt and the purple dress covered in tiny unicorns. 'This?' She held up the skirt in her right hand. 'Or this?' She waved the dress in her left.

Melody shook her head and cast her eyes down. She wheeled up next to Sarah and opened a drawer, pulling out her black leggings and grey t-shirt, pushing them into Sarah's stomach.

'Right. Actually. Good choice.' Sarah put the clothes on the wooden chair under the window.

Melody wheeled over to her bed and began lifting herself out of her chair. Sarah moved closer and leaned over to help, but the steely glare from her daughter made her stop. Right. Yes. Let her do things for herself. Give her back some control. But all Sarah wanted to do was take away her daughter's pain, make life as easy as possible for her.

She knew her own therapist, if she'd bothered to continue with sessions, would tell her not to smother Melody. But if Sarah couldn't take Melody's pain away, what good was she? And who else would? Not Judy the ineffectual. Not Melody's absent father, who barely knew she existed. Not Pierre, who'd returned from France briefly after the accident, but couldn't deal with the trauma he'd been confronted with and went straight back afterwards.

It went against every instinct Sarah had to let go and step back. But she had to.

Smoothing the doona over herself, Melody handed Sarah her favourite bedtime book, the three-in-one *Magic Faraway Tree* collection.

Sarah sat on the edge of the bed, opened to where they'd left off last night, and began reading. When she got to the part where Watzisname tells the children his real name, she slowed right down and paused, waiting for Melody to answer Beth's question 'What is it?'

'Koll-amoo-li-toomarell-ipawky-rollo,' she would sound out in her perfect sing-song voice, a slightly different pronunciation each time they got to that part.

Maybe tonight. Maybe this would be the moment the silence would release her precious little girl.

The air sat thick and heavy around her. Nothing.

Sarah continued to read until Melody's eyes began to close and she tucked her in tight, kissing her on the forehead.

At the door Sarah paused. 'Goodnight, minim.'

Melody wriggled her little fingers. *Goodnight, Mama.* Sarah filled the silence in her mind.

'I love you,' Sarah continued, and performed the rest of the nightly scene in her head, so mundanely familiar. So heartachingly absent.

Melody: *I love you more.*

Sarah: *I love you most.*

She turned out the light and held back her silent tears.

In the dark Sarah climbed the spiral staircase to the small attic in the roof space and opened the creaky wooden door. She flexed her left hand as she brushed past her old cello, forlorn sitting on top of a stack of Granny Rose's boxes, the dust now a thick layer over its once glossy wood. Reaching out, she touched the scroll and ran her fingers over the intricate carving; the once-familiar pull her instrument held for her now absent.

Towards the back of the attic sat a tattered maroon armchair – the armchair Rosalie used to sit in while sipping a cup of tea from her best china when Sarah was no older than Melody was now. She eased herself into its soft cushions and loaded up the latest audiobook on her phone.

She let out a long breath as the narrator's voice slipped through her headphones, breaking the interminable silence.

Ever since they'd left the hospital, audiobooks had become Sarah's one solace, her one escape. The sentences danced through her mind, their rhythm and tempo and pitch comforting, even if she didn't take in each word.

Every night, after she put Melody to bed she'd come up here and sit in the dark alone. Just for a little while.

Tonight's story washed over her, transporting her to the lavender fields of France in 1940, and she imagined herself running her hands over the fragrant purple flowers, waiting for her lover to return from war, the Resistance just . . .

A piercing sound rang through the house and Sarah jumped up, shoving the heavy armchair backwards. She leaped to the attic door and slammed into the cello, knocking it, and a couple of the boxes it was on, tumbling to the floor.

She let them fall.

She took the stairs two at a time and burst into Melody's room. Her little girl was bolt upright, sweat dripping from her pale skin, her body shaking.

Sarah wrapped her arms around her. 'It's okay, minim. *Shh* . . .' She repeated the words over and over, rubbing Melody's back gently until she stilled. 'There we are.' She brushed the sodden hair from Melody's face. 'You're okay. Mama is here.'

With large, pleading eyes Melody looked up into Sarah's face.

'Mama's here. You're safe.'

Sarah felt the tension in her daughter's body dissolve, and sat back, allowing the air to move between them.

'I'll just go get a flannel.' She stood up, but Melody grabbed her arm, her fingers digging deep into Sarah's skin.

'It's okay. I'll be right back.'

Melody shook her head and pointed to her wheelchair.

Sarah lifted her in and pushed her into the bathroom down the hall. She wiped the sweat from Melody's skin with a damp flannel, humming a soft tune the whole time. Melody swayed ever so slightly in time with the song, her eyes closed, as Sarah dried her off.

'There. Is that better?'

Melody nodded and they returned to her bed.

Tucking the pink unicorn bedspread tightly around her, Sarah kissed Melody on the forehead and stepped away, but Melody reached out and took her hand, shaking her head.

Sarah dragged the armchair closer to the bed, the scrape of wood on wood reverberating through the room. She sat beside the bed, still holding Melody's hand.

'Mama will keep you safe.' She knew how empty the words were.

Melody's eyes softened, her lips parted. She turned her head to the side and within minutes her breathing became slow and rhythmic.

And Sarah let her tears fall.

Two

The morning sun broke through the thickly foliaged branches of the Moreton Bay fig in Rosalie's front garden as Sarah waved Melody off. The NDIS-provided car service was always on time for the school run. At first Sarah had resisted the idea of sending Melody to school with a stranger, but it wasn't fair on Ryan to ask him to do it day in, day out and Sarah hadn't driven since the night of the accident.

Melody waved back, blowing Sarah a kiss. 'Have a great day at the zoo,' Sarah called. 'Learn well.'

Melody gave her a thumbs up. *I'll learn my best.*

Sarah was nervous about the excursion, but tried not to show it. Melody's closest friends had accepted her wheelchair and filled the silence with their own excited chatter. But, unsurprisingly, not all the kids in her class were so kind. Sarah hoped the teacher remembered to put Melody with her friends when they split into groups at the zoo. She had emailed him last night to remind him. Again.

Inside, Sarah put away the breakfast dishes, her audiobook playing, and then made her way up to the attic. Melody hadn't stirred again through the night, but Sarah hadn't left her side. She never did when the nightmares came. There was still an hour before she had to leave for the museum, so now was the perfect time to tidy up the mess she'd made in her rush out of there last night.

Dusty shards of sunlight splintered the dark room through the small window on the far wall, bathing Sarah in banded light as she stepped inside. There on the floor in front of her was her cello. She bent down to pick it up, inspecting it all over. There wasn't a scratch on it. How, Sarah didn't know.

Before she rested it against the wall, she held it to her chest, her left hand on the fingerboard. Her fingers wouldn't move. The physio had assured her that her dexterity would return if she was consistent with her rehab, but what would be the point?

She leaned the cello against the wall.

Scattered across the floor were the contents of the boxes she'd knocked over, and Sarah knelt on the floor and started to gather them up. Seven-inch vinyls, yellowed doilies wrapped in pink ribbon, scrapbooks of old newspaper clippings Sarah had seen many times in her youth that used to sit proudly on Granny Rose's coffee table – all came from the brown box with corners that had, at one time, been gnawed on by some sort of tiny creature. The red box closest to the cello was one Sarah had put in the attic when she and Melody moved in. She picked it up and shuffled across the floor to the sheet music that belonged inside. Lying against the wall, just to her left, was a folded-up drawing. Sarah drew in a breath and opened it. A stick-figure Sarah, her mass of tight chocolate-brown curls unmistakeable, was standing centre stage, her long black skirt covered in glitter. She was flanked by the other members of the Five Bows ensemble – drawn much smaller than she was – all of them with red flowers at their feet, big white sails overhead. *Good luck tonight, Mama* was written in the top right corner with a big pink heart below. Inside the heart was Melody's signature, a perfectly drawn music note, a minim.

The night of the concert. The accident. Sarah clutched the picture to her chest.

It should have hung on the fridge with Melody's picture of Ryan-Walrus, but Sarah couldn't bring herself to display it. No one seemed to quite know what to do with Melody's selective mutism, despite the intensive therapy, and Sarah wouldn't risk doing unintentional harm by putting that picture on display. What if it triggered her?

She kissed the love heart and minim and folded the paper back up, placing it gently in the red box.

Over to the right was a round brown leather hatbox. Why hadn't she noticed this before? She knew the answer. She simply hadn't ever really bothered to look. Not beyond the surface of what this room held – old memories and dust, a hodgepodge of Granny Rose's discarded things.

She carried the hatbox over to Rosalie's chair, the weight of it surprising her. Herman would love a vintage hatbox like this. Nestled into the soft embrace of the armchair, Sarah lay the box in her lap. The three locks around the edge were rusted, but in surprisingly good condition. With only a little jiggling, she managed to open the lid.

The smell of must and camphor laurel assaulted her and she sneezed three times. Wiping the tears from her eyes, she looked inside. The box was lined with blue brocaded silk in a floral pattern, and sitting on top of some crumpled blue tissue paper was a pair of white satin gloves. She turned the gloves over, knowing simply by looking at them that her hands were too big to fit them. She placed them by her side and removed the blue tissue paper from the box. Beneath, she found an old camera and a photo album, the brown leather cover cracked around the edges, embossed with the initials R.R.

Rosalie Reynolds. Granny Rose's maiden name and the one she used all her professional life.

Using the white satin gloves as a barrier – her time at the Forgotten Pasts Museum having taught her the harm of fingerprints on old photographs – she opened the cover with a faint creak. Slowly. She didn't want to damage the leather any further. The cloudy white vellum of the cover page had a slight tear on one corner and Sarah was careful not to make it any bigger as she turned to the first photos.

Even in black and white she could recognise a young Rosalie in the first few pages of the album. Her wavy hair stopped above her shoulders, an asymmetrical victory roll that parted slightly to the left – a style she'd kept her whole life, though Sarah mostly remembered it as grey; her thin pointed nose and full smile slightly higher on the right than left, and her piercing eyes that somehow always seemed to look right into you. Sarah would know that gaze anywhere.

Most of the photos, Sarah assumed, were of Rosalie's hometown. A small backwater, according to her grandmother, one better forgotten. Sarah couldn't remember Rosalie ever telling her its name. She'd tried over the years to get Rosalie to tell her about where she'd grown up, about her life before she married Sarah's grandfather and came to Sydney in the mid-1940s. Grandpa had died when Sarah was twelve and she held tightly onto the faint memories she had of him. What she remembered most were his cuddles. He gave the best cuddles. She knew time was no longer on Granny Rose's side, and that when the inevitable came, Sarah's connection with that part of her family history would be lost with Rosalie. But every time she asked she was met with the same answer. 'Now, my darling. There's no point living in the past. Does one no good.'

In the photo, the house behind Rosalie was a proud brick bungalow with beautifully ornate leadlight windows, and it stood in a manicured garden full of blossoming flowers, a car in the driveway, and a large willow tree in the middle of the yard surrounded by a wooden bench. On the next page was a picture of a bike leaning up against a broken fence, which surrounded a wooden cabin – all nestled in bushland. Next to that was a picture of a sweeping vista of hills dissected by a snaking river, the light and shadows playing across the scene mesmerising.

Sarah had seen many of Rosalie's professional photos before – the walls of the main house were plastered with them. Her grandmother was very proud of her time as a photo journalist. But she'd never seen pictures like this anywhere in Rosalie's collection.

She turned the page over. A photo of a dog sitting by a letterbox was next to a white slip of paper with a YMCA logo in the corner. At the top of the page was the heading 'Snapshots From Home League'. Sarah had never heard of the Snapshots From Home League. As she turned each page of the album there were more slips of paper – requests for snapshots – and more photos of homes and families. There were no names printed on the slips, just service numbers and signatures, most of which Sarah couldn't make out.

She pored over the black and white pictures, each mounted carefully in black paper photo corners. Some had notes written next to them – 'Uncooperative but very cute pooch' was written beside the photo of a dog with its back to the camera; 'Rain stayed away' was next to the shot of three young girls standing outside a small cottage, all of them with tight ringlets; 'Cows make interesting companions' was beside the picture of an old farmer with black and white cows in the background. All had a date and place scrawled on the top of the page in Rosalie's distinct neat script. 'Thompson's Ridge, March 1945'; 'Redgum River, April 1945'; 'Wombat Hollow, July 1945'.

Pulling out her phone, Sarah looked up the places, none of which she'd ever heard of. Not surprisingly, it turned out, as they were mere specks in the middle of nowhere, a few hours north-west of Sydney.

As she turned the next page and the next, she noticed Redgum River again. There were at least ten pages of photos with 'Snapshots From Home League' slips, and all from Redgum River and surrounding townships.

She turned another page and below the heading 'Redgum River, September–November 1945' were three photos on the black background. The photo on the left was of a young man in army uniform, his slouch hat cocked to one side, a cheeky grin on his face; on the right was another photo of the same man with a taller broader gentleman standing proud and straight beside him. They were standing outside a wooden cabin – perhaps the same one with the bike out front from the earlier page, though it was hard to tell for sure as it was taken from a different angle. In pencil beneath the photos was written in shaky script 'Edward and Albert'. The third snapshot was of Rosalie sitting on a bike, the tall-and-straight man standing beside her, next to a massive tree. On several pages there were more shots of those two young men – sometimes together, sometimes on their own. Whoever they were, they featured heavily in this album of Rosalie's. There was also a picture of them with a lovely woman standing between them. Their mother, perhaps; she looked a little familiar. Rosalie flipped back through the album to where the 'Snapshot' photos were. There she was. The same woman. Standing in a garden. Beside the photo was a request slip with a signature on it that possibly read E. Davidson, or perhaps E. Dawson. Was one of the two men in all those later photos him?

The alarm on Sarah's phone pinged and she cursed quietly. She had to get to work. Carefully she packed up the album and camera into the hatbox – an idea forming in her mind – and she headed into the city.

*

'Do you know what this is, Ms Blakely?' Herman rocked back and forth on his gold and black brocaded cap-toe dress shoes. 'It might just be the exact break we need.' He fawned over the photo album, open on the lunchroom table, his hands gloved in soft white cotton.

Sarah had hoped she'd stumbled on to something, not that she knew quite what it was.

Herman hooked his thumbs in the lapel of his hunter-green jacket. 'Not even the Australian War Memorial has a collection like this.'

Sarah raised an eyebrow.

'They have similar items from the First World War, when the league got started – pins, posters, that sort of thing. But nothing from the Second World War – it wasn't quite as big then, as I understand it – and certainly not an extensive set of photos and request slips.'

'Really? What exactly was the Snapshots From Home League?'

'Ah, well, soldiers would request, through the YMCA, pictures of home. Something to comfort them. Local photographers would get the request slips, take the photos and the YMCA would send the shots back to the soldiers. Marvellous initiative.'

'That's amazing,' Sarah said.

'Really. The Imperial War Museum in England has a wonderful collection. But here in Australia . . .'

Sarah frowned. 'Surely over the years people have donated such items to the AWM?'

He shook his head and leaned forward, turning the page to admire another set of photos.

'To most people, these photos would simply be family snaps. You know – their relatives, homes, nothing even related to the war, especially without the request slips that accompany the photos in your grandmother's album. And the soldiers who requested the photos wouldn't have a copy of their request form. You have to remember, Ms Blakely, we're talking the nineteen-forties, with no photocopiers, and in wartime supplies of paper were scarce. And years on, even if a family did find photos like this, they'd probably think nothing of them, just another random black and white picture from Grandpa, to get lumped in with all the other memories that collect dust.'

Turning another page, Herman ran his fingers over the velum. 'To have so many photos, from different places and people, *with* the request slips . . .' He let out a long whistle. 'This is historical gold.'

It appeared she had stumbled on to something.

'Is your grandmother rich, Ms Blakely?' Herman stood straight and looked her in the eye.

'What? Why?'

'Oh.' He removed his gloves and pulled his blue paisley silk handkerchief out of his breast pocket and dabbed at his forehead where tiny beads of sweat had pricked through his flawless skin. 'Do not fear. I'm not figuring out a way to make a deal. It's just that, as we discussed, this was a long time ago and during the war. You couldn't just duck into Big W and print as many prints as you wanted for forty-nine cents. Back then, developing film was expensive. I think we can safely assume your grandmother didn't take the request slips and just keep the photos for herself.'

Sarah shook her head. Rosalie had always been the kind of person who, if you gave her a job, did it properly, honestly, and to her best ability. 'Absolutely not.'

'So, assuming she fulfilled the requests and sent the photos to the soldiers through the YMCA, these in the album must be copies.'

'I guess that makes sense.' Sarah shrugged.

'Sarah.' Herman stepped towards her and took her hands in his. He never called her by her first name. And he never, ever held her hands. 'Do you think it might be possible for me to meet your grandmother? For you and I to ask her about this?'

'I . . . suppose.' Sarah had already been wondering what she'd say when Rosalie returned. She was currently on a cruise around the Pacific with two of her younger friends from her cycle club. At the age of ninety-two, Rosalie still participated in the Wahroonga Wheels, a club for cycling enthusiasts aged over fifty-five. Although, with much resistance at first, she'd been using an electronic bike in the last five years, at Sarah and Ryan's insistence.

'Excellent.' Herman dropped her hand. 'Let's sort out the details later. It is ten-thirty and we have a museum to open.'

In the afternoon, Sarah made it home just as Melody returned from school.

'Hello, minim. How was the zoo?'

Melody smiled and clapped and held up the small stuffed animal hanging from her neck. All of the students were allowed to take money for a souvenir, and Sarah had hoped Melody would come back with a koala or cute penguin, perhaps. But draped around her neck was a hideously bright green monkey.

'Right. Well, what are we going to call him?'

Melody shook her head.

'Her?'

Melody cocked her head to one side and pursed her lips. All of her other toys had names: Banana Bunny, Tomato the turtle, Juice the giraffe, Watermelon the whale, Bread the bear.

'What about Bertha?' Sarah suggested, knowing that would never fly, hoping Melody might verbalise her protest.

But she simply shook her head.

'Barbara?'

An eyeroll.

'Matthew?' Surely that would be so ridiculous Melody would have to say something.

She looked Sarah in the eye and her bottom lip began to quiver. Sarah had pushed too far, frustrating her instead of coaxing her to speak.

Quick. Turn this around.

'Mushroom?' She injected as much enthusiasm as she could into her tone.

Melody nodded, her lip no longer shaking.

'Okay. Mushroom the monkey it is, then.' Sarah held out her arm and Mushroom, with the assistance of Melody, shook her hand. 'Nice to meet you, Mushroom.'

Nice to meet you, Mama. Sarah played the response in her mind in the high pitch Melody used for all her play animal voices. The high pitch she *used* to use.

The rest of the week passed in the quiet, slow monotony that had become Sarah's normal, but when Saturday rolled round, she found herself excited for Rosalie's return. Finally, a day that offered something a little different.

In the backyard, Melody and Ryan played a game of chase while they waited for the cycling club's minibus to drop Rosalie home. In the kitchen, Sarah prepared a morning tea of English Breakfast brew, fresh scones from Rosalie's favourite bakery, and strawberry jam and cream.

'Do you always do this when she returns from a trip?' Herman asked.

'Yep. She insists. It's tradition.' Sarah shrugged.

'Tradition?'

'Whenever she used to return from an assignment overseas, my grandpa would take her to one of those fancy tearooms to welcome her back. He and Mum would dress in their Sunday finest and it was a whole big thing. The year Mum died, Rosalie was in New York for some press awards thing and we didn't think she'd want to do it when she rushed back. But she insisted. Said it was even more important with Mum gone.'

'And it's always been scones, jam and cream?' Herman asked.

Sarah nodded. 'She said they were never quite as good as the ones her friend Penelope made, but they'd do.'

'That must have been hard, the first one without your mum.' Herman placed the crockery on the tray Sarah handed him.

'No. Actually, Granny Rose was right. I think it helped us all. I was pretty young, only ten, when my mum succumbed to cancer, and I think the routine was probably comforting. It was like Granny Rose knew I needed it. And maybe she did too. After Mum passed, Granny Rose and I often had high tea together and we'd reminisce about Mum. Granny Rose was always a little sad when we did, but now I know it was her way of keeping Mum alive in some way.'

'Sounds like the two of you have always been close.'

Sarah nodded. 'Yeah.'

And that's why, Sarah thought, it was strange she knew nothing about the album or that part of Rosalie's life.

'Anyway.' Sarah placed the other items on the tray then they headed outside to the large outdoor setting shaded by a giant jacaranda tree. 'So, we continued the tradition and when Rosalie retired, Ryan and I kept it up whenever she travelled. And obviously we still do.'

Herman started laying out the morning tea. 'Well, I love it. I just hope she's okay with me crashing the party today.'

'It'll be fine.' Sarah waved her hand in dismissal. At least, she hoped it would be. It wasn't so much the fact Herman would be there that gave Sarah pause, but rather that Rosalie had no idea why he was there.

A horn honking out front let them know Rosalie had arrived. Melody raced off to greet her, and to see what present she'd brought back, no doubt.

'Hey, Granny Rose.' Sarah bent down and kissed Rosalie on the forehead. 'How was the cruise?'

'Absolutely divine, my darling.' Rosalie's voice cracked with age. 'Sun, sand and open seas.' She patted Sarah on the arm, the long sleeve of her practical aqua linen tunic brushing Sarah's hand. 'And how's my boy?' She looked over to Ryan, her faded grey eyes sparking.

'Awesome as always.' He winked at Sarah as he pushed past her and picked the diminutive woman up, squeezing her in a bear hug.

'Now put me down before you drop me,' Rosalie berated him, not an ounce of anger in her voice.

'You're always safe with me.' He lowered her to the floor and she raised her sun-spotted hands and made sure her coiffed grey hair was still perfectly set in its 1940s victory roll.

'We've got a friend joining us today,' Sarah said, waving at Herman to come over. 'This is my boss, Herman.'

Rosalie cast her grey eyes over him. 'You look like a Christmas ornament.'

Beside her Melody's shoulders shook with silent laughter. Rosalie leaned into her and tickled her side. 'Well, he does,' she whispered.

'It's a pleasure to meet you, Rosalie.' Herman didn't seem offended by the remark, thankfully. Sarah had forgotten to warn him about her grandmother's penchant for speaking rather directly.

They sat at the table overlooking the perfectly maintained rolling lawn and well-tended beds of daisies and roses resplendent in a cacophony of colour, with lavender that edged the beds providing sweet fragrance. Herman poured out the tea while Melody grabbed the largest scone off the plate. She sat next to Rosalie and, as they had started doing these last few months, leaned into her, both their hands tapping out messages to each other. Sarah watched them closely every time, but could never make out their secret language.

Melody ran two fingers across the palm of Rosalie's hand. 'The young princess would like an extra dollop of cream and so would I.'

Sarah obliged, but regretted it almost instantly when Melody splattered more cream over her white t-shirt than should have been possible.

Ryan asked about Rosalie's holiday and she regaled them with tales Sarah was fairly certain were exaggerated for effect.

'I'll show you the photos once I edit out a few of the more . . . inappropriate ones,' she said.

'Speaking of photos, Granny Rose,' Sarah said. 'I was in the attic the other day, and I had a bit of an accident and knocked some things over.'

'My darling girl, there is so much junk up there it should be considered a death trap. Send the lot to the tip.' She tugged on the pearl earring weighing down her left lobe, and Melody copied her movement, though her earrings were imaginary.

'Never.' Herman gasped. 'Attics are caves of hidden treasures.'

Melody leaned forward, her eyes narrowing.

'Tosh,' Rosalie grumbled. 'Caves of personal refuse, more like.'

Sarah picked the album off the ground, where she'd secreted it in her bag beside her, and placed it on the table in front of Rosalie. 'Well, I did find this.'

'What . . . where . . . I thought I'd . . .' Her eyes widened and her body stiffened.

'Granny Rose? Are you all right?' Sarah asked.

Rosalie nodded and squared her shoulders. 'That was a time long past. Another life.' She pushed the album away and wiped her hands on her cream corduroy trousers.

Herman sat forward and opened the album to one of the earlier pages. 'You were quite the photographer, Ms Reynolds, if you don't mind me saying.'

Rosalie narrowed her eyes.

'The composition here – see, with the weeping branches of the trees over the water snaking off to the side – is just superb.'

She tilted her head to one side and sized him up and down.

'And the way you've captured the light in this one, bouncing off the thick trunks, is quite masterful.'

'Are you always such a silver tongue?' Rosalie shot Herman one of her stern looks that suggested you were on the edge of her deciding if she liked you or not. Sarah had seen it many times over the years.

'No, ma'am. Not at all.'

'I can vouch for that.' Sarah nodded.

'I just have an appreciation of the arts,' Herman continued. 'And you are a very good photographer. Where did you learn? If you don't mind me saying, for someone of your generation, it would have been unusual for a woman to be a professional photographer. Which Sarah tells me you were.'

Rosalie laughed. 'I was indeed. As for unusual, you don't know the half of it.' She shook her head. 'To answer your question: my uncle taught me.'

Sarah sat up straighter. It was rare to hear Rosalie say anything about her younger days and she'd never heard mention of an uncle.

'Ber—' she stopped herself, pulling on her earring again. 'A master photographer in his day, who taught me everything he knew. Much to my father's ire. And I fell in love with it. He gave me my first camera and from that day on, I never went anywhere without it.' She looked up to the sky, her gaze distant.

'This camera?' Sarah pulled the old apparatus out of her bag.

'Oh, my.' Rosalie sucked in a sharp breath, her thin lips pressing together. 'Where did you . . . I haven't seen that old thing in a very long time.' She folded her frail arms around herself and Melody reached out and held her hand.

'Granny Rose, Herman is very interested in the photos you took for the Snapshots From Home League.'

'Those silly pictures?' She furrowed her brow. 'My work as a journalist is far more interesting.'

Herman shook his head. 'Your journalistic work was pioneering, Ms Reynolds. Absolutely. I googled you.'

'Did it hurt?' Rosalie quipped.

Herman smiled. 'You were most impressive. But this.' He rested his hand on the photo album. 'This is unique and rather special. I would love to put together a small exhibit, specifically to showcase this.'

'You'll do no such thing.' Rosalie snapped. Standing up she turned and stormed inside.

'But, Ms Reynolds,' Herman called out, and Sarah touched his arm gently.

'Leave it with me. I'll see if I can get any more out of her.'

Inside, Rosalie was sitting on the couch, a mountain of cushions propping her up.

'Granny Rose,' Sarah started, pushing her thick curls behind her ear. 'This photo album is beautiful and the wartime photos tell a little-known story I think a lot of people would find fascinating. If —'

'Sarah, please. Know when to leave well enough alone.' Rosalie reached out and pulled Sarah's hair back around her face.

Sarah took her grandmother's pale hand in her slender fingers. 'These pictures are a treasure. I've never heard you mention anything about doing this during the war.'

'There's a lot about me you don't know, my darling.' Her faded eyes stared into Sarah's. 'A lot of pain and heartache no one should ever have to experience.' Her hard expression softened and weariness slid into its place.

'Well, maybe we can start with the things that aren't painful, then.'

'Like what?' Rosalie looked back at her. The flash of challenge that flared briefly in her eyes was one Sarah was all too familiar with.

Sarah may well have inherited her dad's curls, but her blue eyes and the fiery expression they often conveyed she'd got from Rosalie.

'I don't know. There are a number of photos here from a place called Redgum River. Is that where you grew up? Where you met Grandpa?'

Rosalie's gnarled hands began to shake. 'Redgum River is of no consequence and I'd prefer not to speak of it again.' She stood up and walked away.

Three

Rosalie sat at the bay window of her bedroom, looking down on the garden. Sarah and Ryan had their heads together, throwing glances up at the old house. They wouldn't be able to see her tucked behind her heavy curtain, but they were, no doubt, talking about her.

Sarah had followed her upstairs, but Rosalie had shooed her away, telling her to go look after their guest. Herman was gone now, but Sarah and Ryan were still there.

Rosalie should have measured her response when Sarah brought out the album. Her granddaughter fussed and worried over her at the best of times. This would no doubt set her off. She fussed and worried over everyone too much, truth be told. Especially Melody.

Melody was down there beside them, playing with some flowers.

They coddled that child excessively. Both of them. Perhaps if they stopped treating her like a fragile bird, she'd find her song again. But what would Rosalie know? She'd never heard of selective mutism before, and any time she tried to offer Sarah any advice or ask any questions, she was dismissed. Like she would never understand.

Still, her granddaughter had been through a lot this last year. The accident was bad enough. The aftermath even tougher. And trying to do it on her own. That useless ex of Sarah's certainly couldn't be counted on, even when she and Melody needed him most. Deadbeat. That's what Rosalie had thought of him the very first time she had met him. And his near continual absence over the years had done nothing to disabuse her of that opinion. He'd flitted into town only once since the accident to check on his daughter, stayed two nights on Sarah's couch and flitted right back out again, chasing whatever gig he thought would give him his elusive big break. 'Free spirit' Rosalie's wrinkled tush. It was a term she'd always hated. Ever since . . . well, ever. In her experience it was just an excuse to avoid responsibility. They would see that sorry excuse for a father in another year, maybe, still the deadbeat he always was, still chasing a dream that would never be his.

If only Sarah could find herself a good man. Rosalie knew that didn't fit the feminist view the younger generation had, of course. A woman doesn't need a man and all that tosh. But everybody did, in her opinion, need a somebody to travel life's ups and downs with. Share the joys and burdens. She shouldn't be so hard on her granddaughter, but she couldn't help it. It was her eyes. The expression they so often held. Everyone said they were just like hers, but Rosalie knew the truth. They were far too much a reminder of a time Rosalie really didn't care to remember.

She waited until Sarah and Ryan eventually left the garden before heading back downstairs. What she needed now was a ride, just around the block. Blow out the anxiety of the day's events. As she padded into the living room, she saw it. On the coffee table.

The album.

'Oh, you wily girl.' She shook her head, knowing Sarah had left it there deliberately.

Rosalie hadn't thought about Redgum River in a very long time. Hadn't wanted to. She moved towards the worn leather album and memories broke through the carefully constructed barriers in her mind.

Redgum River
March 1945

Rosalie rode through the quiet streets of Redgum River. It was good to be home. Even if her return was the result of her internship gone wrong. Stupid misogynistic newspaper and its stupid misogynistic editor. Coming home with her tail between her legs was not ideal, but she wouldn't let it break her. In fact, it just made her more determined. Here, in the warm embrace of her tiny little town, she'd lick her wounds and get back on her bike, so to speak.

She pedalled past the shops in Main Street. Old Clancy McCusker, the grocer, waved and threw her an apple, which she caught mid-air. 'Thanks, Mr McCusker,' she called, as she balanced with no hands on the handlebars. Mrs Donaldson was sweeping the footpath outside the newsagency and looked down her glasses as Rosalie rode past, giving a little wave. 'Lovely day, Mrs D,' Rosalie waved back.

Her father would be appalled if he knew that she was careering through town, dressed in 'boy's clothes' no less. But he wasn't here right now. And as long as she avoided the crusty old tattletale Miss Look-down-her-nose-at-everyone Kingston, it was unlikely anyone else would bother reporting her to her father when he returned home from Sydney next week to his country practice.

With the wind blowing through her long blonde hair as it tailed behind her beneath her hat, she felt only bliss.

As Rosalie turned the corner, past the gigantic old red gum that stood like a sentry at the west end of Main Street, she slowed down and circled its wide trunk three times. It never ceased to amaze her how one tree could take up so much room. The three-hundred-year-old grandfather of the town was as wide as any tree she'd ever seen. A few years ago she'd measured its girth and it had taken her forty-five long strides to get all the way around. She often imagined the stories the old tree could tell if it could talk. What it had seen, heard – lovers' quarrels and kisses; the town growing slowly over decades, from one or two tents back in the gold-rush days to the first wooden shack being erected; the general store being built; the main street being dug out and laid beside the river and the first car to drive along it; the people who'd come and gone, made this place home, left it in their wake.

On her third pass around the ancient trunk, she reached out her hand, running it along the brown gnarled base, stretching up out of her saddle, trying to reach where the bark became grey and smooth. Almost. One day she'd stretch far enough.

With a skid of her wheel in the dirt, she turned sharply left and made her way along the narrow strip of short grass that ran beside the river bank. Tall, slim river red gums lined the water and, as she rode further away from town, the thin procession of trees became dense, set back into the bush in a tangled tapestry of green and brown and grey as far as Rosalie could see.

She slowed down as she approached Uncle Bernie's wood cabin and jumped off her bike, gently leaning it against the rotting fence outside. Long tendrils of yellow grass reached up over the once white picket fence, and snaked their way across the trodden dirt path to his front door. Rosalie may have been all grown up now, but this place had lost none of the magical charm it had held in her childhood.

The cabin, disappearing into the tree line, was surrounded by tall river gums, their long branches casting dark silhouettes against the shadows. Even now she wondered if perhaps they were the spindly arms of forest spirits held out to protect hidden sprites and fairies. The roof of the cabin was covered in fallen leaves and moss, the windows at the front frosted with decades of dirt and grime, and five stepping stones made of wood off-cuts led to the front door that hung just slightly askew.

Rosalie hopped across the stones and then jumped with two feet onto the tattered remains of an old door mat. From inside, a gramophone sent soft notes of Vivaldi floating into the air, and the aroma of lavender and lemon myrtle coming from the overgrown terracotta pots on the corner of the veranda made Rosalie smile as memories of her childhood playing make-believe danced through her mind.

Before she could knock on the door, it creaked open and Bernie came out, his thick broad frame filling the doorway. He wrapped her in a tight bear hug. With Rosalie's father away in Sydney so much over the last five years, Bernie had filled the paternal gap in her life and his hugs always made her feel she was home.

'Rose-petal, there you are.' He took her shoulders and stood back, looking at her like he hadn't seen her for years. 'Is it possible you've grown more elegant?'

She brushed her hands over her overalls and frowned. 'Father would say not. Never elegant enough for him.'

'Come in. Sit down.' Bernie removed a pile of newspapers from the dining table. He was always surrounded by newspapers. They were piled on his table, his broken shelves in the living area, in teetering towers in each corner of the cabin – a haphazard depository for local, national and international papers and magazines. One of the joys Rosalie always found when visiting Uncle Bernie was poring over the pages and reading about far-off places and people, and learning about a world that lay beyond the reaches of her expensive education.

Rosalie eased herself into one of the chairs, moving a newspaper so she could sit. On the front page was yet another story about the war, the photo showing troops at rest in a bunker. Rosalie wished she could be there, in the action, making a difference. When she'd suggested as much, her father had bristled. It was 'no place for a woman of breeding. A good marriage is what she needed now'. Rosalie had often suspected the only reason her father allowed her to go to university was a means to put her in front of a suitable future husband.

It hadn't worked.

'Scat, you.' Bernie woke Pineapple, his pet possum, and shooed her away. The creature wasn't too impressed by the interruption and scuttled into the kitchen with a hiss, knocking over pots and pans before she ducked behind a tattered curtain that did little to distract one's eyes from the dust-covered wooden sleepers that made up the internal walls of the cabin.

'How's your mother?' Bernie's words were measured, as always, when he enquired after his sister-in-law, Iris.

None of the adults in Rosalie's life thought she knew much about that summer no one spoke of. They assumed she was too young to remember. But she remembered everything.

'She's well. Have you visited lately?' Rosalie already knew the answer, and indeed Bernie shook his head. Some memories were too dark to live with. Some rifts became too deep to mend.

'What about you, Rosalie? When do you start with the *River Times*?' He beamed with pride.

Rosalie sat with her back straight, years of correct posture drummed into her, while Bernie prepared a pot of tea. 'Next week.'

'You'll show those ignorant city papers you've got what it takes.'

'I hope so.'

The *River Times* was a step down from her internship with the *Sun* – quite a number of steps down – but she had little choice at this point. Her internship had been given as part of an arrangement with one of the university professors. Someone owed someone a favour, it turned out. But after only two months on the job, Rosalie had been rather unceremoniously let go. Cost-cutting, they'd said, because of the war. Funny how it was only her and one other female reporter who were let go.

It was a lesson that smarted, and she was determined never to let it happen again. She would make her own way in this world.

Bernie stood up after they'd finished their tea. 'How about we head out back?'

Rosalie followed him to what he called the Shack. She called it a time machine. Through the overgrown bushes they walked along a path that was barely there until they reached a small clearing. A squat wooden outbuilding sat in the middle of carefully manicured grass, which looked more like it belonged hugging an English manor house than cut into the wilds of Bernie's bush home. Bernie held the door open for her and she stepped inside. Around the white plastered walls rows of string were hung at exact intervals and on each row were black and white moments frozen in time. Landscapes, portraits, studies of nature.

This was where Bernie had taught Rosalie everything she now knew about photography.

They developed the roll of film she'd brought back from Sydney – mostly pictures of the university buildings and cityscapes – and when they finished, she closed the heavy black curtain behind them before they left the Shack, making sure it was secure, allowing no light through, before Bernie opened the door.

Together they strode through the bush down to the river. There it widened and twisted further inland, the sun pushing through the trees and bouncing off the tiny ripples on the gently moving water. Then they headed to Jumbuck Hill.

It wasn't a terribly strenuous hike, but most locals didn't bother going up there too often. Rosalie always thought that was a shame. For them. It suited her and Bernie just fine though, to have the place to themselves.

They emerged from the trees into the clearing that crested the hill and Rosalie drew in a long deep breath, savouring the first glimpse of the view beneath. Redgum River snaked below, cutting a shining dark ribbon through the tones of olive and brown land. To the west, hills bulged and grew until they swallowed the river in their undulating folds. One day Rosalie would like to take a boat and see just where the river went to out there. To the west, it bordered the town, bush on one bank, the shops and Main Street on the other, following the shape of the river. Behind the town centre the haphazard streets and homes of the locals faded into fields of green and yellow. She could see the giant gum standing over the town, and the hint of Bernie's corrugated roof sending glints of reflected sunlight through the bush canopy.

'This never gets tired.' Bernie stepped up beside her and sighed. 'When I go, I want to be buried up here so I can look at this forever.'

Rosalie linked her arm in his. 'Well, thankfully we won't have to worry about that for a long time.'

'God willing,' Bernie nodded. 'Now. Before we take any photos, what do you think you need to consider when shooting landscapes?'

After an hour of being schooled in the concepts of depth and aperture and leading lines, and the ever-constant reminders about composition and light, and something about frames she only half-listened to, Rosalie and Bernie headed back down.

In the Shack, Rosalie stood under the red light of the darkroom watching her pictures emerge. Her shoulders dropped. They weren't bad shots. Not really. But they failed to capture the true beauty and grandeur of what nature provided. She'd thought landscapes would be easier than the close-ups she'd been taking of the natural world, not having to fuss about with tight detail. But it appeared the scope of a sweeping landscape was its own undoing.

'It's easy to lose one's way in a vast expanse of nothing, without some sort of frame to guide your way.'

Ah, so that's what he'd been talking about when he'd mentioned framing. She wished she'd listened more carefully.

'And when there isn't an existing frame, we have to create an arbitrary one. Here. Take this, for example.'

He pointed out a shot of the river and made a rectangle with his fingers. 'Do this.' She did. 'If you'd moved this way . . .' He positioned her hands over the photos so that the curve of the river became the edge. 'And then used that light . . .' He swept his hand over the left corner in an arc. 'Then you'd have had a frame.'

Rosalie let out a sigh and her cheeks burned. If she'd listened to him in the first place, she might have had a chance at making these pictures better. That would teach her to be so cocky. There was still so much she needed to learn.

Sitting tall on her bike, Rosalie balanced carefully as she rode back home with her hands outstretched to the sides, trying to catch the wind. It was a game she'd liked to play when she was young and actually thought she *could* catch the wind. The rush of air against her face and body was still a thrill, though, even without childhood fancy.

As she hit Main Street, she slowed down and grabbed the handlebars.

A woman Rosalie had never seen in town before rushed out of the general store and Rosalie swerved to miss her, falling to the ground.

'Gosh, I'm sorry. Are you all right?'

'I'm fine.' Rosalie rubbed her hip and wished she could rub her buttocks. But even she had her standards.

'Here.' The woman picked up Rosalie's bike. 'Oh dear, that might need some work.' She tilted her head to the back wheel. 'If my boys were here I could get them to have a look. Very handy, they are.' Her expression was full of pride.

'Thank you. It doesn't look too bad. I can probably fix it myself.' Rosalie smiled. Bernie had taught her years ago how to look after her bike.

The woman gave a slight nod of her head. 'Well, good for you. With so many of our lads serving overseas, we ladies must learn to do for ourselves.'

'Is that where your boys are?' Rosalie had been brought up better than to pry into a stranger's private life, but there was a dark look of longing in the woman's eyes, as if she were desperate to talk to someone.

'Yes.' She nodded. 'Well, not overseas right at the moment. They are in Far North Queensland. But they are both serving. I miss them terribly.'

Rosalie couldn't imagine how hard it must be for the mothers who had seen their sons off to war.

'I'm Rosalie.' She held out her hand. 'I don't believe we've met.'

'Lovely to meet you, Rosalie. I'm Penelope Dawson. I only moved to the area last year, after the boys signed up. I live in the worker's cottage on the old Claridge property.'

Rosalie smiled. 'Nice to meet you. I'm just returned home myself.'

'Ah.' A glint of recognition flashed in Penelope's eyes. 'Are you Dr Reynolds's daughter?'

'Yes.' Of course, the bush telegraph had always been efficient, and while the good doctor Frank Reynolds only served the community part-time now, he was still one of its favourite sons.

'Well, it's lovely to finally meet you. You'd be about the same age as my youngest, Albert. He's nineteen.'

'You must be very proud.'

She stood a little taller. 'Yes. Very. But I worry ever so much.'

Rosalie couldn't imagine.

'I send them packages. Socks. Letters. But it isn't the same as having them here. And only Edward writes me. Albert is too much of a free spirit and never was one for putting pen to paper.' She shook her head. 'I wish I could send them some of my famous scones. But they wouldn't last the journey, I'm afraid.' She gave a half-hearted laugh.

'I don't suppose they would. And they wouldn't be the same without lashings of strawberry jam and cream.'

Penelope's laugh became genuine and full. 'Imagine having cream to send.' She exhaled.

Rosalie leaned into Penelope and lowered her voice. 'Are your scones really famous?'

'Yes.' Penelope winked. 'At least, my boys would say so.'

'If I can get you some cream, would you do me the honour of making a batch? We can have a bite together over a cup of tea.'

Penelope clasped her hands in front of her chest. 'I've been saving my butter for a special occasion.'

They made a date and bade farewell.

As Rosalie was about to get back on to her bike, Mrs Donaldson came out of the general store wiping her hands on her green checked apron. 'Rosalie Reynolds, before you ride off, I was wondering if I could ask you something.'

Rosalie smiled. 'Hello, Mrs D.'

'I wanted to see what you thought of this.' She handed Rosalie a piece of card. 'With all the photography you're doing, and with you starting at the paper – what an exciting turn of events that is – I thought you might be the right person for this job.'

Rosalie turned the card over in her hand. It was white with black and red printing. In the top left corner was a logo – a red triangle with YMCA in the middle. In bold red type was the heading 'Request For Home Snapshots'. The card had sections filled out in neat script, with a home address, a service number and squadron details.

'They did this in the Great War too, the Snapshots From Home League, you know? Very popular it was then.' She pushed her grey-speckled hair back beneath the tattered snood she wore. 'My Jeffery said the photos he received while he served in Gallipoli were a godsend.' When she said her husband's name, there was the lightest pause, and Rosalie's heart went out to her.

'My sister Linda, you remember Linda, don't you? She volunteers with our regional YMCA and I help her when I can, and you see, when this came through last week, she thought I might know someone in the area who'd be happy to take it on.'

Linda was right to ask her sister. Mrs Donaldson, general store and post office proprietor, was the eyes and ears of the entire river area. There was nothing she didn't know about pretty much everyone in all the townships around. And she was a force. If you wanted something done, it was she to whom you went.

'Of course, I have no idea how to use a camera myself,' Mrs Donaldson continued, 'and we're expecting a few more of these to come through from fellows from around these parts who'd appreciate a photo or two from home. There are so many local boys who signed up, you know? We've only had a few requests before now, and the Jenson boy, from River Downs – you probably know him: small, freckles all over his face – he would take the odd snap here and there, but now he's moved to the big smoke. In search of work, I believe. The requests that have come in are from various parts of the district, so it would mean traipsing all over the countryside, which is why I haven't asked Bernie. But then I thought of you.'

Mrs Donaldson had always been one to talk. On and on she went until she was forced to take a breath and Rosalie could interject.

'I have to be getting on, Mrs D, but I'd be happy to oblige.' She tucked the card into her pocket. 'I would very much like to do something to help the war effort.'

'I knew it.' Mrs Donaldson clapped her hands.

'I just wish I could do more. This seems so . . . so insignificant.' Rosalie got her on bike.

'Never underestimate how big a small gesture can be. Especially in the darkest of times.' Mrs Donaldson squeezed Rosalie's hand, the earnest look on her face piercing Rosalie's heart. 'This will make more of a difference than you can imagine.'

Rosalie wasn't sure about that, but it was at least *something* she could do, she supposed. And it would help keep her busy while she tried to reassemble her life here.

The next day, Rosalie stood in front of the home of Private Jones over in Thompson's Ridge, the next town down river, to take her first shot for the Snapshots From Home League.

Mrs Jones, Millie, who couldn't have been much older than Rosalie, looked perfectly serene with a toddler on her hip while she posed for photos. Frederick seemed far too serious a name for the two-year-old who smiled and giggled continuously, his tight red ringlets constantly falling into his face.

'Just like his daddy,' Mrs Jones said, as she brushed her son's hair away from his eyes.

'Da-dad.' Frederick clapped.

'Freddy Snr enlisted before we found out I was pregnant. He's been home on leave a couple of times, but he's missed so much.'

Millie placed the child on the floor and he ran around her, popping under her apron and back out again, making faces at Rosalie.

Rosalie reached for her camera and Frederick inched towards her, his head tilted to the side, his eyes never leaving her, full of curiosity. She took a photo of him as he took one more step, and the click of the shutter saw him jump back. And then he giggled, a high-pitched joyful sound, which had Rosalie smiling broadly.

She managed to take a few good shots, at least she hoped, in between Frederick pulling funny faces at the camera and Millie laughing till she snorted. Rosalie suspected Freddy Snr might appreciate a shot capturing his son's cheeky nature. And Millie looked ever so pretty when she laughed. Rosalie would see how they turned out when she developed the film.

'Thank you,' Millie said, when Rosalie finished. 'I don't own a camera and every week Frederick changes so much. Freddy will be so happy to receive this.'

Rosalie could tell Millie was holding back tears and she reached out and touched her shoulder.

'I'll get them back to the YMCA straightaway.'

'Thank you.' Millie's eyes glistened. 'Truly.'

Rosalie rode off, heading back to Redgum River with her heart beating faster than her pedalling required. Yes. This was most definitely something tangible she could do. She hoped Mrs Donaldson would have more assignments soon.

Rosalie pushed herself away from the photo album, away from her recollections, before she lingered there in the depths of her past, where darker memories lurked.

She walked over to her glass doors. Outside, a magpie was hopping across the grass and it stopped, turned its head towards her and stared at her with one tiny black eye.

'What?' she asked, and it tilted its head. 'I can't. If I allow Sarah and Herman to exhibit those photos, it will open a Pandora's box of questions.'

The magpie hopped closer to the door, its head bobbing up and down.

'Well,' Rosalie huffed. 'That's easy for you to say. You're not the one who'll have to answer the questions.' She folded her arms across her chest.

For more than seven decades she'd kept that part of her life locked tightly away. What good would it do now to open it up? She glanced over to the album.

No.

Redgum River had to stay buried in the past where it belonged.

Four

Rosalie was nothing if not stubborn. Sarah had tried various approaches in the last few days, but she simply couldn't get her grandmother to talk about the photo album or Redgum River. It was time to change tack.

After Sarah had put Melody to bed, she sank into the sofa by the dining room table and opened her laptop. Time for Google to shed some light. She looked up Redgum River and found a poorly populated historical society page. There were a couple of black and white photos of the town, unannotated; one badly written paragraph about the town's beginnings; and a sign-up form for anyone wanting to contribute to the society. The page hadn't been updated in five years, judging by the last entry, and Sarah wondered if the society even was a proper thing, or if they simply hadn't adapted to modern technology. Her guess was probably the latter given how small towns usually kept great records of their history.

She searched more, this time using Trove. Herman had introduced her to the site, which was full of amazing historical collections from libraries, universities and museums all around the country.

She put in Rosalie's name and key words like 'history' and 'journalist'. It didn't take long for Sarah to find the body of Rosalie's work that she already knew about. She added 'Redgum River' and 'newspaper' to the search parameters and found an archive of a publication called the *River Times*, with dates ranging from 1905 to 1945.

She scrolled through page after page of the archived newspapers. Her eyes were red and dry by the time she found a reference to a Dr Reynolds in an article from 1927.

Sarah did the maths. Rosalie would have been a year old. Was this her father? Sarah had no idea if her great-grandfather had been a doctor, but it seemed to fit.

Stretching, she moved into the kitchen and, as the old grandfather clock in the living room struck 10 p.m., she made a cup of coffee. Black. No sugar. Strong.

Sitting back on the sofa, she drained her cup, feeling the caffeine kick in. She scrolled to the next edition and the next in search of Rosalie.

After another hour, Sarah was coming to the end of the archives, and the end of her hope of finding what she was looking for. Not that she knew what that was exactly. But she did know she hadn't yet found it. She'd found plenty of mentions of Iris Reynolds – who, it seemed, must be her great-grandmother – and her work with the CWA sprinkled through various editions, and article after article about Dr Reynolds – the fetes he opened, how proud the town was of their very own doctor doing such important work in Sydney and how lucky they were to have a man like him in their midst. And there was the odd reference to Dr and Mrs Reynolds' daughter, Rosalie. Bingo. Sarah knew she was looking in the right spot, but everything so far had been regular town news. Nothing to suggest why Rosalie was so reluctant to speak about that part of her life.

In the wee hours of the night, she opened the last edition of the *River Times* that had been digitised, and she drew in a deep breath.

March 1945. A bake sale. The article was written by N. Payne and R. Reynolds.

'There you are,' Sarah whispered.

Rosalie had never mentioned writing for her local paper, only ever speaking of her work with *Life* as her start in journalism. Perhaps she'd decided her work with the *River Times* simply not worthy of mention. But, if her family were such an integral part of Redgum River life, as they appeared to be, why had Rosalie never mentioned anything about the town?

Friday afternoon rolled around again, and Sarah sat, as always, in the pink armchair, watching Melody draw on the wall of the therapist's room. She had gone into the session hopeful after last week's appointment, but that hope soon dissolved as Melody simply went through the hour, step by step, contentedly moving through the motions, nothing changing, not even the Play-Doh piquing any interest or slightly altered response in her daughter.

At the end of the session Sarah picked up her bag without word, gave Melody a hug and wheeled her outside, her already broken heart splintering just a little more.

The sun was low in the sky and as they made their way down the ramp onto the footpath, Ryan pulled up. Before he could ask Sarah how the session went, she got him on to the topic of his work, which she knew would keep him talking till they got home.

'And then, Mr Bossy-wouldn't-know-a-gable-from-a-skillion-if-it-bit-him-in-the-butt came in.' Ryan threw one arm in the air. 'How that man runs one of the top architecture firms in the country is beyond me.'

'It sounds like things are getting worse.' Sarah felt for her cousin. He was a talented architect, but over the last couple of years that firm and the ridiculous hours they expected from him had sucked all the joy out of a job he once loved.

'Maybe I should just chuck it all in and do something wild and crazy. Join a circus . . .'

From the backseat Melody clapped.

'. . . or start designing bespoke glitter bunkers for doomsday preppers.'

Sarah laughed. 'I think prepping is more of an American thing. And I'm not sure how much those sorts of people would be into glitter.'

'No. It's a thing here too. The Aussie preppers. I saw a documentary about them recently. And why wouldn't you want to be surrounded by glitter if the world was coming to an end?' He shrugged.

Melody clapped her agreement. She would most definitely want to be surrounded by glitter if the world was coming to an end.

'I don't think I have an answer for that,' Sarah laughed.

'See. I should give this more thought.'

'Or,' Sarah drew out her words, 'less drastic, maybe you should go out on your own. Be your own boss.'

He nodded. 'I could, I suppose. But you know what your pop used to say. "Sometimes you need to shake things up . . ."'

Sarah sighed. '". . . to settle things down."'

Ryan reached across the van's bench seat and put his arm around her shoulder.

'I'm not sure he was ever thinking of glitter bunkers, though.' She shook her head.

He squeezed her tightly. 'Hey. You never know where you might find the right solution.'

Sarah laughed. That may well be true in many circumstances, but she was fairly sure glitter bunkers weren't the answer to her problems.

*

That night Ryan joined her and Melody for dinner and after Sarah put Melody to bed, she sat with him on the sofa, each of them with a glass of wine.

'So, I've been doing some research,' Sarah said, and filled him in on the *River Times*.

Ryan rubbed his chin. 'It is a little weird she's never mentioned that. But maybe, given where she ended up career-wise, she's embarrassed about her humble beginnings?'

'Maybe.' Sarah frowned.

They looked at each other a moment and then shook their heads in unison.

'No. She'd have bragged about how far she'd come,' Sarah said.

'Yep. She's definitely hiding something.' Ryan laughed.

Sarah took a gulp of her wine. 'But how are we going to get her to tell us?'

He shook his head. 'I don't know. If I knew how to get reluctant people to open up,' he hit her knee, 'you and I would have had a few different conversations over this last year. You're the expert on closing the past off, cuz.'

That hurt. But he wasn't wrong.

Sarah stared ahead, refusing to make eye contact.

'Have you been back to Dr Mitchell?' Ryan's question hung between them. 'Or that cute counsellor – what was his name? Liam?'

Sarah glanced at him. 'You only want me to keep seeing him so I can introduce you.'

Ryan shook his head. 'While that wouldn't be a bad outcome, all I want is for you to get the help you need.'

'I'm fine.' She turned her gaze away. 'I'm fine. I didn't find that talky-talky stuff any good anyway.'

All that focus on opening up about what had happened, facing fears, giving her guilt some sort of physical form, like a drawing, so she could morph it, erase it . . . blah, blah, blah. Such crap.

Sarah didn't want to erase her guilt. She didn't deserve to. She deserved to sit with it always.

'Besides, my focus has to be on Melody.'

Ryan reached across and tilted her chin so that she had to look at him. 'Sar-bear?'

She narrowed her eyes. 'If you spout some bullshit about pouring from an empty cup, you'll be wearing this.' She raised her wineglass.

Ryan threw his hands up in surrender. 'I'm just saying.'

'Well, don't.'

'All right.' He scooted a little closer on the couch. 'What are we going to do about Granny Rose then?'

Sarah pushed her irritation aside. Ryan's heart, as always, was in the right place. And if she wasn't so pigheaded, another trait she got from her grandmother, she might have even admitted that part of him was right. Deep down she knew his clichés about drawing from an empty well and fitting your own mask first were, on some level, true.

But for now she had a daughter to help, a museum to save and a mystery to solve. And that was more than enough to deal with.

Five

Rosalie returned from her ride around the local park on Saturday morning, pink-cheeked and rather exhilarated. She hadn't been convinced when Sarah and Ryan had first suggested the e-bike – how could it possibly compare to the real thing? – but to shut them up she'd tried it and though she'd never admit it to them, it was a relief to have some help with the pedals at her age.

As she pulled up outside her house, she noticed that funny little boss of Sarah's standing at her front door. Hank, or Horatio, or whatever his name was, dressed up to the nines as if he were about to attend the theatre back in the days when people made an effort for such things.

'Ms Reynolds.' He removed his purple pork-pie hat. 'Lovely to see you again.'

Rosalie pulled her shoulders back, trying to appear straighter, which was no mean feat at her age. 'Good morning. I can guess why you're here.' She fixed him with a stare that she hoped would see him cower.

But the nerve of the man – he simply smiled.

'It may not be quite what you think.' He took a step towards the house. 'I thought we could have a chat over some special Vietnamese tea.' He winked and opened his teal brocade waist coat to reveal a small flask in the inside pocket. 'I hear there was a certain way you liked it when you were reporting from the front line in the sixties.'

Despite herself, Rosalie grinned. It had been a long time since she'd had one of her special Vietnamese teas. She had to hand it to him. He'd clearly done his research. While she wasn't about to give in to him, the least she could do was indulge him for the effort he'd gone to.

She raised her chin and looked down her nose. 'Come in, then.'

At the dining table, Herman set the teacups and handed Rosalie the flask. She sploshed a healthy dose of the sweet-smelling whisky into her black tea.

'It was the only way to get through the day sometimes.' She sighed as she lowered herself into the chair. Herman sat beside her and dripped the tiniest amount of the good stuff into his tea.

'I have read many of your articles, and articles about you and your work. Your time in Vietnam and Lebanon, the Falklands – every major conflict throughout the seventies and eighties, I believe. You had quite the interesting career.'

'Yes. I did. And yet that's not why you're here, is it? The Snapshots From Home League. What possible appeal could such a small part of a war, a war that has, if you ask me, been explored to death . . . what possible interest could some inconsequential photos be to you, or to anyone else, for that matter?'

Herman adjusted his legs and leaned forward. 'I think you'd be surprised. Your Snapshots are a part of the war that not a lot is known about, and your collection is expansive. May I ask you a question?'

'You're here, so I suppose so.' Rosalie sat back in her chair. There was an innate intelligence to this man, and she was quite interested to see what he would ask her. Not that it would sway her decision, but she enjoyed intelligent debate.

'I suspect if the only concern you had was that people wouldn't be interested in your photos, you wouldn't be holding them back with such ferocity.'

Rosalie forced herself to breathe with steady rhythm. Perhaps she should have been warier of this man.

'Really? Well, I think perhaps you're fishing in an empty pond.'

Herman studied his teacup and turned it three times before responding. 'Maybe I am. But for someone who has quite literally seen and done it all; seen the worst humankind has to offer, witnessed horrors I can't even imagine,' he shook his head, 'I am curious as to why some "inconsequential photos", as you put it, taken in a small country town have you . . . spooked.'

'Spooked?' Rosalie's laugh was strained, but she hoped Herman wouldn't notice. He barely knew her, after all. For all he knew it was her usual laugh.

'I'm sorry, Ms Reynolds. It's none of my business. And the Snapshots really aren't why I'm here.'

'Really?'

'Really. I have to admit my curiosity got the better of me and I may have googled Redgum River.'

Rosalie didn't fully understand the internet; in fact, she tried to stay away from technology as much as she could.

'I found something interesting I wanted to bring to your attention. Because I'm a little worried about Sarah.'

'Sarah?'

'Here, let me show you . . .'

Half an hour later, Herman left and Rosalie had to lie down. He'd shown her only a few photos before the bright glare of the laptop screen had begun to hurt her eyes, but the way he described the place . . . She couldn't ignore that what he was suggesting made a lot of sense.

And yet it did mean going back.

Redgum River
Early April 1945

Rosalie's first week at the *River Times* didn't exactly go the way she'd hoped. She'd had visions of chasing down stories of local crime or conducting interviews with prominent figures in the area. Instead, she fetched coffee for Neville Payne, the editor, filed old stories in a cabinet that seemed to have no order or system to it – which she corrected within the first two days – and answered the phone. If it rang.

On Friday afternoon Neville called her into his office. Though 'office' was a slight stretch of the word. It was more of a separation from the main area, delineated by a wooden partition on which a gold plaque hung, slightly askew, marked 'Editor'.

'Ah, Miss Reynolds.' Neville pushed his glasses up his nose as he squinted up at her. 'Sit, sit.' He waved his hand in the air in the general direction of the wooden chair opposite his desk.

Rosalie sat and noticed the desk slightly slanted down in one corner. She made a mental note to shove some folded scrap paper under the offending leg.

Neville stood up, adjusting his red suspenders then putting his hands on his hips. He seemed to slant in the same direction as his desk, and Rosalie wondered if he would straighten up too when she fixed it. He paced three steps to the left, and three to the right.

'You've proven yourself quite useful since you've been here.' His tone indicated she should be grateful for the compliment. 'And resourceful.'

Rosalie hoped alphabetising the filing cabinet wasn't going to be the crowning glory of her illustrious journalism career.

'So, I think it's time I sent you out into the field.'

She sat up straighter, her heart beating faster. 'Thank you, sir. I won't let you down. I covered many stories in my time at univ—'

He held up a hand. 'Yes. I'm well aware of your stint at the university paper. But here . . .' he spread his arms out and spun around, looking at the printing press with obvious pride, '. . . here in the real world, we're dealing with real people and real stories. Not a bunch of puffed-up, privileged activists who would sooner forget the cause they were fighting for if another one came along.'

Rosalie pressed her lips together and held her tongue.

'I know this rag may seem like a backwater press to someone of your education and upbringing, Miss Reynolds, but the stories we tell matter to the people in this region. If you pay attention, you might just learn a thing or two about the human side to storytelling that an expensive education can't teach you.'

Rosalie shifted in her seat, a lifetime of polite breeding preventing her from speaking up and correcting her boss. She knew she was lucky to have this job, and she was tough enough to put up with whatever challenges Neville Payne threw her way. Especially if it meant she would eventually work her way to a position at one of the larger city papers.

'So,' he continued, as he turned to face her again. 'The school is holding a charity bake sale this weekend with all proceeds going to the Red Cross. I'd like you to cover it. Take photos. Interview the families on what it means to do their bit for the war effort. That sort of thing.'

Her first story in the field. Granted, a school bake sale was hardly the stuff of legend, but if Rosalie impressed Payne with this, surely he'd assign her other, more interesting stories.

'Now, go home and rest up before tomorrow.'

From the side of the building the newspaper office was housed in – right next to the bakery and the post office – Rosalie picked up her bike, which was leaning against the red brick wall, and secured her hatbox in its basket, before riding off down Main Street and heading home.

Saturday morning burst to life with bright blue skies and a hint of warmth in the autumn day. Dressed in a sensible blue shirt-dress, Rosalie rode to the tiny school a few blocks away from Main Street, the breeze she created cool against her skin.

The school, comprised of three white-washed stone buildings spaced out around a large quadrangle, was buzzing with activity by the time she arrived. There was a marquee under which some tables sat, with a sparse offering of cakes and breads and slices laid out on white table cloths. Rosalie wondered if the families who'd provided such fare had used all of their rations for this day. Granted, things out here in the country weren't as tight as they were in the city, with many households and farms producing their own eggs and butter, and everyone around here willing to share and help each other out. But there was a lot of sugar on those tables, and sugar was in short supply everywhere.

Behind the marquee, a ball toss was set up: the giant head of a circus lion had been cut out of wood and painted in bright colours, and children were already lined up waiting for their turn to see if they could throw the small beanbags through his gaping mouth.

A group of men over on the right had taken up either end of a giant rope, ready to test their strength, and on the left young boys and girls ducked and weaved around each other, doing the 'heel and toe', as a small band played behind them.

Rosalie got out her camera and started taking pictures, at first trying to capture the scale of the event. But there was something missing in her shots, she knew, pretty as they were.

'Hello there, Rosalie.' Mrs Donaldson stepped up beside her.

'Hello, Mrs D.' Rosalie took her notebook out of her hatbox.

'I thought you journalist types preferred those large leather shoulder bags.' Mrs Donaldson said, raising an eyebrow.

'Well, it would probably be more practical,' Rosalie smiled, 'but I kind of like my little hatbox.'

'It does suit you.'

'And where,' Rosalie spread her hands before her, 'does this all come from?'

Mrs Donaldson linked her arm in Rosalie's and steered her around the grounds. 'Well, all the fixtures and structures are either from the school or the church. Stuff they've had for years, used for fetes and fairs and the like, in times more certain than now.'

As they passed the giant lion head, Rosalie noticed the flaking of the paint and the chips from the wood's edge. When she'd been a student here, before becoming a boarder in Sydney for high school, they had used that same lion, she was sure.

'As for the cakes,' Mrs Donaldson pointed to the marquee, which Rosalie now noted was fraying at the bottom seam, 'as you know, we're not quite as affected by rationing here as in other parts of the country, and for items like sugar we scrimp and save for a few months, go without. It's no hardship compared with the sacrifice those serving are making.'

Rosalie wriggled free of Mrs Donaldson's grasp and took a photo of the cakes laid out before her with their bright reds and yellows and whites against a green gingham tablecloth.

Three young girls, who Rosalie had noticed dancing when she arrived, came running up to her and Mrs Donaldson, one with a posy of fresh flowers in her hands. Their mother, Rosalie assumed from the identical blonde curls they all wore, stood behind them with the red-star badge of the Australian Comforts Fund pinned to her threadbare shirt.

'From our garden.' The youngest of the sisters presented the posy to Rosalie.

'Can you spare a pence or two for our forces?' the middle sister chimed in.

Rosalie reached into her pocket and pulled out her small purse. She took out five shillings. 'They are very beautiful flowers. I think this should suffice.' She handed the coins to the oldest sister, whose eyes grew wide.

'Thank you, Miss . . . Reynolds, isn't it?'

Rosalie nodded. She recognised the woman but couldn't remember her name.

The mother smiled and handed Rosalie a pamphlet adorned with the ACF logo, outlining where the funds would go.

The youngest sister handed Rosalie the posy. She pushed it back into the little girl's tiny hands. 'I'm actually here working today.' Rosalie tapped her camera. 'So, do you think you can hang on to it for me?'

The little girl nodded. 'The flowers are my daddy's favourites.' The smile she wore was full of sadness. 'I hope he comes back soon.'

Rosalie looked to the mother, who mouthed 'New Guinea', and Rosalie's chest tightened. She looked back at the sisters. 'I hope so, too. With Mummy's permission, would you girls like your photo taken?' The two eldest girls smiled, the youngest jumped up and down.

'It's for the *River Times*. And if you drop by the office at the end of next week, you can grab a copy for yourselves.'

The mother frowned and Rosalie noticed the dresses they each wore had been mended many times over.

'It's a free service we offer to anyone who stars in one of our stories.' Rosalie hoped her little fib would be okay. Neville kept the photos the paper used filed away – badly filed till Rosalie's arrival – but there was no reason Rosalie couldn't make an extra copy for this family.

'Thank you, Miss Reynolds.'

'Rosalie.' Rosalie held out her hand.

'I'm Dorothy Arnold. Dot. And these are my girls, Tess, Peggy and Bonnie.'

Now Rosalie placed her. Dot was on the CWA with her mother. 'Now, girls, where do you think we should take this photo?'

The girls looked at each other. 'Next to the cakes?' the middle sister suggested, and Dot blushed.

'Hmm.' Rosalie looked around for a better spot. She knew what Dot was thinking – if the girls stood that close to the cakes, they'd want her to buy some. 'What about over there?' She pointed to the cluster of trees near the lion head. 'You will look really pretty over there and be the focus of the shot. We wouldn't want to lose you with so many cakes to distract us.'

The oldest girl nodded and herded her sisters over to the trees.

The bright sun was filtered through the leaves, softening the light, and the three girls stood, the youngest in the middle with the posy, their smiles forced as they stared at the camera. Rosalie crouched down so she was at a better angle.

'Why does your dad love these flowers so much?'

All three girls started talking at once and that did the trick. They forgot about Rosalie's camera altogether as they became animated about whether it was their father who'd planted the flowers, or Dot, and whether the white ones were his favourite, or the pink.

As they argued, Rosalie took their photo. Through her lens she captured the toothy smile of one, the serious eyes of another and the thoughtful expression of the third, the dappled light hitting the pastel petals of the posy.

'Thank you,' Dot said, as they finished and the girls ran off.

'How long has your husband been serving?'

A tear glinted in Dot's eyes. 'Gordon? Since the beginning.

Enlisted straight away. He was in Europe at first, but was recalled with everyone else.'

Two of Dot's girls started pulling each other's hair. 'Excuse me,' she said, now even more flustered, and she ran off.

For the rest of the morning Rosalie took photos and interviewed families: the wife who'd seen her husband off to war for the second time, worried this time he might not come back; the father whose sons had enlisted, and was now running his farm with the help of his neighbour's daughters; the thirteen-year-old boy whose sister was a nurse, he wasn't sure where, who didn't want to worry her with the news their mother was ill.

Rosalie sighed. At university it had all been about causes and intellectual debates and posturing about events so very far away from their safe bubble. And while she knew what was happening in the world, and here on their own soil, it had somehow been a distant thing.

This, though? This was real. Just as Payne had said.

'So, which will you use?' Payne asked her at work on Monday morning. 'What angle will the story take?'

Rosalie laid the best of the photos out before him. All of the shots were good. Pretty pictures. Nice portraits. But many lacked any kind of real depth. She didn't show him those ones.

'This is my favourite.' She pointed out the photo of Dot's girls she'd snapped just as they'd finished their debate about their daddy's favourite flowers.

Payne nodded. 'It has real emotion.'

'But is it enough to tell the story?' Rosalie asked. 'Won't people want to know about the activities and how much money was raised, and where it will go?'

'Yes. Of course. But at the end of the day, all storytelling – and mark my words, photos tell the most interesting stories – has to be about the human experience behind the facts and details and moments. Otherwise, what's the point? You must find a way to combine the two. Words that will tell the facts, and pictures that tell the heart. It's an art form that few journalists manage to truly achieve. They usually only master one or the other.'

'What about this?' Rosalie pushed her notebook in front of him. 'With these three shots?' She laid out the one of Dot's daughters, one of the cake table when it was at its busiest, and one of a young boy sitting at the end of the tug-o-war rope as the sun was setting, dirt all over his threadbare trousers, a forlorn expression on what should have been an innocent face, as he gazed at the empty end of the rope.

Payne sat silent for a moment. A long, agonising moment. And Rosalie held her breath.

He looked up at her, smiled and nodded.

When the paper finally came off the press, Neville handed Rosalie a copy.

'Your first story, Reynolds. What do you think?'

Rosalie looked at the front page, a tear in her eye. She should have been bothered by the by-line – 'N. Payne and R. Reynolds' – but she was so proud of her story she pushed aside any annoyance at the inclusion of Payne's name. She'd never had the front page when working on the university publication, and even though this was a less prestigious paper, she couldn't help but feel proud. This wasn't just a story she'd covered for the sake of *news*. This actually meant something to the people who called the river towns home, all the families up and downstream, all the farmers in the hinterlands that would read this tonight. There might not be any lauding from peers of journalistic merit with an article like this, but Rosalie didn't mind. This was different. This was personal.

'Thank you, Mr Payne.'

He gave her a curt nod. 'Call me Neville. We might make a decent journalist out of you yet.'

Not all of her memories of Redgum River were difficult, thought Rosalie. If there was a chance the music therapy idea Herman had floated could help Melody, help Sarah, wouldn't it be worth going back there? Maybe. But she could not undo what was done. Not make up for the pain and loss. Not give back what was taken away.

How could you make peace with a past whose pieces could never be put back together?

Six

As Sarah and Melody headed across to Granny Rose's for Sunday roast, Sarah trudged behind her daughter trying to muster some semblance of enthusiasm. But perhaps enthusiasm was too ambitious. Interest? Presence? Yes. She'd settle for presence. Settle for forcing her mind into the moment at hand instead of the dark corners it had been hiding in lately.

Melody's nightmare last night had nearly been Sarah's undoing. Her daughter's scream, Sarah's inability to calm her down quickly, the blue-black cloud of despair that had settled over her in the early hours of the morning as she watched over Melody. The last thing Sarah felt like doing today was putting on a smile and engaging in happy conversation. But she would. She always would. For Melody. She could never let her see just how broken her mother was inside.

What she wouldn't do today was bring up the museum or the album or the article in the *River Times*. She didn't have the energy for that discussion on top of the effort it took to simply appear fine. She'd sit back, put on her smile, let Ryan charm as he always did, and let Melody enjoy Granny Rose's company.

As they approached the French doors to the living room, she

was greeted by Ryan, chef's hat on as usual, the aroma of honey and rosemary wafting through the grand old home.

'Good evening, young ladies.' He bowed. 'Welcome to Restaurant Ryan. I'll be your server tonight.'

Melody giggled in her silent way and Sarah managed a genuine smile. Soft voices coming from the kitchen danced on the air.

'Do we have visitors?' Sarah frowned.

'One.'

'Who?'

Ryan pulled a face.

'Who?' Sarah said more forcefully.

But Ryan didn't have time to answer, as Rosalie came bustling into the living room, followed by Herman.

What was he doing here?

Sarah drew up whatever remaining strength she had to get her through the next hour or so; enough strength to get her through the evening until she could collapse into bed and repeat the charade of having everything under control tomorrow. And the next day. And the next.

'Ah, there you are.' Rosalie walked over and kissed Melody on the forehead. 'I was beginning to think you weren't coming.'

Sarah looked at her watch. They were only five minutes late.

'Of course we're here,' Sarah said. 'Where else would we be?'

'I could think of a few places.' Ryan winked.

'Really?' Rosalie raised an eyebrow. 'And where, pray tell, would you go in that rust bucket of a van of yours?'

She tapped something into Melody's hand and Melody responded with her ghost giggle.

'Isn't it about time you traded her in?' Rosalie suggested.

'I cannot believe you would even say that, Granny Rose.' Ryan put his hand to his chest. 'Gertie has been with me through thick and thin.'

Sarah rolled her eyes. Ryan had bought that ugly eyesore when he was eighteen and he loved it for reasons Sarah couldn't comprehend. It looked like it had been pieced together from different vehicles, an awful melding of blue and yellow and grey panels and touch-ups. She'd thought once he'd landed the job with Lowrie and Lowe, he'd upgrade to a vehicle more suited to his shiny new role in a prestigious architect firm. But his love for Gertie only seemed to grow the more his job demanded of him.

'She's got plenty of miles left in her. Just like you.' Ryan shot Rosalie a cheeky grin and Sarah could tell from the turn of Rosalie's lips that his charm was working once again. 'All she needs is a makeover.'

'I hope you're not suggesting *I* need a makeover.' Rosalie frowned, touching the soft white curves of her victory roll, her eyes sparkling with adoration.

'You can't makeover perfection.' Ryan sauntered off into the kitchen and Sarah resisted the urge to mime vomiting.

'Hi, Herman.' She turned her attention to her boss. 'I wasn't expecting to see you here.'

'Ms Reynolds invited me to join you. Your grandmother and I have been chatting about something that we'd like to talk to you about.'

'About the museum?'

'Not exactly.' He shook his head.

She frowned and looked to Granny Rose. 'What's going on?'

Rosalie raised her hand. 'Now, hear me out.'

Sarah had the distinct feeling she wasn't going to like what her grandmother had to say. 'What's going on?'

'As I said, hear me out.' Rosalie nodded to Herman and he pulled out his laptop.

'What's this?'

'An idea I think you really need to consider,' Rosalie said.

Sarah leaned forward and looked at the screen. 'A *music therapy retreat*? Seriously?' She stared at Rosalie.

'I'd never heard of such a thing until Herman mentioned it, but I've been doing some research on the topic, lots of reading and googling on the YouTube . . .'

Ryan stifled a laugh as he placed the roast in the middle of the table.

Rosalie shot him a look. 'And the benefits are real. It's all right there . . .' She waved her hands in the general direction of the laptop.

Sarah shook her head. She was well aware of music being used as a therapy tool. Though she didn't have any academic knowledge of it, she was most definitely attuned to the connection between music and emotion, and music's healing value. She had thought of it before, many times since the accident, but had ruled it out.

Sarah asked Melody to fetch some serviettes. She shouldn't discuss this in front of her.

She rubbed her temples. 'I . . . I don't . . . How can revisiting the very thing that is the root of her problem actually solve it? I can't expose her to any more trauma.'

'Sometimes,' Rosalie reached out her hand and patted Sarah's leg. 'Sometimes the root of the problem *is* the solution. With that in mind, I'm willing to do you a deal. If you agree to take Melody to the retreat, I'll agree to give the museum my photos.'

Sarah frowned. 'Blackmail?'

'An incentive.' Rosalie smiled.

Ryan looked at the laptop. 'It might be worth considering, Sar-bear.'

'But why a retreat? There would be any number of therapists we can see after school right here in Sydney?' Sarah wondered what else was going through her grandmother's mind.

'Oh.' Ryan smiled and nodded.

'Oh what?' Sarah turned to him.

He pointed to the address on the screen, which Sarah hadn't seen. Redgum River. Sarah snapped her head towards Rosalie.

'Because I'm coming with you,' Rosalie announced.

'You're what?'

'I'm coming with you.'

Sarah's mind raced, trying to order the thoughts bouncing into one another. A music retreat. Rosalie so reticent to discuss her past before, now wanting to actually go to Redgum River. A road trip. Time off work, time away from school.

'This is crazy. To get any value out of it at all, we have to be there . . . God, I don't know. How long? What about school?'

'Holidays are coming up,' Ryan chimed in, pushing his thick brown hair off his forehead. That hair of his really could star in its own rom-com, Sarah thought. 'And who cares about a few weeks extra off school?'

Sarah did. Taking Melody out of school, an environment she was comfortable in – surely that wasn't a good idea. 'No. I'm sure we can find a therapist here, if you're insisting this is something I should try.'

'Sorry, darling, it has to be Redgum River,' Rosalie said. 'That's the deal; that's where we need to go.'

'But I can't . . . you know I can't . . . how would we get there?'

'I can take us,' Ryan offered.

'What? What about your job?'

'Lord knows, I need to get away from that wretched place. I don't know how much more of it I can take, to be honest.' His shoulders dropped. 'You could do with getting way too,' he whispered in Sarah's ear.

Melody came back into the room, a packet of serviettes in her lap.

'How do you feel about a family holiday?' Rosalie asked her.

Melody's eyes grew wide and she smiled.

'That settles it.' Rosalie started serving up the roast.

Anger rose in Sarah. Panic. 'This is completely crazy.'

'Or is it a glitter bunker moment?' Ryan put his arm around her.

No. This wasn't anything glittery. This was her grandmother bulldozing her into something she didn't want to do. What about Melody's current therapy? What if exposing Melody to music in this way made things worse? She looked at her daughter, who gave her a reassuring nod. But Melody didn't know what she was agreeing to, so her being on board didn't really count.

Ryan and Herman started listing all the pros about the idea and Sarah studied Rosalie's expression.

She saw something she hadn't seen in her grandmother's eyes in a long time. Fear behind her determination.

'Is it really that important to you that it's this particular retreat?'

Rosalie nodded.

'Why?' Sarah narrowed her gaze.

'Because it's time to go home.'

Home.

Sarah couldn't get the word out of her head as she turned the light off in Melody's room later that night after three 'one more chapter's of *The Magic Faraway Tree*. Dropped so casually as it was by Rosalie, and with no further explanation.

Home.

She'd pushed, tried to get Granny Rose to say more, but the stubborn woman had simply lifted her chin into the air and changed the subject.

Growing up, Sarah had heard tale after tale of her grandmother's exploits, the fearless photojournalist, a regular pioneer of her time. A life punctuated by war zones, and coups and exotic locations. And while she'd never heard much of anything from before Rosalie was married, Sarah had always assumed it was because nothing could compare to her exciting professional life.

Home.

It was a word Sarah had never heard Rosalie use before. Not when she spoke about her travels. Not when she talked about her life in Sydney.

The house. My house. Our house . . .

Where your grandfather and I settled . . .

Returning to base after an assignment. . .

But never *home.*

Such a simple, everyday word. Such a strange word when it came from Rosalie.

On Wednesday afternoon, with Melody doing homework, Sarah sifted through the notes she'd made of imagined scenarios of Rosalie's secret life left behind in Redgum River, from the banal – she had fallen out with her parents – to the ridiculous – they were a family of spies who'd had to relocate after the war.

None of which made sense.

All of which led Sarah to the conclusion that she had to find out the truth. Rosalie's terms were clear. So, Sarah sat at the dining table with a glass of Berocca and her laptop. The thought of spending more time staring at a screen searching for answers released a tightly held groan from deep within. But she couldn't go into this lightly. There was more at stake than just finding out Rosalie's truth. This also involved Melody. And where she was concerned, there was no such thing as doing too much research.

She typed in the website for the retreat and scrolled through every picture and paragraph, clicked on every link to every study and supporting document, watched every video there was. She was surprised by just how extensive the field was, and, she had to admit, the more she read and saw, the more she wondered, was it worth a try?

Wasn't *anything* at this point?

She rolled her neck in a feeble attempt to release the tension that not enough sleep and far too much stress had seen her carry for too long. Always in her neck and shoulders. Always present.

Later that night, after Melody was tucked up in bed, Ryan paid her a visit and they went out into the carefully cultivated rose garden that made up her private courtyard. Rosalie's gardener still came once a week to tend to the grounds, thank goodness, as Sarah had never had a particularly green thumb.

Before they had a chance to sit at the rusted outdoor setting, Ryan turned to Sarah.

'I did it!' he whisper-shouted.

'Did what?'

'I quit.'

'What the . . .' She lowered her voice, not wanting to wake Melody. 'You *quit*? I thought you were just going to take some time off.'

He nodded. 'I was going to. But the thought of having to go back there afterwards . . .' he shuddered. 'I just couldn't bear it. So I quit.'

Sarah sat down in one of the chairs. 'Right. Well . . . congratulations. That's a big decision.'

Ryan sat opposite her. 'Yep. So that means we can all go to the retreat. You are going to the retreat, right?' he asked.

Staring out into the tranquil floral vista, Sarah tucked a curl behind her right ear and twirled it around her finger. 'I don't know.'

'Come on, Sarah.'

'I just . . .' she shook her head. 'What if it does more harm than good?'

He frowned. 'Finding out more about Granny Rose's past, you mean? Like, what if it turns out she's a murderer?'

Actually, the thought of that was at least intriguing. She laughed.

'Well, that, but also . . . Melody . . . It's just so . . . hard. I read everything, learn what I can, try to figure out what's best. But what if . . .' Sarah stood up and took a step forward, rubbing her hand on her hips. She spun round and threw her hands in the air. 'What if I make the wrong decision? What if I try this and it doesn't work, or it sets her back, or . . .' her hands fell beside her. 'God, I don't know.'

'But what if it does work?' Ryan stood beside her. At six feet, he was a good head and a half taller than her. 'Can I be honest, with you, Sar-bear?'

Sarah let out a small laugh. 'When are you ever not?'

'Oh, you don't want to know how much I really hold back. What's up here,' he tapped the side of his handsome head, 'compared to what comes out here.' He pointed to his mouth. 'Sometimes I deserve a medal for the things I don't say.'

'Do you now?'

He nodded, his rom-com hair flopping forward across his left eye.

'Right then. Out with it.' Sarah braced herself for whatever crazy idea or criticism was about to come spilling forth. Ryan wasn't usually one to put her down, but his warning about being honest sent a shiver of unease down her back. Was he about to pile on too? Like everyone else – the tone in the GP's voice, the looks from the school mums, the shakes of the head from the therapist. She felt as though everyone was always thinking she was letting her daughter down, that she wasn't doing enough.

He reached across and held her hand. 'I cannot tell you how proud I am of you, Sarah. How strong you are. How brave. You are the best mum in the whole entire world.'

Sarah stared at him. That was not what she'd expected him to say.

'You are.' He moved around to face her straight on and held her shoulders. 'There isn't a thing you wouldn't do for that kid. But I've watched you over the last year get so weighed down with guilt. And then worry about doing what's right. I think you've forgotten that sometimes it isn't actually about what's *right* at all.'

Sarah frowned.

'I think you have been so caught up in trying to help Melody that you've backed yourself into a corner. You've become so consumed with guilt and the need to fix things that the fear of doing something "wrong" has paralysed you. I know you, Sar-bear. You were this fearless creature growing up. And now you're frozen. Locked in an endless loop of but-what-if.'

Her bottom lip began to tremble. 'But . . . Melody needs me . . . for me to . . .' Sarah fumbled her words.

'I know you're exhausted.' He raised his hands and cupped her cheeks. 'Maybe this isn't just about Melody. Maybe it's about you, too.'

'*I'm* fine . . . I'm . . .'

He lowered his voice. 'No. You're not. You're anything but fine. It's time to let go. Forget about what's "right" for once.'

'But if I can't do what's right, what should I do?' Sarah's voice caught in her throat.

'I don't know. Maybe something crazy.' He winked. 'A . . .

'. . . glitter bunker moment,' they said in unison.

Seven

Rosalie hadn't seen much of Sarah and Melody this past week, and she shouldn't have been surprised. It wasn't exactly fair, springing Herman's idea of the retreat on her at dinner and then using him to further her cause. She really ought to be ashamed of herself.

Except she wasn't.

Every night since Sarah had found the album, Rosalie struggled to find sleep. Every night she was plagued by dreams of a time long ago, and she knew deep down they wouldn't go away until she dealt with whatever this was: clearing out any regrets and bad memories before her number came up, or simply the triggering of memories to resurface because of a seemingly innocuous photo album.

But that album was anything but innocuous. Those photos had meaning, consequences. And she knew they were going to continue to haunt her until she faced them and the power they held over her.

The clock on the mantle ticked past two as the memories stirred.

Redgum River
April 1945

Rosalie rode her bike up the dirt road to Penelope Dawson's house, a canister of cold cream in her basket. Three days ago, Mrs Donaldson had given her a few new Snapshot requests, including one from Edward Dawson. Today she could kill two birds with one stone. Make good on her promise to visit Penelope for scones and fulfil a Snapshot request.

Rosalie's tyres crunched as she pulled her bike to a stop outside Penelope's house. As the old worker's cottage of a once sprawling farm, it was a fairly rudimentary home, but the neat flower boxes at the entry and the sparkling cleanliness of the place spoke of much care.

Penelope opened the screen door and greeted Rosalie with a smile. 'So lovely to see you again, Miss Reynolds.' She wiped floured hands on her faded blue apron.

'Please. Call me Rosalie. We cannot stand on formalities over a canister of cream.'

Mrs Dawson licked her lips. 'Right you are. Come in, then, love. No point standing around catching flies.'

The aroma that wafted through the room was quite simply heaven. 'Oh my,' Rosalie said. 'They smell divine. You weren't exaggerating about your famous scones, were you?'

Penelope's eyes sparkled. 'Well, you haven't tasted them yet, so maybe hold back on the praise.' She pulled out a chair at the dining table and indicated Rosalie should sit.

Taking her first bite, Rosalie couldn't help but let out an exclamation of delight. 'Oh. Mmm. These are . . . without doubt, the best . . .' she swallowed, '. . . scones I've ever had.' And that was saying something, as she had frequented a number of posh tearooms in Sydney.

'Really?' Penelope pushed out her chest.

'Really.'

'That is very kind of you. Thank you.'

'And this jam!' Rosalie licked the drips off her fingers. 'Please don't tell my mother I did that.' She smacked her lips together.

The laughter that Penelope tried to stifle was light and airy.

When they finished their tea, Rosalie plucked up the courage to fish her camera out of her hatbox.

'I actually have something to ask you.' She pulled out the Snapshots From Home card and gave it to Penelope.

'That's my Edward's signature.' She gasped, looking at Rosalie with wide eyes.

'Yes. The YMCA organise for photos to be sent to the lads. Would you be happy to have your photo taken?'

A soft red flushed Penelope's cheeks. 'I . . . well . . .' She pushed her blonde curls behind her ear. 'I mean, of course I'd do anything to give my boys a smile. But I'm hardly in a state.'

Rosalie reached across the table and took Penelope's hand. 'You are perfect just the way you are right now. Do you think Edward would want a photo of you like this, exactly as he pictures you, warm and safe back home, or all made up not looking yourself?'

Penelope nodded. 'You're right. Though,' she stood up, 'I do have a little rouge left over from before the war.' She scuttled off down the short hallway.

Outside in the garden, Rosalie picked out a backdrop of distant gum trees and some lovely pink flowers in the foreground. Penelope fussed with her green cardigan, doing up its wooden toggles and undoing them again. The soft morning light was shining on her blonde curls and Rosalie thought she looked rather beautiful.

Penelope put her hands in the pockets of her cardigan and looked at Rosalie. 'Is this okay?'

'Why did Edward request a photo of you in the garden?' Rosalie had to get her to relax. She was far too stiff for a good photo. 'Why not baking? Or in front of the house?'

'Oh, well . . .' The smile that spread across her face was full of warmth and Rosalie snapped a shot.

'Oh, goodness. I wasn't ready for that.'

'Try to imagine I'm not here.'

'Right. Okay. Well . . .' she turned to the roses at her right and Rosalie repositioned herself and crouched down. 'If it were Albert who'd put in the request, then we'd be taking this photo with my scones, for certain.' She laughed. 'Never could get enough food in front of that one.' She shook her head. 'But Edward. He's my quiet one. He's always loved a garden, no matter where we lived when they were growing up.' She looked up at Rosalie. 'They're too young, you know. Both of them. To be serving.' A single tear fell down her cheek.

Rosalie stood up and stepped towards her. She only knew what she read in the papers, but she suspected any age was too young to be at war.

'I can't imagine what it's like for you.' She put her hand on Penelope's shoulder. 'Hopefully this will help bring them both a small piece of joy.'

Penelope nodded. 'I hope so.'

Rosalie took a few more photos until she was certain she already had quite a few good shots, and as the sun reached its peak in the sky she took her leave with a promise to visit again soon for more scones.

She took the scenic route home, along the river and through town, and was surprised to see her father's car in the drive when she returned. He wasn't due back for another couple of weeks.

Betty, their maid, greeted Rosalie at the door with a wet cloth and Rosalie washed her face before going inside.

'Father, it's good to have you home.' Rosalie greeted Frank with a kiss on the cheek. 'We weren't expecting you, were we?'

Frank pushed his hands into the pockets of his tan trousers and shook his balding head. 'No. I've had a schedule change. At dinner we can talk about the why.'

That night Betty served Rosalie, Frank and Iris a delicious joint of roast beef with carrots, and Frank opened a bottle of red from his cellar. He poured out three glasses and then turned to Rosalie. 'What do you say to accompanying me to the St Vincent's charity gala in a few weeks?'

'Me?' Rosalie dropped her fork and it clattered on her plate, making her mother jump. He always took Mother with him to the gala and Iris was far more adept at flattering those Frank was no doubt trying to impress than Rosalie ever could manage.

'Yes. You. I think it would be nice to have my journalist daughter on my arm to show off how proud I am of her. And you never know who you might meet at a gathering like that.'

Rosalie could see straight through this. There'd be lots of eligible bachelors there, and Frank was quite determined that she shouldn't wait too long to find a husband.

Rosalie narrowed her eyes. 'But I have to work.' That was a good excuse.

'I've already spoken with Payne and he's agreed to give you the week off, if you will write a small piece for the paper about it.'

'Really?' *How dare he speak to Neville behind her back.* Rosalie shouldn't have been surprised, though. He was always bulldozing his way through other people to get what he wanted. And what he wanted was her to find an appropriate match.

'Yes. You can take a few photos, maybe of your dear old dad, to show how far the support in the country towns can reach. A nice follow up to your ACF piece.'

Rosalie sat a little taller. Perhaps she could turn this to her advantage. A whole week in Sydney was appealing. Something altogether exciting and different to photograph. And something that might garner her recognition beyond the *River Times*. And there weren't just bachelors at these galas. Everyone of importance in the business world would be there. The editor of the *Herald*, perhaps. Surely he'd go to something like that, and perhaps she would have the chance to make herself known to him.

'I *guess* . . . as long as it's all right with Mother?'

Frank looked sternly at Iris, who nodded her assent.

'So it's settled then.' Frank raised his glass.

Rosalie smiled with anticipation.

Three weeks later, under a perfectly clear autumn morning sky, Rosalie drank in the view outside the car window, as sprawling buildings spread before her. She and Frank were approaching the Harbour Bridge and she leaned forward to see the criss-crossing metal arch rising above her. Every semester, after a few weeks' break in Redgum River, when Walter, her father's driver, would bring her back to the Women's College where she'd stayed during her studies, they crossed the bridge, just like now. And every time it took her breath away and she knew she was back in the place where her dreams had wings and hope.

The gala wasn't for another two days and Father would be busy with meetings until then. But Rosalie was sure she could amuse herself, her camera in hand.

When they arrived at the Australia Hotel in Castlereagh Street, a porter rushed outside to greet them at the car and carried their cases up the grey and white marble stairs, past the red Doric columns into the fine establishment's marble foyer. The two rooms

Father stayed in when he was working in Sydney were appointed with blue velvet armchairs, large four-poster beds, and gilded paintings that hung on walls covered in rich wallpaper.

Rosalie looked out to the street below, the cars driving past, the people bustling by, and smiled. There was enough time for her to go for a stroll, maybe to Hyde Park, and take some photos before dinner. She slung the camera strap around her neck, put on her hat and headed off.

The afternoon light pouring through the canopy of Moreton Bay figs offered interesting shadows and light and Rosalie spent far longer than she should have taking photos there. As she ambled back to the hotel she stopped outside the Theatre Royal and took a photo of the art deco façade.

'Are you going to see a show?' A man's deep timbre made her jump.

'Ah, no.' She turned around and stepped back. The gentleman stood tall, his bright blue eyes boring into her, his perfectly symmetrical smile full of warmth.

'You're a photographer?' He nodded to the camera in her hand.

'Yes. A journalist, actually.' She stood taller, attempting to match the confidence oozing from him. When she was studying at university she'd met any number of men assured of their own worth and place in this world, but there was something about this gentleman, his gentle poise, that didn't raise her hackles the way those boys had.

'That's impressive. I've never met a lady journalist before.'

Ah, but that rose her hackles. 'Well, now you have.' She turned on her heels and strode away.

'I'm sorry, ma'am.' He caught up to her and fell into step beside her. 'I didn't mean to offend you. I think it's swell, really.'

She wasn't sure what to make of his tone. Was he genuine, or mocking her?

She stopped outside the entrance to the Australia Hotel. 'Thank you. Good evening, sir. This is me.'

'Wait. I don't have your name.'

'Why would you need my name?'

'So I know when I read one of your articles.' He grinned and Rosalie felt herself thaw slightly.

'I doubt very much you'd be reading one of my articles.'

He clutched his hands to his chest as if she'd wounded him, and she couldn't help but smile as she ascended the steps into the hotel. She turned back before the bellhop closed the glass doors for her and the man took his hat off, rolled it up his arm and flicked it back up on to his head. He bowed and winked and walked off down the street.

The evening of the gala was the most perfect first of May night, with clear crisp skies and a chill in the air giving Rosalie the perfect excuse to don a fur shrug over her pink satin gown. While she certainly preferred the practicality of overalls and simple shirt dresses in her daily life, the moment she did get to dress up, she embraced it with full enthusiasm.

The gala was held in the grounds of the hospital under a series of marquees: the larger, main marquee for the VIP guests, with two smaller marquees either side. At the entrance to the big marquee two men dressed in white dinner jackets stood at attention checking everyone's invitations. The procession of guests, decked out in fine frocks and handsome tuxedos, entered slowly to the sounds of a small string ensemble playing Irving Berlin. Inside, there were chandeliers lit with candles, topiary trees and blue and white crepe bunting.

Rosalie frowned. She'd spent the past few days before coming to Sydney taking Snapshots for soldiers from humble homes and families, and the sad hungry look in the eyes of one of Corporal Pierce's three children, as they posed for their photo with their scrawny dog, Rex, haunted her as her father escorted her deeper into the marquee.

Father left her beside the punch table to 'attend to business', with the promise of returning before she'd even notice he was gone.

She took her camera out of the pink handbag she'd stowed it in and looked around for her first composition for her *River Times* story. She took a photo of the punch table, small platters of canapés creating dappled dots in the distance. Moving to the side of the marquee, she photographed her father meeting a rather dashing man around his age, perhaps slightly older, as they shook hands in greeting. The man had an air of authority about him, and something a little familiar Rosalie couldn't quite put her finger on, but from the number of people waiting to greet him, Rosalie assumed he was the famous Dr Burton. Tonight's host, her father's boss at the hospital. Dr Burton was in charge of Frank's rotations as he tried to secure a permanent job as a physician at the hospital.

With her father occupied, Rosalie continued to take photos – of the musicians, of the couples who'd begun to dance, of the men crowding around the auction table discussing what they might bid on, and of the large paper thermometer that took up the back corner of the marquee. A blue arrow with a white pound symbol painted in the middle pointed about a quarter of the way up the thermometer.

'This is where we're at with our fundraising goal,' a young man nearby told her. 'Perhaps your husband will be willing to make a donation to the hospital, or bid on one of the auction items.'

'I'm not here with a husband,' she responded, and a deep voice from behind made her turn around.

'I'm certainly glad to hear that.' The man from outside the theatre smiled at her.

'You?' Rosalie's cheeks warmed. His blonde curly hair had been slicked back and his tux showed no signs of false opulence, fitting perfectly over his tall, broad frame.

'Me.' He agreed confidently. 'And you?' He held out his hand and she allowed him to brush hers with a kiss. 'I'm Henry.'

'Rosalie.' She smiled politely and scanned the room.

'Are you looking for someone in particular?' Henry bent down and whispered in her ear. She could smell the orange juice and champagne on his breath and she stepped away.

'My father. He's here somewhere.'

'I'm sure he'll turn up eventually. In the meantime, why don't we have a little bit of fun?' There was a twinkle of mischief in his eye and Rosalie frowned, wondering how she could politely remove herself from this uncomfortable encounter.

'Don't worry. I promise you'll be impressed.' He put his glass down, and picked up another, pointing to the arrow on the thermometer, then back to the drink. 'The punch is a little watered down, rations and all, otherwise that arrow would be much higher.' Henry frowned. 'What do you say we do something about it?'

'What can we do?' Rosalie stared at him.

He looked at her camera. 'Well, this lot here are all about status and flaunting that status. That's why they get invited. Why don't we use that to our advantage?'

Rosalie had no idea what Henry was talking about.

He went over to an attendant, whispered to him, placed something in his hands, and the man shucked his jacket. Henry took off his tux and put on the attendant's jacket. Removing the bottle of champagne from the ice bucket on the table next to them, he emptied the ice into a nearby pot plant and, looking rather pleased with himself, said, 'This will do nicely.'

Rosalie frowned, not keeping up with him at all.

'We need this.' He pointed to her camera. 'And this.' He straightened his jacket and tucked the bucket under his arm. 'What do you think?' Henry asked her. 'A shilling a shot?'

Rosalie stared at him. 'That's highway robbery.'

'Not for this lot. Especially if they think they might end up in the newspaper.'

'But they won't.' Rosalie put her free hand on her hip.

'They don't know that. And they can pick their photo up from the hospital foyer next week.'

Well, if they were going to get a photo out of it, and the funds were for a good cause, Rosalie could probably go along with the plan. She made Henry promise that he wouldn't pretend the photos would be published anywhere.

'There.' Henry pointed to a fine-looking older couple at the punch table. 'Sir and Lady Fernsby. Old money.'

Henry introduced Rosalie to the couple and told them she was with the Sydney *Herald*. She shot him a glare. They posed dutifully and slipped a few shillings into the bowl. Henry thanked them for the generosity and moved Rosalie away.

'I asked you not to do that,' she said crossly.

'I'm sorry. But it did work. Next?' He pointed to a young couple at the auction table.

'No.'

'No?'

'Have you never heard the word before?' Rosalie stood her ground and straightened her shoulders.

'Not often, I have to admit.' He put his hand on his chest. 'I won't do it again. I swear. Just donations for a photo. No mention of newspapers.'

Rosalie looked into his eyes and he held her gaze. She decided to believe him.

They spent the next hour moving through the marquee together, Henry selling the idea of Rosalie capturing the historic moment for posterity – no mention of newspapers; Rosalie positioning the couples so the light was optimal. The more money that was in the bucket, the more people seemed to donate.

Eventually Henry and Rosalie found some empty chairs and Rosalie sat while Henry fetched two drinks.

'I'd say that was rather successful, wouldn't you?' he said as he returned and handed her a glass of water. He was having another glass of punch.

'I have to admit, we did raise a lot of money.' She lifted her glass in salute.

'You're a great photographer,' Henry said.

Rosalie shook her head. 'How would you know? You haven't seen the pictures yet.'

He shrugged. 'I can tell. You put your subjects at ease. You were calm, kind. And while I may not know a lot about lighting, you seemed to know what you were doing.'

Rosalie allowed herself to relish the compliment. 'What do you know a lot about then, Henry? If not lighting.'

Henry laughed and blinked his eyes as if trying to force them to focus. 'Sorry?'

'What do you do? Why aren't you serving in the war?'

He frowned, just for a moment before the grin returned. 'I'm in my final year of a medicine degree.'

'Oh?' It was hardly surprising, she supposed, given they were at a hospital fundraiser.

'Third son of a third generation of doctors.' He raised his glass and took another gulp.

'Ah, there you two are.' Frank strode toward them.

Rosalie got off her stool and Henry rose too.

'Henry!' Father slapped him on the shoulder.

Rosalie stepped away. A niggling tingle shot up the back of her neck. 'You two know each other?'

'I was hoping to introduce you myself, but it appears Mr Burton was too quick off the mark for me.'

'Mr Burton?' Rosalie narrowed her eyes.

'Ah, I see the children are acquainted.' The man Father had greeted when they arrived was beside them.

'Dr Burton, may I introduce you to my lovely daughter, Rosalie. Rosalie, Dr Burton.'

Rosalie's mouth dropped open. 'Dr Burton. And this is your . . .' She looked at Henry.

'My youngest son, Henry.'

The third son . . . Rosalie's stomach tightened.

'I say, Reynolds.' He turned to Frank. 'You said she was a pretty thing and you weren't lying.'

'Father?' Rosalie fixed Frank with a glare, her mind racing.

'Why don't you two take a spin around the dance floor? Get to know each other better.' Frank leaned towards Rosalie and whispered, 'He's a good man,' before moving off with Dr Burton.

'Are you . . . all right, Rosalie?' Henry asked.

She could feel her cheeks burning. 'I . . . you . . . your father . . .' she said through gritted teeth. 'Outside the theatre . . . did you know who I was?'

Henry at least had the decency to cast his gaze down and appear sheepish.

'This was all a set-up?'

'No, it wasn't, Rosalie. I swear.' He looked up at her with wide glassy eyes. 'Our fathers are colleagues and yours did mention to me that you were coming to the gala with him. I wanted to meet you outside of this charade . . .'

Charade was right. She knew her father wished her married, but surely he wouldn't stoop to this – he and Dr Burton doing each other a favour. A wife for Doctor Burton's youngest son, a promotion for Frank. She had flashbacks to her failed internship. She had no intention of being anyone's pawn again.

'Good evening, Henry.' She turned and marched out of the marquee.

'Rosalie?' Henry caught up to her.

'Leave me alone.'

He ran his fingers through his thick blonde hair, releasing his curls. 'Please, Rosalie. It isn't what you think.'

But Rosalie was sure it was. 'Was this your father's idea, or mine?'

Henry frowned. 'Neither. Yes, they have spoken of you, but just like any fathers speak of their children. I was simply intrigued to meet you. That's it.'

'Then why didn't you say who you were, when we met outside the theatre?'

She waited for him to reply, but he simply swayed in front of her.

Before she could storm off again, a buzz of voices from the marquee echoed across the grass. Rosalie looked over to see people running towards each other, men shaking their heads, women covering their mouths with gloved hands.

A waiter scuttled past.

'Excuse me,' she called. 'What's going on?'

'Hitler, ma'am. They're saying he's dead.'

Rosalie started after him as he scuttled away.

'Rosalie. Wait!' Henry ran after her. 'Did he just say . . .'

'Come on.' She pulled out her camera, and Henry followed her, dumbstruck.

Inside the marquee, the band had stopped playing and guests were huddled in small groups. Whispers of 'Could it be?' and 'Maybe it's a hoax' and 'You can't trust those Krauts' rumbled through the charged air.

Rosalie snapped a few photos, capturing what might, or might not be a moment in time to remember.

'Rosalie.' Her father stepped up beside her.

'Is it true?' she asked.

Frank shrugged. 'We don't know. We're waiting for confirmation. Put that away.' He lowered her poised camera. 'Now's not the time.' And they waited with everyone else under the marquee for news.

———

Ryan coughed as he entered the room, pulling Rosalie back to the present.

'Are you okay, Granny Rose?' he asked. Always such a considerate lad.

She nodded. 'Sometimes it's just hard to get to sleep is all.'

He put his arm around her. 'So it seems.' He pointed to the light coming from the guest house.

And Rosalie knew, as hard as it would be to go back home, she had to do it – for herself and for her granddaughter.

Eight

Tarakan Island, off the coast of Borneo

May 1945

Edward leaned up against the rough trunk of the tree, the canopy of the jungle offering scant relief from the rain. Despite the downpour, there was no respite from the humidity. Beside him Albert heaved off his kit, his eyes closed, catching a few moments of rest before they were, no doubt, expected to move off again to trudge through the squelching mud that sucked the very energy from every man in their platoon.

With a swat of his left hand, Edward killed two mosquitos, the blood smearing across his palm. Another couple of bites to add to his collection. From his breast pocket he pulled the black and white photo of his mum out of the velum pouch in which he kept it, removing it carefully, making sure he covered it from the rain with his slouch hat.

She looked beautiful, a wistful expression on her face as she tended her flowers. He turned the photo over and read the note on the back once more:

> I hope this photo of your mother brings you some joy. She is keeping well and thinks of you often. We took scones together this day. They were delicious. Thank you for your service. R.R.

The script was impossibly neat and delicate, and Edward wondered if perhaps a woman had taken the shot, as unlikely as that was. Or perhaps her husband or brother had, and she'd simply penned the message on his behalf. No man he knew had script as flowing as that. However it had come to pass, he was awfully grateful. For the photo the YMCA had sent him, and for those few words. It was one thing to hear from his mum herself; another thing entirely to hear from someone else that she was well. And to know these two had shared Penelope's famous scones – the simple knowledge filled him with warmth. He worried about his mother constantly, back home all alone.

Thunder rumbled in the distance. Always hot. Always wet.

When he next got the chance, he'd write to his mum. Perhaps when this wretched march was over they might have a few dry moments at base to indulge in such a thing. Still, at least they could move out here in the jungle, as cumbersome as it was. And that was better than the days they'd spent cramped together on the transports over to the island. Edward shuddered at the memory of the relief to finally disembark, only to be met with a shoreline aglow with orange flames and the thick black smoke of burning oil. The Japs had set fire to it all. The oil tanks burned. Torpedoes exploded around them. Random bombardment and rifle fire cut through the strange thick blackness surrounding them. They'd taken the beach and air strip and now they were pushing inland to secure strategic positions on the island.

There was no point trying to write home when they were surrounded by the wet like this. The pencil scratchings would simply wash away from the flimsy scraps of paper Edward tried to save for letters. When they got to their destination and were out of the rain, perhaps his mood would improve too. And that would be better for writing home anyway – to try not to let the misery of this place seep into his words.

Albert stirred beside him, attempting to smile. At least, for now, this hellish place hadn't broken him. At least, for now, Edward could push his guilt aside that he hadn't been able to talk his younger brother out of signing up.

'We'll get to travel.' Albert had said excitedly when he told Edward his plans. 'See places we could never even dream of.' His green eyes had sparkled as he'd pushed his long ginger curls out of his eyes. Those curls were gone now, of course, his hair cut close like the rest of them. It didn't suit him, not framing his open face quite right.

Nothing Edward had said could dissuade Albert from enlisting and there was no way Edward was sending his baby brother off to war alone, so he'd joined up with him, the need to protect him, like he'd done his whole life, driving his determination.

He should have tried harder to stop him. This was no place for Albert. This was no place for any of them, really. But sweet, gentle Albert . . . Edward tried to cope with the sporadic explosions, the snipers, the oil and the mud, by telling himself they were all things one should expect from war. But Albert had expected adventure. Not death. Not blood. Not guts pouring out of the man next to him when he triggered one of the booby traps set across the island. On their third day, Albert had frozen still beside Private Bennett, watching the man's insides spill out, his mouth set somewhere between a disbelieving line and a horrified grimace.

For the very first time Edward had seen fear in Albert's eyes. And though he tried to hide it, Edward knew his brother was terrified deep down inside.

'Right, men,' the commanding officer barked. 'Time to go.'

The order was met with silent movement, the men too exhausted to protest.

Thick jungle and treacherous hills impeded their progress, not to mention pockets of Japanese resistance.

Albert pulled himself up slowly. Edward caught the briefest flash of fear behind his brother's eyes before Albert masked his inner darkness with his usual goofy smile.

'I cannot wait to see her again,' Albert said, nodding at the picture of their mother before loading his heavy kit on his back, making sure his banjo was secured to his pack. Who brought a banjo into the middle of the jungle in the middle of a war? Albert. That's who.

Edward tucked the photo away in his pocket, pushed his steel helmet down tight on his head and squared his shoulders.

'Let's go, Albie.' He rested his hand on his brother's shoulder.

And they marched off in the rain, pushing through the thick mud as they made their slippery descent into whatever hell was waiting.

Nine

Ryan's words had been swirling around Sarah's mind for the last few days. He was right. She was frozen with fear. Stuck.

It would take a huge leap of faith into a very scary unknown, though, to get unstuck. And despite Ryan's recollections of her fearless youth, Sarah was pretty sure there was no bravery left inside her anymore. She couldn't even bring herself to drive a car. Where was the bravery in that?

So she fired off a string of emails to the head therapist at the retreat, Joshua Chung, some with information of her own – the accident, details of Melody's condition – and question after question about the retreat and the therapy.

She also researched Mr Chung himself. Degrees from Sydney's UNSW and UTS, clinic work in Hong Kong and London, and a warm smile on his profile picture on the retreat's website.

'Are you the answer, Mr Chung?' she said out loud. 'Can you help my baby girl?'

Sarah had no idea. But as she stood outside Judy's office on a wet grey Friday a week later, still no sign Melody's therapy sessions were making any progress, she could feel her resolve hardening: she had to do something. Anything.

She helped Melody into Ryan's van and climbed into the front seat.

'So, do you still want to come to Redgum River?' she asked him.

'Yes.'

'I got an email last night. A spot has opened up.' Her hands began to shake and she sat on them to hide her nerves from both Melody and Ryan.

'You know *I'm* up for it. Are *you*?' He flicked a quick glance her way.

'I have absolutely no clue. So what have we got to lose?'

Ryan grinned. 'That's my fearless cousin back.'

She was quite sure that he knew just how petrified she was, but she appreciated him pretending otherwise.

Two weeks later, Rosalie stood with Sarah and Melody on the street outside Rosalie's home, waiting for Ryan to pull Gertie around the front.

'Ready to hit the road?' he called out as he pulled into the kerb.

Sarah shrugged. Melody clapped. Sarah had explained to her, in a roundabout way, what the purpose of the trip was. She hadn't wanted to blindside her daughter, and she understood the importance of Melody feeling like she had some say in her own treatment. That had been drilled into Sarah from every medical professional they'd seen. But she'd played down the therapy side of things a little and emphasised they were going on a holiday, likening the retreat to a special camp. And Melody was very excited about going to camp.

'Ready as I'll ever be.' Rosalie handed him her red suitcase. 'Question is, will this old piece of junk make it?'

'Gertie has never let me down yet.'

'Mmm.'

'Ryan, can you tell Granny Rose we're not taking her bike?' Sarah pointed at Rosalie's e-bike leaning against the curved sandstone wall that surrounded Rosalie's property.

'Why not?' Rosalie put her hands on her hips.

'Well . . . it isn't . . . I mean . . .'

'I can pop it on the roof rack.' Ryan picked up the bike before Sarah could protest any further and hoisted it on. When he finished securing it, he helped Rosalie climb in the back of the van.

Sarah settled Melody next to Rosalie, making sure she had her favourite colouring pencils with her, before hopping in the front. With everyone inside, Ryan started the engine. 'Who's ready for an adventure into the unknown?' he called over his shoulder and Sarah swallowed the lump in her throat.

With the radio playing softly, they headed out of the city. The drive would take around four hours, long enough for Sarah to talk herself in and out of this being a good idea a hundred times over. At least that was one advantage of having Granny Rose and Ryan with her: she couldn't just quietly turn around and slink back home, pretending this never happened. She had no choice now but to see it through.

Beside her, Ryan began singing along with the radio, quite out of tune as usual. He'd been doing that a lot since he'd resigned. Singing. It was good to see a lightness return to him that had been missing for so long. She just wished . . .

Sarah cast a look back to Melody, who frowned, eyes darting around.

Sarah placed her hand on Ryan's leg and shook her head. He stopped, mouthing 'Sorry' to her.

Looking back again, Sarah saw the agitation in Melody dissolve, and she let out a silent sigh. This was going to be a long four hours.

Rosalie was uncharacteristically quiet. Sarah hadn't seen her grandmother so withdrawn for years. Whatever must Redgum River mean to her? She didn't like seeing Granny Rose like this.

But it was too late now. They were on their way. Besides, Sarah had broken her number one rule and had allowed the tiniest speck of hope to lodge deep down inside. The more she'd read about the retreat and music therapy in general, the more she'd corresponded with Mr Chung, the more she knew they had to try it. She'd sent so many emails to the poor man, he was surely dreading her arrival, but he had answered her incessant questions with compassion and insight each time.

Ryan shifted in his seat beside her. He would have shaken his head at her if he'd known how obsessive she'd been in the lead-up to this trip. And she wouldn't have blamed him. Sarah couldn't pinpoint the exact moment she'd disappeared fully and become this anxious, serious, unrecognisable version of herself. It wasn't the accident, surprisingly, though that was certainly the moment her life changed irrevocably. It wasn't the dark, endless days in the hospital. It wasn't the first time she saw Melody in the chair, or even when they realised she had stopped talking. It wasn't moving into Granny Rose's guesthouse, leaving behind the home she'd created for her young daughter, or when she'd given up on her own therapy. Not the first time after the accident when she went to drive a car and froze, unable to even open the door. She'd actually laughed at herself when that had happened. The first time. Much less laughter the second.

When Sarah looked back over the last year, she could see her old self there, sprinkled throughout those moments in full colour, able to make a joke here, offer a sassy retort there. But somehow, somewhere, the colour ever so slowly leached away until there was only this grey version of herself left.

A version she didn't particularly like, but one that had taken over completely.

An hour out of the city Sarah began to nod off.

'Recognise the landscape, Granny Rose?' Ryan called over his shoulder, jarring Sarah awake.

'Indeed. Not much has changed.' The response was forced, Sarah could tell. She turned around in her chair and saw Rosalie staring out the window as the tall gum trees sped past. The first words she'd said all trip.

What was the old duck hiding? And, more importantly, why? Sarah studied her grandmother, thankful for the distraction. It sure beat the script that usually ran through her head – *how will today go, when will there be a breakthrough, remember to go to the chemist and buy more catheters, wash the sheets after the sweat from last night's nightmare, remember to check if there's a ramp at that place, make sure there's no loud music at that party . . .*

Wondering about Rosalie's past and making up stories of why she had never mentioned Redgum River was a strange kind of relief. Perhaps her grandmother was a teen delinquent and had got run out of town; or maybe she'd exposed the mayor's ill-doing in an article for the *River Times*, and he had her run out of town; or had she fallen in love with a married man and then had to take her broken heart as far away as she could, vowing never to return . . .

'What are you staring at, my darling?' Rosalie's voice broke through Sarah's imaginings.

'Huh? Oh sorry. Nothing.' Sarah turned back around.

'Do you think they'll have decent food at this retreat?' Ryan asked and Sarah allowed herself a little chuckle.

'Always thinking of your stomach.' She shook her head. 'It's self-catering, remember.'

He rubbed his belly with one hand, and Sarah's heart beat faster, willing him to put both hands back on the wheel. 'Food is life, Sar-bear.'

'I did look into restaurants and cafés for you, though.'

'Of course you did.' His gentle expression held no hint of mocking or judgement. 'You know. This time away is a chance for us too. Neither of us having to be on top of everything all the time.'

She did know that, and it frightened her. Four weeks at the retreat. Four weeks when someone else was in control. Four weeks of nothing but focus on Melody: fine. Four weeks of focus on her: not so fine.

He lowered his voice. 'I've been doing my research too, Sar-bear.'

She shot him a look of surprise.

'Yes, I have. Do you think I'd let just any old nutjob have a crack at my Melody?' He shook his head. 'Yes, I've done my research and we're in good hands at this place. All of us.' He winked. 'You just need to . . . what would Melody's favourite Disney princess say?'

Sarah shook her head. 'Let it go?'

'That's the one.'

'You know, technically, Elsa's a queen, not a princess.'

'You don't always have to be right,' he grumbled. 'Sometimes it's fun not having all the answers. The unknown is often where the magic lies.'

After a quick pit stop they hit the road again and half an hour away from Redgum River they passed through a tiny village – Wombat Hollow read the sign – nestled in the hills. Old weatherboard cottages painted in blues and creams and whites hugged the narrow road, thick green foliage spilling over their rooves and wrapping around their sides in a warm embrace. There was a small café with intricate fretwork sitting on the bend in the road and Ryan slowed right down to get a better look. Sarah knew he was making a mental note to come back and check it out in more detail later. He may have walked away from his job, but he'd loved architecture and design for as long as Sarah could remember.

As they left the village behind them, driving slowly due to the winding road, Rosalie mumbled something Sarah couldn't quite make out. She turned around and was met with a forced smile. Quickly Rosalie broke eye contact and leaned over towards Melody, who had put her colouring aside. The two of them engaged in one of their secret conversations. Sarah's heart splintered, as it always did when she witnessed the communication she wasn't a part of – a thousand tiny splinters of lost moments she could never experience.

She turned back around and focused on the road ahead, struck by the vibrancy of the green all around them. Was it always this lush here, she wondered. Perhaps. Though, if her extensive research was correct – local climate, population, industry, history, anything she could find out about the area – these parts had had a lot of rain lately. As Sarah watched the rich lime and emerald and olive greens roll past, she wound down her window to breathe in the colour.

Crisp. Clean. Fresh.

Deeply she inhaled.

Cool. Serene. Calm.

She exhaled.

In. Out. The tranquillity surrounding her seeping into her soul.

'Here we are.' Ten minutes later Ryan pointed to a sign on the side of the road: 'Redgum River'. Thick, deep script painted white was carved into a dark-brown slab of wood.

Behind her, Rosalie made a faint squeaking sound and Sarah turned to check on her. She sat straight and tall, hands folded in her lap, her expression perfectly poised, a thin smile. But her eyes. There was no hiding the trepidation in her grey eyes.

'Have you got the map on your phone?' Ryan asked. 'Not that I think it will be too hard to find anything in a place like this.'

Sarah turned back around and pulled out her device. 'Yep. Follow this road and then, just north of town, it veers to the left, and we take the first left after that.'

Melody clapped from behind.

The road they were on seemed new, or at least newly tarred, and skirted the edge of what Sarah assumed was the centre of town on their left. A row of buildings lined the street, their striped awnings painted in various combinations – white and lilac, grey and pink, lemon and blue. Each awning corresponded with a sign that hung from its wooden beams. A newsagent, a butcher, a hairdresser. A few people milled about the street in no apparent hurry and the midday sun cast a bright, almost neon, glow over the town.

Every now and then, between the buildings Sarah caught a glimpse of the river, speckles of sunlight bouncing off the rippled water. On their right was a lacework of wide streets lined with a hodgepodge of old weatherboard cottages, brick bungalows – some in their original dark-red skins, some painted white – and a sprinkling of modern houses that didn't seem to belong.

As the road swung gently to the right, the town and houses dissolved into thick bushland and Sarah wondered if they'd missed a turn. But when she looked back at the map on her phone, the blue dot that was them was heading in the right direction.

A smaller road forked off to the left and Ryan turned down it, the dense grey-green curtain of tall gum trees opening up to a clearing. The road bulged into a cul-de-sac and at the end of it a driveway led to a large wooden building that echoed a colonial homestead. Dotted around the clearing were smaller cabins that seemed to have been deliberately aged to blend in with the bush surrounds.

'I guess we're here,' Sarah whispered, the weight of hope and fear choking her words.

Ten

Rosalie sat frozen inside Gertie. Not able to get out of the van. Not willing. She should have listened to her inner doubt last night and pulled the plug on the whole ridiculous idea. She'd been moments away from texting Sarah and making up some mystery illness to get her out of coming. What was the point of her going back to a town she had left so long ago, to echoes of a life she'd turned her back on? Granted, she had suggested this trip, but she realised she had been foolish to do so.

Yet as she'd picked up the phone, she couldn't do it. She'd never backed down from anything life had thrown at her, and there was no escaping the part of her, deep in the recesses of her soul, that seemed to be urging her to return.

Closure. That's what the touchy-feely brigade called it these days. Well, she'd lived far too long, seen and done far too much, to bother with such nonsense. Yet, here she was, back in a place she swore she'd never return to.

There was a time in her life, most of her life actually, when the unknown was exciting. Right now, though, she could have done without the unknown. One had no way of predicting what the ripple effect might be. Good, or bad. Rosalie's career had taught her that, and back then she'd relished it. But work was different. She could always handle whatever a story threw at her. In her personal life those sorts of surprises were more difficult to negotiate.

Redgum River
May 1945

Those days after the news of Hitler's demise had seen Neville and Rosalie work around the clock filtering through various stories that came in – the German delegation to Lüneburg Heath; a few days later Eisenhower's acceptance, in Reims, of Germany's unconditional surrender; Stalin signing the text of surrender the day after.

In Berlin, on the night of Tuesday 8 May, it was official. The war in Europe was over.

'Go and capture what's happening out there.' Neville had waved his hands in the general direction of Main Street as the news broke in Australia. 'I'll man the fort here.'

As Rosalie had walked through the centre of town, she was met with both joy and caution. People were happy, of course. But there had also been hesitation in the air. The war in the Pacific was not over. For these folk, whose sons, brothers, and husbands were still fighting, the hardship was far from finished. She'd thought of Penelope with Edward and Albert somewhere over there.

Outside the post office, Rosalie had seen Millie and Dot huddled together. Frederick and the girls had danced in the street with other children, but the women could only give Rosalie a half-smile as she'd approached.

'What do you think this means for our lads?' Millie had asked, her eyes wide.

Rosalie had shrugged. 'I think it means there's room for hope.' What else could there be? If there wasn't hope, then what?

By the end of May things had returned to normal in Redgum River. Mostly. Rosalie had taken on more assignments from Mrs Donaldson, and Neville was starting to give her more responsibility at the paper. Life had found a certain rhythm in the chaos and uncertainty, a rhythm Rosalie didn't mind.

One Sunday, the threat of winter in the air, Rosalie left church with Penelope and headed back to her place for tea.

'I'm so pleased you came by. This arrived for you on Friday.' She handed Rosalie a folded piece of paper.

Rosalie frowned.

'It's from Edward,' Penelope said. 'I wrote to him after you took those photos of me and told him all about the work you're doing here. I'll let you read it while I put the kettle on.'

Dear Miss Reynolds,

My mother speaks very highly of you, and I wanted to thank you for the lovely photo you took of her. I fear she is lonely there in Redgum River, though she does not say it in her letters. I can read between the lines, however. I am grateful she has a friend in you. I showed the picture to my brother, and of course all he could talk about was our mother's scones and how he can't wait to eat them again. Perhaps when we are home, we can eat scones all together.

Thank you again for your kindness.

Yours, Edward

Rosalie let out a sigh. Edward taking the time to write to her, when he was in Lord knew what type of horror, touched her heart. She would have to make a point of visiting Penelope more often, and reassure Edward his mother was fine.

An idea scratched at the back of Rosalie's mind as she thought of Penelope and Millie and Dot. Was there something more she could do for them?

'Tea's ready,' Penelope called, and Rosalie tucked the letter into the pocket of her overalls. 'I hope you don't mind him writing to you.'

'Of course not. It's nice to know the photo was appreciated.'

'He writes every chance he gets. Albert's never been one for putting pen to paper. But Edward writes for both of them.'

'I can't imagine how much you must miss them.'

Penelope simply smiled.

As they drank their tea and nibbled on slices of stale tea loaf, Rosalie tucked a stray strand of hair back into her snood and floated her idea. 'If I organised a picnic for some of the families I've taken photos for, would you come?'

'Oh, that does sound interesting.' Penelope started to clear away the table and Rosalie joined her. Together they nutted out the details as they washed the dishes.

When Rosalie got home, she couldn't wait to write to Edward of her plan.

She opened her compendium and pulled out a piece of soft pink paper.

> Dear Private Dawson,
>
> I have seen your mother again this week, and I feel you are, regarding her loneliness, very perceptive, despite your physical distance. But I have a plan. There are many here missing

their loved ones as this infernal war drags on. And while there is talk of the end being nigh, until that day there is still much that can be done to ease the suffering of families of those who serve. I'm planning a picnic with some of the families for whom I've taken Snapshots. I hope it will be a success.

Yours, Rosalie

She addressed the envelope with the details Penelope had given her. In the morning she would send it off on her way to work.

A week later, on a cool Saturday morning in June, Rosalie grabbed the picnic basket Betty had prepared and put it on the back of her bike.

'Don't be late home.' Father appeared in the kitchen doorway, his hands in his pockets. 'Your mother and I expect you back for dinner.'

She rode to the north end of town, where the river widened and the bank was covered in lush green grass, before the bush encroached on the water's edge. Penelope was already there and waved to her as she approached, a large red-and-white checked picnic blanket spread before her.

Rosalie pulled up and Penelope helped her unpack. Dot was the next to arrive, with Tess, Bonnie and Peggy in tow, Peggy carrying a posy of daisies, which she gave to Rosalie.

'Thank you for inviting us,' Dot said. The girls took a look at the food and their eyes widened in a silent plea to their mother. 'Go and have a game of chase first. We need to wait till everyone arrives.'

Millie arrived with Frederick on her hip, a gentle smile on her face. Once Dot's girls realised there was a toddler to play with, they crowded around Millie, scaring poor little Frederick with their intense attention as they each tried to take him from his mother to play.

Eventually he relaxed, thanks to the patience of Tess, and all four children ran off to the river's edge and started throwing sticks into the gently running water to see which one would make it to the bend upstream first.

Rosalie grabbed her camera and started taking photos.

Mrs Donaldson arrived, a plate of biscuits in hand and Rosalie headed back to the picnic blanket.

As the midday sun warmed the grass beneath Rosalie's bare feet, Frederick lay asleep in Millie's lap, exhausted from more games of chase and stick racing than he'd probably ever had in his life. Bonnie was also curled up next to Dot, though she wasn't asleep, and Peggy sat in a patch of clover by the river, while Tess made a garland for her out of the tiny white flowers.

'. . . so I guess we'll have to wait and see.' Mrs Donaldson seemed oblivious to the fact Rosalie hadn't been listening. 'Perhaps this is something you can follow up? Oh, look who it is heading our way.' She tucked her hair behind her ear and pointed to the figure walking along the river bank.

Rosalie looked up to see Bernie coming towards them. He held his hand up in greeting and headed to the group.

'This seems like the right way to spend a morning.' He smiled.

'It is indeed.' Mrs Donaldson extended her hand in invitation. 'Would you like to join us, Bernard? There isn't a lot of food left, I'm afraid, but plenty of jovial company.'

'I could do with a drink, if you've got any.'

Rosalie poured him the last of the lemonade. 'Have you been out wandering the wilds again in search of that elusive perfect shot?' She nodded to the camera around his neck.

'Always.' He grinned.

'You're a photographer too?' Penelope stood up.

'Taught my niece everything she knows.' He winked at Rosalie and she introduced Penelope and Bernie properly.

'Perhaps you could take a photo of the group, Bernie, all of us together?' Penelope said.

'It would be my pleasure.' He bowed his head.

'Including you, Rosalie.' Penelope smiled.

'Oh . . . I . . . I don't . . .'

'Don't tell me,' Millie said, 'the photographer doesn't like being photographed?'

'True.' As much as she loved being behind the camera, she hated being in front of it in equal measure. 'There's never once been a photo taken of me I've liked. Not since I was a baby.'

'That's because you haven't let me take one,' Bernie said.

He got everyone in position, standing with the river behind them, children in the front. He made jokes until everyone lost their stiffness and then shot a quick-fire series of photos before Bonnie took off, chasing something in the grass around one of the large river gums that stretched up river.

The group splintered and Bernie stayed and chatted to everyone for a little longer. Rosalie knew it was probably time to pack up, but she still had some photos left on the current roll of film, so she moved about taking a few last pictures.

She crouched beside Tess and Peggy, who were sitting once again in the clover patch, and took a close-up of them with the pretty white flowers in their hair.

A second 'click' made her look up. Bernie was there with his camera, and a wicked smile on his face.

'Oh no, you didn't?' Rosalie stood up. 'Don't you dare print that!'

'You might be surprised how good it is,' Bernie said.

'I doubt that very much.' She glared at him.

'We'll see.'

Rosalie turned on her heel shaking her head and started packing up the picnic basket. Dot helped her, and together they had it done in no time. When Rosalie looked over to Bernie, she saw he was in deep conversation with Penelope.

'Thank you, Rosalie.' Millie stepped towards her. 'This was the best day we've had since . . . well, thank you.' She gave Rosalie a hug.

'Yes, thank you.' Dot wrangled her daughters around her.

'Perhaps we can do it again sometime?' Penelope said, as she folded up her picnic blanket.

'I'd like that,' Dot said.

'Well.' Mrs Donaldson dusted her hands together. 'I guess that's settled. Shall we say in another fortnight's time?'

Everyone nodded and one by one they headed off.

Rosalie rode home, her arms out wide, joy in her heart. As she rounded the bend in their street leading to their house with its imposing façade looking over the cul-de-sac, she screeched her tyres to a halt. In the driveway was a black Jaguar she'd never seen before. No one in Redgum River, or anywhere near here, had a car as fancy as that.

Her breathing quickened and she felt a flush at the back of her neck.

'Are you coming, Granny Rose?' Sarah's gentle voice broke through Rosalie's memories. 'Are you okay?'

Rosalie blinked, wondering what excuse she could muster to stay in the van.

None, apparently.

Sarah helped her out, which was unnecessary, of course. As Rosalie put her foot on the ground, she looked out at the scenery and stumbled.

'Whoa,' Sarah said, and shook her head. 'Maybe it's time we looked at getting you a walker.'

Rosalie shot her a look. 'You'll do no such thing. I'm perfectly fine.' And to prove it, she did a little jig as she made her way around to the back of the van where Ryan and Melody were waiting for them.

Sarah shook her head, a smile touching the edges of her mouth.

Rosalie knew there was nothing wrong with her. Not physically, anyway. Her wobble had nothing to do with her ability to walk or stand, and everything to do with the clearing she was standing in.

Eleven

Ryan had parked Gertie in one of the spaces marked by the grey stencilled paint of large gum leaves on the asphalt. The car park was large, each space at least half as wide again as those in the city, and swept in an arc around the cul-de-sac. Wooden logs were spread evenly around the arc, separating the parking from a manicured lawn of deep green.

Sarah stretched after the long car ride. They were here. They were really going to do this. Unless she quickly put Melody back in Gertie and sped away. But there was more than one problem with that plan. There was nothing else for it, she guessed. 'Shall we?'

Rosalie brushed away Sarah's proffered hand and stepped ahead of them. She stopped in the middle of the wide path lined with small grevillea bushes that ran right through the middle of the neat lawn.

'Are you sure you're okay, Granny Rose?' Sarah asked, when her grandmother let out a deep sigh.

'It's changed,' she whispered. 'But also it hasn't.' She frowned.

'You know this place? The retreat?' Sarah took her hand and found it was shaking.

'Not the retreat. But this place . . .' She pointed towards the grounds and shook her head.

'Granny Rose?' Sarah brushed a stray strand of the white-grey hair from Rosalie's face.

For the briefest moment there was a storm of emotion in those old grey eyes – longing, love, fear, sadness – but it dissolved quickly and the resolute expression Sarah was used to returned.

Ryan wheeled Melody up level with them. 'Well, are we going to stand out here all day or are we going to check in?'

Sarah drew in a deep breath. 'I guess we're checking in.' She inched forward towards the main building. It lay at the end of the path, squat and round, as if it had somehow sunk over a long time, rather than having been built just a few years ago. It was clad in thick slabs of wood, left unpainted. The grains and shadows of grey-brown shifted in the light, reflecting the hues of the surrounding gum trees.

On either side of the main building the path split and branched into meandering turns to the cabins behind. Each cabin was clad in the same natural grey-brown wood as the main building, and nestled in its own small clearing surrounded by towering gums.

The fresh tang of eucalypt danced on the cool air, surprisingly delicate given how thick the bush was. Three rainbow lorikeets rushed by in a blur of red, blue and emerald, and Melody reached up in the air as they tweeted their hello. From somewhere in the distant underbrush, a lyrebird sang out its distinctive whip.

The family stopped at the end of the path and the gentle dance of leaves overhead welcomed them. In that moment of quiet, Sarah could hear the gentle sound of the river running somewhere behind the trees. Then a man stepped through the large sliding doors in front of them, dressed in tan khakis and a sage-green polo shirt, the Redgum River Music Retreat logo embroidered on the left chest in white. He walked down the ramp to greet them.

'Welcome. You must be Sarah?' He shook her hand. 'And you must be Melody.' He knelt down and gave Melody a high-five. He reeled back and shook his hand in mock pain at the power of Melody's hit, and it garnered the intended response, Sarah supposed, with Melody giggling silently at the man now sprawled out on his bottom before her.

'I'm Joshua Chung.' He jumped up and brushed himself off.

Sarah smiled. He looked a little different from his picture on the website – a sprinkle of grey at his temples, his eyes even warmer. His comforting smile seemed genuine and, she supposed, was useful at putting his clients at ease.

'I'll show you to your cabin and you can get settled. Why don't you lead the way?' He bent down and whispered something in Melody's ear. She turned her chair around and headed off down one of the paths that swung to the right behind the main building, as if she knew exactly where she was going. Joshua walked beside her, every now and then talking softly to her, his quiet mumblings the only sound to break the gentle rhythm of the bush song of rustling leaves, lyrebird whip, and the babbling of running water.

Within moments they were standing in front of a cabin at the end of the property, backing onto a clearing that led to the river. Sarah stared at the scene. The river was much wider than she'd observed when they were driving through town. The tall gum trees around the cabin were like sentries, their lop-sided branches opening their arms in welcome.

'This is one of our newest cabins. There are three bedrooms.' He opened the wooden door. 'One for Mum and partner, and one each for you two special ladies.' He pointed at Melody and Rosalie.

'Oh no.' Ryan put up his hand. 'We're not . . . ewww.'

'This is my cousin.' Sarah stepped in.

'Oh. *Sorry*. Right.' A slight pink blush tinged Joshua's cheeks.

'The booking didn't specify. It was all a bit rushed and last minute, I suppose.'

'We'll take the one with the two beds, won't we, minim?' Sarah said, and Melody gave her a thumbs up.

'Right. Good.' Joshua said. 'Well, there's a small kitchenette too, and some information on the dining table for you.'

Rosalie pushed past him and inspected the inside.

'Our first session isn't till tomorrow morning,' he said to Melody, his easy-going confidence returning. 'So, for now, just get settled and wander around here a bit, or go explore in town. Make yourselves at home.'

'I'd like to go into town,' Rosalie said.

'Excellent. Sunday afternoons are very popular with people from neighbouring towns and villages visiting – for the bakery, ice creamery and picnics by the water.' Joshua smiled and gave Melody another high-five as he left.

Sarah unpacked her and Melody into the bedroom with two single beds, and Ryan helped Rosalie with her suitcase in the second bedroom before throwing his duffle bag into the third.

The cabin was small-ish with white-washed walls that allowed the intricate grain of the cut wooden logs to show through. The bedrooms were furnished with comfortable beds and standalone wardrobes, also whitewashed. There was a small living room, with a sage-coloured sofa covered with cushions printed with gum leaves and wildflowers in shades of grey, russet and green. The small kitchenette comprised a hotplate and microwave, and above the butler's sink set into a wooden benchtop, a wide window framed the rich bushland outside.

Sarah stood at the window taking in the view.

Ryan walked up beside her and wrapped his arm around her. 'Careful. You might get used to this and never want to go home.'

'Hardly.' Sarah smiled. She had to admit, though, being away from all the reminders of the accident and the life that was no longer hers, the lost promises of a future that would now not be – being so far removed from what had become her life – did stir a calmness within her.

'Are we heading into town, then?' Rosalie's question was more of a demand.

Ryan looked at his watch. 'I don't see why not. Shall we?'

Rosalie nodded.

'Are we all going?' Ryan asked, looking at Melody.

She answered with a nod.

'I wouldn't mind having a look,' Sarah said.

'All aboard, then.' Ryan opened the cabin door and everyone piled out.

They parked at the far end of town and took a stroll up Main Street. They passed a busy little supermarket and three cafés, all with tables and chairs at the back that spilled onto the riverbank adjacent. Each café was full of people drinking tea and coffee and eating cakes.

The riverbank was dotted with picnic tables and wooden benches, each occupied by families or couples. Children were running around playing chase, a few people had fishing lines dangling in the water. The grass sloped gently down to the river that wound its way past the town and through the thick green surrounds, a path running parallel, full of people ambling along.

'Oh, Granny Rose. This is stunning.' Sarah reached out and touched her grandmother's shoulder.

'It was always a pretty spot. Though none of this was here back then.' She waved her hands in the direction of the picnic tables. 'We just did it the old-fashioned way.' She nodded towards a young family spread out on a picnic blanket.

'It must have been idyllic growing up here.'

Rosalie nodded. 'It was. Mostly.'

'I can't believe you've never been back.'

'Things aren't always what they seem on the surface.' Rosalie squared her shoulders and walked ahead of them.

Sarah shot Ryan a look. 'We've got her here, though,' he said. He pushed his hair back. 'Or, maybe she got us here. Either way, now that we *are* here, I have no doubt whatever she's hiding will come out.'

As they caught up to Rosalie along the main street, they passed a two-storey pub, standing tall with an upstairs balcony that wrapped around the whole building, heavy with late lunch-goers or perhaps afternoon drinkers, all looking over the river, a chorus of merry voices stretching out towards the water.

Next to the pub was a post office with an old magazine rack at the front and a community noticeboard screwed into the wall, which was almost completely hidden by old and new scraps of paper offering this, selling that. 'Three white kittens free to a good home'; '1993 Ford for sale: one owner'; 'Farmhand needed, must be okay with mucking out stalls'.

Rosalie stopped.

'This is where it all began,' she whispered.

'Granny Rose?' Sarah stepped closer. 'Where what began?'

But Rosalie simply righted herself and moved on.

They ambled along the street some more, until the road swung to the right, following the path of the river.

Ryan let out a long whistle when he noticed it, and Melody grabbed Sarah's hand, shaking it furiously. She spread her fingers wide.

'Yes, it is a very large tree, minim.' Sarah nodded. 'And it must be very old. Did you used to play in it, Granny Rose?' she asked.

But, again, Rosalie didn't answer. She'd taken a few steps forward and had tilted her head to the side. Sarah joined her.

'Is that music?' Sarah caught a few notes floating on the cool afternoon breeze. They moved through the crowd of people, just a few steps, and around the corner, under a tall white rotunda down by the river where the shops ended, Sarah could make out a couple of old men, busking, it seemed. A family stopped in front of the wooden structure, blocking Sarah's view, as crowds moved along the riverbank. She turned around to get the others to follow her, and saw Rosalie's face. She looked positively stricken.

'Granny Rose?' Sarah asked. But there was no response.

Twelve

Rosalie blinked, the figures blurring, the twang of a banjo fading, the lyrics of Porter's 'In the Still of the Night' swirling in her mind. She wanted to move to get a better look, but her legs wouldn't budge. She tried to focus on Sarah's distant voice, but her mind was pulling her away.

Redgum River
June 1945

Her heart racing at the sight of the Jaguar, Rosalie leaned her bike up against the side of the house as quietly as she could, trying to slow her pulse. Low voices, male voices, rippled on the evening air mixed with the melody coming from the gramophone playing Cole Porter. Her father was talking with someone who sounded familiar. The lilt. Yes. She did know that voice. What was *he* doing here?

Inside, Rosalie found her mother sitting straight-backed on one of the dining chairs, her father pacing the floor with his hands shoved into the pockets of his expensive suit trousers.

In the corner of the room Henry stood, proud, tall, relaxed.

Rosalie cleared her throat before she entered and her father turned around, a look of horror briefly crossing his face when he saw the dishevelled state she was in, overalls smudged with grass stains, hair wisping in every direction. There was no point even trying to make herself look presentable, they'd all seen her, so she simply strode into the room, head high.

'Ah. There you are.' Frank's smile didn't reach his eyes.

'Hello, Father. Sorry I'm late.'

'It's our guest you should be apologising to.' Her father nodded towards Henry. 'You remember Mr Burton.'

'Good evening, Rosalie.' Henry bowed his head in greeting. 'It is lovely to see you again.'

Rosalie's stomach clenched. 'Nice to see you too.' She may not look the part of somebody raised correctly right now, but she could still remember her manners. 'Are you staying for dinner?'

'Yes. Your father was kind enough to extend me an invitation.'

Rosalie shot Frank a cold smile.

'Come,' Iris said. 'You get changed for dinner. Betty is about to serve up.'

Rosalie skulked away, washed her face, reset her hair and returned in a simple lemon-yellow shirt dress.

Beneath the table, she wriggled her toes as she ate. Above the table she tried her best to give no sign of the discomfort coursing through her veins. She would suffer through this dinner for the sake of her mother, who, Rosalie noted, looked thrilled to have Mr Henry Burton supping at her table, and she'd make polite conversation as if he was the charming, innocent caller he was pretending to be. Not the liar she knew.

After dinner, Frank invited Henry to the study. 'I have a very fine drop of whisky I've been saving.'

Yes. Please. Disappear. Rosalie wished she could say the words out loud.

'Actually, sir.' Henry said. 'I was wondering, with your permission of course, if I could perhaps speak with Rosalie.'

Rosalie flinched, and Iris looked at her with irritation.

'Of course, young man.' Frank looked pleased. 'Why don't you both go out in the front yard and sit under the stars?'

Outside, the night air was warm and the black sky silky. The stars twinkled in their eternal watch, looking down on Rosalie from far above. Under any other circumstances, it could have been considered quite a romantic evening.

Henry directed Rosalie to the wooden bench that encircled the large trunk of the jacaranda tree in the centre of the garden. It had been there for as long as Rosalie could remember, and she'd often sat under it reading or dreaming of a life travelling the world with her camera.

She sat there now wondering what on earth Henry wanted to say to her.

He sat down next to her. 'I owe you an apology, Rosalie. Not only for my behaviour on the night of the gala, but also for not being entirely honest the day we met.' He ran his hands through his blond curls, and the rueful expression on his face seemed genuine enough.

'I don't understand why you thought you had to hide who you were.'

The slight inebriation at the gala she could forgive. But Rosalie did not like feeling she had been manipulated.

'For that I can only blame the caution my family name requires of me. I was aware our fathers intended us to meet at the gala. My family has been trying to convince me to take courting seriously, but every young lady they introduce me to only sees my name.' Henry dropped his gaze. 'I wanted to meet you before they introduced us. So we could form our own opinions of each other.'

'Well, Henry Burton, that plan may well have backfired.'

He nodded. 'I know. I'm sorry.'

Rosalie believed him, but he'd made an assumption about her in his explanation that she wasn't comfortable with. 'For the record, Henry, I have no intention of being matched with anyone, and I certainly have no interest in your surname.'

'I know that Rosalie. And I admire your independence and ambition. I hope we can move forward as friends.'

'I suspect we aren't suited to be friends.' She stood up.

'I'm not so sure about that. But, I guess time will tell.' He smiled at her. 'I'll take my leave of you now, and look forward to our next meeting.'

He headed in to bid farewell to Frank and Iris, leaving Rosalie standing there, her words of refute unspoken.

After Henry had left in his purring Jaguar, Rosalie's pulse was racing – with anger or daring, she wasn't sure. Henry had rattled her, and she wasn't sure what to make of that.

When her parents retired, Rosalie sat at her dresser sorting through the week's photos, placing them in envelopes ready for her to deliver to the YMCA. One photo was left over. The extra copy that she'd made of the group picnic shot. She turned it over and penned her message on the back.

Dear Edward,

I hope this photo brings you both relief and joy. The picnic I organised was a great success and, as you can see, your mother had a splendid time. I do believe she made some firm friends, as did we all, and we are already planning our next get-together. So please rest in the knowledge that your mother is no longer lonely and I will be looking out for her until your safe return, which I hope is soon.

Yours, Rosalie

The following Sunday, as Rosalie sat in the garden drinking tea, Iris came to speak to her. 'Henry will be here for supper shortly. Can you please wash up?'

'What? Why?' Rosalie couldn't believe her ears.

'Because our families are connected, he's a lovely young gentlemen, and he'd like to get to know you.'

'But what if I have no interest in getting to know him?' Rosalie wasn't sure if she did, or not. But she was certain she didn't want others deciding that for her. 'Mother, I have no desire . . .'

Iris raised her hand. 'My darling, I know how important your . . . career . . . is to you and that you are not interested in your father's and my efforts to see you happily settled. But perhaps if you would just open yourself to the possibilities out there—'

'Mother, *really*?' Rosalie couldn't believe Iris was going to pursue this.

'Just get to know him. As a friend. If something more comes of it, wonderful, if not, so be it. Continue with your journalistic pursuits.'

Rosalie knew her parents weren't going to let this go. She squared her shoulders. Fine. She would get to know Henry, and then, when there was nothing to the relationship, they could all move on.

When Henry arrived, he was, of course, the perfect gentleman. Frank quizzed him about his studies and Iris asked him about his life outside university. Rosalie said very little, but she did find herself smiling at the story he told of the rugby team's latest loss, which involved torrential rain, soaking mud and men normally proud of their sporting prowess slipping and sliding all over the field.

Once they finished their simple dessert of strawberries and cream, Frank and Iris made up a feeble excuse of having to attend to some correspondence and left Rosalie alone with Henry.

Rosalie folded her napkin and placed it on the table, muttering something about being tired herself.

But Henry wasn't deterred. 'I'm staying in town for a week. Maybe we can start fresh and be friends.'

She turned to face him and looked him in the eyes. 'Does this have anything to do with my father's job?'

'No.' Henry put his hand on his chest. 'I know you have no reason, yet, to believe I'm an honourable man, Rosalie. But I genuinely like you and want to be your friend.'

Rosalie wasn't sure whether to believe him or not but she was willing to give him the benefit of the doubt. This time. Besides, she wasn't as naïve as they all thought; she was perfectly capable of protecting herself.

'I'm not sure there's enough in Redgum River to maintain the interest of someone who's used to a fast-paced city life,' she said.

'On that point, my dear Rosalie, I think we shall have to agree to disagree.' He held her gaze intently and her traitorous cheeks burned.

'Right . . . um . . . I'll be at work tomorrow.' Her voice was soft.

'Would it be all right if I visited you at the paper?'

'I'm not sure how Neville would feel about that.'

'Of course.' Henry's face fell. Rosalie was beginning to see that he wore his emotions openly.

'But if you come just before knock-off then perhaps I can give you a *quick* tour of the office.'

Henry smiled. 'I would like that very much.'

*

Monday quickly turned into a nightmare when there was a problem with the ink delivery system to the press. And as the afternoon rolled into early evening, Roy, the printer, was covered head to toe in black not long before the paper was due to be distributed and they still hadn't sorted the issue. Neville was shouting in a way that Rosalie had never seen him do before, his face turning redder by the moment.

'Why's there a damn smudge there?'

'I thought you said it was the bloody roller that was the problem!'

Rosalie had never heard him swear before.

'For god's sake, we'll never get this out on time!'

At exactly the wrong moment, Henry strode through the front door of the office. Rosalie turned around, her wild hair escaping from her snood and poking out in all directions, her face nearly as red as Neville's.

'Who the hell is that?' Neville shouted at Rosalie. 'And why is he in my damn press office?'

Henry stepped forward and put himself between Rosalie and Neville. 'That is no way to speak to a lady, sir.'

'Henry, it's fine.' Rosalie tried to remain calm, although Henry's intrusion into her workspace was not helping this already fraught situation.

'I'm not speaking to a lady,' Neville barked. 'I'm speaking to my employee.'

'Our printing press doesn't appear to be working,' Rosalie said to Henry.

'Do you mind if I take a look?' Henry asked Roy.

'Be my guest.' Roy stepped aside.

'Seriously? Reynolds, who the hell is this man?'

Rosalie was relieved that Henry had his head so buried into the machinery that he hadn't heard Neville curse at her again. 'He's . . . a friend.'

Neville put his hands on his hips. 'And does he know a damn thing about printing presses?'

Rosalie spread her hands out wide. 'I have no idea.'

It turned out that Henry did indeed know something about printing presses. Within ten minutes of he and Roy working together they had the problem sorted and the familiar sound of the turning rollers and the *swish*, *swish*, *swish* of the broad sheets of paper as they transformed from blank masses to black and white masterpieces of the written word filled the air.

'Right! All hands on deck to get these babies bundled and ready to despatch.'

Neville, it appeared, had forgotten about who the hell Henry was and why he was there, and had them all scrambling to get the paper out.

Once they were done, he sat back in his chair at his desk, wiping his brow with a blue-and-red polka-dot handkerchief. 'Well done, team. I didn't think we could do it.' He looked at Henry. 'To whom do I owe my gratitude?'

'The name is Henry Burton.' Henry held out his hand and Neville shook it vigorously.

'Well, Mr Burton, I don't know where you came from or how you did what you did, but thank you for saving my arse today.'

Rosalie could see that Henry was about to pull up Neville for his use of bad language in front of her again, but she shot him a look that she hoped he would understand as *don't you dare*.

'How did you know what to do?' Roy asked.

'I work on the paper at the university. Our press is smaller than this one, but I've seen a similar problem.'

Neville stood up and slapped Henry on the back. 'Well, however it came to be, I owe you a beer. Now, head off, the lot of you, and make sure you're not late tomorrow.'

Once she was sure Neville and Roy were nowhere near, Rosalie turned to face Henry.

'I guess it was lucky I was here today,' Henry smiled.

'Yes.' Rosalie's tone was terse. 'Thank you for helping Roy fix the press.' She turned her back and walked out of the office building.

Henry followed her, catching her with only a couple of long strides, his face contorted with confusion. 'You're mad at me? For helping fix the press?'

Rosalie shook her head. 'No, for that I am grateful. What I am not grateful for is you trying to defend my honour with my boss. How will I ever be accepted as just another employee if my boss can't speak to me the way he speaks to a man?'

'Oh . . . I'm sorry, Rosalie. I didn't realise . . .'

'You made me appear like a fragile little woman who needs a man to save her. Do you know how hard I have had to work to prove myself?'

'Oh gosh, Rosalie.' Henry raised his hands in contrition. 'I didn't mean to undermine you. I just can't abide anyone, especially someone in a position of power, speaking to a woman like that. I'm really sorry.'

Once again Henry's emotions played out across his face and Rosalie could see he was embarrassed.

'Okay.' She softened her tone. 'But please don't do it again.' Rosalie packed her hatbox on to her bike. 'I'd better get a wriggle on. It's getting late.'

Henry put his hand on the handlebars of Rosalie's bike. 'You're not seriously going to ride home, are you?'

'It is how I normally get there.' The corners of Rosalie's mouth turned up.

'At least let me take you to dinner first. To apologise for embarrassing you at work. And then I'll drive you home.'

'And what do we do with this?' She pointed to her bike.

Henry shot her a confident grin. 'Didn't you know? This is the exact reason they build these cars with soft-top rooves.' He folded the rooftop down and sat the bike on the back seat.

'Ah yes.' Rosalie folded her arms in front of her chest. 'I read that somewhere. *Pop the roof down so you can take a stranger's bike on a lovely tour of the countryside,* I believe the advertisement said.'

Henry's laugh was rich and deep. 'Let's go, Rosalie, before I decide to take your bike to dinner and leave you here.' He held out his arm and she took it.

The local pub, with a restaurant looking over the river, was hardly the kind of flash establishment Henry would have been used to. But they did serve a decent meal, even with rations, and the service was always attentive and friendly.

Henry was the perfect gentleman over dinner, and Rosalie had to admit she enjoyed his company.

'I've been looking back through your articles,' he told her as the waiter cleared the table. 'You're very good.'

'Thank you.'

'And this is what you want to do? I mean, as a career?'

'Well, the *River Times* isn't my dream job, but journalism, photojournalism in particular, yes. I know a woman isn't supposed to . . .'

Henry raised his hands in defence. 'I think it's great. And I think you have talent. Genuinely.' He held her gaze and Rosalie knew he was telling the truth. 'So, what is your dream job?'

Rosalie hesitated. Would he laugh? Tell her it was impossible? If he truly wanted to be her friend, like he claimed, then he'd do neither.

'I would love to work for *Life* magazine.' There. She'd said it out loud.

'Ah, just like Margaret Bourke-White.'

Rosalie's eyes widened. He knew her idol?

'She is amazing, but I reckon you could match her, given the chance.'

Rosalie laughed. 'That's very flattering. But for a start I'm not sure how I'm going to get that chance. Nonetheless, I'm going to darn well try my hardest to make it happen. Somehow.'

Henry fidgeted with his tie, avoiding eye contact with her.

'What?' She fixed him with a steely gaze.

'Please take this with the intention it is given, and don't read anything into it.'

She lowered her voice. 'What?'

'I have a friend who works for *Life*. He's overseas at the moment, but when he returns I could introduce you.'

Conflicting thoughts crashed through Rosalie's mind. Was Henry doing this to garner favour with her? No. He clearly knew she'd see straight through that. But an introduction to a *Life* reporter? What would he expect in return? She blinked. 'Why? Why would you do that?'

'Because, despite your best efforts to believe the worst of me, we are friends. And I believe in you.'

His last four words pierced her protective armour. He believed in her? No one had ever told her that before.

'I don't know what to say.' She looked down.

'You don't have to say anything. But if I don't get you home soon, I'm sure your father will have a few things to say. Shall we?'

He stood and moved behind her chair, pulling it out for her.

From the driveway, Henry walked Rosalie to the front door and bade her goodnight with a delicate kiss to the back of her hand. She watched him as he walked back to his car and waved as he drove off. Was he the entitled scoundrel she'd first pegged him for? That night in Sydney still teased the edges of her opinion of him.

Didn't all our tiny parts make up our whole? Or was our whole more than that? Could we lose those undesirable fragments if our better sides were given the chance to flourish? Rosalie didn't know.

———

'Granny Rose?' Sarah was saying.

Rosalie blinked. She was being manoeuvred to a bench outside one of the shops. So deeply buried in memories of her past, Rosalie had barely registered they were moving.

'Are you all right?' Ryan's voice this time, and as he helped her lower herself on to the bench, her focus returned to the now.

'I'm fine.' At least, she thought she was. Apart from seeing ghosts. 'I probably just need something to eat.' She hoped Sarah would believe that, though she knew there was little conviction in her voice.

Ryan left and returned with coffee and a biscuit. 'Thank you.' Rosalie mustered a smile, hoping she would convince them.

After she finished the coffee, they moved on with Ryan's arm tucked tightly under hers – completely unnecessary, but she'd allow him to feel useful – they made their way back to the retreat. As she walked, Rosalie turned her ear to the sounds around her. Children laughing, bells ringing above shop doors, plates clanging from one of the cafés.

No music playing.

Returning to Redgum River, Rosalie knew there'd be ghosts. She just didn't realise they'd seem so real.

Thirteen

Tarakan Island

Mid-June 1945

Edward lay in his makeshift cot, a few nights' rest back in camp just what his unit needed after weeks in the muddy jungle. They'd lost two men last week. One down the side of the mountain, one to a Japanese sniper bullet. The man had dropped without sound, right there in front of Albert, red blood mixing with the brown sludge beneath their feet. The men around him had immediately sprung into action, Edward taking out the Japanese shooter before he could kill anyone else. Before he could kill Albert.

It was the first enemy Edward had killed directly, though he was sure other actions he'd taken had probably resulted in loss of life. But he'd learned, since signing up, the need to put events and feelings into tiny boxes and lock them away in separate compartments deep inside his soul. Never opening them. Never looking inside. There was no other way to survive. He wasn't sure Albert was managing this, though.

Often at night, Albert was restless beside him, fitful, his face contorted. And since the sniper attack, it had got worse.

Just before the sun began to rise, the men beside him stirred. They had only two nights in camp, but it would have to be enough to steel them. Last night's hot stew when they arrived tasted just as good as Christmas dinner with all the trimmings, a far cry from the rations they ate when on the move – hard Weet-Bix dipped in cold coffee, and tinned beef.

As the camp came to life with easy chatter and relaxed movement, Albert rose from his cot next to Edward, the haunted look in his eyes dissolving when he saw his older brother.

'Morning, grumble bum.' Albert smiled.

'Morning, cyclone.' They gave each other a quick pat on the back.

Beneath his touch, Edward could feel Albert's protruding bones. They'd need more than a night's serving of stew to build up their waning strength.

Albert pulled out his banjo and started plucking a quiet tune. A few of the men stopped momentarily, nodded, and went on with packing up their kit. The soft sounds from the banjo were a far cry from the rowdy sessions the brothers used to enjoy jamming together before they'd condemned themselves to this godawful place. They were both talented musicians, not that life had afforded them the luxury of any formal training. Their father, Lester, had won the piano that now sat in their mother's small cottage back in Redgum River in a poker match when Edward was fourteen, Albie twelve, and the family were living in Sydney's Surry Hills.

The boys had been mesmerised by the large wooden instrument that none of them knew how to play. They'd all looked at it like it was from outer space.

'Now what?' Penelope had said, her hands on her hips as she shot her husband a look.

'I don't know,' Lester had shrugged.

'Why couldn't you have wagered actual money? That would have been far more useful,' said Penelope.

Young Albert had approached the piano with soft steps and opened the lid, placing a few fingers on the keys. He'd tapped away, testing it out, and after a little while, even though the instrument was out of tune, he'd manage to play 'In the Mood'.

Penelope had stood there, her mouth wide open, as had Edward.

'Our son's a prodigy,' Lester had declared. 'Our ticket out of this mess, love.' He'd embraced Penelope and twirled her around.

Edward had also given the keys a go, but wasn't as good as Albert. Still, over the next few months, they managed to teach each other how to play, and quite well. And every time Lester returned from the pub down the road, another wager won, he'd have in his hands a new instrument: a harmonica, a dinged-up trumpet, a guitar missing one string. Albert could play them all soon enough.

By the time Lester brought home a banjo a few years later, he was dragging his son around local entertainment halls, trying to make a quick buck to pay off his drinking and gambling debts. Edward went with them and shielded Albert from as much as he could, thankful he was too young to understand what was happening. Edward tried to make a game of it and when the brothers went busking in the park on Saturdays together, Albert thought it was just for a lark. He had no idea they were helping to keep the family afloat.

When Lester died of influenza in the winter of 1939, leaving the family destitute, they'd taken Lester's old truck, the piano, the banjo and their few belongings, driven out of the city and never looked back. The boys chased work, Edward taking any job he could, never staying in one place too long. Always taking the piano with them. Just before they joined up, they'd settled Penelope in Redgum River, the piano with her, promising they'd return to play it together after the war.

Edward tried not to dwell too often on those memories of happy music.

Out of the shadows a curdling scream echoed. A flash of light on the perimeter. A shout. *Ra-ta-tat-tat* punctuating the air. Another dawn raid.

Albert dropped his banjo and picked up his rifle. Half-dressed men scrambled into position and fired back. The Japs retreated into the dark scrub and a unit from the company pursued, the others remaining to check on the wounded.

Only three men were hurt, two with flesh wounds, their buddies bandaging them up.

'Eddy!' Albert screamed, and Edward turned to see his younger brother cradling another soldier, Private Tom Smith, in his arms. Blood pooled around them.

'Are you hit?' Edward shook Albert's shoulders.

'No.' His eyes were wide. 'That's all Tommy.'

Edward motioned for the medic who patrolled with them. He patched Tommy up as best he could and once it was clear to do so, the stretcher bearers evacuated him to the base at Agnes, miles away across rough terrain.

The medic exchanged a glance with Edward. They both knew the chances. With a gentle nudge, Edward pulled Albert away and they both tried to wash the blood off.

The unit sent to chase down the attackers returned at midday, the older men solemn, the younger with an air of triumph.

'They won't be bothering us again,' a young private gloated.

In the afternoon the company returned to Agnes, their position no longer safe. Tommy was dead when they arrived.

Orders filtered through that they'd be heading out again in the morning and in the hazy heat of the setting sun as they waited, Edward lay on his cot as sweat dripped down his bare back, his woollen puttees drying at the end of the khaki canvas.

Beside him, Albert played a silent tune, his fingers dancing over his banjo as if he were playing a concert, yet not touching the strings. He wore a far-off gaze and Edward wondered what place his brother had retreated to.

'Mail's in.' A call from the mess tent roused him.

Men from all over camp gathered around the company clerk as he called out the names of recipients.

'Private A. Dawson.'

Albert laid his banjo down, moved forward and snatched his letter mid-air. 'Told you Mum loves me more.' He shouldered Edward. He said that every time he received a letter, even if Penelope wrote to Edward too. Which she always did, they just didn't always arrive at the same time.

Edward still hadn't got Albert to reply to their mother, his younger brother insisting, 'You have a far better way with words than I do.'

Edward knew he was hiding his embarrassment – their constant moving around when they were younger, missing school, had left Albert struggling with reading and writing. Edward knew that Penelope wouldn't mind how basic a few scratched lines from her youngest son were, but no amount of encouragement from him would make Albert pick up a pencil.

Edward waited as other names were read out, and men scurried back to their cots or the shade of a tree to open their mail. The last letter came out of the bag, ten men waiting eagerly to see if it was for them.

'Private E. Dawson.'

Edward put up his hand and took his envelope. But it wasn't his mother's handwriting. He took it back to his cot and tore it open. It was from Rosalie, the photographer from Redgum River. He read it over and over again, the few words she'd written bringing him comfort. To his relief, she was looking out for Penelope. He wondered if Rosalie was young, like him and Albie, or his mother's age. She and his mother had formed a friendship, it seemed, so that was a possibility. It didn't matter, he supposed. Any kind of comfort here was to be welcomed.

After reading the letter three more times, he folded it and put it in his Bible with his other letters from home and the photo of his mother.

After dinner the men of their battalion sat around the large tree in the middle of the camp while Albert played soft, gentle music. An old Irish folk tune their father had taught them, 'The Rising of the Moon', and a few of the men sang the lyrics quietly. They finished with Cole Porter's 'In the Still of the Night' to ease the men into a quiet evening, before they would head into the unknown once more when the sun rose.

Fourteen

Back at the retreat, Ryan helped settle Rosalie in for an afternoon nap. Sarah was sure her grandmother would resist the suggestion, but Rosalie willingly conceded a rest might just be in order.

Ryan emerged from the bedroom. 'So, Miss Melody. How about . . .' he pulled a satchel out from under the coffee table in the living room, '. . . some craft time before dinner?'

Melody smiled and clapped her hands.

'Off you go, Sar-bear.' He stepped closer to her and whispered, 'have a little break.'

Grateful, she squeezed his hand, left the cabin, and wandered through the tall gum trees until she reached the winding river. It was flowing quicker than she thought it would, fallen leaves from the trees above sailing past her as they danced on the water's surface.

Breathing in the air thick with the tang of eucalypt, she lowered herself onto the river bank, stared into the green-brown cellophane of rippling water, and pushed down the tidal wave of anger, anxiety, fatigue and sorrow that was always dangerously close to bursting forth.

The constant worry over Melody, the desperate need to find answers, and now the concern over Rosalie – it was all welling up inside her. Her grandmother had always been a force and Sarah often thought of her, despite her advanced years, as invincible. But lately – a stumble here, muffled words there, her vagueness today – she'd noticed a fragility to Rosalie that shouldn't have been surprising, but was nevertheless unsettling. And Sarah didn't know if she had it in her to carry one more weight. She knew it was wrong to feel this way, but she just wasn't sure she was strong enough.

'But you have to be strong enough,' she said out loud, running her hand over her scar. 'You have no choice.'

'No choice about what?' A deep voice from behind startled her.

She turned around to see Joshua only a few steps away.

'Sorry,' he said. 'I didn't mean to disturb you.' He hesitated and stepped back.

Sarah shook her head. 'No. It's fine. I was just enjoying the view.'

'And contemplating some big questions?'

'Something like that.'

'We do get that a lot here. May I?' he asked, pointing to the patch of grass beside her.

'Sure.'

'Anything I can help with?' Joshua sat, not too close, and to Sarah's relief, he didn't force her to make eye contact.

'This particular issue, probably not.' While she was hoping he would be able to help with at least some of her problems – far too desperately hoping, in fact – she was here to help Melody, not herself.

'Ah.' He ran his fingers through this his thick brown hair. 'Well, you never know. We'll see how the weeks pan out, hey?'

'I guess. It's very peaceful here.'

'It is. That's why we chose this spot for the retreat.'

'The river is beautiful.'

He nodded. 'And she's flowing pretty strong at the moment. We've had a lot of rain recently.'

'So, it isn't always this green?' Sarah spread her hands over the carpet of lush grass they were sitting on.

'Actually, it is. Unless we're in drought, which we most definitely aren't at the moment. In fact, this is the first sunny spell we've had for a while. You've come at the right time.'

'Lucky for us.'

'Yes, we had to rush to get your cabin finished in time – the new additions have been taking longer than we were hoping. But the retreat owner convinced the contractors to get it done.'

'I'll be sure to thank them if we meet.'

They sat in a peaceful silence for a while before Joshua asked, 'Is this your first time to Redgum River?'

'Yes. First time in the area. But my grandmother grew up here.'

'That's interesting,' he said. 'It's always nice when old locals return.' He laughed. 'I bet it's changed since she was a girl?'

'I imagine. She's never really talked about her childhood.'

Joshua squared his shoulders. 'I grew up here, lived here all my life.'

'And how did you end up at the retreat?'

'The owners used to run music lessons out of their place here. They taught me piano and flute and a few other instruments when I was a kid, and after uni I came back home, set up my own counselling practice, and one day, over a cuppa, the idea for this retreat was born.'

'Sounds like a perfect match.'

'It's worked out well. We've grown quite a bit over the last few years, adding cabins and courses.'

'How many instruments do you play?' Sarah asked. It had been a while since she'd hung out with any musicians.

'Three quite well, four very badly.' He smiled, the warmth Sarah had seen in his interaction with Melody resurfacing. 'I've never tried the cello, though. I have to say, you are by far the most accomplished musician we've had at the retreat.'

Sarah shot him a look.

'I googled you.' He shrugged.

'You google all your guests?' She narrowed her gaze.

'Not usually. But in your emails you mentioned the accident after the concert. I'm so sorry for what happened – it must have been terrifying.'

Sarah stared ahead, not trusting her words and simply nodded.

'Anyway, we're glad your family's here, and I hope we can help Melody.'

'I do too.' Her voice was barely a whisper.

Joshua turned to Sarah. 'Have faith in the process.'

Faith, in anything, was something Sarah had sorely lacked for some time now. She wrapped her hands around her knees and brought them to her chest. Silence fell and she stared at the river.

After a few moments, Joshua's gentle voice danced across the space between them. 'Maybe while you're here, you could teach me some cello. I'm a quick study.'

Every muscle in Sarah's body tensed and she flexed her right hand. 'Oh, it's . . . been a long . . . ah . . . I didn't bring my cello with me . . . I mean, you know . . .'

'We have one in our collection.'

'Ah.' Sarah cast her eyes down and focused her gaze on the grass beneath her. She plucked a blade from the dirt and played with it between her fingers then put her hands on the ground behind her, ready to push herself up and remove herself from a conversation she didn't want to have. But when she looked up and met his dark eyes, his expression full of kindness, her need to escape dissolved.

'Of course,' Joshua said. 'I understand if you're not ready to play again, though. Do forgive me if I was too pushy. I'm usually much more tactful and cool.' He shook his head.

'Cool?' Sarah pursed her lips together.

He ran his fingers through his thick hair and grimaced. 'Did I just say that? That is actually a word I've never used to describe myself before. Or anyone else for that matter. I think maybe I'll head back before I say something else I might regret.'

He stood up and brushed his trousers down.

Sarah stifled a laugh. 'See you later, Mr Cool.'

Joshua's cheeks tinged pink and he turned away. After taking two steps, he stopped and looked back at her with serious eyes.

'You are strong enough, by the way. The fact you're here tells me that. Despite how it can seem, life never truly saps our strength completely. It feels like it.' He nodded. 'Too often, sometimes, I know. But there's always a tiny bit of it left, right down in the very bottom of the ocean inside us, and sometimes we just have to wait for the tide to change so we can find it again.'

Sarah drew in a deep breath and held his gaze, biting her bottom lip.

'My grandmother always used to say, "Chuán dào qiáotóu zì rán zhí." Loosely translated it means, "When the boat gets to the end of the wharf, it will go straight with the current." You know, it will all work out.' His voice was full of knowing and Sarah almost believed him. For five glorious seconds the hope she carried deep within her, the hope she dared barely ever acknowledge, flared, warmth and light washing over her.

Sarah stayed by the river a little longer, waiting until she was sure her path back to the cabin wouldn't cross with Joshua's. Not that it would have been a bad thing, she just wasn't sure she could deal with any more of her own emotions right now.

She hauled herself up. *Back unto the breach.* Something Rosalie always used to say when on assignment.

When she got to the cabin, she found Ryan and Melody had abandoned craft and were playing in the clearing – some sort of hybrid chasing–hiding game that only the two of them knew the unspoken rules of. Melody waved to Sarah, a broad grin across her face as she pushed her chair behind a bush. She raised her finger to her lips, and silently shushed her.

Sarah shushed back and winked. She could see Ryan pretending to look behind one of the big gum trees that surrounded the property, his exaggerated movements as he stalked the area and comical expression of surprise when he couldn't find her drawing a guffaw from Sarah.

Melody frowned and silently shushed her again.

'Sorry,' Sarah mouthed, and she tiptoed to the cabin, mimicking Ryan's absurd steps. When she reached the porch, she collapsed onto the railing, laughing. A proper good belly laugh that hurt her stomach muscles.

She'd forgotten how good that felt.

As she watched while Ryan and Melody continued their game – this time it was Melody's turn to hunt him down – Sarah saw an old man walking down the path towards the main building, the Stave. Sarah thought it a poetic name for the place in which therapists and clients came together – named after the five lines that music pieces were written on, where notes, rhythm and harmony came together. The man was met by a tall woman in the same sage polo shirt Joshua wore and she helped him up the ramp with a gentle arm around his shoulders.

Sarah wondered how many of the clients at the retreat would be elderly. Would there be anyone else here Melody's age? She'd find out tomorrow, she guessed. The lightness that had washed over her just moments ago was pushed aside by her old friend Worry, and again she questioned whether she'd made the right decision bringing Melody here.

A sound from inside the cabin interrupted Worry and Sarah headed inside to see if Rosalie was all right.

When she entered, Sarah found her grandmother standing in the middle of the kitchenette–living space, fiddling with the strap on her bike helmet.

'You're not seriously thinking of going for a ride, are you?' Sarah stared at her grandmother.

'No.'

'Good.' Sarah let out a sigh of relief.

'I'm not *thinking* about it.' Rosalie turned to her and shot her a grin. 'I'm *going* for a ride.'

'What? Granny Rose . . .'

Rosalie held up her hand.

'I'm feeling perfectly fine. And some fresh air will do me the world of good.' She pushed her teal and silver helmet onto her head, squashing her usually neat hairdo against her cheeks.

'Then go for a walk. I'll go with you. Down to the river, perhaps.'

'Sarah, my darling.' Rosalie stepped towards her and took Sarah's hands in hers. 'You seriously need to stop worrying about everything and everyone. I'm fine. And even if I wasn't, at my age there's no point worrying about it anyway.'

'But . . .'

'No buts. I know life hasn't been kind to you recently, my darling, but not every day is one to fight and conquer. It's okay to just *be* sometimes.'

Sarah frowned. Her grandmother wasn't one to get philosophical. At least not with her.

Rosalie reached up and touched Sarah's cheek, her wrinkled hand cool yet surprisingly soft. 'Simply enjoying the day can be a victory in itself, you know. Maybe you can find some space to breathe while we're here. What do you say?'

Sarah took Rosalie's hand in hers. It had been a long time since her grandmother had shown her such open affection.

'Now. Let me go for a ride, like a good girl.' Rosalie disentangled herself from Sarah's grasp and Sarah felt the absence of the touch keenly, surprised by just how much she didn't want to let go.

Rosalie's expression softened. 'It will be okay. You and Ryan bought that e-bike because it was safe, remember. If I'm not back by supper, you can send out a search party.' She laughed, a crackling deep sound and Sarah smiled. 'Just make sure they're cute.'

'Granny Rose!'

'I'm old, dear. Not dead. Not yet.'

Rosalie turned and strode outside. Sarah followed her around the back where her bike was parked.

'Ride safely,' she called, and Rosalie waved her hand in the air.

Just up the path at the back of the cabin, Sarah saw a makeshift workbench. Made of three chunky weathered sleepers lying on top of two old wooden A-frames, the workbench was home to a small collection of terracotta pots – some plain, some with painted white stripes decorating their girth, all with potted flowers in them. Yellow pansies, pink geraniums and lavender. Under the workbench was a big metal watering can, and what was maybe a locked toolbox.

Was this another therapy on offer at the retreat? Gardening?

As she made her way back to the edge of the clearing in front of the cabin, she saw Ryan and Melody coming in from their game, Melody waving frantically at her.

'You two look like you've been having fun.' Sarah stopped in front of her daughter and smoothed Melody's wayward hair from her brow. 'Euw.' She wiped the sweat on her jeans. Melody ghost-giggled. 'Straight into the shower for you, young lady.'

Ryan stood with his hands on his hips, droplets of sweat pushing through his t-shirt.

'And you're next.' Sarah shook her head.

From behind her, Ryan flung his arms around her and she stiffened briefly before relaxing into the embrace. 'Next time you should join us,' he said.

She wrapped her arms across his, holding him tighter to her.

'Who are you and what have you done with my cousin?' he asked.

Sarah laughed. She'd avoided acts of physical comfort with anyone except Melody since the accident, fearing a tight hug might break her, squeeze out the tears she refused to cry.

'Are you okay?' he whispered in her ear.

She nodded, glad she didn't in fact burst at the seams in his embrace.

'Really? You haven't . . .' he squeezed her a little tighter, 'it's been a long time since you've hugged me like this.'

'I know.'

'Not that I'm complaining.' He pushed himself back. 'But this probably isn't the best moment.' He released his hold and shook out his t-shirt.

'You're gross.' Sarah shook her head.

'But you love me anyway.' He winked, and headed inside.

And there it was again. The sense of void when Ryan pulled away. She wrapped her arms around herself and followed him in.

Fifteen

Tarakan Island
July 1945

Edward removed his boots and puttees and wrung out his sodden socks. Looking down the line of cots, all the men in his unit were doing the same. Today's skirmishes had been fast and brutal, but at least they had all made it back to camp relatively unscathed.

The small island of Tarakan may have been declared 'secure' by the powers that be a few weeks ago, but there were pockets of resistance from remaining Japanese troops still fighting for their Emperor, and every couple of days on rotation Edward and the rest of his unit would head out to ensure the security of the area.

Once his gear was taken care of, he grabbed the small rucksack that contained his Bible and notepad and walked to the edge of camp. He ducked and entered a hollow that had been created as a parasitic fig had, over time, sapped its host tree dry of life. It was a tight squeeze for his large, broad frame, but the root coiled inside the space, all the way to the top, offered a convenient perch on which to sit. Edward was sure he wasn't the only one who used this hiding place for some solitude, but he'd not yet been disturbed when he sought refuge in the tree's cool embrace. He'd never realised before enlisting how much he valued being alone.

Nibbling on one of the bland pieces of hardtack from his ration pack, he took out his letters from Penelope and read them over, as he always did when he found quiet moments. With the most recent letter he'd received, she'd also sent a photo and he removed it from his left breast pocket where he kept it and stared at it as he'd done every chance he'd had since he'd held it for the first time. Not that he needed to look at it again. The beautiful face was burned into his memory.

Her long blonde hair in wild disarray around her face, her soulful eyes radiating kindness, her soft smile full of life and joy. She was side-on to the camera, unaware, it seemed, that the photo was being taken. And she was an angel.

Rosalie Reynolds.

Every chance he got he drank in every feature, reread the letters she'd sent him, her words carrying new light. Now when he slept – in the snippets and snatches he stole between the constant sound of intermittent gunfire, Japanese raids for food, the chaotic explosions, and the noise of his fellow soldiers in camp – he'd close his eyes and see her face.

He wished he could stay in the sanctuary of his hollow tree forever, but he knew soon someone would be looking for him. They were doing a double patrol today. They had set out early this morning – an uneventful march to the south – and after a brief rest now, would be heading out again this afternoon.

Opening his notepad, he touched the tip of his pencil to his tongue.

Dear Rosalie,

My mum has written to me about your visits and the group of friends you have assembled. I hope one day to get home and meet you all. Wouldn't that be something?

Right now, I can hear music coming from the camp, floating across the heavy hot air. Albie must have pulled out his banjo again. Yes. A banjo in the middle of a war. It is not the strangest thing I've seen here, believe me, and it gives us moments of pleasure – joy, even. Joy can be such a fragile thing. But even in this hellish quagmire, there are moments of it. Do you play an instrument? I play a few. Perhaps at that picnic when we are returned, Albie and I can play for you all.

Take care, Rosalie, and thank you for the kindness you extend my mother.

Yours,

Edward

He walked back into camp, and the unit made ready to pull out on the next patrol.

As the bright afternoon sun beat down on their backs, the men marched north on a perimeter sweep. They hadn't come across any snipers for the last few days. With each patrol there were fewer encounters with the enemy, every day new Japanese soldiers surrendering.

Pop, pop, pop.

Gunfire peppered the air from behind the tree line.

The men dropped low, Edward pulling Albert down with him, every set of eyes searching the nearby jungle. Was this a lone sniper, or had they stumbled across a unit?

The firing became heavier.

With no clear target to aim at, Edward and the rest of his unit started shooting back into the tree line.

'Over there!' someone called out.

They concentrated their fire on a movement in the trees. Crouched down they crept forward. There was a break in the enemy fire as they advanced on the position, showering the shadows with bullets. Another movement in the trees.

'Kiska!' The warning cry that a Japanese grenade had been seen.

Edward looked up and saw the small projectile heading straight towards them. The men scrambled. Albert stumbled.

The grenade fell. The ground exploded.

Sixteen

As soon as she was out of sight of the cabins, Rosalie removed her helmet and ran her hands through her hair, fluffing it up as best she could. Long gone were the days when her thick wild blonde mane was her pride and joy. Just another one of those infernal reminders that her youth was now decades behind her. Still, she may be grey and an awful lot thinner on top now than she used to be, but helmet hair, as the young ones called it, was nevertheless not something she could abide. She wouldn't go fast, the equivalent of a leisurely Sunday stroll, and she would pop the helmet back on before she returned, avoiding any looks of disapproval from her granddaughter. Sarah meant well, she knew, but if Rosalie hadn't earned the right at ninety-two to throw caution to the wind, then what was the point of any of it? Surviving war zones, travelling the world, beating Father Time at his own game. Though she was a little more cautious in her old age than she ever used to be: there was no point tempting fate to come knocking any earlier than it had to. She just wasn't as cautious as her granddaughter would like.

Riding through the thick forest of gum trees, she bumped and bumbled along, taking it slowly until she emerged from the fallen leaves and twigs, beside the river. Where once there was nothing but a slight wearing down of the grass along the bank, the paved path that she'd seen in town continued to meander its way alongside the water. Thankfully, though, there was no one else around this far up-river.

She picked up speed. Not as fast as she used to ride the river-bank all those years ago, of course, even with the tiny motor helping her.

Just a little faster.

The wind whistled past her ears and she let out a loud whoop, stopping just short of taking her hands off the handlebars and throwing her arms into the air. She might have been fearless, but she wasn't a fool.

The familiar sweet aroma of the river – the delicious blend of water, dirt and eucalypt – filled her senses and for a moment she was a teenager once more. How many times had she ridden this very route? Far too many to count. Echoes of feelings borne long ago danced through her mind; of freedom and daring, of joy and excitement.

Of love and sadness.

The path certainly made it easier to travel along the river than it had been in her youth, but even an e-bike could be tiring. She slowed down and looked around, uncertain. How far had she come? She didn't recognise any of the landmarks from her youth. She should have passed the fallen gum by now – the one that looked like a glove. Where was the knoll that marked the edge of Redgum River, telling her she was truly in the wilds? And was that a house, over there in the distance, on a new road?

Rosalie swung her heavy legs over the bike frame, confused. This was not how she remembered things.

The sun began its slow descent in the sky and Rosalie knew she should turn back.

Then she saw it. A sight so familiar to her, as if she'd only been here yesterday. The two gums, leaning up against one another, just atop the rise, hiding the entrance to her secret spot. The grove.

She rested her bike on the ground, left the path, and picked her way over the twigs and shed bark, her breath shortening as she approached. When she reached the twin trees she stretched out her hands to steady herself, leaning against one of the smooth grey trunks.

'Hello, dear friends,' she whispered.

She ducked under the lowest branch, her hips and knees protesting the depth of the move.

'Come on, old girl,' she groaned, as she pushed her way through the low-hanging leaves.

Emerging from the hidden entrance, she drew in a deep breath. The grove was exactly as she'd remembered it. She inched towards the old tree, rubbing her cold hands in front of her. As she got closer, she could see the jagged initials and heart carved deep into the smooth grey trunk and she was nineteen once more.

Redgum River
July 1945

Rosalie sat opposite Penelope at her dining table as she read out the telegram she'd received that morning.

Rosalie took in her words as the poor woman's face crumpled.

Explosion. Injured. Alive.

Penelope let out a strangled sob. Tears fell down her cheeks. Rosalie embraced her tightly. 'There, there. He's alive. Focus on that.'

When Penelope calmed, Rosalie fixed her a cup of tea. 'I don't suppose they can tell us how badly he's been injured,' Penelope said, looking at Rosalie with wide eyes.

'I imagine not. At least not by telegram.'

'They only mention Albert. Nothing about Edward. He wouldn't have left his side. Not ever. What if —'

Rosalie stopped her. 'You can't think that. If anything had happened to Edward, you'd have heard.'

'No news is good news?'

Rosalie nodded with false conviction. Her work at the paper had taught her one thing about news coming from the battlefield – it wasn't always reliable, and rarely was the timing of it accurate. It was *possible* something had happened . . .

No. She wouldn't let her mind go there. She had begun to think of Edward as a friend and she couldn't bear the thought of him being hurt.

Penelope sipped her tea, the shake in her hand rattling the cup on the saucer. 'Oh, my, look at me.' She tried to laugh it off.

'It's all right, Penelope. You've had quite a shock. The tea should help a little.'

It spilled over the edge of Penelope's cup.

'Or perhaps a walk in the garden?' Rosalie suggested.

'Yes.' Penelope nodded. 'Will you walk with me?'

'Of course.'

Arm in arm they strolled in the long grass, back and forth past the lavender and winter roses that were in full bloom. The scent was heavenly and belied the heaviness they both felt.

'You're right. I'm sure Edward is okay.' Penelope's soft voice whispered on the air. 'He's my strong boy. Always protecting us. But Albert, he's full of joy, a free spirit. But it's fragile.' Her voice caught.

'Maybe I can see if Neville has a contact in the service who can give us more information.' All Rosalie wanted to do was alleviate Penelope's anguish.

'Thank you. You have been a good friend to me. To all of us Snapshots.' Penelope smiled at her. 'What would we do without you?'

'Oh, I'm nothing special. And you'd all do just fine without me.'

Penelope shook her head. 'Don't underestimate what you've done for us. What you do. With your picnics and thoughtful reporting and photos. When we lose you to some big city paper or magazine, we will feel your absence keenly.'

They linked their arms again and continued walking.

'Well, we won't have to worry about that for a while. I don't think any Sydney publication is going to notice me just yet.'

Penelope raised an eyebrow.

'What?' Rosalie asked.

'Well, I overheard Dot the other day, who heard it from Mrs Donaldson, who'd been talking to her cousin, that a certain handsome gentleman had designs on enticing you to the big smoke.'

Rosalie stopped and looked at Penelope.

'Henry and I are just friends.'

'Mmm.' Penelope tilted her head and pursed her lips.

'What?'

'Nothing. It's just in my experience, men and women are never just friends.'

Two could play at this game. 'Are you and my uncle just friends?'

Penelope blushed, her dignified lack of response speaking volumes. She cleared her throat. 'All I know for certain, is that I'm very glad you're here and that you came into my life.'

'I'm glad too.' Rosalie wrapped an arm around Penelope, and they headed back inside.

When Rosalie got home her father was there, having arrived back from Sydney earlier that day. That evening Betty served them a dinner of richly flavoured cottage pie.

'So, Rosalie. How was your week?' Father took a sip of his red wine.

'The week was fine. Mr Payne seems willing to give me a little more responsibility. But I was over at Mrs Dawson's today. She's received bad news about one of her sons. He's been injured.'

Iris raised a hand to her chest. 'Oh, dear.'

Frank nodded. 'War. It always takes a toll. These are uncertain times. Have you heard from Henry since his last visit?'

She resisted rolling her eyes at the lack of subtlety. 'Yes. Quite a few times over the last couple of weeks.'

'He's a lovely young man,' Iris said. 'And from what your father says, Rosalie, he's going to graduate with top honours.'

'Perhaps you will get to plan that wedding after all, dear.' Frank said to Iris.

Rosalie dropped her fork. 'We are *friends*. There'll be no planning any weddings.'

'You could do a lot worse than Henry Burton.' Iris looked at her sternly. 'I don't know why you're so resistant to the idea of security. That's what you need. What we all need.'

'Perhaps I want to make my own mind up about things.' Rosalie's voice rose.

'Rosalie. Mind your tone.' Frank snapped. 'Your mother is right. You could do a lot worse.' He raised his hand before Rosalie could protest. 'You've always been too headstrong for your own good. Men like Henry do not come along often. Opportunities like this don't come along often.'

Opportunities for whom, Rosalie wondered. 'I'm sure they don't,' she said with as little rancour as she could manage. 'I might retire to my room now.'

Rosalie left the room burning with irritation.

As she readied for sleep, Iris tapped lightly on her door and came in and sat on her bed.

'Why, Mother?' Rosalie plonked herself down beside her. 'Why are you and Father pushing so hard for a match with Henry? I could have a future, a good one, with my work.'

Iris smoothed her yellow silk dress over her knees. 'There's no security in it, my darling. What do you think will happen when this war is over and the men return? They'll not sit idly by while the women are doing their jobs. There is only certainty in a good match. A good match to a good man, with a steady job. That's what you need. Look at what happened with Violet.'

Rosalie looked into her mother's eyes. Iris very rarely spoke of her sister.

'You were too young to remember how hard it was.'

In fact, Rosalie's memories of that night were vivid. Iris's gut-wrenching howl. The desolate look on Bernie's face.

'Bernie is a good man and I know he loved her. But he couldn't provide for her properly. The life of an artist is no life for a marriage. Moving around, changing work, no financial stability. When she fell pregnant, I begged her to come home, but love is blind.'

'Auntie Violet always seemed so happy to me.' Rosalie had fond memories of her mother's sister.

'She was.' Iris nodded. 'But happiness isn't enough, my darling. It wasn't enough to . . .' Her voice wavered.

To save her. Or the baby.

Tears welled in Iris's eyes and she let them fall down her cheeks unhindered. 'If Bernie had got her here to your father sooner, he might have been able to . . .' She shook her head. 'That nomadic lifestyle they led . . .' She sighed. 'You cannot blame me for wanting a stable life for you, Rosalie. Not after what happened. And it wasn't just Violet and the baby. Bernie was never the same again. And he never forgave your father for not saving his wife and child. He's become a recluse. I want more for you. I want the best for you.'

'I understand,' said Rosalie. 'I do. But times are different now. And I am not Bernie or Violet.'

The anguish that played across Iris's face tore at Rosalie's heart. But she couldn't give up her dream, and she wouldn't settle for the sake of security.

Iris composed herself and sat straight with the elegant poise her upbringing had trained into her. 'I cannot force you to do anything you don't want to do. But please promise me you won't close yourself off to . . . other . . . possibilities, just because your mind is set.' Her gaze was full of desperate longing.

'I promise.'

A few days later, at the *River Times*, Neville announced he was taking a week of holiday and leaving Rosalie in charge. She nearly threw her arms around him when he told her, but managed to control herself.

In charge. Of a real paper. This was it. Really something she could put on her resumé.

With Neville gone, Rosalie made a few small changes to the edition she would put out in his absence – including more photos than usual and ensuring those on the front page were larger than he normally allowed. After all, it was still considered an innovation to have news on the front pages of a paper instead of classifieds and notices. Roy grumbled about having to change the press, but when the papers were printed and he checked them, he did crack a small smile.

Most of the townsfolk warmed to the new look, though a few of the old timers mumbled their disapproval. Rosalie chose to ignore them.

Not long afterwards, Rosalie headed to Sydney at Henry's invitation. He had indeed set up a meeting with his friend at *Life*, and despite her minor misgivings about his motivations, Rosalie knew it was an opportunity she couldn't pass up. All she needed was the introduction and then she would let her work speak for itself.

She sat in the posh tearoom on Elizabeth Street Henry had picked for the meeting and touched the album lying on the table in front of her one more time. If Henry's friend didn't turn up soon, she was going to wear a hole in its cover.

Henry raised his hand to the waiter and ordered another pot of Earl Grey. 'Are you sure you don't want anything to eat, Rosalie?'

'I'm too nervous to eat.'

'You've got nothing to be nervous about. Reggie will love your photos and your work. If this isn't a sure thing, I don't know what is.'

'What if he doesn't come?' Rosalie would give Henry this one chance to confess that it was all a ruse just to get her to Sydney and make her spend time with him.

'I've known Reggie since we were too young to even bathe ourselves. And I don't think he's ever been on time for a meeting in his life. Relax. He'll be here. Trust me.'

That was another reason she was here – to find out if she could truly trust Henry.

A moment later, a man wearing a tweed jacket stumbled up the front step into the tearoom. Three waiters scurried over to help him and all eyes in the tearoom looked that way.

'See.' Henry beamed. 'I told you he'd come.'

Rosalie took a closer look at the man causing the commotion at the front. He looked more like a bumbling professor than he did a hard-nosed newsman. With the help of the waitstaff he picked up the papers he'd dropped during his unceremonious entry and now he was waving to Henry. As he tried to adjust his jacket, the top few papers fell from his arm and he juggled them, nearly losing the lot once more.

'Are you sure that's him?' Rosalie asked.

Henry let out a chuckle. 'That is most definitely him.'

Once Reggie had made it to their table, knocking into a waiter and falling into a customer along the way, Henry relieved him of his papers and placed them on the spare chair. He made the appropriate introductions and ordered Reggie a slice of teacake.

'So, this is the young lady you've been telling me all about.' Reggie finished shaking Rosalie's hand and sat down.

Heat rose in Rosalie's cheeks, and she felt Henry shift beside her.

'And what has Henry been saying about me?' she asked Reggie and raised an eyebrow.

'Oh, nothing for you to worry about. He's simply been singing your praises.'

Rosalie took a sip of her tea to give herself a moment to catch the thoughts fluttering around inside her head.

'Henry tells me you're quite the photographer. And that you're even running your own regional newspaper.'

Rosalie shot Henry a look. 'I'm afraid he has exaggerated somewhat. I *work* in a regional newspaper and have been left in charge once while the editor was away.' She pulled out a copy of one of the *River Times* she'd brought with her. 'This is an edition that was printed on my watch.'

Reggie looked through the newspaper and Rosalie tried to read the expression on his face, but there was nothing to give his feelings away.

'As for my photography, I am rather proud of it, but I know I still have much to learn.' She pushed her photo album towards him.

'And I told you all about the work she's been doing for the Snapshots From Home League.' Henry leaned forwards on the table.

Reggie nodded. 'Yes, you did.' He looked up from the album and turned to Rosalie. 'I have to say, your work is quite impressive. We don't have a lot of female photographers or journalists in this country. I'm sure I don't need to tell you that. But, with the likes of Margaret Bourke-White paving the way in the States, *Life* is more open to the idea than a lot of others.'

Rosalie's heart began to beat faster and, despite herself, she could feel her hope rising.

'My boss might consider taking on someone like you, once you've had a little more experience.'

And just as quickly her hope dissolved. Where was she going to get more experience from?

'Of course . . .' Reggie winked at Henry. 'With the backing of a family like the Burtons – didn't your father and the editor study at university together, Henry? With the Burtons' support, perhaps there'd be something more we could do.'

Dissolved hope flared into anger. Rosalie took her album back and closed the cover. 'Thank you for your time today, Reggie. It was a pleasure meeting you.' She wanted to stand up and storm out of the tearoom, but she knew that such an outburst would undoubtedly reach her father, so she swallowed her pride and sipped her tea while the two old friends caught up.

Outside the tearoom, the men said goodbye with hearty pats on the back and Reggie tipped his hat to Rosalie with a promise to look at her work again.

Henry turned to her, his grin broad. 'There you go. That went well, wouldn't you say?' His smile fell as he took in her expression. 'What's wrong? You heard him – he loved your work!'

She shook her head. 'As long as I'm attached to your family, yes, my dream can come true. I certainly heard that part.'

'Oh, pay no attention to that. He was genuinely impressed.'

'You don't understand, Henry, do you? If I can't get a job on my own merit, then I don't want the job. I shouldn't have to be *associated* with the right family. My work is good enough on its own.'

Henry took her hands in his. 'I know it is.'

'Then why didn't his remark bother you? For that matter, how do you know *I'm* not just using our friendship to get ahead professionally?'

'Because I know you wouldn't do that. As for the rest, that's just how business is done. It's not what you know, but who you know. If our friendship happens to get you ahead, then I'm fine with that.'

She pulled away. 'Well, I'm not.'

'Then perhaps you're being naïve. This is the way the world works.'

Anger flooded her veins. Perhaps she was naïve, but she didn't like him pointing it out so blatantly.

'Was this all part of some plan?' she asked. 'To get me to like you more? To make me indebted to you?'

Now Henry looked angry. 'No. And I thought by now you'd have realised that my feelings for you are genuine and that all I want is the best for you. I don't want you to like me because you *have* to like me. I want you to like me simply because you do. I thought I made that clear when we first met.'

Rosalie slumped. She didn't know what to think. 'I'm sorry, Henry. These circles you move in – everyone trying to use everyone to get ahead – I don't know if I'm cut out for that.'

'Then I'll changes circles.' He shrugged.

'It's not that's easy.'

'It's as easy as we want it to be.' His words were soft. 'Rosalie, you may not realise it yet, but you have captured my heart. And I will do everything I can to prove to you that we would make a good match.'

'That's just it, Henry. I don't want a match.'

She looked into his deep blue eyes and saw pain.

'Never?'

'I don't know. Maybe. One day. But I want adventure. I want to carve out a life for myself first. Maybe there'd be room for marriage.

Maybe not. But it wouldn't be a *match*.' She stepped back, then forwards again. 'Match sounds like a business arrangement. If it happened, it would be something that grows, not something that is forced or arranged or agreed upon. I'm sorry, Henry.'

Henry drove her back to the Australia Hotel and walked her to the door.

'Rosalie.' Henry looked at the ground in front of him and then raised his gaze, capturing Rosalie's eyes. 'Please know my affection for you is genuine and I want to make you happy. Please give me a chance to do that.'

'Thank you, Henry.' Rosalie's voice cracked. 'For everything. Perhaps, can you give me some time?'

'Of course.'

One clear Sunday afternoon, Rosalie rode towards town, picking up speed, allowing the wind to pull her hair out of its bobby pins as she felt the cold rush on her face. Riding past the river, she let go of the handlebars, threw her arms back and lifted her head to the warmth of the sun.

'Rosalie!' a woman shouted.

She swerved, and, unable to regain control of her speeding bicycle, fell to the ground in a heap.

'Oh my, miss. Are you all right?' A man hobbled towards her and stood over her, his hand outstretched ready to help. She looked up into his bright green eyes, a swirl of mischief and haunting darkness. A warm smile sent shards of electricity through her heart. She took his hand and her breathing quickened.

'Miss? Are you all right?' He repeated the question as he helped her to standing.

'Yes, I think so.' She looked at the peppering of tiny scars that had torn across his face, the glimpse of a bandage beneath the collar of his shirt.

Once she was steady on her feet, he let her hand go and she instantly missed the warmth of it. The man before her was average height, slim, leaning heavily on the walking cane he held in his left hand, which was disfigured with burn scars.

'Rosalie?' Penelope ran up to the two of them, concern etched into her face. 'Are you hurt?'

'No. A little bruised, perhaps.' She looked from Penelope to the man and back again.

'I'm so happy we ran into you, Rosalie. This is Albert! They told me he wasn't coming home till next week, but then, *poof*, like magic, he arrived last night.'

Rosalie looked between the two once more, slowly registering what Penelope was saying. Her mouth dropped open.

'Nice to meet you, Rosalie,' Albert said. 'Mum and my brother have both talked about you.'

She cleared her throat. Gathered herself. 'It's lovely to meet you, too. And wonderful to have you back home safe.'

He grinned, dimples creasing his cheeks and Rosalie thought her legs might buckle beneath her.

Rosalie pulled her hand away from the tree and the faded images of her youth dissolved. Her much older legs were in danger of buckling again, under the weight of her memories.

This was too much. Too hard. She scrambled out of the clearing and away from there as fast as her ageing body could carry her.

Seventeen

Sarah's heart raced as she hurried along the path beside the river. Were they even going in the right direction?

'It's okay.' Joshua's calm voice did little to quell the fear rising inside her. 'We'll find your grandmother.'

She turned to look at him. 'What if she headed into town?' Maybe they should be heading south, not north.

'Someone would have seen her.'

He was right. Maybe. Joshua had made a few calls before they left the retreat and no one he'd spoken to had spotted Rosalie.

'She said if she wasn't back to send out a search party.' Sarah ran her hands over her scar as she often did when worried. 'But I didn't think she meant it. I thought she'd go for a quick ride by the river and be back right away.'

'She can't have gone too far. I mean, she isn't exactly in the bloom of youth,' Joshua said calmly.

Sarah shook her head. 'Oh, you don't know her. She's part of a cycle club and she has a steely determination like no other. With the bike being electric, who knows how far she could have gone. It's just . . .'

'Just what?'

'Well, she's had a few turns lately.' Sarah cast her gaze towards the river, the water running even faster than she'd remembered it was this morning. 'What if . . .'

Joshua reached out and put a gentle hand on Sarah's shoulder. 'Let's not go down any drastic paths of thinking. Maybe she just went further than she meant and has taken her time finding her way back.'

Sarah hoped so. Though even that made her anxious.

'Rosalie?' she called out, her voice echoing across the river. 'Granny Rose?'

They continued walking, and every now and then Sarah checked her phone. Ryan had stayed behind with Melody, and Sarah was hoping he'd send her a message, or call, and say Rosalie was back there wondering what all the fuss was about.

'Rosalie?' Joshua shouted.

They'd been looking along the river for a while now, the fading light hindering the search. And with every minute that passed, Sarah found it harder and harder to curb her fear. If they didn't find her soon, they'd have to call the police.

'There.' Joshua grabbed her hand and pointed down the path to a flickering light.

Sarah ran towards it.

As she got closer, the familiar figure came into focus.

'Rosalie?' The breathless word barely audible.

'Sarah? Is that you?' Rosalie's voice rang out, not a hint of angst in its chime. 'What are you doing out here?'

'Looking for *you*.' Sarah bent over to catch her breath, as Rosalie pulled her bike to a stop beside her.

'I'm right here.'

'Do you have any idea what time it is?' Sarah asked as Joshua strode up beside her.

'Five-ish?'

'Try six. We've been looking for you for half an hour.'

'Why on earth would you do that?'

'You said if you weren't back . . .'

'Oh, that's just an expression, Sarah.' Rosalie waved her hand in the air.

Joshua cleared his throat and Rosalie looked at him then back to Sarah.

'Oh.' She nodded. 'Sorry, my darling. I didn't mean to worry you. Just lost track of time.'

'Just lost track of time?'

Rosalie patted Sarah's arm. 'It happens. Shall we head back?' She pushed off on her bike, riding a little ahead.

Sarah turned to Joshua, exasperation rising in her.

He smiled. 'All that matters is she's safe. This is now just a pleasant evening walk with the sun setting.'

Sarah tried to focus on the bright orange fading to black in the distance, the dark silhouetted branches of the gums against the evening sky framing the view.

'My favourite place on earth.' Joshua said.

Sarah turned to look at him. 'Really?'

'Yep. I've travelled quite a bit.' Joshua listed a handful of exotic destinations – Egypt, Sweden, Canada – and Sarah suspected he was holding back, not wanting to come across as boastful. 'But this place beats them all. What about you? Have you travelled?'

They continued along the path, Sarah's gaze moving between Joshua and her grandmother, now some way ahead. 'A little. When I was younger, I went overseas with the youth orchestra a couple of times. And before I had Melody, I had touring opportunities.'

She told him of her favourite trip, to Spain a few years ago, but so fresh in her memory – the centuries-old cathedrals and concert halls she'd played in. 'But with Melody's dad not around, I tried to keep my work closer to home.'

Joshua nodded. 'And now?'

The question snuck up on her. Perhaps it was the relief at finding Rosalie, or the beauty of the night, but the words came out of Sarah's mouth before she could stop them. 'I haven't played since the accident.'

'I see. Injury?' He looked at her flexing hand.

'Sort of. I do need to get back to physio, but it's not just that . . .' Sarah tried to find the right words. 'I don't want to do anything that might upset Melody further, push her further into herself.'

Joshua looked at her with kind eyes, and words she had no intention of uttering spilled forth.

'And to be perfectly honest, I don't know if I want to play again. Before the accident it was such a big part of our lives. But now it's just a terrible reminder . . .'

Looking up at the sky, Joshua nodded. 'I get it. I do. Maybe now you're here, though, you can let some of that burden go. Lay it on us. That's what we're here for. And take some space to find yourself a little. Our therapist Phoebe has every Wednesday free. Even if it's just to grab a nice hot chocolate. Might help.'

Sarah stopped dead in her tracks. 'Oh, no, I'm fine . . . I don't need to . . .'

Joshua slowed down, stopping a couple of steps from her. 'It's okay, Sarah. We all move through trauma in our own unique way.'

She put her hands on her hips. 'If you start on at me about the seven stages, I swear to God . . .' She knew she was stuck somewhere in a messy quagmire of denial and guilt and anger and loneliness. She didn't need him to spout some generic rhetoric at her.

He raised his hands in the air. 'I wasn't going to.' The corners of his mouth turned up in a soft smile. 'All I'm saying is that you guys being here at the retreat is something new and different you're trying. Be open to whatever it presents. Maybe nothing will change. Maybe it will. Just be open and . . . well, who knows.'

No worthless promises of quick fixes. No empty guarantees that if they follow the program to the letter, they'll get results. No hollow assurances that it is only a matter of time.

Just 'who knows'.

'Maybe it's time to let some of your old self come back to Melody. And maybe some of her will come back to you.'

No one had ever quite put it like that.

Sarah's shoulders dropped, and a small smile touched the edges of her lips.

The low sound of rumbling thunder rolled over the evening sky somewhere in the distance.

'Storm coming?' Sarah asked.

Joshua shook his head. 'It sounds far away. We've had so much rain lately I've not been able to get into the garden nearly as much as I like, so I hope it *stays* far away.'

'You're a gardener?'

'I dabble.' He shrugged his shoulders.

'Are you two coming?' Rosalie called from further up the path.

Joshua tilted his head in her direction and Sarah nodded. 'We'd better catch her up.'

Back at the retreat, Rosalie parked her bike against the cabin wall and sauntered inside, greeting Melody and Ryan as if she had no care in the world.

'Good night, Sarah,' Joshua said, at the bottom of the ramp. 'See you in the morning. I'm looking forward to getting to know Melody better in our first session.'

'Good night.' Her shoulders tightened. Tomorrow it was. Make or break.

Or . . . who knows.

The first rays of sun pushed through the opening of the curtains in the living space, as Sarah padded around the room, trying not to disturb the others. She hadn't slept much – at all, really – her mind racing from one flustered thought to the next, and she'd given up all hope of nodding off as the clock on her phone ticked past 4 a.m.

Six o'clock now, it was still another two hours before she had to have Melody up and ready for her first session. Staring at the walls inside their cabin was doing nothing to calm her nerves, so she wrapped her yellow cardigan around herself and headed out into the cool morning air.

There was a light on in the Stave across the clearing, and one of the other cabins was stirring. But the air was still. A light dusting of rain sat on the grass – Sarah had heard it coming down a few hours earlier – but the sky, just waking up, showed the promise of a clear day.

A clang from behind the cabin rang out on the still air and Sarah jumped.

'Come here.' A deep whispered growl followed by another clang.

Sarah stepped off the porch and edged around the side of the cabin. She didn't know what she would do if it were some sort of burglar. But she figured the chances of that around here were probably pretty slim. Although there was that one horror movie she'd watched as a teenager, set in the bush . . . no, don't be so silly.

Placing her hands on the cabin wall, she popped her head around the corner, hoping she would be so stealthy and quick that whoever was there wouldn't see her. But she didn't pull her head back quick enough. She didn't pull it back at all.

She stared, open-mouthed, at the sight just up the path.

Next to the gardening bench Joshua crouched, in a grey tracksuit, hands in a clump of dirt spilled under the table, a . . . Sarah blinked . . . yes, a possum perched on his shoulder.

'You are in so much trouble, young lady,' he growled under his breath.

Sarah stifled a laugh. 'Young lady?'

Joshua jumped up and whacked his head on the table.

'Oh, god, sorry.' She rushed over to him but stopped a few feet short when the possum lifted its head and stared at her – like a genuine death stare.

'No. My bad.' Joshua rubbed his head. 'I shouldn't have been poking around. But this little mischief-maker couldn't help but get into my geraniums.' He ran his hand down the possum's tail, which curled around his fingers. 'All the eucalypt leaves in the world at her fingertips and she still goes for these.' He picked up the smashed pot and tidied up the mess. 'I hope we didn't wake you.'

Sarah shook her head. 'No. I've been up for a while.' *The whole night.* 'So is . . . she . . . your pet?'

Joshua laughed. 'No. It's not legal to keep possums as pets. But I'm not sure she understands the concept. Her family has been here for generations, so the owner tells me, and she thinks she runs the joint.'

Sarah smiled. 'Did you say these were your geraniums?'

He looked down. 'Ah yes. Sorry. I meant to have them out of your way before you arrived, but I got busy. I can maybe come back this afternoon and clear them out.'

Sarah frowned. 'No. They're not in my way. When you said you dabbled in gardening, I didn't realise you meant here at the retreat.'

He nodded. 'I live in an apartment in town. So the owner lets me indulge my green thumb here.'

'What's all the racket?' Rosalie huffed, Melody rolling behind her. 'You lot could wake the dead.'

That was a slight exaggeration, Sarah thought, though her grandmother's hearing had always been top notch.

'Lucky our little minim was already up, and Ryan has popped the kettle on.'

'Sorry, Rosalie.' Joshua grimaced. 'This rascal sometimes has a mind of her own. She should be all tucked away for the day by now. Too much time among the humans.' He shook his head.

Melody tugged on Rosalie's arm and tapped something into her hand. 'Melody would like to know if the creature has a name,' Rosalie said to Joshua.

'She does, actually.' Joshua stepped closer to Melody and she reached out her hand to touch the possum.

'Oh, I don't know if that's a good idea.' Sarah moved closer to Melody's chair. 'She might bite.'

Joshua pulled up short. 'She's more afraid of you than you are of her, I can assure you,' he said to Melody. 'But maybe your mum is right. Just until you get to know each other properly.'

Of all the fleeting times Sarah had contemplated getting a pet for Melody as a companion – a cat, a dog, a goldfish, a hamster – she'd never entertained the idea of her daughter 'getting to know' a possum.

Joshua knelt where he was so that he, and his possum, were at eye level with Melody, yet, to Sarah's relief, a suitable distance away.

'Melody,' Joshua said. 'This is my friend Pineapple.' The possum nudged Joshua's neck. 'Pineapple the tenth, actually. Or maybe it's eleventh. I've lost track. Pineapple, this is Melody.'

At the mention of the possum's name, Melody clapped her hands and stared at Sarah, her mouth agape. Sarah covered her own open mouth with her hand.

'It's a funny name, isn't it?' Joshua said.

'Not as funny as you might think,' Sarah smiled. 'Melody names all her stuffed toys after food and drink.'

'Ah, I see. Rosalie?' Joshua frowned, looking up. 'Are you okay?'

Sarah turned to her grandmother. Her hands were holding tightly onto Melody's wheelchair.

'Granny Rose?'

Rosalie blinked. Three times. Cleared her throat. Twice. Then she turned on her heels and stormed off towards the tree line behind the cabin.

'Is she all right?' Joshua stood up.

'I have no idea.' Sarah shook her head. Once more, she was at a loss to explain her grandmother's behaviour. 'I'd better go after her,' she said. She pointed to the tall gum trees. 'Would you mind staying with Melody? Take her back in to Ryan?'

'Of course not. We'll be fine, won't we, Melody?'

Melody gave an emphatic nod.

Sarah kissed her on the forehead and hurried off into the bush. This was just about the very last thing she needed this morning.

Eighteen

Tarakan Island
July 1945

Edward sat in the mess tent barely touching his food. He hadn't felt much like eating since the attack. His superficial wounds had healed quickly enough, but it wasn't the cuts and the abrasions, the shrapnel or the lingering ringing in his ear that had done the real damage that day. It was his distress over Albert's injuries. And his inability to have kept his brother safe.

Each night he dreamed of the attack, and in every dream he saw the look of terror on his brother's face the moment before the explosion. And then, afterwards, his blood mixing with the mud around them. If only he had pulled him away. If only he had seen the man behind the trees in time to take him down.

Albert had suffered terribly in the makeshift hospital on base as the medics fought to save his leg. He was there just twelve hours before being taken to the hospital ship. Edward was devastated to come back from patrol to find Albert had gone without the brothers having had the chance to say goodbye. There had been no word on his condition in the few days following and Edward knew it might be weeks before he found out how Albert was going.

It was lonely here without him, but Edward was relieved his brother was out of this hellhole. Pushing his untouched plate to the side, he took out his picture of Rosalie, a sense of calm washing over him.

He imagined what it might be like when he got home – a healed Albie strumming on the banjo while he played piano, Penelope baking scones in the kitchen, Rosalie watching on.

Perhaps it was foolish to hang on to such an image. He still had to survive the war, and while skirmishes outside base had all but ceased, getting out of here alive was no guarantee. He'd heard whispers ever since he'd enlisted that the war was coming to a close, and those whispers hadn't proven true yet. Even if he did make it home, when life returned to normal after the war, which it inevitably would, he had no idea what normal would look like for him, for Albert. For Rosalie.

Did she have a sweetheart? Was he serving too, with her waiting for him to return? Was she already married with three little children running around her ankles? His mum hadn't mentioned anything in her correspondence – the minute detail she included was around gardening and cooking and everyday town gossip.

Still, if foolishly imagining what things *could* look like gave him even a small amount of comfort, then he would happily play the fool.

Nineteen

Rosalie knew that you could never hope to return home without facing your past.

But a furry little creature? What business did a blasted possum have setting off such a reaction in her?

So much of Rosalie's energy these days was poured into convincing everyone around her that she was, in fact, not as old and incapable as they thought; that she still had her faculties about her. And all it took to destroy that fragile façade was a possum.

Sarah wouldn't let this go, of that Rosalie was certain.

A large gum tree stood in her path, so she turned left and continued walking. Another tree in her way. She turned right. Twisting and turning between the tall timber guardians of the bush, without any regard for which way she was going, Rosalie came to a stop in a small clearing. And right there, through that small gap in the grey and brown, she swore she could see the back of the retreat's main building. She hadn't gone far. But clearly she'd gone in anything but a straight line.

Not wanting to head back just yet – humiliation was not something she suffered lightly – she stepped further into the clearing and the dirt beneath her feet levelled out into what was once a path.

Could it be?

She looked back at the main building, reoriented herself. It had to be. But surely it wasn't still there. In her head she calculated the distance – eight more steps, maybe a few more given her stride wasn't quite as long as it used to be – and she measured it out.

One, two, three . . . ten, eleven.

'Oh, my.'

A fallen branch covered in decades of leafy and twiggy debris, new growth sprouting from its fertile cracks and crevices, hid it well. But there was no mistaking it.

The Shack.

Rosalie let out a long sigh as she picked her way over the branch to get a closer look. As it was too dilapidated for her to venture inside, she sat on a smooth old stump and leaned against one of the rotting walls of the place that was once her sanctuary.

Redgum River
July 1945

Rosalie rode over to the Dawsons' on a fine Saturday morning and arrived to find Penelope in the garden tending her roses. She waved as Rosalie approached, then put her fingers to her lips. Wiping her dirt-spattered hands on her apron she walked down the neat path to greet Rosalie.

'Is everything all right?' Rosalie asked.

'Oh, yes. Of course.' Penelope's voice seemed for a moment unnaturally chirpy. 'Albert is still sleeping. He's still recovering, after all, and is taking a little time to adjust to being back home.'

The forced smile Penelope wore gave Rosalie pause.

'He should be up soon.'

There it was again. The overly bright tone.

'Is there anything I can do to help?'

'Oh, thank you, dear. No, I don't think so. He's still in pain, is all, and sometimes he needs to sleep it off.'

Rosalie noticed the catch in Penelope's voice. 'Is everything okay?'

'Will you give me a hand while we wait?' Penelope passed Rosalie a trowel, ignoring the question.

Half an hour later, a noise from inside the house caught their ears and Penelope stiffened beside Rosalie.

'I'll just go see if he's up for visitors.' She scuttled inside before Rosalie had a chance to respond. A few moments later, standing on the porch, she waved Rosalie over.

Sitting at the dining table with cup of tea in his hand, Albert smiled as she entered. He stood up and nodded to Rosalie. 'Hello there.' He grinned and his dimples deepened. 'I was just having a cuppa. I can't tell you how much I missed a good cup of tea when I was over . . . there.'

'Did you not have tea when you were serving?'

'Oh, we did. It was like nectar of the gods. But now that I'm home, I realise just how bad that tea was.' Albert pulled a chair out for Rosalie and she sat down. 'And we most definitely didn't have my mum's scones.'

Penelope pulled out a tin with a fresh batch of scones wrapped in calico inside.

'Nothing in the world beats these.' He smiled.

'On that I would agree with you.' Rosalie held up her teacup and Albert clinked his with hers, the warmth in his eyes as they held Rosalie's gaze sending heat shooting though her veins.

As they ate scones and drank tea, Rosalie asked Albert about his time serving. A flash of something dark crossed his face, ever so briefly, before his smile returned. 'In journalist mode, I see.'

'Oh. Sorry. It's just that we only hear what they want us to know. I guess I was hoping for a more honest account.'

A brief look passed between Penelope and Albert.

'Let's not talk of such things over tea.' Penelope stood up and fussed with the knitted cosy covering the pot. 'Didn't you want to ask Rosalie about her photography, Albert?'

A broad grin returned to his face. 'Yes. How did you get into it?' He leaned forward.

Rosalie told him about Bernie and her time at university and her work with the *River Times*. And each time she asked him a question about himself, or Edward, he turned the focus back to her.

'It sounds like you've got quite a career ahead of you.' Albert sat back, a look of admiration on his face.

'I hope so. I have a way to go yet, though.'

'You're just being modest.' Penelope patted Rosalie's hand. 'A local star, you are. Now, what's on your agenda for the rest of the day?' Penelope stood to clear the table.

'I'm heading to Wombat Hollow actually, to take a Snapshot for a family.'

'Wombat Hollow?' said Albert. 'There's a guy from there back on base. Different unit to ours, though. Corporal Langford.'

'That's him! That's who the request came from,' Rosalie exclaimed.

'Do you think I can come with you?' he asked earnestly. 'To meet Ralphy's family would mean the world to me.'

'I'm sure they'd really like that. I'll head home now and be back with Walter and the car in about . . . an hour?'

'Thank you, Rosalie. I really appreciate this.'

On the way out to the Langfords, Albert asked Rosalie about her Snapshots work.

'Tell me more. Why do you do it? Do you write to everyone you take photos for, or just my dreamboat of an older brother?'

'Dreamboat?'

He shrugged. 'Tall, broad. Blond hair like Mum. Not this red mess.' He shook his head.

'Oh, I don't know about that.' The words tumbled out of Rosalie's mouth before she could stop them. Thankfully, Albert didn't react.

She cleared her throat and changed the subject, telling him all about the Snapshots initiative and her involvement. 'I don't write to everyone. But Edward wrote to me and because of my friendship with Penelope, I replied. And now . . . now I guess you can say we're friends.'

'He enjoys your letters. I only had Mum's to look forward to, and I can tell you, anything we get from home is a blessing. I think what you're doing with these photo things is bloody fantastic. They mean more to the men than you can possibly realise.'

Rosalie had hoped, and always believed, that the Snapshots she was taking were a brief moment of light in the darkness of the soldiers' everyday. But hearing from Albert just how much they meant touched her heart.

'Thank you. That means a lot. What a shame,' she smiled, 'that you didn't put in a request, then I could have sent you something as well. I'm curious, Albert, if you had, what would you have asked for?'

Albert scratched the fiery stubble that covered his jawline, his green eyes narrowed in thought. 'Hmm. Now that's a tough one. If I don't say a picture of my mum, that probably makes me a bad son. But I kept her real close in here –' He tapped the left side of his chest '– and I had Edward's photos to look at.'

'Well, what did you miss most of all?'

He paused a moment, a pained look passing across his eyes. 'The music. I had my banjo over there with me, but it wasn't the same as Edward sitting at the piano, Mum bustling about with food and having a good old singalong. And the scones. Silly, isn't it? In the middle of a bloody war zone and I missed music and scones.' His eyes clouded over with sadness.

Rosalie swallowed the lump in her throat. 'I don't think that's silly at all. They're happy, comforting memories of home. It makes perfect sense to me.'

Albert smiled. 'So, I guess I would have requested . . . Mum sitting on top of the piano, holding a plate of scones.'

Rosalie laughed. 'Well, that would have been the most creative request I've received.'

'Would you have done it?'

'Sure. As long as Penelope was up for it. And I reckon she'd do anything for you two.'

He nodded and murmured, 'You're right about that. She's one in a million.'

At the Langford's place Albert hobbled around the yard with the family kelpie and Ralphy's younger brother, who Rosalie guessed was maybe twelve years old, while she spoke to Mr and Mrs Langford. She told them Ralphy had requested a photo of the whole family around the tree he'd planted with them before he'd joined the army.

After she got the shot, Albert sat with the couple, talking to them at length. Rosalie stayed just out of earshot, watching their expressions move from concern to pride to comfort. Whatever Albert was saying was having an impact on them. She raised her camera and adjusted the zoom, capturing the moment, full of depth and heart. Her eyes pricked and she had to look away.

In Redgum River, Walter pulled the car up to the Dawsons' house and Penelope got up from her crouched position in the garden.

Bernie was beside her, his hands also covered in dirt. Together, they greeted Rosalie and Albert. 'Why don't you stay for dinner, Rosalie?' Penelope said. 'I'm sure it won't be anything like you're used to, but we'd love to have you.'

'I hardly see you anymore, Rose-petal. Even Pineapple is missing you.' Bernie put his arm around Rosalie. 'Say yes.'

'Of course. I'd like that.' She looked at Walter, who gave her a short nod.

'I'll let Betty know and come back around eight,' he said.

Penelope clapped and Albert flashed his dimples.

It was a dinner of sausages, and soggy carrots and peas, but it was served with love and the conversation was so lively Rosalie hardly even noticed the vegetables drowning in their own water.

'Sure beats army rations,' Albert said, as he cleaned up the last of his sausages.

'Well, that isn't much of a compliment, is it?' Penelope quipped. 'Perhaps I should send you back over there until you learn to appreciate your mother's cooking.' She shot him a look that was supposed to be of admonition, but the happy lines crinkling around her eyes and the broad smile she wore gave her away.

After dinner, Rosalie moved to the piano and noticed it had been dusted.

'Do you play?' Albert was there beside her, a tea towel in his hands.

She nodded. Her father had insisted she learn when she was a child as part of her becoming an accomplished young woman, and while she loved the instrument, she'd hated her tutor, Mrs Grey-bun-too-tight-for-her-big-head Yeats, whose methods included hitting Rosalie over the knuckles with a wooden ruler. It had worked, she supposed. Rosalie could play exceptionally well. But her childhood music lessons had sucked the joy out of playing and she hadn't touched a piano since just before she started her degree.

'It's been a while,' she sighed.

'She plays beautifully,' Bernie called from the kitchen, where he was helping Penelope with the washing up.

Albert leaned across her, his scent of lemon and earth tickling her nostrils, and he opened the fallboard, flicking the music rack open.

'What's this?' Rosalie ran her finger over a deep curly scar in the wood that reminded her of a possum's tail.

A look of guilt washed over Albert's face. 'I may have put that there when my pa won this beauty in a poker match.'

'A poker match?'

He put his hand on his chest. 'Not a word of a lie. These are my initials, see?' He traced his fingers over the scar and Rosalie could follow the stylised A and D.

'Ready to play?' He moved the stool into position for her.

'Oh . . . I . . .' She looked up into his eyes.

'Go ahead. I prefer my banjo, anyway.' He picked up the string instrument that had been leaning against the side of the piano.

Rosalie took a seat. 'What would you like me to play?'

'Whatever you want,' Albert said.

'I don't really know any popular music.' Her cheeks warmed with embarrassment.

'Can you sight-read?'

'Of course.'

'Edward can too. Taught himself. I can a little, but I play mostly by ear.' He moved to the other side of the room and rummaged in an old trunk that was sitting there. 'I think something in here should do the trick.' He returned with a pile of sheet music.

Rosalie riffled through the pages. Most of them were torn or crinkled but the music was still clear. There were pieces featuring all the big names – Ellington, Holliday, Berlin, Crosby, Porter – a plethora of music far more exciting than anything she had played as a child.

'Where did you get all these?' Rosalie looked up in wonder.

'Edward and I used to gig a bit.'

'This is amazing.'

'Pick one and we can give it a try.'

She eventually settled on a few pieces and placed the sheets on the music rack.

'You lead. I'll follow,' Albert suggested.

Rosalie started with 'Cheek to Cheek', conjuring images of Fred and Ginger as she quickly scanned the music before letting her fingers touch the keyboard. It was a song she knew well to sing, so she hoped that would make up for her never having played it before.

She rested her fingers on the keyboard, tapping out the first few notes gingerly, almost as if she were afraid of the instrument. Or afraid of how badly she would play it. But a few bars in she started to relax as her fingers loosened and years of training flowed through her. As she picked up the speed, playing with more confidence, Albert lifted his banjo. While she played the melody, he strummed the chords, improvising embellishments as he found his rhythm.

From the kitchen Penelope sang softly. Albert looked down at Rosalie, and she thought perhaps she caught a glimpse of wetness rim his eyes as she glanced up.

'All right, maestro.' Albert put his banjo down after the third song. 'What's next?'

Rosalie tapped her chin with her finger. 'What about . . .' She pulled out the music for 'In the Still of the Night', one of her favourite Cole Porter songs.

Albert smiled. 'This is Mum's favourite.'

'Oh, it is!' Penelope came over. 'Why don't you play the piano with Rosalie for this one?'

'I'm game, if you are.' He looked at Rosalie.

She shuffled over to make room on the stool for him. 'You take the low. I'll take the high.'

Albert laced his fingers together and pushed his arms forward giving them a good stretch. 'I'll do my best.'

Rosalie counted them in and it was as if they'd been playing together for years. Albert let her set the tempo and seamlessly played along with her. As she watched his fingers dance across the keys without him reading the music, she nearly stopped playing. If this was him playing by ear, how good would he be if he'd had lessons?

Behind them Penelope sang, Bernie looking on with a doe-eyed expression, and now Rosalie could hear her properly, she realised how beautiful Penelope's voice was. She murmured to Albert, 'Jeepers.' His smile deepened and without missing a note he gave her a little shoulder bump.

As the clock struck eight, they wrapped the evening up.

'Thank you for such a wonderful time. I can't remember when I last had so much fun,' Rosalie said to Penelope. It sure beat dinner at home, with her parents' constant questioning of her and less than subtle hints of their vision for her future.

'It was our pleasure.' Penelope wrapped Rosalie in a tight hug. 'I hope we can do it again sometime.'

'I'd really like that,' Rosalie said.

Penelope patted Albert on the back. 'Could you see our guest out.'

When they reached the steps of the porch, Rosalie turned to face Albert. 'I really did have a fabulous time tonight. Thank you, Albert.'

'You are very welcome.' He took a step closer, stopping just inches away. 'I really enjoyed playing that duet with you.' His voice was low, his eyes boring into her.

Rosalie swallowed hard. 'So did I. You're much better than you give yourself credit for. I hope we can do it again one day.'

'I will make sure we do.'

Rosalie turned around and steadied herself on the railing before stepping off the porch. She breathed in the cool night air and walked towards the waiting car, not daring to look back.

Rosalie tossed in bed. Down the hall, the grandfather clock struck twelve.

Giving up on sleep, she slipped out from under her quilt and threw her overalls on over her nightdress. Grabbing her camera, she tiptoed out of her bedroom and down the hallway, making sure she was quiet so she didn't wake Mother or Father.

Quietly unlocking the back door, she stepped out into the dark night, picked up her bike and walked it down the driveway. Once she was at the end of the street, she mounted and rode through town until she reached the large red gum at the edge of the river turning north. Guided by the moonlight she found her way to the hidden grove she thought of as hers, pushing her way under the two gum trees that had grown with interlocking branches at their top.

Leaning against the sturdy trunk, the sound of the river babbling behind her, she set up the tripod she'd brought with her and took photos of the trees' silhouettes against the dark night, remembering what Bernie had taught her about night-time photography. As she looked up at the stars that punctuated the sky, she allowed her colliding thoughts to dissolve away. She sat down and put her arms out beside her, trailing her hands through the soft cold grass beneath, her eyes closed.

The sound of footfalls set her senses on alert and she stood up again. There was a shadow moving along the riverbank – shoulders slumped, head bowed low.

Rosalie's heart pounded in her chest and her palms began to sweat.

She held her breath.

The figure stopped by the water just down from her and lowered himself onto the grass. With his back to her, Rosalie had the chance to move quietly away unseen. She'd have to leave her bike leaning up against the trunk of the tree – the wheels and the chain would alert the intruder to her presence. She could always come back for it tomorrow.

The figure reclined in the grass, soft moonlight casting gentle light on to their face. She crouched through the small opening towards the man.

'Albert?' she whispered.

He gave a start and turned around. '*Rosalie?*'

She exhaled and relief washed over her.

'What are you doing out here in the middle of the night?' he asked.

'I could ask you the same thing.' She stopped a few feet away from him. There had been a wildness to his eyes when he'd called her name but before her now it dissolved and the warmth in his green eyes returned.

'I find it hard to sleep,' he told Rosalie. 'Sometimes I come down here where I can hear the running water and look up to the stars.'

'It's a fair way from your home. Can you not just lie in your garden and look at the stars from there?'

He raised an eyebrow. 'And what is it you're doing out here?'

'I have a secret spot.' She helped him up and guided him through the trees. 'You can get some really great photos here at night.' She indicated the camera on the tripod pointing up to the night sky, which was peppered with tiny white stars.

'Can you not just go in your garden and take them?'

'I don't want to risk disturbing my parents.' She smiled. 'Oh . . . touché.'

'Have you ever really looked up at the stars? I mean *really* looked at them. I didn't until I was serving. Every night I'd look up, searching for the Southern Cross.' He sat back onto the grass and Rosalie sat next to him. 'Looking for a piece of home, I guess. But it's different over there. It was always much lower in the sky.'

'Really?'

'Ah-huh. The sky moved differently, even though we were still in the southern hemisphere. Funny how we can have an unwavering belief that things are absolutely the way they are, and then we find out they're not.'

Rosalie raised her arm and pointed to the Southern Cross. 'So if we were over there now, and looking up, where would it be?'

'Hmm. Everything would be shifted . . .' he took her hand and moved it down so it pointed much lower, '. . . that much. That's where it would be.'

Rosalie forced herself to focus on her breath, rather than the fact he was holding her hand.

He coughed, and let go.

They sat there in grass, side by side, their hands nearly touching but not quite, as they looked up at the stars, silent. The air was still, the night quiet.

Sarah's voice cut through Rosalie's reverie. 'Granny Rose! I've been looking for you everywhere.'

Her granddaughter was pulling a rather comical face, Rosalie thought, as she launched herself over the fallen branch.

'Well, here I am.'

Sarah shook her head. 'So I see. Are you okay?'

Rosalie tried to think of a plausible excuse for running off like that, but came up empty.

'The possum,' she answered simply.

'The possum?'

'Yes. She, he, it, whatever,' she waved her hand in the air, 'reminded me of something from a long time ago.'

'A possum named Pineapple reminded you of something in your past?'

Was the woman going to repeat everything Rosalie said?

'Yes.'

'What?'

'Nothing important.'

The little folds between Sarah's eyes deepened. Did she know frowning like that wasn't good for her complexion, Rosalie wondered?

'If it wasn't important, why did you take off?'

Rosalie paused. 'Because sometimes the smallest of memories is a stepping stone to ones buried deeper.'

'That's beautiful, Granny Rose,' said Sarah.

'Maybe.' Rosalie shrugged. 'Depends on where the stepping stones lead.'

'And they led you here?'

'Ah, well, arriving here was quite by accident.'

'And where is "here", I wonder?' Sarah looked at the ruined shack behind them.

Rosalie drew herself up taller. She couldn't avoid this forever. After all, it was part of the reason she'd insisted they come to Redgum River in the first place – to help her find a way to set her story free.

'This is where I learned.' Her words came out in a whisper.

'Where you learned what?'

'Darling, if you're going to repeat everything I say, we're going to be here for a long time. This is where everything started. This place – well, a version of it, once belonged to my Uncle Bernie.'

Sarah fidgeted beside her and Rosalie knew she was fighting to decide which of the many questions she must have to ask.

'Was this your uncle's house?' Sarah stood up and looked around the shack.

'No.' Rosalie laughed. 'Of course not. Even in this state, you can see how small it is. This was our darkroom.'

Sarah spun around and stared at her.

'Bernie was the one who taught me how to take photos, and we developed them here. All of the Snapshots were developed right inside there.' She pointed to the mess of broken wood.

Sarah picked her way around the Shack, trying to get a better look inside.

'I know you have many questions, my darling. And I will answer them. But you have to let me do it in my own time. I need to find a way to reconcile my memories, now I'm here, process them all after so long.'

Sarah nodded.

'Besides, shouldn't we be getting back? Preparing for Melody's first session?'

'Yes.' Sarah looked at her watch. 'Yes, we should. Here.' She held out her hand and Rosalie took it, relieved that she didn't have to figure out how to get off that stump all by herself.

She was also relieved Sarah didn't, for the first time in a long time, make any kind of fuss or concerned comment. 'Let's go,' was all she said.

Rosalie nodded and thought back once more to those green eyes that had haunted her for so many years.

Twenty

Back at the cabin, Sarah rushed around the kitchen clearing the breakfast dishes, while Ryan and Melody played a card game on the coffee table. Rosalie was in her room 'freshening up', as she called it.

They had walked back in silence, arm in arm, a gentle moment between them they hadn't shared for a long time. Today, Sarah had seen something in her grandmother that she'd never seen before. Vulnerability. And vulnerable was not a word anyone would use to describe Rosalie.

Whatever she was hanging on to from her past, it was clearly affecting her. Sarah was desperate to know what it was, but she knew she would have to be patient and gentle in pushing for the truth. There was definitely much more to uncover than she'd first thought. More than just the story of the old black and white photos in a dusty album.

She stacked the last of the plates in the drainer and turned around, putting on her happiest, most enthusiastic smile, hoping no one would see through her bubbling nerves.

'Right, then. Who's ready to get this started?' She injected excitement into her voice.

Melody raised her hand and smiled, though Sarah could see the hint of apprehension behind her warm brown eyes.

'Born ready.' Ryan stood up and Melody shook her head. 'I'll be there with you in spirit.' He ruffled her hair and she swatted his hand away. 'You ready, Granny Rose?' he called out.

'No need to shout, my darling.' Rosalie sauntered into the room and Sarah noticed the extra care her grandmother had taken with her makeup and hair. The two of them were going to spend some time 'exploring Rosalie's old stomping ground' was how Ryan put it. 'Being dragged around against her will' was Rosalie's description. From Sarah's Google search, she wasn't sure there was too much of interest to see, but if it meant the two of them were out of her hair and she could concentrate on Melody, then great. And at least if Ryan was with Rosalie, that was one less thing to worry about.

All four of them bustled out of the cabin, and on the path in front of the Stave they went their separate ways.

'It'll all be okay.' Ryan leaned over to Sarah and whispered in her ear.

She hoped so. Lord knew how much she hoped so.

Melody waved Ryan and Rosalie off and turned to look up at her mother. Again, Sarah mustered a convincing smile, and with all the confidence and calm she could dredge up, they went inside.

The glass sliding doors opened into a large foyer, colours of sage and beige greeting them. There were three large soft sofas around the edge of the foyer, their velvet cushions slightly worn but clean. Over each sofa a crochet blanket hung in that haphazard way that you knew was perfectly styled, one a patchwork of hexagons, one in wavy stripes, the other in swirling rounds. In the middle of the open space, a small wooden table sat with a bouquet of yellow banksias, red proteas and silver-green gum leaves spilling over the tall glass vase. In front of the large floral display was a sign that read, 'Just a note' – the 'o' written as a music note – 'to say welcome'. There was a delicate scent of eucalypt in the air and on the walls were photos of what Sarah assumed were the local surrounds, all framed with repurposed branches, roughly cut to size.

One of the photos was larger than the rest and Sarah stepped closer.

It was of a small wooden cabin nestled among a forest of tall gum trees, shards of light streaming in between the branches. It was stunning. A plaque beneath the frame read 'Morning Contemplation, Bernard Meyer, 1939'.

Bernard . . . Bernie? Could this possibly be the uncle Rosalie had mentioned this morning?

Sarah stood back.

'Gorgeous, isn't it?' Joshua's voice came from behind.

She turned around. 'It is.'

Joshua gave Melody a high-five and then they did some sort of finger-waggle thing that made Melody's shoulders shake with her ghost giggle.

'That was the original cabin on this site,' Joshua explained. 'Where I did all my music lessons as a boy.'

Wait? What? 'You were taught by Bernie?' Sarah pointed to the plaque, and she tried to do the maths in her head.

'No. I never got to meet Bernie. Before my time. We only demolished that cabin five years ago so we could purpose-build this.' He spread his arm and did a slow twirl. 'I've got a lot of fond memories of that place. But this . . . this was worth letting all that go.'

'It certainly is impressive.' She looked around. Surrounding the foyer was a series of rooms that branched out like spokes on a wheel, and from the glimpse Sarah had, it appeared each one was comfortably furnished in different colours. The one closest to where they were standing was in russets and wood tones; the next in pastels of purple and lemon; one with primary colours; one, she arched her back for a better look, in black and white and grey.

'We have four therapy rooms,' Joshua said. 'And over there,' he pointed to the room that branched off the far end of the foyer, 'is our performance space. We hold meetings in there, dinner, special events, concerts. Actually, on Thursday the Vital Voices are having a concert here.'

'Vital Voices?'

'It's a choir we run out of the local nursing home, for people with dementia and cognitive issues, and their families, and we all sing together and have morning tea and leave our worries at the door and just . . . be.'

Sarah tilted her head to the side. 'That sounds really special.'

'Yeah. It is. I'm so lucky. The choir is actually how all this began. The owners . . .'

The squeal of a young child running through the foyer made them both turn around. A little boy, maybe five years old, came running up to Joshua and crashed into his legs. 'Hey there, Vinny.' Joshua knelt down. 'Good to have you back again.' Vinny threw his arms around Joshua's neck before running back to his mum. A young woman, dressed in the retreat's sage polo, greeted the family and they headed into the pastel room.

'Vinny's one of our regulars.'

'Regulars?'

'We have all sorts of clients here. Some from the local area who come once a week as "day clients"; some, like Vinny, who come every couple of months and use the retreat as respite therapy; some who stay at the retreat for a block of time, like you; and the choir and the outreach programs we run. It all depends on the needs and outcomes of the client . . . Sorry, I slipped into business mode there.'

Sarah shook her head. 'No. Don't be sorry. I'm blown away, to be honest.' She still could barely believe such a place existed.

Melody wheeled over to them.

'Well,' Joshua put his hands on his hips, 'enough of that. Miss Melody doesn't want to hear all about boring business, do you?'

She frowned and shook her head, then smiled broadly.

'I wonder,' Joshua moved slowly and Melody followed him, 'if maybe you can help me with a pesky intruder I have in one of my rooms?'

Sarah walked behind them and they entered the room decked out in wood tones. She was grateful he hadn't chosen the one with primary colours, as it reminded Sarah of the therapist's room back home.

There were three tan armchairs in seemingly random positions facing in different directions, pictures of gum trees on the walls in the same frames as the foyer, a large umber beanbag in the middle of the room, a few instruments scattered about – a guitar, some bongo drums, a recorder, bells. And then she noticed it. In the corner of the room, partially hidden behind one of the armchairs, and a carelessly thrown blanket. Its endpin poking out.

A cello.

Sarah fought to swallow her gasp.

Melody hadn't seen it yet. But if she did? Sarah's heart beat quickly. What was he thinking? She was about to have a go at him, tear Melody out of there, but then he pointed up. Melody and Sarah raised their heads. In the opposite corner to where the offending instrument loomed, on the open beam of the ceiling, was a possum.

'I think Pineapple likes it in here because the colours are just like her natural habitat, but it's a bit warmer,' said Joshua.

Melody smiled and waved to the possum.

'Maybe we can stay in here and just make sure she doesn't do any damage.'

Melody saluted Joshua and put her serious face on.

'She gets in there,' Joshua pointed to the porch, 'if we forget to close the door properly.' He winked at Sarah, which Melody missed, her gazed fixed on Pineapple. 'Maybe you can keep guard, Sarah, in case she has any friends who think it's a good idea to join her.'

Melody hadn't noticed that Pineapple was sound asleep, as all nocturnals ought to be this time of day.

Without taking her eyes from Pineapple, Melody nodded and pointed out the door. Sarah stood there for a moment, not sure what to do. She wasn't keen to leave her daughter alone for their first session.

Joshua tapped his nose and nodded to the chair on the porch. It was angled in such a way that Sarah would be able to see everything going on in the room. She nodded. Once she was outside, Melody lowered her arm, and Joshua sat in the armchair under the beam Pineapple was perched on, a guitar in his hands. Melody, fixated on her task of watching the sleeping creature, had her back to the cello.

Sarah narrowed her gaze. Perhaps none of this was as haphazard as it appeared. With gentle movements, Joshua began to strum on the guitar. It was a slow tune, a melodic soft sound floating on the air. Joshua played, Melody watched Pineapple, and Sarah sat still, breathing in and out. In and out.

Half an hour passed, and as far as Sarah could tell, nothing had happened. Joshua kept playing, sometimes telling a story, or asking a question between songs. Melody didn't take her eyes off Pineapple, and Sarah remained still on the porch.

'You have done a very good job there, Melody,' Joshua said, resting the guitar against the armchair. 'I reckon Pineapple would have run amok if it weren't for you watching her like that.'

Melody sat in her chair, her shoulders back, her chest out, her chin high.

'Do you think maybe you can come back this afternoon and make sure she's still behaving herself?'

Melody nodded emphatically. Joshua gave her a high-five. 'Excellent. I'll see you then.' He nodded at Sarah, and she came into the room. Both Joshua and Melody seemed rather pleased with themselves.

With Ryan and Rosalie out and about, Sarah and Melody headed into town for lunch. They found themselves a little café overlooking the river, aptly named The River Runs, and ordered burgers and fries. There was a gentle bustle about the town, people shopping, people walking along the river, and Sarah enjoyed watching the comings and goings in silence. Melody scoffed down her burger in record time and indicated to her mother that she wanted to explore along the river.

At the part of the riverbank where the town began to melt into the bush, they came to the extraordinarily large tree they'd seen on their first day. A little further up the bank, Sarah could see Ryan in some sort of downward-lion-lily pose. What was he doing in a yoga class? She waved, but he didn't see them. Melody's attention was solely on the tree. With a broad grin across her face, Melody leaned into her chair and pushed her wheels harder. She only got once around the tree before conking out and turning to Sarah to ask for help with pleading eyes.

Sarah took the handles of the chair and pushed Melody around the enormous trunk. Throwing her arms in the air, Melody made a spiral motion with her hand.

'You want me to go faster?' Sarah laughed.

Melody nodded.

'Okay . . . But don't blame me if you get dizzy!'

Melody made a whipping action with her hand.

Two more turns around the tree, as fast as Sarah could go, and she'd had enough. How long had it been since she'd done anything even remotely resembling vigorous physical activity? Far too long, apparently.

Melody slapped her leg with her hands and turned around to look at Sarah.

'Oh, minim. I don't know if I can go again.' She bent over and put her hands on her knees.

But Melody wouldn't be deterred. She put her hands together under her chin in a prayer-like motion and looked at Sarah with puppy-dog eyes.

Sarah drew in some deep breaths in preparation.

'What are you two doing? Running the Gumtree Olympics?' Joshua walked towards them, his hands on his hips, a smirk across his face.

'More like the chariot race in *Ben Hur*,' Sarah laughed. 'Are you on your lunch break?'

'Yep.' Joshua nodded. 'Katie and Phoebe have back-to-back sessions today, so I'm going to grab them something to eat too.'

'Well, we can highly recommend the burgers from The River Runs café.'

'Ah, I see you've found the local favourite. Best Mexican chickenburger this side of Sydney.'

'We had the beef burger, didn't we, Melody?'

She nodded.

'And we weren't disappointed.'

Melody shook her head, then grabbed Sarah's arm, giving it a good tug.

'I'd better . . .' Sarah frowned.

'This one's on me.' Joshua extended his hands. 'May I?' he asked Melody.

She hesitated, but only for a moment, and then nodded, bracing herself for the lap around the tree, one arm in the air.

'Ready, set . . .'

Melody lowered her arm.

'Go!'

Clearly, Joshua was far fitter than Sarah and he had Melody around that enormous trunk and on a second lap before she could even tell him to be careful. After three laps, Joshua slowed down and pulled the wheelchair up in front of Sarah.

'I reckon that might do it. Don't want to tucker myself out.' He smiled at Sarah. Kneeling down, he spoke to Melody. 'I'm definitely going to need your help this afternoon. One of the other kids left their apple out and Pineapple got a hold of it . . .'

Melody raised her hands to her mouth.

'Let's just say, she ran around the retreat for half an hour on a sugar high that would put a toddler to shame.'

Melody smiled gleefully. Sarah suspected the tale was a total lie – surely nocturnal Pineapple was still safely asleep in the rafters.

Serious face on, Melody tapped her chest twice and then saluted. *Deputy Melody, on the case.*

Joshua said goodbye and started towards the town centre. Sarah, forcing some energy back into her legs, ran a few steps to catch up with him.

'Is it all right if I ask you a question? About this morning?'

'Of course.'

'You didn't try to get her to play any kind of music. I thought . . . I mean from my research . . . I thought, well, I thought there'd be more music.'

'It will come,' Joshua said. 'First, we have to build trust. Melody's only known me five minutes, and while *I* think I'm a pretty cool and fun guy, she needs to come to that realisation herself, in her own time.'

Sarah raised an eyebrow.

'What?' asked Joshua.

'You did it again.'

'What?'

'Called yourself cool.'

Pink touched Joshua's bronze cheeks.

'Which makes me automatically uncool.' He shook his head. 'Well, luckily she didn't hear me say that.' He looked over to Melody, who was leaning over the side of her chair picking clover flowers.

'Your secret's safe with me,' Sarah laughed.

'Phew. Then we still have hope. See you in a couple of hours.' Joshua turned on his heel and hurried to the shops.

Sarah thought about what Joshua had said. The logical, university-educated, intelligent woman in her knew he was right. Therapy was about connection. That was one of the problems with Judy. Sarah had been too frightened to do anything about it, and every day she'd berated herself for not having had the courage to explore other options. But connection took time and the emotional mamma-bear inside just wanted to help her baby girl. Straightaway. A click of the fingers.

As she walked back to Melody, who'd nearly finished the clover-chain necklace she was making, Sarah reminded herself she had at least now finally been brave. That they were here and trying something new, and she had to give it a chance.

Twenty-one

Rosalie stood at the end of the street, leaning on the handlebars of her bike. She'd been there now for at least twenty minutes and if she didn't move soon, surely one of the residents in one of the houses would notice the strange woman standing staring into space, and call the police.

But she couldn't move. Not a step.

She'd managed to steal some time to herself by ditching Ryan, convincing him that yoga was something he should try. She would be absolutely fine on her own – what trouble could she possibly get into in broad daylight?

'Promise me you'll be home before dark,' Ryan had said, before kissing her on the forehead. 'Otherwise, that worrywart cousin of mine will have my arse on a platter.'

'Of course.' Rosalie had smiled sweetly. 'We can meet in the car park at five-thirty and return to the cabin together, and she'll be none the wiser.' They shook on it.

And now, after wandering through town, she found herself standing at the entrance to the cul-de-sac, and she couldn't move.

She could see it there, up the hill. Her old home. Exactly as she remembered it – grand, the jewel of the street, perfectly maintained, as if she'd only left yesterday, not more than seven decades ago. Other than some rather unfortunate choices of flowers in the garden, it looked exactly the same. Even from here she could see the jacaranda with the wooden bench wrapping around its trunk.

The moment she'd caught sight of it, she'd frozen. Unable to go down the street to the childhood home she'd only this morning been so desperate to visit. Unable to turn and walk away.

Redgum River
August 1945

The large river redgum cast a broad shadow across the picnic blanket, and Rosalie leaned her back onto the sturdy trunk as she watched her friends enjoy their time together.

Penelope and Bernie were in quiet conversation, and Dot and Millie had laid themselves in the grass and were giggling at a shared joke. Albert had joined them on the picnic; he was down by the water watching the children play a game that Rosalie couldn't make heads nor tails of. It wasn't tip, or kick the can, or hide and seek, but some combination of every childhood game she knew. There was an awful lot of joyous laughter coming from the bank of the river.

Rosalie caught herself looking over at Albert yet again and forced herself to refocus on Mrs Donaldson nattering away beside her.

'Do you really think the Americans have something that will stop the war with the Japanese? There are all sorts of rumours, but this isn't the first war I've been through, as well you know, and not the first time this time around we thought we were nearly through it.' She sighed. 'Surely you have inside knowledge, being in the news game? Some sort of indication or whatnot. I do hope the rumours *are* true. This war has gone on long enough. If you ask me . . .'

Rosalie's gaze drifted back to the riverbank. Albert was sitting on a log smiling and laughing as the children played around him. She could tell he wanted to join in, but he still had a long road to recovery ahead of him. Beside him his walking stick lay against the log and he tapped it absentmindedly. Little Frederick ran towards him waving a stone in the air and when he dropped it next to Albert, Albert flinched. Rosalie took a step in Albert's direction, but he looked up at her with a half smile. Rising slowly off the log he squared himself and took a few steps away from the children.

'And I really think it's appalling, don't you agree?' Mrs Donaldson's voice broke through Rosalie's distraction.

'Oh . . . ah . . . yes.' It was usually safest to agree with Mrs Donaldson.

'You're rather taken with him, aren't you?' Mrs Donaldson nodded towards Albert.

'Excuse me?'

'Penelope's lad. He seems like a lovely young man.'

Rosalie didn't dare respond, not trusting the rather confusing swirl of her emotions.

Albert headed towards the picnic blanket with the children following him. From one of the bags he pulled out a container of his mum's scones, and from a metal canister he dolloped a large blob of cream on each one with a shaking hand then gave them to Tess, Bonnie, Peggy and Frederick, who took their prizes and sat under the large gum.

He lowered himself down beside Rosalie and Mrs Donaldson cleared her throat and moved over to Dot and Millie. Albert leaned back on his elbows. 'Bernie called in the other day. With flowers for Mum,' he said, with a twinkle in his eyes.

Rosalie raised her eyebrow. 'Did he now? I'd say for him that was a pretty bold move.' The sun bounced golden flecks of light off Albert's ginger curls.

'Then I should probably thank you for bringing them together. She deserves some happiness, after . . .' He paused. 'My dad wasn't a very good husband. He gambled. Lost everything we had, more than once. They, Mum and Edward, think I don't know. They think they managed to shelter me from it. But you can't shelter anyone from something like that. I saw it. I knew what was happening.'

The light she'd glimpsed in his eyes was gone, and in its place was the darkness of someone who'd seen too much. She reached across the grass and touched his hand.

'I'm sorry.' She had no other words.

He tried to smile. 'I shall give her my blessing. Edward may not be so thrilled about it, though. He's been the man of the house for so long now, always trying to protect everyone.' He shook his head. 'He takes it all too seriously, you know. Life.'

'Not like you.'

'Nope. Not me. Far too much to enjoy to take any of it too seriously.' Albert hauled himself up, opened a bag he and Penelope had brought with them and took out his banjo. Frederick scrambled to his feet and clapped, Tess and Peggy stood, their eyes wide, and Bonnie shoved the last bite of her scone into her mouth and brushed her hands down her dress.

'Are you going to give us a concert?' Tess asked.

'No.' Albert walked down the grass and the children followed. So did Rosalie. 'I was thinking we could play something a little more my pace. Statues?' He strummed his banjo and started to play a tune. The children began to dance, moving with joyous abandon, arms and legs twirling in wild rhythms, not necessarily in tune with the music. Rosalie lifted her camera from its usual home around her neck and snapped a few shots.

'You too, Miss Reynolds.'

'Oh, I think . . . maybe I shouldn't . . .'

She looked around at the children, their faces beaming. Penelope grabbed Bernie's hand and dragged him down to the group. 'Life's too short and often too sad,' she whispered in Rosalie's ear, and started dancing. Bernie stood next to Penelope swaying gently. Rosalie lowered her camera, allowing the music from Albert's banjo to wash over her. Her hips moved from side to side. Then her feet. Frederick slipped his hand into hers and she mirrored his chaotic twists and whirls.

A moment later, Rosalie realised the music had stopped. Everyone else had frozen in silly poses.

'You're out.' Peggy pointed at her.

Rosalie raised her hands to her flushed cheeks.

'Why don't we let Rosalie off this time. A practice round for everyone,' Albert said.

Tess put her hands on her hips. 'Well . . .' She looked at Rosalie. 'I suppose. But only one practice round.'

'Thank you.' Rosalie smiled. 'I'll pay more attention from now on.'

Albert began playing again and Rosalie danced and froze, smiled and laughed. After three rounds only she and Tess were still in.

'Right. The championship round,' Albert announced. 'Bonnie, Peggy and Frederick, you be my judges.'

The three children flanked him and wore very serious expressions. Albert struck the banjo and this time when he finished his tune, Rosalie watched Tess out of the corner of her eye to make sure the girl had stopped, and then danced a few more steps.

The children rushed forward. 'You're out!' They circled Rosalie and threw their arms around her, pulling her to the ground.

'Oh my. I . . . didn't hear . . . Albert . . . stop,' she said between cackles of laughter.

'Tess is our winner!' Albert called.

Lying in the grass with the children piled on her, Rosalie could hardly breathe, but she made no move to get them off her or to stand up. They all cheered from where they were.

'Ah, ahem.' A voice rumbled over the group. Rosalie looked up and in front of her stood an upside-down Henry, his hat in his hand.

The children slipped off her and she scrambled to her feet. 'Henry! I had no idea you were visiting.' She straightened her green shirt dress and made a feeble attempt to neaten her hair, which she could only imagine was sticking out in all directions.

'Clearly.' He frowned. 'I called on you at home, but Betty said you were at your picnic. I hope you don't mind me stopping by.' He glanced at Albert.

'Of course not.' She introduced him to everyone.

'Ah, Penelope. I've heard about your famous scones. Would I be lucky enough that you have any here today?'

Rosalie smiled. 'I think there may be one or two left.' She headed back to the picnic blanket and Henry followed, placing his hand in the small of her back, guiding her to walk with him.

She stepped out of his touch as Dot and Millie made small talk with him, and as a new game of statues started up, the sound of Albert's banjo dancing on the air, Rosalie looked over her shoulder, catching Albert's eye. She sent him a fragile smile, and he nodded in response before Frederick, yawning, climbed onto the log beside him.

'Do you think it's true,' Dot asked Henry, 'that the Americans will end the war soon?'

Henry inched closer to Rosalie's side. 'Truman was pretty clear in his address at Potsdam last month that he would ruin Japan. The whispers among my friends are that it may well happen. And soon.'

'My Gordon will come home.'

The look of hope in Dot's eyes tore at Rosalie's heart.

'Hopefully they can all come home safe.' Albert stepped up to the group. He'd left the children playing by the water's edge and their laughter carried on the cool breeze that was now rippling over the riverbank.

Henry stiffened beside her.

'Well,' Mrs Donaldson said. 'Let's remain optimistic but not get too carried away.' She started packing up the empty plates and containers.

Everyone chipped in and the picnic was all cleared away in a matter of minutes.

'Shall I walk you home?' Henry asked Rosalie.

She glanced at Albert, who was picking up Penelope's basket. His expression was blank.

'Your father invited me to stay for the afternoon and have dinner.'

Rosalie forced a smile. 'Yes, that would be nice.' Her father had been away and Rosalie had enjoyed not having to deal with his pointed remarks about Henry being a fine catch, and his connection to Reggie, and her chances of securing her dream job.

With warm hugs and kisses on cheeks and hands ruffling children's hair, everyone took their leave. Rosalie let go of her embrace with Millie and stepped towards Albert. He gave a pressed smile, a quick nod and turned to leave.

Rosalie's heart dropped.

*

Dinner was a dull affair later that night, with Frank holding forth on various topics to assert his authority, all to impress Henry, no doubt. Still, it meant Rosalie didn't have worry about too many questions being directed her way.

She and Henry spoke intermittently on the phone, about his studies, the *River Times*, the war, and she enjoyed their conversations. But he was still just a friend.

'So how long will you be here?' Iris asked Henry when Betty brought out their trifle for dessert.

'I was thinking a week.'

Rosalie swallowed.

'A nice break before I have to head back and knuckle down for final exams.'

'And then we will have to refer to you as Doctor Burton,' Frank said. 'It has a nice ring to it, doesn't it, Rosalie?'

'A title is neither here nor there,' she said with a shrug. 'But I know Henry will make a fine physician and his patients will be lucky to have him.'

'Well, it's still a long road ahead, but I am looking forward to completing this phase,' he said.

'And a fine woman by your side to complete the picture.' Frank looked at Rosalie.

Rosalie blushed and opened her mouth to protest, but Henry spoke. 'In time, that would be wonderful. Right now, I am able to count your daughter as a friend and that is enough.'

There was an awkward silence.

'A good friendship is a strong foundation for a relationship,' Iris said, coughing gently.

When they'd finished their trifle, Frank stood and said to Iris, 'Why don't we leave these two to see out the evening?'

Henry rose and bade them goodnight.

'If it's all the same to you, Henry,' Rosalie said, before he could sit back down again. 'I will retire as well. Neville wants me in early in the morning.'

'Of course.' His disappointment was clear, but his good breeding prevented him from pressing her. 'Walk me out?'

She nodded.

Henry opened the front door and when they stepped out into the yard, stopping by the jacaranda tree he took Rosalie's hands.

'You've been quiet tonight.' He looked a little hurt. 'Should I not have come?'

'No. It's fine. I just wasn't expecting you.'

'I've missed you.' Henry lowered his voice. 'Between your work and my study, it's been too long since I was able to look upon your beautiful face.' His thumb tickled the back of her hand.

'Henry.' She lowered her gaze. Images of Albert flashed in her mind; his green eyes, his warm smile, the electricity when their hands touched.

'I know. Just friends. But that doesn't mean I'll give up on us. I think we could have something special.'

Rosalie knew she really ought to shut down any hope he still carried. But she was coming to value his friendship. Nor could she bear the idea of hurting him any more than he seemed to be now. Perhaps, with time, his feelings would simply fade.

But how much time would it take? How much time did she have before she could no longer deny her heart belonged elsewhere?

She tried to think of something to say but Henry spoke first. 'I'll wait. However long it takes. Good night, Rosalie.' He leaned down and kissed her on the cheek.

Regret filled her.

How easy it would be to love Henry.

How impossible.

A car came speeding around the corner, startling Rosalie into the present.

She tore her gaze away from her childhood home and looked at her watch. Oh, good lord, she was going to be late again. In her younger days, she could get from her house to the other side of town in no time. But now, even with the aid of a small motor, it was an entirely different matter.

She mounted her bike and pedalled as fast as she could. As she rolled through the main street in the fancy bike lane that now ran all the way around town, a horn tooted behind her. How dare they? Surely they could see she was going top speed, and she wasn't in anyone's way there in the blue zone.

'Hey, gorgeous lady, you need a ride?' a voice called out.

She spun around and was greeted by the cheeky grin of Ryan. He pulled Gertie to a stop beside her. 'I waited for you as we agreed, and when you didn't show, I figured I'd come see how far away you were.' He turned on his hazard lights – a modern habit Rosalie had noticed drivers adopting to give them permission to do whatever they wanted – and helped Rosalie and her bike into the van.

As they drove back to the retreat, Rosalie was grateful the only question Ryan asked was how her afternoon had been.

'Just lovely,' she lied.

In fact, it had been quite unsettling. Would all her time here be the same? Perhaps she should sit down with Sarah tonight, tell her about the photos – and then convince Ryan to take her back to Sydney where she could leave this place firmly behind her where it belonged.

Except it would never be firmly behind her, would it? Here she was, in her nineties, a lifetime and more lived, loved and lost, and her past still haunted her. The memories threatening to drown her.

No, she would stay. See this through. Find – she really hated to use the word – closure. Whatever the goodness that meant.

Twenty-two

Over the next few days, Sarah sat on the porch outside Melody's sessions and watched on. As far as she could make out, Melody was perfectly comfortable in Joshua's company, the two of them already having formed some sort of bond. Over the last year Sarah had become an expert in Melody's body language and she could tell from the relaxed drop in her daughter's shoulders, the softness in her smile, and the way her head tilted to the side when Joshua spoke, that Melody thought of him as a friend.

Still, she couldn't stop the tendrils of quiet despair creep over her tightly held hope.

Every day for the last four days, morning and afternoon, Joshua sat in the arm chair strumming his guitar while Melody sat with him, her watchful gaze always on Pineapple sleeping in the rafters. The only thing that Sarah did notice was different was that each day the blanket covering the cello in the corner of the room was peeled back ever so slightly.

This morning's session was proceeding as usual, and Sarah felt herself nodding off in the chair on the porch, sleep ever unreliable since the accident. She shook her head to stay awake and for the first time since they all arrived in Redgum River, she wished that she was out adventuring with Ryan. Not that looking at the architectural details of old homes and buildings was anything she was interested in. Nor was his newfound passion for yoga. But anything would break up the monotony of her time and help quell the rising fear inside her that this was not going to work.

She stood up and stretched her arms out wide, rolling her neck from side to side, when a strange, low sound came from inside the room. She turned around to see Joshua voicing odd but melodic sounds as he strummed the guitar. A hum. An oh. An ah. Quietly. Gently. In time with the music.

Melody looked at him and smiled.

Sarah held her breath.

After a few moments, Melody stopped watching Joshua and returned her vigilance to Pineapple.

As the session came to an end, a very long thirty minutes later, Melody gave Joshua a nod and a small clap.

He saw them out into the morning's clear cool air and Melody started wheeling down the path.

'Sarah, I know it may not seem like it, but that was progress this morning.'

'Really?' she asked.

'Yeah. Some of the things we watch out for are the little cues in the body language. Until this morning, she wouldn't even look at me while I was playing. Today she did. And after only seven sessions, that's pretty amazing, given the trauma and guilt that she's working through.' Joshua reached out and squeezed Sarah's arm. 'I'm really hopeful, Sarah. And I can't wait for our session this afternoon. Don't discount the baby steps. They all add up.'

Sarah wanted to believe him, desperately. But she also didn't want her hopes to get too high only to come crashing down again. She said goodbye and followed Melody back to their cabin, where Rosalie was sitting outside.

She'd been doing that a bit. Choosing to sit on the porch and stare into the trees rather than go exploring with Ryan. Even going off on her own on her bike – which Sarah was perfectly aware of despite Rosalie's attempt to hide it from her – seemed to have lost some of its appeal.

'How was your morning?' Rosalie asked, without taking her eyes off the trees in the distance.

Melody gave her a thumbs up as she wheeled into the cabin, no doubt going to help herself to the chocolate chip cookies that were waiting for her on the dining table, just like she did after every morning session with Joshua.

Sarah shrugged. 'Joshua seems to think it's going well. But I don't know. I just wish there were . . . more substantial, obvious, signs. Touching an instrument. Uttering any kind of sound.' She eased herself down into the white wicker chair beside her grandmother. The thick cushion was more comfortable than it looked, and Sarah let out a sigh as she sat down.

'I guess all you can do, my darling, is trust in the experts.'

Sarah wished she could. She had been trusting in them for so long now to no avail.

'You've always been pretty good at reading people, Sarah. What's your take on Joshua? I know he's highly qualified, but is he a good fit for Melody?'

Sarah's instinct said yes, though she wasn't sure she could trust her own judgement anymore. Rosalie reached out and took Sarah's hand in hers. 'I know you've been through a lot, my darling. More than anyone should have to bear in a lifetime. And I know that means it can be hard to trust that the universe isn't going to turn your life upside down again. But even the darkest of days, the most uncertain of situations, don't endure forever.' Rosalie's voice cracked as she said the last words.

Sarah blinked quickly and saw a tear roll down her grandmother's lined face. With her forefinger, Sarah brushed it away.

'They sound like the words of experience, Granny Rose.'

'They are. And hard learned. So don't ignore them.' She winked.

Sarah leaned over and gave Rosalie a hug. From the corner of her eye she saw the old photo album resting against Rosalie's leg. She reached across and picked it up.

'Is this what you've been doing with your time? Looking through these pages?'

Rosalie shook her head. 'I've only just pulled it out this morning.'

Sarah opened the pages of the album and turned them slowly until she got to where the Snapshots started.

'It's funny looking through these now that we're here,' Sarah said. 'Seeing the river in real life, the town centre. It hasn't changed much in all these years, has it?'

'Not a lot.' Rosalie's voice was dripping with sadness.

'Is that a bad thing? Coming back home and finding it so familiar?'

It took a moment for Rosalie to answer, and Sarah turned the page while she waited.

'That depends, I guess, on the nature of the memories one has of home. Not all memories, even if familiar, are comforting.'

'What about this one?' Sarah pointed to the photo of a boy and his dog in the dirt. There was so much joy in this picture, she couldn't imagine there was any sadness attached to the memory.

Rosalie looked at the shot and a small smile touched the edges of her thin pale lips. 'That was a good day.'

Sarah turned the page. 'And this one?' She pointed to one of the pictures that featured the same two handsome men. 'These fellows seem to pop up quite a bit. An old beau, perhaps? Or two, you scoundrel.'

Rosalie's smile dropped. 'Don't be ridiculous!' she snapped, and shut the album, catching Sarah's finger in between the pages with a pinch. 'I'm going to have a lie-down.' She stood up. 'I'm tired.'

As her grandmother retreated into the cabin, Sarah stared after her, unsure of what had just happened. She opened the album again and looked once more at the photos. When Sarah had first discovered these, she assumed that Rosalie's reluctance had to do with the war and what she must have endured at the time. But her reaction just then? This was personal, of that she was now sure.

She pored over the photos, looking – the trouble was, she didn't know what for. Her eyes stopped on a photo of a wooden cabin among the gum trees. A familiar wooden cabin. And out the front a smiling Rosalie and the same two men who, it seemed, had caused her to storm off just now.

Bernie's cabin. The same picture hanging in the Stave.

With delicate care, Sarah removed the photo and placed it inside the pocket diary she kept in her handbag.

In the afternoon, Sarah took Melody to the Stave a few minutes before her session was due to start. While they waited in the foyer, Sarah moved to the large framed picture on the wall and pulled out the smaller photo, holding it up to make the comparison. Yes. It was most definitely the same cabin. The one that had once stood in this very spot. The one that Rosalie's uncle, Bernie, had lived in. The one that Rosalie and her two mysterious men had stood in front of for this photo.

'You're nice and early.' Joshua came out of one of the rooms. 'I love it when my clients are keen. What have you got there?'

'It's a photo from my grandmother's album. I thought I recognised the cabin and was just comparing.' She flashed him the picture.

'Yep. One and the same. Is that Rosalie?'

Sarah nodded. 'I don't know who the men are, though.'

Joshua leaned in to take a closer look and squinted, shaking his head. 'Well, why don't we get started seeing as you're already here?' he said.

Melody clapped her hands and wheeled towards them.

The minutes ticked by, with Joshua playing the guitar and vocalising melodic sounds, Melody watching Pineapple. Although, if she wasn't mistaken, Sarah thought that Melody spent a lot more time looking at Joshua today. And for that she was relieved. Not just because, as Joshua proclaimed, it meant that she was making progress, but also because, as Sarah had entered the room, she'd noticed the cello more exposed than it had ever been, only a small portion of the blanket now covering the neck of the instrument.

As Joshua strummed away at the guitar and continued to make sounds, Melody wheeled a little closer to him and started bobbing her head in time with the music. He very quickly, almost imperceptibly, gave Sarah a quick glance.

Small cues.

Just before he reached the end of the tune, he played a wrong note.

Sarah sat forward.

Joshua was clearly an accomplished musician, and this was a very easy piece to play. It was one Melody had learned when she was only five.

Joshua paused. 'Sorry.'

Melody glanced at Sarah, and she fought to remain calm under her daughter's gaze. She gave her a gentle smile.

Turning back to Joshua, Melody tentatively put her finger on one of the frets, guiding Joshua to the right note.

'Thank you.' He smiled and started playing again, Melody swaying gently to the tune. As he played the song from beginning to end once more, Melody gave him a thumbs up when he reached the part he'd fumbled just a moment ago.

That was no small cue.

That was a whopping great big one.

Even Sarah could recognise that. Melody hadn't touched an instrument, any instrument, since the accident.

She wanted to whoop and jump up and down and scream and twirl around. She wanted to run into the room and wrap her arms around her baby girl. She wanted to hug Joshua and run into the bushes and shout hooray. But she sat there, frozen, holding her breath, too scared to move or make a sound in case she shattered the moment and ruined any chance of Joshua building on this.

The session came to an end and Melody waved goodbye to Pineapple. Joshua walked them out and as Melody raced through the foyer, he slowed his step and turned his shoulders towards Sarah.

'Good job today, Mama.' He smiled at her.

Sarah frowned. 'Me? I didn't do anything.'

'I saw you nearly pass out when Melody corrected my false note. But you held it together, and that encouraging smile you gave her was just perfect.'

'So, does this mean . . .' She dared not utter the question.

Joshua put up his hand. 'All it means is today was a good day. Recovering from trauma is rarely linear, as I'm sure you know.' His warm smile did little to ease Sarah's concern. 'Take today as a win. What happens tomorrow, who knows.'

*

Back at the cabin, Melody was playing quietly with her art set, drawing a picture of a possum lying in a tree, music notes instead of leaves spilling off the branches. Rosalie was still in her room and Sarah could hear the faint sound of snoring coming from behind the door.

Three thumping steps on the porch saw her rush outside to quiet Ryan, returning from his yoga class.

'*Shh*. Granny Rose is sleeping.'

He frowned. 'Is she okay?'

It was a fair question. Despite her advancing years, Rosalie was not usually one for an afternoon nap.

'I think so.' She had no idea.

Ryan's phone rang and Sarah could see, to her surprise, Herman's name flashing up on its screen. 'Oh, hey, Herman,' Ryan said. 'How's it going in antiquities land?' He skipped down the ramp and continued the conversation away from the cabin, well out of Sarah's earshot.

Sarah put her hands on her hips. What was her boss doing ringing *Ryan*? As if she didn't have enough to worry about already.

He returned ten minutes later, holding out his phone. 'He wants a quick chat.'

Sarah shot him a look, which he expertly ignored. She took the phone. 'Hi, Herman. Is everything okay?'

'Yes, of course. I just wanted to check in with you and see how you were going with your grandmother. Are you any closer to cracking her reluctance to give us the photos?'

Did realising there was more to the story count? 'Um, maybe. We were looking at them together today, so that's a step in the right direction.'

'Okay. Well, keep me posted. She's an amazing woman. I hope you can find a way to heal whatever it is in her past she's been keeping secret.'

Me too. 'Thank you. Do you want Ryan back?'

'No. That's fine. I'll chat to him again next week.'

'What are you two . . . ?' The phone went silent. Herman had hung up.

'All good, Sar-bear?' Ryan danced towards her and took his phone back.

'Yes. Why is he calling you?'

Ryan smiled that dazzlingly cheeky smile that always got him out of trouble when they were teenagers. 'Just something we're working on. All will be revealed in time.' He did a little jig as he backed away.

Sarah shook her head. Great. More unanswered questions. She couldn't cope with more unanswered questions.

'Is it okay if I go for a walk? I could do with a bit of a refresh, I think.' She rubbed her temples.

'Sure thing. I'll watch these two princesses,' Ryan grinned.

Sarah had no idea what Ryan and Herman were up to, but she had to admit it had been a long time since she'd seen Ryan this relaxed. She stepped out into the fresh air. If only she could find a way to relax too.

A walk along the river was exactly what Sarah needed. Questions were swirling around her mind – what were Herman and Ryan up to, for starters? Who were the two men in Rosalie's album? And why had Rosalie nearly dismembered her when she'd asked? But as she ambled along the gently winding bank, surrounded by green grass, the soft sound of water running, the scene framed by tall, elegant gums, her questions dissolved. Perhaps she could stay here by the water for the rest of . . . well, forever. Forget her problems.

No, they were waiting for her back at the retreat. She really should return – it was nearly time for dinner.

As she approached her cabin, she realised the gardening table was no longer at the side of the building.

A familiar clink-clank sound drew her to the other side of the Stave, and there was Joshua at the very same wooden trestle.

'Oh, hey. I thought I'd get this stuff out of your way so I don't disturb you again. I've been making the most of this weather while it's still dry.'

'It's a cute set-up. How long have you been gardening at work?'

'Ever since I started here.' He wiped his dirt-covered hands on the towel at the end of the table and turned to her and smiled.

'Gosh, your boss is a lucky man.'

Joshua shrugged. 'Well, technically I'm the boss. Eddy Dawson owns the place but he's getting on a bit and he tends to let me run it my way.'

Eddy. There was an Edward in the album. And a Snapshots request from an E. Dawson. Surely not . . .

'What's Eddy's story?' Sarah asked.

'He's had an interesting life. Grew up here. Fought in the war. Fabulous musician. He hasn't been around lately, but when he's back I can introduce you? For now I'd better get this stuff cleared up before dinner.'

She nodded eagerly. It was a long shot, but if Eddy, Edward and E. Dawson were the same person . . . Well, what did that even mean? Until she was sure, it was probably best not to mention anything to Rosalie. If they weren't, there was no point. If they were, it was potentially huge.

The Wednesday of their second week at the retreat was a designated rest day. Sarah wandered through the gardens at a loss as to what to do. Ryan was taking Melody and Rosalie out for lunch in Wombat Hollow. Sarah had been all set to go with them, but Ryan had insisted she take some time for herself.

Trouble was, she had no idea what to do with herself.

At the back of the retreat there was a wooden bench seat tucked away under the gums, with splatterings of moss growing around its edges. Sarah sat down with a perfect view of the retreat cabins, a glimpse of the river in the distance. She turned her gaze to the canopy of grey-green leaves above.

'Oh, hello!'

A woman dressed in the same uniform as Joshua's was coming towards her. Sarah shielded her eyes from the sun. It was one of the therapists. She held out her hand. 'Hi. Sarah, isn't it? I'm Phoebe. We haven't officially met yet.'

As Sarah shook her hand, the rainbow-coloured bangles on Phoebe's right wrist jangled. They were the same bright colours as the scarf in her grey hair.

'Hi.'

Phoebe sat beside her and pulled out a wrapped lunch. 'This is my favourite spot to take a break.' She pushed her glasses on top of her head. 'The only bad thing about a retreat rest day is the amount of paperwork I have to catch up on. Popping out here gives me a moment of serenity.'

'I guess there would be a lot of paperwork in this job.'

Phoebe laughed. 'A burden that comes with the territory. But it's not too bad. It may not be the most exciting part of my job but it's also not the worst.'

'Oh?'

'I love my job immensely, but some days are harder than others – occasionally it can be a bit overwhelming.'

Sarah had never really given any thought to what it must be like to be on the other side of the couch. The stories Joshua and Phoebe, and Judy, must have to bear. 'So, what does a therapist do, when therapy gets a bit too much?' she asked.

'I drink a lot of hot chocolate.'

'Joshua mentioned your hot chocolate,' Sarah laughed.

'I do make a cracking mug. Pop by any time and we can shut out the world for just a moment and lose ourselves in chocolatey comfort.' Phoebe's phone rang. 'Looks like my lunch break is over.' And she bustled off back to the Stave, leaving Sarah wondering how she was going to fill the afternoon.

Twenty-three

Rosalie had been avoiding bringing up the incident with the album with Sarah. She hadn't meant to slam it down on her like that. She'd just panicked and, well, that's what had happened. She owed her granddaughter an explanation.

She could, she supposed, make something up, but her granddaughter was too astute for that. Rosalie always said she would have made an excellent journo. She could sniff out a lie with the best of them.

No. Rosalie would have to come clean – but first she must get things clear in her own head. She needed to see the photo in the Stave that Sarah had mentioned. So, with the retreat winding down for the day, she pulled on her grey cardigan and wrapped it tightly around her as she slipped out of the cabin.

At the Stave, she pushed open the cold glass door and looked around. Thankfully, no one else seemed to be there. She'd been wanting to take a peek inside this place since they arrived, but with so many families (six, if she'd counted correctly) coming and going all day, she hadn't felt it was her place to set foot in the therapy building.

Until now.

Inside, she made her way around the edge of the foyer, taking a peek into each of the rooms. Which one did Melody use, she wondered? As she went, she scrutinised the photographs on the walls, some of which were actually pretty good, recognising the local landscapes. Then, she spotted it. The large picture on the centre of the wall. Unmistakable, with its composition and use of light – she could spot her uncle's work anywhere.

She touched the frame and read the plaque; his name engraved there causing her to smile. 'Hey, Bernie. I'm so pleased a piece of you is still here,' she whispered.

At the end of the sweeping wall she spotted a door with a sign that read 'Staff only'. She made her way towards it, wondering what she'd find, her journalistic instincts to investigate still strong. She passed a large room; well, more of a small hall, really. There were chairs stacked in the corners and music stands in an arc to one side. Off to the side of the stands was a very old piano. She walked over to the golden-brown instrument and ran her hands over its smooth frame. Oh, the familiarity. It had been a long time, though, since she'd tinkled any ivories. Looking around to double check no one was there, she sat on the stool and opened the fallboard. A tingle ran up her spine. Her fingers hovered over the keys, anticipation rippling through her. As she lowered her hands, she stopped. There. In the top right corner of the fallboard. A carving. A very familiar carving, that always reminded her of a possum's tail. She ran a shaking finger over the deep scar.

'Oh lord.' She exhaled. This was . . . but how?

She closed the fallboard, folded her arms over it and rested her head on her arms. What was the universe playing at? It seemed awfully determined to ram old memories down her throat. It was playing dirty, that's what it was. She was here, wasn't she? In a place she swore she'd never return. To pass the photos, part of her history, down to Sarah, before the good Lord called her home. Wasn't that enough? Surely punishing her every time she turned around with visceral reminders of everything she'd worked so hard to forget, was simply cruel.

But then, if Rosalie had learned anything in all her years on this planet, it was that the universe could be cruel.

Redgum River
August 1945

Rosalie arrived at the newspaper office on Monday morning and rested her bike against the side wall. She tried to push the memories of last night aside. Henry was here and he'd made a move Rosalie hadn't been expecting, and she had no idea what to do about it.

Neville was in already and sitting at his desk. Rosalie poured him a coffee and had started preparing the plates for the printer when the phone rang, and Rosalie picked it up. A curt voice asked for Neville and she handed over the receiver.

'Right. *What?* Are you sure?' He waved to get Rosalie's attention. 'When? Right. Damage?' He scribbled furiously on the notepad that was always on top of his desk. He covered the mouthpiece with his hand. 'Rosalie. Stop what you're doing. Breaking news.' He went back to his call, and Rosalie studied his expression. Intrigue mixed with . . . horror?

She leaned over the desk and tried to make sense of his scrawling scribble. 'Hirosh . . . ama . . . ima? Bomb. Massive blast. Flattened'. The last word was underlined. She held her breath.

'Right then.' He finally let out a long sigh. 'I'll stay by the phone. Ring back whenever you have more.' He hung up and looked at

Rosalie. 'Clear the front page. The Yanks have dropped an atomic bomb on Japan. They've wiped out the city of Hiroshima.'

Rosalie opened her mouth, but no words came out. She went cold. Neville continued to fill her in on what he'd learned, which was only sketchy detail at this stage. Still, it was enough to make Rosalie feel dizzy as hope and fear coursed through her. Could this be it? The end of the war? But at what cost?

The evening paper went out late with the headline 'Rain of Ruin' splashed across the front page.

Over the next two days Neville and Rosalie barely left the office as information and stories came in and the utter devastation of the bomb became clearer. Truman was talking of ultimatums and last chances and, for the first time in its history, the *River Times* became a daily edition.

On Wednesday morning Henry turned up at the office with a basket full of hot pies and cold homemade lemonade. He waltzed over to Neville's desk and started laying out the fare.

'Courtesy of Mrs Donaldson. All of you look like you could use a break.' He beckoned Roy over and the printer joined them.

Neville ran his fingers through his greying hair as he bit into one of the pies. 'Ah, that hits the spot.'

Roy mumbled his agreement.

Rosalie was too tired to say anything. Almost too tired to eat, except she knew she had to somehow keep her strength up. She'd spent the last couple of days staying back until midnight, sifting through the stories and information that were landing, coming back to the office by 5 a.m. to start working on the next edition. Still, she wasn't as exhausted as Neville. He'd taken to sleeping under his desk, just in case a phone call came in the middle of the night.

'I've been speaking with my mate Reggie, and it seems things are heating up in the states,' Henry said to Neville.

'That's what I'm hearing,' Neville nodded. 'Rosalie, why don't you go home early tonight? This is far from over. We've got some big days ahead of us.'

'I . . .' Rosalie didn't want to leave the office. She wanted to be right there where it was all happening.

'Get some rest. Over the next few days I want you to get out there,' he waved his hand toward the door, 'and capture the reaction of the townsfolk. Maybe we can add a personal element to everything that's coming in on the wire.'

Rosalie tried to muster enough energy to protest, and in that hesitation she realised that all the stories they were printing were coming from sources overseas, or their affiliates in Sydney. Stories that revelled in the 'terrifyingly devastating bomb' and said it would be instrumental in bringing the war to an end. Nothing they were publishing in the *River Times* was their own. Perhaps Neville was right. They could add an element here that was missing. It wouldn't make the front page, or even page two or three, but it would be their little part of history told.

As her colleagues enjoyed the tasty sustenance Henry had brought with him, Rosalie left the office for some fresh air. They'd be back at the press shortly, pushing out the evening edition.

Outside, she enjoyed the warm sun washing over her. She rolled her shoulders and stretched her arms to the left, then right.

'Are you all right?' Henry stepped up behind her.

She turned and nodded. 'It's been a big few days.'

'It has.' There was a look of regret in his eyes.

'I'm sorry your week here has been . . . well, not what you expected.'

'This is what you were born to do.' Henry said. 'I'd never take that away from you. And it will be over soon enough. But I'm heading back to Sydney now.'

'I'm sorry.'

'You don't need to apologise to me, Rosalie.' He leaned in towards her. With one hand he cupped her chin and raised her lips to meet his. His other hand slipped behind her back, and he pulled her in tight. His kiss was soft and tender, but there was no denying the want behind his gentle touch.

His lips were soft and sweet, and she allowed herself to forget, for just a moment, that anything else existed. Just for a moment.

She pulled away. 'Oh, Henry . . .' She sighed, her head begging her to accept this wonderful man before her; her heart screaming no.

Henry ran his thumb up her arm. '*Shh*. I just need you to know how deeply I feel for you. No pressure. I'll come back to Redgum River soon.' And with that, Henry strode off down the street to his car.

The following day, Rosalie leaned against the office wall, soaking in the midday sun as she took just a few minutes to rest and eat a quick sandwich, when Neville called out.

'Get in here, Reynolds. Now!'

She rushed inside.

'They've dropped another bomb. Nagasaki.'

Rosalie drew in a deep breath, squared her shoulders and walked over to Neville's desk.

At the end of the day, Rosalie rode through town. Main Street was humming with people gathered in small groups huddled over that day's edition of the *River Times*. She dismounted and pulled her camera out of the hatbox strapped to the back rack of her bike.

She snapped a shot of a group of young men gathered outside the pub, a triumphant air to their mumblings as they read. Dot and Millie were outside the hairdressers, their expressions a mix of weary anticipation. Rosalie nodded to them silently and continued to wade through the heavy air of expectation that had settled over the town. Beside the post office was a small group of older women, Mrs Donaldson at their centre, murmured words of gentle understanding passing between them. Rosalie captured the women huddling together with her camera. A picture of their solemn hope next to the bold excitement of the younger lads in the pub would tell the story of tonight.

Instead of heading home for supper, Rosalie made her way to Bernie's shack. She would get these images developed tonight so they were ready for Neville in the morning. Who knew what tomorrow would bring? Father and Mother wouldn't be expecting her for dinner. She hadn't made it home for supper once this week.

All the lights in Bernie's cabin were on when she rode up to his property and she could hear muffled voices coming from inside the house. She wanted to head straight in there and let the warmth she knew could be found behind the thick wooden door wash over her. But she had to finish her work for the evening first.

After developing her film, the pictures even better than she'd anticipated, she dragged her weary feet along the cobbled path and heard music floating on the evening breeze. She didn't bother knocking when she got to the front door, pushing it open gently and slipping inside.

There was now no doubt Penelope and Bernie had been spending an awful lot of time together, the neatness within the cabin walls evidence of their growing relationship. The piles of newspapers and magazines stacked in one corner of the living room were now the only trace of Bernie's clutter left.

'Ah, look who's here,' Bernie said, as he turned around and saw Rosalie.

Albert was there with them, and his gaze met Rosalie's, the light in his eyes as he looked at her sending a shiver down her spine, followed by doubt as she thought back to the last time she'd seen him – the hurt in his eyes when Henry had shown up at the picnic. And doubt flared into guilt as she remembered Henry's kiss.

Penelope, standing in the kitchen as if she'd always been there, an apron tied around her waist, bustled over to Rosalie. 'Hello, stranger. It's good to see you. That Mr Payne has a hide keeping you from us the way he has this week.' She wrapped her in a tight embrace. 'You look pale. Have you been eating properly?'

Rosalie frowned.

'I thought not. Sit. Dinner will be ready in five minutes.'

Unsurprisingly, the topic of conversation over dinner was the war, the bombings, and what it all meant.

'Surely the Japs will surrender now.' Albert cut his potato in half and stared at it on his fork, an unreadable expression on his face.

'War is an unpredictable beast, isn't it?' Bernie said. He looked over to Penelope, who frowned. 'But I think there is room to hope.'

'We just want our Edward back,' Penelope said. 'My boys back together. And for this whole mess to be over finally.' She reached across the table and squeezed Albert's hand.

'You know Edward, mum. He's as determined as they come,' Albert said. 'He'll stay safe and come home and then start bossing us all around so much we'll wish he was away again.'

'Don't you speak like that.' Penelope looked horrified.

'I don't mean away at war.'

'I should hope not. You may joke, but I know you miss him as much as I do.'

'I miss having him accompany my music. Although,' he said, 'I may have found a replacement.'

Rosalie smiled. 'I think you'll find you're on your own tonight. There's nothing here for me to play.'

'I have an old guitar,' Bernie said.

'I've never learned guitar.'

'Well, now's as good a time as any,' Albert said.

When dinner was over, he motioned for Rosalie to come with him to sit on the couch. After showing her a few chords, he decided she was ready. Together, with Albert leading, they played a jaunty song that Rosalie wasn't familiar with. There were hints of American swing and jazz, and it didn't take her long to pick up the tune.

Bernie and Penelope tapped their feet along to the music. After two more songs, they began cleaning up the dishes and Rosalie's newfound energy began to fade. 'I should probably get home. Get some sleep and ready myself for whatever tomorrow will bring.'

'I'll walk you out,' Albert offered, and saw her to the door.

'Thank you for making tonight so much fun, Albert.' Rosalie hoped her voice wasn't as shaky as her hands she was holding behind her back. 'I really needed that.'

'That's the beauty of music.' Albert played with the collar of her white blouse, a shiver rippling down her spine. 'It's always there when we need it. To comfort us. Lift us up. Even in our darkest hours, it can find its way into our soul and bring us hope.'

Rosalie stepped around him and stumbled, the fatigue she'd been pushing aside the last few days claiming her.

Albert caught her. 'You're exhausted.'

'I'll be okay.'

He shook his head. 'Wait here.' He helped her down onto a nearby log.

When he returned, he was wheeling Rosalie's bike. He mounted it and tapped the crossbar. 'Hop on.'

Rosalie frowned. 'What about your leg?'

'I'll manage. I'll ride you home. You're so tired, you're likely to fall off if you're on your own.'

Rosalie couldn't argue with that. It was as if she had suddenly hit a wall. Her legs were shaking so she sat side-saddle on the crossbar, the metal rod biting slightly into her. Albert put his arms on either side of her to hold the handlebars and she could feel the warmth radiating from his body.

As he started to pedal, she wobbled.

'Lean against me if you need to.' His whispered breath tickled her ear.

She rested her shoulder against his chest and he shifted his arms to encase her a little more securely.

The cool night air danced over her skin as Albert rode them through town, leaving goosebumps peppering her arms, her senses more awake than her fatigue should have allowed. She gave him directions to her house and as they rolled into her street, he slowed down.

'This one at the end of the cul-de-sac.' Rosalie pointed to her house. The lights in the front room were off, and she breathed a sigh of relief. Her parents would hardly approve of her arriving home in this fashion.

Albert steadied her as she dismounted the bike. 'Your chariot has arrived, madam.'

'Thank you, sir.' She exaggerated a curtsy. 'Really, though.' She took a deep breath. 'Thank you.'

'Any time. What would you like me to do with this?' He was still holding the handlebars of her bike.

She told him to leave it against the side of the house and he did so, making his way back to where she stood under the branches of the jacaranda tree.

'Good night, Rosalie.' Albert kissed her on the cheek, lingering a moment longer than friendly propriety dictated he should.

Her words caught in her throat.

His hand ran down her arm and before it trailed away, she entwined her fingers with his.

'Rosalie . . .'

She nodded.

He lowered his head and stopped, his mouth an inch from hers. She arched up, closing that last tiny chasm and he kissed her. Full of want, passion and care, his lips parted and he took her deeper. She pressed her hands against his chest, and his moved around her back, pressing her body against his.

She groaned.

He pulled his head back, his hands still grasped around her waist. 'I think I should go, before I stop being a gentleman.'

Heat rose in Rosalie's cheeks and all she could do was nod.

He reached up and tucked a stray hair back under her snood. Pressing his lips together, he took three steps back.

'Good night, Rosalie.' His voice was deep, gravelly, and the moonlight offered just enough illumination for her to see the haunting look in his eyes.

'Good night, Albert,' she whispered.

She watched him walk away, her whole body thrumming with excitement. But as he disappeared into the night shadows, guilt pushed excitement aside as she thought of Henry.

Rosalie hauled herself away from the piano and sighed. So often they had played music together. The banjo, the guitar, the piano. This piano.

'Can I help you?' A soft male voice from behind nearly startled her off the stool. She swivelled around and saw Joshua standing in the dim light. 'Rosalie? What are you doing here?'

'I thought I'd check the place out.'

Joshua smiled. 'Isn't she a beauty?' He nodded to the piano. 'We inherited her when we set up the retreat. Cost an absolute bomb to restore her, but I think it was worth it.' He ran his hands over the ancient wood. 'She plays beautifully now. Do you play?'

'I used to. A long time ago.' She didn't dare tell him she had played this very piano. He would think her mad. *She* was beginning to think she was mad.

'Maybe tomorrow you can join our Vital Voices choir and play for us.'

Rosalie stood. It was definitely time to get out of here. 'Oh, I might be a little too rusty for that.' *And if I touch those keys, who knows what memories will come flooding back.*

'Well, you're most welcome if you change your mind. Now, I really do need to lock up . . .'

'Of course. I should be heading back.'

Rosalie let herself back inside the cabin. Perhaps if she shut her eyes tight enough in bed tonight and thought of humdrum things – doing a tax return, cleaning tiles with a toothbrush – she could block the universe from intruding on her thoughts.

Perhaps.

Twenty-four

Tarakan Island
August 1945

Dragging himself across base, Edward wiped his brow. The humidity was worse than usual today. Sweltering. Wet. Sapping the energy from every life form around. Even the feral cats that liked to come into camp to scrounge for food couldn't bother mustering anything that resembled movement. It was almost as if the whole place was holding its breath.

Waiting.

Edward joined the rest of his unit in the mess tent as they crowded around the radio waiting for the latest news. The reports were unfathomable. Twenty thousand tons. Edward couldn't even imagine how much that was. The nervous anticipation among the men was palpable.

There had been whispers for so long now that the Allies were close to ending the war. But this time it was real. And now they were all . . .

. . . waiting.

'All right, gentlemen and not so gentle men.' Private McDonald stood on one of the tables. 'We're opening the betting again.' He waved his notebook in the air.

The men gathered around flapping pound notes in the air, shouting out dates of when they thought the Japanese would surrender. Someone shouted out 'Tomorrow!' which was met with raucous cheering.

If only *that would be true*, thought Edward.

As the men scrambled to place their bets, Edward slipped away from the crowd. He wouldn't place a bet. Didn't want to jinx anything. He kept his hope deep inside him and let others wear theirs openly.

He lay down on his cot, the weight of the air pressing down on him. From his rucksack he pulled out the latest letter from Rosalie and read it again. How many times had he read her letters? Ten? Twenty? He'd lost count.

Dear Edward,

I enclose a picture of your brother, mother and me. We have spent some time together since Albert's return. He is a wonderful musician, though I am sure I don't need to tell you that. We have played together on occasion and I am the weak link, my skills on the piano no match for his. My uncle Bernie, who is courting your mother, took this photo. Albert is concerned you might not approve of their relationship, but I can assure you Bernie is one of the best men I know. Albert sends his very best. Take care over there. We are all looking forward to your safe return.

Yours,

Rosalie

Edward looked at the picture Rosalie had sent, unable to take his eyes off her beautiful face. Her perfect smile, her sparkling eyes. He hoped with all his might the destruction the Allies had brought on Japan the last few days would do as intended and finally end this infernal war.

Twenty-five

There was no sun on Thursday morning streaming through the curtains into the cabin. Outside, thin grey clouds were building, and a cool breeze rippled through the trees. Sarah stared out the window and yawned.

Again, she'd woken at three and couldn't get back to sleep. But this time there was an element of excitement to her fitfulness: she was looking forward to this morning's session. Baby steps, or great big giant leaps, either she would take. When she was putting Melody to bed last night, she'd noticed a calm about her daughter that she hadn't seen in a long time – the way she'd laid her head on the pillow as Sarah read to her, the loose hold of Banana Bunny instead of her usual tight grip.

The rest of the cabin began to stir, and Sarah popped the bread in the toaster and started setting the table, looking forward to what the morning would bring.

When Sarah and Melody arrived at the Stave, Melody settled into her usual spot and Joshua began playing the guitar. The cello was now in full view, still in the corner of the room, but uncovered.

Joshua had placed a few other instruments randomly around the room – a bongo drum, a ukulele, a recorder – but Melody showed no interest in any of them. She simply nodded her head in time to Joshua's strumming and as he sang – words this time, not just sounds – her hand began to tap. But there was no other interaction. She barely looked at him today.

By the end of the session, Sarah felt like they were back at day one. Joshua had warned her there might be setbacks. Was this a setback?

Melody raced out of the Stave when they were finished, giving Sarah a few moments alone with Joshua before he had to see his next client.

'I know it feels like a big deal, Sarah, but it's perfectly normal,' he said. 'Remember, I said this wasn't going to be linear.'

She shook her head. 'I know. I just . . .'

'Got your hopes up?'

She nodded.

'Hope is a good thing. I'm really pleased with how things are going. This is only the second week and she's come so far. Bring her to the choir concert this afternoon.'

'Are you sure that's a good idea?'

He nodded. 'I think being around music when the focus is not on *her* might be a good thing.'

'Like a group therapy sort of thing?'

'No. A not-therapy thing. I think it will be good for her to see other people with challenges enjoying music in a non-therapy setting, in a fun setting.'

Sarah wasn't sure, but he'd been right so far about everything else. 'Okay.'

'Before you go, can I ask you something?'

'Sure.'

'Was your grandmother a musician?'

Well, she wasn't expecting that. 'No. Not that I'm aware of. I know she loves music. But she wasn't too thrilled when my mum married a muso, nor when I got together with one. Though, to be fair, she was right about him.'

Joshua laughed. 'Ah yes, we musicians sometimes get a bad rap. Unreliable, heads in the clouds . . .'

'That doesn't even come close to describing my waste-of-space ex.'

'That bad, huh?'

'You've no idea. Why do you ask? About Rosalie, I mean?'

'Oh. Well, last night I was working late – never-ending paperwork with this job – and the doors were open. As I was leaving, I found her at the piano. There was just something about the way she sat on the stool; the way she touched the piano. Like it was an old friend. I know to anyone else that would sound silly, but . . .'

'It doesn't sound silly.' Musicians often recognised like souls. Sarah had seen it in Melody the first time she touched her cello. It was like she belonged there.

'I thought you'd get it. And, though she tried to hide it, I swear she'd been crying.'

Crying? Sarah had seen her grandmother cry a grand total of twice in her life. When Sarah's mother, Lynne, had passed away – the image of Rosalie, broken, sobbing, beside her daughter's coffin, the only part of the funeral Sarah still remembered, burned into her ten-year-old mind – and when Grandpa had died two years after that.

'Are you sure?'

'I'm not certain, but that's what it looked like,' said Joshua.

'I don't know. Ever since I unearthed that album, the one that photo you saw is from, she's been off. She grew up here, and I thought it was just the nostalgia of coming home that was upsetting her, or making her so uncharacteristically . . . distracted. But now I think maybe there's more to it.'

He spread his hands wide. 'Why don't we try something? Do you think you can get Rosalie to the choir concert this afternoon?'

'What will that do?'

'It's just a hunch.'

'Okay.' Sarah was willing to try anything at this point.

As she passed the staff room, Phoebe waved to her, a steaming mug in her hands. She lifted it and raised an eyebrow. 'Join me?'

Could she? Could she shut out the world, just for a moment and lose herself in chocolatey comfort? It smelled so good.

'Five minutes.' Phoebe waved her over.

Five minutes. Sarah nodded.

Back at the cabin, Sarah paced the floor. She'd spent half an hour with Phoebe and told the woman more than she had intended. But there was something about that mug of hot chocolate that had seeped into her, relaxed her, and she'd let stuff out she hadn't spoken about to anyone. Maybe it was drugged. Maybe she should avoid Phoebe and her hot chocolate for the rest of their time here. Except she'd already said she'd pop in again. And she had enjoyed the woman's company. Funnily enough, Phoebe also played the cello.

Stop. You have other things to worry about right now. Like how she was going to get Rosalie to this concert. She had no idea why Joshua had suggested it, but her gut was telling her she really needed to try.

'Why on earth would I want to listen to a choir full of old people?' Rosalie protested, when Sarah asked her.

Ryan stifled a laugh.

'That's enough from you, young man.' She waved her gnarled finger at him.

'I just think it will be nice for all of us to enjoy the afternoon together. Apparently, they put on a pretty good afternoon tea.'

From the couch, Melody clapped her hands.

'I'm not dressed for afternoon tea.'

Nope, that hadn't worked.

'You look fine. Besides, there's supposed to be rain over the next few days, so this might be the last chance you have to get out of the cabin for a little while.'

Rosalie rolled her eyes. 'Oh, all right then. You lot go ahead, and I'll join you after I get changed.'

Ryan, Melody and Sarah made their way to the Stave, and once inside, Sarah forgot all about trying to persuade her grandmother into who-knew-what. The room was absolutely humming.

Over by the windows on the far wall was a long trestle table covered in a white tablecloth laden with every cake, slice and sandwich imaginable. Melody's eyes widened when she saw the feast, and she put her hands in front of her chest. *Please, Mama*, the unspoken plea.

'Come on then, minim.' Ryan stepped beside the wheelchair and walked with Melody towards the spread.

In the middle of the room people mingled, chatting quietly, greeting each other, sipping on cups of tea, smiling with a warmth Sarah could almost feel. Among the throng of family and friends of the choir, Sarah recognised many of the retreat guests, and they nodded to each other, and her, as they looked around the room.

Phoebe and Katie, the youngest therapist at the retreat whose dyed pink hair was tied back in a ponytail, were busy steering the members of the Vital Voices choir, recognisable by the teal scarf each one of them wore, into their positions in front of the music stands.

Joshua stepped up beside Sarah. 'What do you think?'

'I think . . . I think *wow*.' Sarah had no other words.

'Wait till you hear them sing. Before that, though, there's someone I'd like you to meet. Is Rosalie coming?' He looked around.

'She said she would. She's just getting changed.'

Joshua guided Sarah over to a small cluster of choir members standing in the far corner and tapped one of the gentlemen on the shoulder. The man, standing tall and proud despite his clearly advanced years, turned around and greeted them with a smile.

'Eddy, this is Sarah,' Joshua said. 'Sarah, this is the owner of the retreat, Eddy.'

The old man blinked and wavered on his feet. With a slight shake of his head he pulled himself up straight again.

'It's nice to finally meet you.' He held out his hand and as Sarah shook it, he squeezed hers ever so gently.

'Finally?' she asked.

He shook his head again. 'Oh. I . . . I've been a fan of your work for a long time. The symphonic orchestra and the Five Bows.'

Sarah's heart beat faster at the mention of her old ensemble.

'How are you finding the retreat? Is Joshua treating you right? Your accommodation?' Eddy's words came so fast it was hard to tell where one question ended and the next began. 'And your grandmother? She's travelled with you, hasn't she?' He looked around the room. 'Is she here?'

Sarah was beginning to think Rosalie wasn't coming. 'Ah, I'm not sure she's feeling up to a concert.' Her gut was telling her to cover for her grandmother.

Eddy nodded, and Sarah noticed a slight rounding of his shoulders.

'I have been meaning to drop by. To welcome you all. But . . . I just . . .'

A few tentative notes cut through the din of the room, and people began to hush. The choir jostled into their final positions – taller members at the back, shorter members, and those with walking frames and needing chairs, at the front. While the majority of the choir appeared to be over the age of seventy, there were younger members too. Sarah noticed a young boy who couldn't have been more than eighteen.

'That's Brandon,' Joshua whispered in her ear. 'He suffered a brain injury last year. The only time he smiles now is when he's singing.'

A lady with blue-rinsed hair and pink glasses that framed grey eyes clapped her hands in an attempt to ready everyone.

'That's Phyllis. She's ninety-eight and calls the shots.' Joshua laughed. 'She was one of our first choir members when we started five years ago.'

The man next to Phyllis sat with his face turned up to the ceiling, dark sunglasses on.

'Archie. He's sixty-three and was a university professor up till a couple of years ago.' Joshua pointed out five or six more of the choir members before a few more notes rang out from the piano as everyone settled.

A tap on a music stand from Katie. A nod from the pianist. And they began. Melody wheeled over to Sarah and squeezed her hand.

Oh, no. This was a mistake. They should go.

The first few bars of 'Singing in the Rain' filled the room and Sarah held her breath. Melody looked up at her, frowned, clenched her jaw. Her I'm-trying-to-be-brave face. Sarah looked around, wondering if they could slip out without anyone thinking they were rude. She made a move, but Melody pulled on her hand and pointed to Brandon. Every member of the choir was swinging, in their own time, to the music, but Brandon was waving his arms in the air like he was at a rave. Melody smiled and let go of Sarah's hand.

Sarah exhaled.

A round of applause at the end of the song resulted in a very deep bow from Phyllis.

The choir drew a collective breath to start the next song. Sarah recognised the tune from the opening bar, and Archie started clicking his fingers. They launched into Cole Porter's 'Anything Goes', with Phyllis singing the chorus much higher than the rest of the choir, a look of pure joy on her face. But it was the pianist who caught Sarah's eye. His fingers danced across the keys with a grace and precision that was spellbinding.

'That's Eddy's brother, Albie. A very fine musician,' Joshua said. 'He was my teacher when I was a kid. We don't get many good days with him anymore, but when he's playing . . . oh, it's a privilege to watch. He hardly speaks now, but he sings with the choir sometimes.'

Sarah wasn't the only one who'd noticed a master at work. Melody wheeled over to him, looking back at Sarah and pointing to his wheelchair. *Just like mine.* She sat there near him and watched every note he played in wide-eyed wonder.

In the middle of the next song, one of the choir members joined Katie at the front as a second conductor, her back to the choir, waving an imaginary baton at the audience. Despite the flamboyant display in the middle of the room, Sarah couldn't take her eyes from Melody.

When the next song started, Melody shifted in her chair, pulled her shoulders back and moved her fingers in the air as if she was playing a keyboard of her own.

Sarah grabbed Joshua's arm.

He smiled down at her. 'Sometimes the breakthroughs happen outside of therapy.'

'Sorry.' She let go.

'It's fine. It's a big moment.'

Big moment didn't even begin to describe how Sarah felt.

For three songs, Melody stayed near Albie's side, her fingers playing every note in the air. Between each song, she looked over to Sarah. Abandoning all pretence of staying calm and not making a big deal out of small things, Sarah beamed back at her little girl.

'And for our last song,' Katie addressed the audience, 'one of our favourites, "In My Life".'

The audience clapped and cheered at the announcement. Phyllis bowed. Again.

'You can't beat the Beatles for bridging generational divides.' Joshua was clapping with the rest of the audience.

Eddy moved from the back of the choir and pulled the piano stool up next to his brother. He picked up a violin that Sarah hadn't noticed was leaning against the piano, placed his chin on the chinrest and readied his bow.

Panic coursed through Sarah, and she took a step towards her daughter.

'Wait.' Joshua's gentle voice stopped her. 'Look at her.'

Melody's eyes were still focused on the piano keys. But what if she freaked out when she noticed Eddy and his bow?

As if reading her thoughts, Joshua leaned in. 'Phoebe is right there. She's watching.'

Sarah looked at the therapist, standing just a metre or so from Melody, and Phoebe gave her a quick nod.

'Are you sure?' Sarah turned to Joshua.

He nodded. 'We've all got our eyes on her and we're ready to move if necessary.'

The song began and Melody didn't take her gaze off the piano. Sarah didn't take her gaze off her daughter.

With the last line of the song sung with intense emotion and gusto, the audience erupted into a standing ovation. Brandon thumped the air, Archie swayed back and forth, Phyllis bowed again and again.

Eventually the audience sat back down, and the choir applauded the brothers. Eddy turned Albie's wheelchair around and the two men took a bow. Melody was smiling at Sarah.

'Albert?' A tiny high-pitched voice came from behind Sarah.

Standing there in the entrance to the room was Rosalie, her mouth open wide, her eyes fixed on the brothers.

'Granny Rose? Are you okay?'

There was no answer, just the stare. Sarah looked to Eddy, who was surveying the room. When his eyes met Rosalie's, he dropped his bow. Melody startled at the sudden movement and a look of terror washed over her.

'Oh shit.' Sarah moved smoothly but quickly towards her, Joshua behind.

Also with slow, calm movement, Joshua picked up the bow and handed it back to Eddy. 'It's okay, Melody. Look around. Everyone's okay.'

The room was full of smiles and laughter and happy chatter.

Melody didn't look convinced.

Albert reached over for Melody's hand.

She gazed at him.

He nodded towards the piano.

She pulled a face.

He started tapping out a simple gentle tune and, without skipping a note, looked to her and waited till she started to mimic him. He gave a smile and a nod.

Sarah turned around to find Rosalie, but her grandmother was gone.

What she wanted to do right now was to gather Melody in her arms, take her away, embrace her and never let her go again. But Melody seemed calm, smiling at Albert. And Sarah wanted answers.

'May I speak with you both?' She forced her voice to stay level as she addressed Joshua and Eddy.

With Albert providing background music, the choir, the families and friends and the retreat guests mingled by the food. Sarah waved Ryan over.

'Stay with her?' She looked at Melody.

He nodded.

'And if you see Granny Rose, don't let her out of your sight.'

'She was here?' He frowned.

'Yes, but now I don't know where she's gone.'

In the foyer, away from the crowd, Sarah turned to Eddy and Joshua, who had obediently followed.

'What is going on?' Sarah asked, confused.

Eddy lowered his head. 'I'm sorry. I didn't know if she'd come . . .'

'Come to the performance? Or to the retreat?' Sarah forced herself to stay calm.

'Both.' He shrugged.

Joshua put his hand on Eddy's shoulder. 'What's going on, Eddy?'

'When your inquiry came through, Sarah, and I heard about Melody's story, I knew Joshua here could help her. But I thought it best to keep a low profile when you arrived. I was worried about Rosalie . . .'

'Why?' Sarah shook her head. She was now certain he must be the Edward, the E. Dawson from the photo. She just didn't know what that meant.

Eddy rubbed the white stubble on his chin. 'Your grandmother obviously hasn't told you. Unsurprisingly, I suppose. She wouldn't know I was here. Wouldn't know I was still alive. I probably shouldn't be at my age.' He forced a laugh, but his eyes were serious.

'We knew each other when we were younger. Much younger. There is some . . . history between us. Between the three of us.' He gestured his thumb towards the room. Towards Albert.

'Is that why Sarah has a photo of you and Albie when you were young?' Joshua asked the old man.

Sarah stared at him. 'You knew? When I showed you that photo, you knew it was Eddy? And Albert?'

'Well, I thought I recognised them because I practically grew up in their house taking music lessons and the walls were covered with old photos.'

'But you didn't say anything?'

'I could see you hadn't made the connection. You're here because of what happened to Melody. My job is to focus on her. I didn't feel it was my place to lob a distraction your way when I had no idea, either, what that photo was or what it meant for you all.'

Sarah shook her head. Pushing through the confusion, she started to piece things together. 'When Rosalie told me about this place, and I applied for Melody to come here,' she put her hands on her hips, 'did you know who we were?' she asked Eddy.

He at least had the decency to cast his gaze to the floor. 'I . . . I did. And I made sure your cabin was finished quickly so you could come.'

'Why?'

'I owe Rosalie. More than she knows. I thought if the retreat could help your family . . . help Melody. It would be the least I could do.'

'*The least you could do*? What does that mean?' Sarah narrowed her gaze.

'That's . . . complicated.'

She threw her hands in the air. Clearly Eddy wasn't going to give her any straight answers. Just like Rosalie.

'So why are we only meeting you now? And like this?'

Eddy looked weary, but Sarah needed answers.

'As I said, I wanted to keep a low profile at first. And Albie has been unwell. I didn't want Rosalie to see him like that. Not after all this time. I knew this would be hard enough on her as it is.'

Sarah turned to Joshua. 'I don't . . .'

'Eddy, just who *is* Rosalie to you?' Joshua asked. His concern for Sarah was obvious in his eyes.

'I think it's probably best if Sarah speaks to Rosalie first,' Eddy replied quietly.

'Oh, I will.' Sarah sighed. 'As soon as I find her.'

Twenty-six

Rosalie hadn't moved so fast in years. Decades.

Edward. Albert. There, *right in front of her*. She'd stood in the doorway as the choir sang that last song, frozen in place, looking at a mirage. But the music was real. As real as it had been all those years ago. No one could play like Albert.

She knew, however, when Edward looked her in the eye, that it was all real. He was really standing in front of her. Violin in hand, Albert by his side.

Except it wasn't quite Albert. His eyes – so distant – hadn't registered her.

When Edward had dropped his bow, she'd panicked, and in the confusion had high-tailed it out of there as fast as she could, back to the cabin where her bike was waiting for her. She'd mounted it without thought and rode away. Not stopping until she found herself back in her secret spot by the river, where she now sat on the fallen log, hugging her legs tightly.

Away from the memories.

Except they were always there. Waiting for her.

Redgum River
August 1945

In the days after the second atomic bomb was dropped, Rosalie spent more time than ever at work. She even went into the office over the weekend, and the first Saturday edition of the *River Times* was printed. Often Albert waited outside the office for Rosalie to finish, and he'd walk her home. Or double her on her bike if she was tired, Rosalie perched on the crossbar, cradled in his arms.

This morning, six days after the second bomb, Rosalie arrived at the office at eight on the dot. Neville was already inside and looked like he hadn't slept a wink. The makeshift cot he'd set up in the corner of the office was as neat as Rosalie had left it yesterday.

Without word she made him a coffee and placed it in front of him on his desk.

'Thank you, Reynolds.' He sighed.

'Did anything come in overnight?' She sat opposite him.

He nodded. 'Lots of whispers. The Japanese have been presented with the terms of surrender.'

'What? There's been nothing on the wireless.'

'Well, it could go either way, I guess. Until the powers that be . . .' he waved his hands in the air, '. . . know for sure, they won't be saying much.'

Rosalie ran her eyes over the torn-off leaves of paper spread across the desk between them. Numerous ideas for headlines were scribbled across their tops, accounting for every possibility that the next twenty-four hours, or more, might bring. From the war ending to the war escalating; from another bombing to drawn out negotiations. No wonder he looked so ragged.

'Well, I'm here now and can man the phones. Why don't you get some rest? You look like death warmed up. And barely warmed at that.'

'Thank you, Reynolds, for your blunt assessment of my appearance.'

'You're welcome.' She moved around the table and took him by the shoulders, guiding him to the cot and pushing him down. He groaned his disapproval, but within seconds of his head hitting the pillow, he was snoring loudly.

While he slept, Rosalie organised the scattered papers on his desk into groupings of similar headlines – five piles in total. Then she set about tidying the rest of the office up, which she'd been neglectful of this last week.

At 9.10 the shrill ring of the phone echoed through the office. Neville stirred as Rosalie picked up the receiver.

'Yes, he's right here.'

He sat up and took the phone. As he listened, he closed his eyes and let out a sigh, then clicked his fingers and Rosalie picked up a pencil and started taking notes as he repeated what was being said.

'London. Japan has accepted the terms of surrender. Unconditional. Emperor accepts Potsdam Declaration. Americans on standby in the Philippines. Show of naval might . . .' Rosalie's hand flew across the page as she took down every word, underlining the day's date. August fifteenth.

When Neville eventually hung up he looked at Rosalie with wide eyes. 'Turn the wireless on.'

Rosalie did as requested. Just before 9.30, the stirring tune of Elgar's 'Pomp and Circumstance Military Marches' rang out through the tiny speakers of the office radio before Ben Chifley was introduced. His words pierced the air. 'Fellow citizens, the war is over . . .'

Rosalie froze, her pencil poised above her notepad. As Chifley continued to address the nation with details, she started taking notes.

Neville reached over and put his hand over hers. 'I can take care of this. You get out there and capture the reaction.'

She stared at him a moment. How could he ask her to miss this momentous occasion?

'These words will be the same in every paper across the country,' Neville said. 'But what happens out there, that is unique to us. That is where the real news for us lies.'

A wave of understanding hit Rosalie. She jumped up and grabbed her camera, careering out of the office.

At first, people emerged in quiet pairs from the buildings that lined Main Street, looking at each other in silent disbelief. When they realised they'd all heard the same announcement – that it was actually true – tears broke through their fragile veneer and they hugged each other.

Slowly the street began to fill, as people were drawn to seek out others – to verify, to share, to cry, to celebrate. Rosalie captured as many comings together as she could. Soon, children were running and riding up and down the street, trailing red, white and blue flags behind them, the joy on their tiny faces a blur as they sped past.

Dot and her three girls came running towards her. 'My daddy's coming home,' Tess called, throwing herself into Rosalie's arms.

'Can you believe it?' Dot grabbed Rosalie's shoulders. 'Do we dare?'

Rosalie nodded. 'It's true.'

They shared a look of restrained joy. Yes, Japan had agreed to surrender, but the official formalities took time. The fighting wouldn't stop until the ink was dry, and they didn't know when that would be. Until the men and women were back on home soil, they couldn't fully celebrate.

By midday there was bunting hanging from every shopfront and a long line of tables running right up the centre of Main Street.

Every colour of tablecloth was being brought out and vases of flowers appeared from nowhere. As the townsfolk descended on the centre of town, they brought with them plates and bowls of food, placing them in the middle of the tables.

'Rosalie!' Penelope's familiar voice rang through the crowd and Rosalie spun around to greet her. 'Is it really true? I mean, I listened to the radio, but it still seems like a dream.'

'It's true, Pen.' They hugged.

'My Edward?'

Rosalie smiled. 'He can come home.'

Penelope tightened her embrace.

Behind Penelope, Bernie and Albert walked towards Rosalie, Albert carrying his banjo, Bernie his guitar. Albert's eyes darted around the gathering crowd.

'I hope you're getting some good shots.' Bernie hugged her when they reached her.

'Of course. I may well run out of film though.' She patted her pockets.

Bernie handed her three canisters.

'Thank you!' She kissed him on the cheek and he steered Penelope towards another group of celebrators. Rosalie didn't know their names, but everyone was a friend today.

Despite the knowledge that there would still be some dangers ahead, no one was going to let that spoil the joy of the day. A moment of hope and relief, and excited expectation was surely allowed after so much dark.

A child ran past them, waving a flag, shouting happily and Albert tensed.

'Rosalie.' He stepped closer to her, his shoulders relaxing.

'Hello.' Rosalie wanted to throw herself into his arms, and, given the scene before them, she probably could have and no one would have batted an eyelid.

'This is . . .' He shifted from one foot to another.

'I know.' To hell with it. She wrapped her arms around him and he kissed her intently.

And no one noticed.

Millie slowly pushed her way through the crowd carrying Frederick. When she reached Rosalie and Albert, no words were exchanged, just a warm embrace.

Bernie appeared beside them again. 'What do you say, son.' He patted Albert on the back. 'Shall we head over there where it's a bit quieter and play a few tunes?'

The two of them disappeared and when Rosalie turned around, she saw her mother and father walking up the street. Iris had tears streaming down her face and Frank, all too aware from his work at the hospital of the toll war took, allowed himself a small smile. 'This is marvellous,' Iris said as she saw Rosalie, and she clasped her hands in front of her chest.

Music began to play and the crowd looked over to the steps of the small town hall in the centre of Main Street. There Albert and Bernie sat with their instruments, and an old man Rosalie didn't recognise stood beside them with an accordion. Bernie counted them in and on three they began a rendition of Glenn Miller's 'In the Mood'. Albert always looked so content when he was playing music, Rosalie noted.

All around them people started dancing in the street and Rosalie lifted her camera. There was almost too much for her lens to take in, but she remembered some of Bernie's advice. *Focus on the details. They're what show us the big picture in the end.*

She zoomed in on a couple, an old woman in her eighties and a young man who can't have been more than fifteen, dancing a twostep. She moved over to the tables and captured a shot of four children eating scones, a Union Jack and an Australian flag discarded on the table in front of them. In the crowd she captured Dot and Millie spinning around with the children, and an old veteran from the Great War, dressed in full uniform, his medals proudly on display across his chest, sitting with Frederick in the gutter, playing jacks with him in the dirt.

Rosalie took a photo of Mrs Donaldson standing in the doorway of the post office watching proceedings, her hands in the pockets of her apron. Her happiness seemed subdued, Rosalie thought: she knew the cost of this war wouldn't be over for a long time after the men and women returned home: Mr Donaldson was still only a shell of a man after the last war. When she noticed Rosalie there, she gave her a slow nod.

Rosalie turned her camera to the trio who were still playing up a storm, and captured them from side on, the blur of revellers behind them creating a unique background. Then she lowered her camera and simply took it all in.

Albert looked over to her and heat skipped across her skin.

The next moment, Rosalie was grabbed from behind and twirled around.

'I thought I'd find you here with your camera.' The familiar deep voice washed over her.

'Henry?' She turned in his arms and he didn't let her go. 'What are you doing here?'

In all the excitement of the morning, she'd forgotten he was due back today.

He brushed her hand. 'How fortuitous I was already on my way here when the announcement came over the radio. There's nowhere else I'd rather be today.'

'Henry . . . I . . .'

'Ah, hello, Dr Burton.' Frank slapped Henry on the back with gusto.

'Dr Reynolds.' Henry shook his hand, his other arm wrapping around Rosalie's waist.

'Rosalie, your mother is a little overcome with all the excitement, so we're going to head home.' Frank gave Iris a pointed look.

Henry turned to her. 'Shall we move somewhere a little less crowded?' He guided her to the small alley that separated the post office from the greengrocer. From there they could still see the celebrations taking place, but it was a little quieter.

'Henry . . .'

'Rosalie.' He grabbed her hands and held them tightly. 'I won't pressure you, I promise. But now that I've graduated and the war is over, I was hoping, maybe, you would now consider me, offer a poor aching heart some hope.' He held her hands to his chest.

Rosalie lowered her head. 'Henry. You are a good man. I care for you . . .' Her words faltered.

'But?'

She turned her gaze to Albert on the steps of the town hall.

'Ah. I see.' His expression dissolved. 'You have feelings for him?'

'I . . . I think I do.'

Henry stared at her. 'You know how much I can offer you.'

'But that is not reason enough to be with you, Henry. I'm so sorry.'

Henry straightened his shirt. 'What about your work?' he asked. 'Are you going to throw away your career for him?'

Rosalie knew he was speaking from a place of hurt, desperate to get her to reconsider. 'I have no intention of giving anything up. Do you remember when I told you I didn't know if there'd be room for marriage in my life? I have no idea what the future holds for Albert and me. But it will not stop me chasing my dream. And he will understand that or he won't be part of it. Regardless of all of that, though – my feelings for him, for you – I cannot change them.'

Henry's shoulders dropped. 'Right, well, I'll bid you good day, Rosalie. But know my heart belongs to you, whether you want it or not.' And he walked away, without looking back.

Rosalie felt weak. She stepped back out into the crowd and looked to the steps of the town hall. She caught a glimpse of Bernie, but Albert was gone.

Try as she might later that night, Rosalie couldn't fall asleep. The day had been too much – too happy, too sad. She slipped into her overalls at midnight and slid out the back door, riding off in the dark to clear her head. The town was quiet and dark, the remnants of the bunting flapping in the breeze the only reminder of the momentous day that had passed.

As she left the sleeping town behind and approached her secret place, a faint and familiar twang, distant, soft, floated on the night air. In the small clearing, she found Albert sitting on a thick woollen rug, strumming his banjo. Beside him was a rucksack, behind him a pillow.

'Camping?' she asked, as she slowed her bike to a halt.

He startled and looked up, surprise on his face when he saw Rosalie before him.

'Yes, actually.'

'So, not just a midnight stroll because you couldn't drift off?'

He shook his head. 'Ever since you showed me this place, I come here often and camp out. Let that stunning view put me to sleep.' He turned on his side and fixed his gaze on her and she had to look away, back up to the sky.

'Today was . . . I don't think I have the words for what today was.'

He nodded. 'You and the toff, huh?'

'What?'

'Henry. I saw him with you. You two are an item?'

'No. Absolutely not. We're just friends.'

'Does he know that?'

Rosalie sighed. 'He does. Now. And maybe we aren't even that anymore.'

'You turned him down?'

'Yes.'

'Why? I imagine by every possible measure he'd be a good catch.'

Rosalie looked Albert in the eye. 'He is a good catch. He's just not . . . *my* catch.'

Albert took Rosalie's hand and a shiver travelled up her spine. 'Rosalie,' he said, 'I can't offer you what a man like Henry can. All I can offer you is my love. And it's yours if you'll have it.'

Her heart raced, her pulse thrummed. 'That's all I need.'

Rosalie pushed aside the past. As much as she didn't want to face anyone, she knew she had to return to the retreat. Running off like this again was only creating more questions.

With her body aching and weary, she mounted her bike. By the time she'd made it back, the sun was casting long shadows across the ground. Unsurprisingly, Sarah was waiting for her on the porch. Rosalie parked her bike beside the cabin and walked up the ramp towards her granddaughter.

'Are you okay? Where did you go? This running off business is starting to become a habit with you.' Sarah's words spilled out.

'Yes, I'm fine.' Lie. 'I went to get some fresh air.' Half-truth. 'And the last isn't as easy a question to answer.' Truth.

Sarah's expression was a mix of worry and confusion.

'Is Melody okay?' Rosalie's concern for her great-granddaughter was genuine. So was her need to not have to answer serious questions right now.

'I think so. When Eddy dropped his bow, the sound . . . the look on her face . . . She was spooked. But Albie calmed her down.'

'Albert?'

Sarah nodded.

'He always did have a charm. Knew just what to say.'

'He didn't speak. Apparently, his dementia is pretty bad and he doesn't say much anymore.'

Sadness washed over Rosalie. Her poor Albert.

'Who are they, Granny Rose? Edward and Albert? They are clearly more than just a couple of old friends.'

'Yes. Yes they are. I will tell you, my darling. But may I ask you a favour first?'

Sarah's eyes narrowed. 'I suppose.'

'Before I answer all of your questions, and I know you must have many, I need to have a few of my own answered. I'm not entirely sure I have the full story myself. Can you give me this leeway? I promise you we will sit down and I will tell you everything.'

Her granddaughter had always been compassionate, and Rosalie was sure Sarah would recognise how important this was to her.

Sarah let out a sigh and raised her hand, extending her pinkie finger, just like Melody did when making a promise. Rosalie smiled and they locked fingers.

Sarah went back inside, leaving Rosalie standing there as a light rain began to fall.

Twenty-seven

The next morning Sarah and Melody headed over to the Stave for their last session of the week. Joshua greeted them in the foyer, and before following Melody into their room, he pulled Sarah aside.

'How's Rosalie? How are you?'

'I'm not sure.' She shrugged. 'Were you able to find anything out?'

He shook his head. 'Eddy wouldn't say anything. I wish there was something I could do.'

'Actually, I'd like to visit him. Do you think that would be possible?'

Joshua tilted his head. 'Oh. Okay. Are you sure?'

Sarah had been thinking about it for half the night. What happened yesterday, seeing Rosalie, the strongest, most capable woman she knew, run off like that again, frightened her. What could possibly have happened all those years ago that her grandmother would keep having these strong reactions? She needed to investigate the brothers herself, just in case she had to protect Rosalie.

'Yes. Do you think that would be okay?'

'I don't see why not,' Joshua said. 'We've got choir practice up at the nursing home this afternoon. Why don't you come with us? Bring Melody too.'

'Great.'

'Shall we?' He stepped to the side so Sarah could enter the therapy room ahead of him.

Joshua started by tuning his guitar, Melody sitting in front of him. He turned the tuning peg of the E string and Melody pointed her finger up in the air.

Sarah sat forward in her chair.

'Sharper?' Joshua asked.

Melody nodded.

He plucked the string again. Melody frowned and pointed down.

'Too far?' He laughed and she grinned.

Every string he tuned, Melody pointed sharper or flatter until it was just right.

Joshua settled himself on the chair, stretching out his left leg, kicking the bongo drum on the floor. Melody's shoulders shook with a silent giggle.

As Joshua sang and strummed his guitar, Melody looked from him to the bongos and back again. He gave her a slight nod and she picked the drum up and sat it in her lap.

Sarah nearly stood up but restrained herself before she distracted Melody.

First there was a head bob. Then a tentative, quiet pat with soft fingers on the bongo's stretched skin.

Dooom, blatt; dooom blatt . . .

Almost imperceptible but, yes, Melody was playing the bongo drum.

Ever so slightly, Joshua increased the tempo of the tune he was playing, and Melody adjusted to meet his beat.

To stop herself from jumping up and down, which would most certainly be a distraction, Sarah held on to the arms of the chair she was in, her knuckles white with the grip.

Again, Joshua picked up the tempo. Again, Melody followed his lead. As the tempo raised, so did the volume with which Melody played, until the sound she made reverberated through the room.

Sarah's heart raced. Her daughter was playing a drum.

Her daughter was playing a drum!

The crescendo was building, that sweet moment in a piece of music when you could feel the anticipation of the climax, and as they reached the final note, a guttural scream echoed around them.

Sarah opened her eyes and flung herself out of the chair, stopping halfway across the room when she realised Melody had dropped the bongos on the floor and had covered her mouth.

'It's okay, Melody.' Joshua's voice was low, calm. 'We're all okay.'

She turned and looked at Sarah.

Stay calm. Don't overreact. Just smile. Oh, god; oh, god.

Sarah grinned at her daughter and clapped.

Melody lowered her hands from her mouth, and a tiny smile tickled the edges of her perfect pink lips.

In the last ten minutes of their time together, Melody didn't make another sound, just moved her head in time with Joshua's songs. But it didn't matter. Today she had made a sound. One beautiful, perfect, purposeful sound.

'Awesome job today.' Joshua raised his hand and Melody whacked it with a high-five that left a momentary red mark on both of them. She wheeled off in the direction of the cabin and Sarah turned to Joshua. 'Thank you.' Her bottom lip trembled. 'I . . . that . . . she . . .'

'Breathe.' Joshua smiled.

'Thank you.'

'Just remember, baby steps.'

Why was he talking about baby steps? That was one massive giant leap.

'We still have a lot of work to do, but that . . . that was a good moment,' he said.

It was a great moment.

But Sarah knew he was right. She'd allowed her hopes to take flight before and that hadn't ended well.

'Meet you back here this afternoon, say three o'clock?' Joshua asked.

'It's a date.' Sarah's cheeks flushed. 'I mean . . . an appointment . . . or . . .'

Joshua laughed. 'I know what you mean. It's nice I'm not the only one putting their foot in their mouth for a change.'

'Right. Three o'clock. See you soon.' Sarah hurried after Melody.

Sarah was relieved that Ryan had no yoga on that afternoon and he could take Melody for lunch. They'd barely seen him the past few days, he'd been so busy with his newest obsession. Not that Sarah begrudged him. She could see in his lightness of step and the calm joy that seemed to surround him now that this quietness, the change of scene, were exactly what he needed.

She headed back to the Stave, where Phoebe had a cup of steaming hot chocolate ready for her in her office. There was no talk of the accident, or Melody, or anything to do with that part of Sarah's life. It felt as though they were just two friends nattering over a comforting drink.

Except . . . it wasn't. Sarah knew it was therapy in disguise. But she didn't mind.

Today along with the hot chocolate, Phoebe also had a cello waiting. 'I just thought, if you felt up to it, maybe we could look at this piece together.' She pulled out some sheet music from her drawer. 'I've been wanting to play it for a while, but nobody here is skilled enough to help me learn it. I thought maybe you could give me some pointers.'

'Did you just?' Sarah pursed her lips. 'That is incredibly . . . subtle of you.'

Phoebe spread her hands out wide. 'What can I say? The hot chocolate works in mysterious ways.'

Sarah laughed.

'Seriously, though.' Phoebe leaned in. 'Only if you want to.'

Sarah hesitated then took the music. They were, after all, just two friends having a chat, she told herself. A chat that happens to be about a cello. She trusted Phoebe.

Yet she couldn't bring herself to play the instrument. Fractured images and sounds filled her mind – the cheers from the Opera House audience, the streetlights flashing past as they drove, Melody dropping the bow, the screeching crack of the truck – guilt flooding her. No. She couldn't play. But she did touch the cello's neck while showing Phoebe how to play the opening bars. It was a very strange sensation. Trepidation mixed with longing.

Phoebe played quite well and, sitting there letting the melancholy sound of the cello wash over her, Sarah felt the part of her she'd locked away a year ago open ever so slightly.

In the afternoon, Sarah and Melody met Joshua as planned and he took them to visit Edward and Albert.

The nursing home was to the east of town, in a quiet leafy street surrounded by Federation homes and California bungalows. Tall gum trees partially hid the front of the house, hugging it, protecting it. It was a two-storey red-brick Federation home, with a wide front verandah supported by timber porch posts painted white that reached up to white gingerbread scrollwork that sat under the eaves. The leadlight windows and door panels showed motifs of roses and vines in red and green and pink, and were framed in white wood.

Joshua held the wide door open for Sarah and Melody. The foyer, once a reception room, Sarah guessed, was expansive, the walls painted a soft grey, the ceiling white. A modern pendant light fitting hung from an ornate ceiling rose, casting soft light into the open space. A pink sofa sat off to one side, a wooden sideboard on the other next to a reception desk. A young woman with jet-black hair and bright-blue nails greeted Joshua and waved the three of them through.

In front of them was a wooden staircase arcing up to the second floor and behind it Sarah could see a lift.

'Through here.' Joshua guided them to the back of the house, to what Sarah guessed was a more recent addition, which housed a dining hall.

Katie was already there setting up, arranging chairs into a horseshoe facing the large French doors that looked out on to a well-manicured lawn edged by neat lavender hedges. She greeted them with a happy smile and wave, her pink ponytail bobbing with the movement. Sarah and Joshua helped her with the last few chairs and one by one the residents started trickling in.

When Sarah saw Eddy and Albert, Eddy helping his brother with his walker, her stomach churned. What was she actually doing here? What did she hope to achieve? She hadn't exactly thought this through – what questions she'd ask, what she'd do with the answers, if she got any. But it was too late now. They were here.

Eddy looked over to her and gave her a slight nod before he set Albert up at the piano. The second Albert was in front of the instrument, his posture straightened.

Melody tugged on Sarah's arm.

'Of course. Over you go.'

Melody clapped and started to move, but stopped. She frowned and pointed to her wheels.

'Oh,' Joshua nodded. 'Albert only uses a wheelchair outside the home. Company regulations.'

Seemingly satisfied with the answer, Melody wheeled over to the piano.

'Why don't you take a seat over there.' Joshua pointed Sarah to a couple of spare chairs near the piano. 'The choir rehearsals are Katie's baby, but sometimes she needs a hand wrangling this rowdy mob.'

Joshua was right. The rehearsal was messy and chaotic. And absolutely joyous. Melody mirrored Albert's movements on the piano and every time they had to stop because Phyllis had lost her place, or Brandon started dancing, or Archie let out a loud whoop, she frowned at the interruption and shook her head. Sarah had to stifle a laugh. It seemed her daughter had inherited her perfectionism. She was far too young to understand, however, that this in front of her *was* perfection. Sarah was only just beginning to understand it herself.

The choir practised three songs – two they'd been working on for a few months, and one new one. At the end, as everyone dispersed, Katie came over to Albert with a handful of sheet music in a teal folder.

'I'm thinking of this one for our next concert.' She handed him the music. 'What do you reckon?'

He looked at the pages briefly and nodded. Laying the sheet music face down on the top of the piano, he began to play ABBA's 'The Winner Takes It All'. And he was note-perfect, his rhythm and dynamics sublime.

Melody looked up at Sarah, her mouth agape.

Sarah raised an eyebrow. *Yes, my darling girl. Just like you.* One look at a piece of music and Melody could play it.

When Albert finished the song, he started again, this time singing the lyrics. Melody nodded along. It was a song she knew well. People assumed, given Sarah's training and job – former job – that the only music listened to in her house was classical. But that couldn't be further from the truth. Yes, Mozart and Bach and Vivaldi were on high rotation, but Sarah loved a good pop song as much as anyone, and in between concertos and arias and sonatas, Queen and ABBA were played, of course, and Maroon 5, the deep tones of Lewis Capaldi, and recently the soundtrack from *The Greatest Showman*, Hugh Jackman on repeat.

Albert's voice, while not strong, was pleasant and he sang through the first five verses with ease, and moved into the sixth. The rules. The gods. The dice. But as he sang the last line of the verse, he stumbled, as if he'd forgotten what the god's minds were as cold as. He stared at his fingers hovering above the keys, went back a line a tried again. Still the word didn't come. Another attempt. Nothing. His shoulders tensed. Sarah stood up. Should she help? She waved Joshua over.

Albert began again. This time from the beginning, and as he reached the same line in the song, Sarah held her breath. *You've got this, Albert.*

He paused.

And Melody lay her tiny hand on his, guiding his finger to the next note and whispered 'ice'.

She looked around in panic, as if one tiny utterance would bring her world crashing down. Joshua knelt beside her. 'Well done. Thank you for helping Albert. Sometimes he gets a little stuck.'

With wide eyes, Melody looked at her mother, and then turned her gaze to Albert. He started playing again, picking up from 'ice', and Melody tapped the side of her head. *Understood.* She swayed in time to the music while Albert finished the song, but didn't say another word.

Sarah's mouth was dry. Joshua stood up and came back over to her. 'Baby steps,' he said. And she nodded, holding back the screams of joy inside her.

Katie clapped when the song finished. 'Yes. I think that will make a lovely choir piece, don't you?'

Albert nodded, his eyes sparkling.

'We often have a cuppa outside after choir practice,' Eddy said, joining them by the piano. 'The rain is holding off. Shall we?'

He guided Albert out to the yard and Melody wheeled along beside him. Once outside at the long wooden table and chairs, Albert sank back into himself.

From the backpack she always carried with her, Melody pulled out her crayons and sketchbook, handing Albert a blank page. Together they began to draw.

'Those two seem to have hit it off.' Joshua nodded towards the pair.

Eddy coughed.

'I hope it's okay I brought Sarah with me today,' Joshua continued.

'Of course. It's nice to have the opportunity to see you again, Sarah.'

Sarah sensed the tension in the old man's voice. Was he worried about the questions she might ask? Should he be?

She opened with something simple while she tried to figure out exactly what she wanted to say. 'How long have you been living here?'

'Three years now,' Eddy answered, taking a sip of tea. 'We lived at the retreat before that. When it became clear Albert needed more help than I could provide, I moved him in here.'

Sarah frowned. 'But you seem . . .' Gosh, how did she say it without offending him?

'Oh, I could live on my own still.' He nodded. 'But I couldn't abandon him. He's my baby brother. So I moved in too.'

Sarah found that both sweet and sad. 'Was it hard to leave your home?' Rosalie had always been adamant that the only way she was moving out of her home was in a box.

Eddy shrugged. 'Once we knocked down the original cabin to build the retreat, it wasn't really home anymore.'

'Bernie's cabin?'

Eddy's eyes flashed. 'Yes. How much do you know? About your grandmother when she lived here?' He looked over to Albert.

Sarah let out a sigh. 'That's pretty much it. I know her uncle Bernie used to live in a cabin where the retreat now is. And that she has photos, including lots of you and Albert, in an album, but she refuses to talk about anything to do with them.' From her tote bag, Sarah pulled out the album and handed it to Eddy.

He opened the pages. At first he smiled as he looked at the pictures. But his smile dropped and his eyes faded with each page he turned.

'Your grandmother . . .' He sighed, running his thick, age-spotted finger over one of the Snapshots. 'My goodness, she was talented.' He shook his head.

'And the three of you were friends?'

He nodded.

'And you knew who I was when I applied for Melody to come here?'

He cast his eyes down quickly before answering. 'When Rosalie and I . . . lost touch, I followed her career. What an amazing career that was.' He shook his head. 'There wasn't ever much about her family in the press.'

No. Rosalie had worked hard to keep her private life just that.

'But there were . . . snippets. Enough.'

Something wasn't quite adding up here. 'What aren't you telling me?'

Eddy looked off into the trees. 'Out of respect for Rosalie, and those who can't speak for themselves, I don't think it's my place to say. I really do think you need to ask her.'

For those who can't speak for themselves? She looked over to Albert.

'Sarah, can I ask you something?' Eddy rubbed his cleanly shaven chin.

'Yes.' She narrowed her gaze.

'What happens if you don't like what she tells you?'

'What?' What was that supposed to mean?

'Sometimes when we go looking for the truth, what we find isn't what we expect. What we find is pain. Sometimes for ourselves. Sometimes for others.' He shook his head.

'Maybe,' Sarah said. 'But I think it might be a little late for that.'

'Hard to put the genie back in the bottle?' he said.

'Something like that.' And she didn't *want* to put the genie back in. She wanted to know what happened here all those years ago; and now they were here, she knew it was unhealthy for Rosalie to be sitting on these secrets, considering the way she'd been behaving these last two weeks.

'For what it's worth,' Eddy leaned across the table and rested his large hand on hers, 'know that I'm sorry.'

'Sorry? For what?'

'For my part in it. Please. Talk to Rosalie.'

Eddy got up and left, taking Albert with him.

'Hmm.' Joshua furrowed his brow. 'That didn't really help, did it? We can come back tomorrow and try again, if you like.'

'No. He's right. I need to talk to my grandmother first.'

*

As they left the nursing home, Melody stopped behind Sarah and Joshua.

'What is it, minim?' Sarah asked. 'Did you forget something?'

Melody shook her head and put her finger to her lips in a silent *shh*. Her eyes darted to the trees at the edge of the nursing home and back again.

Sarah craned her head, but saw nothing there.

'Come on. Let's go back to the cabin.'

Melody nodded, and they piled into Joshua's car.

Sarah's head was spinning. When she'd found the album and Rosalie had insisted on coming to Redgum River, she'd gone through so many possible scenarios in her head. But none of them came close. Now she had no doubt that Rosalie was hiding something much deeper and darker than she'd imagined.

Twenty-eight

Rosalie stepped out of the shadows once she was certain Joshua had driven off. God bless her great-granddaughter for not blowing her cover. She thought she was caught there for a moment.

She made sure her bike was safely locked up outside the nursing home, silently thanking Phoebe for the directions. She smoothed her blouse and trousers with shaking hands, set her shoulders back and strode towards the entrance with false bravado.

The lovely nurse inside escorted her to the dining hall, where she said she'd bring Edward to meet with her.

Rosalie paced, albeit slowly, up and down the grey lino, her heart thumping heavily against her chest.

The familiar deep voice of her younger days echoed through the room. 'Rosalie?'

She turned around. 'Edward.' Of all the things she could have said, should have said, it was the only word that came out.

Behind Edward, Albert shuffled into the room, leaning heavily on his walker. Edward pulled the piano stool out for him and Albert started to play. A quiet, gentle tune, from a lifetime ago.

'Would you like to sit?' Edward pulled a chair out for Rosalie at a nearby table and she lowered herself onto it with as much grace as she could muster.

'Thank you.' She stared at him. 'It really is the both of you.'

'Yes.' He nodded.

'When we first arrived, I thought I saw you playing music in the rotunda.'

'Then you probably did. We sometimes busk. When Albert's up for it. Like the old days. When we do, I feel like I have my brother back.'

'How bad is it?' She looked over to the man who was once her world.

'Bad. The only relief is when he's playing – he has forgotten none of that. He sings with the choir, and sometimes when he's playing like now. But he hasn't spoken in nearly three years. Nothing coherent.'

Rosalie's heart broke for Edward. The burden of pain always fell to those left behind. 'I'm so sorry.'

'Thank you, Rosalie.'

Perhaps now wasn't the time, but she had to know. 'I saw that Sarah was here just now. What did you tell her?'

He shook his head. 'Nothing. That we were friends. That she needs to speak to you.'

She looked up at him and met his eyes. The swell of emotion – of relief and sadness, of regret and pain – was almost too much to bear.

Eventually, Edward broke the silence. 'She showed me the album. I can't believe you kept it all this time.'

'Of course I did.'

So much unsaid.

'I'll give you two a few minutes alone if you like.' Edward tilted his head towards his brother.

'Thank you.'

After Edward had left, Rosalie pulled up a chair next to the piano. Albert looked up, still playing his song and he smiled at her, his green eyes shining as bright as they had the last time she'd seen him all those years ago. Her Albert.

'Rosalie?'

She almost gasped out loud. Edward had said . . . oh, it didn't matter.

'Yes. Hello, Albert.'

'Meet me in the grove after work?'

'Of course.' Her heart tightened.

He nodded and returned his gaze to the black and white keys beneath his fingers. When he looked back up, the light she'd seen was gone. Her Albert was gone.

'Oh, Albert.' She choked back tears and scuttled out of the nursing home and rode away from there as fast as she could, memories crashing in all around her.

Redgum River
September 1945

Rosalie hopped off her bike and laid it in the grass beside her as she sat down by the river. It had been another long day at the paper, filing stories about the demobilisation of troops, the release of POWs, and the aftermath of the formal signing of the Instrument of Surrender. Rosalie had thought she was busy during the war. Apparently, the ending of hostilities meant she was even busier.

She removed her snood, shook out her hair, and lay back in the grass. The sun was setting, casting a golden shimmer across the water and an ethereal light across the sky. She closed her eyes.

Just for a moment she'd lie here before heading home. Home to the still disappointed expressions of her parents. It had been three weeks since Rosalie had turned Henry down, and it appeared Frank and Iris were not going to forgive her.

Frank's anger had been manifest. He had shaken his head and called her a foolish girl who knew nothing of how the world worked. Iris had cried. Rosalie had tried to get them to understand that she didn't love Henry. But her mother had simply replied, 'What's love got to do with securing your future?'

Perhaps all they needed was time. Though Rosalie held little hope that all the time in the world would alleviate their disappointment and frustration with her.

Soft footfalls behind made her sit up. Albert and Penelope were walking towards her, arm in arm, Bernie behind them carrying two fishing rods.

Rosalie and Albert had been spending as much time as possible together in the weeks since that night in the grove, but always at Penelope or Bernie's house. Never quite alone, at the insistence of Albert. Rosalie was quietly relieved at this, because while her skin burned at his touch, that night had frightened her – the intensity of her feelings, the all-consuming power of their connection.

That wasn't the only reason Rosalie wanted to be careful about the pace of their relationship. Turning down well-to-do, well-connected Henry had garnered her parents' ire, as expected. Telling them it was because she was in love with an injured soldier of no means would have quite possibly provoked their fury. She would have to wait until the Henry-storm had settled, then integrate Albert into their lives slowly, hoping that at some point they would be ready to see the light in him she saw.

'Hello, you three.' Rosalie sat up. 'Out for an evening stroll?'

'Yes. Some fresh air before supper.' Penelope smiled. 'Fish, if either of them catches anything, or shepherd's pie if they don't.'

Albert leaned in to Rosalie, his warm breath on her ear sending a tingle down Rosalie's spine. 'My money's on shepherd's pie.'

Bernie gave him a nudge. 'Have a little faith.'

'I have faith in shepherd's pie.'

The two of them headed down to the river bank and threw in their lines.

Rosalie turned to Penelope. 'Any news from Edward? When he might be coming home?'

Penelope shook her head, her smile falling. From what they understood, it might still be some time before demobilisation would see the men return.

'How's work, Rosalie?' Penelope changed the subject.

Rosalie filled her in on the last two days as they sat by the river bank.

'Gosh, it sounds like you could do with a holiday.' Penelope pulled up her sleeve and Rosalie saw a bruise.

'Are you hurt?' Rosalie leaned forward.

'Oh, no. A bump.' She smiled uneasily and rolled her sleeve down again. 'Trying to do too much on my own in the garden, and I had a nasty fall.'

'Are you okay?'

Penelope turned her gaze to the grass, pulling down on her sleeve.

'You really ought to get Albert to help with anything too much for you. One of the advantages of having him home.' Rosalie tapped her on the leg.

'Well, I don't like to ask. Not with his leg giving him so much trouble. He has . . . enough to think about. No need to worry about me.'

After half an hour there were no bites on either man's line and they gave up and joined Rosalie and Penelope on the grass.

Mrs Donaldson came bustling over. 'Ah, just the people I was hoping to run into. I wanted to talk to you about the rotunda drive.'

Last week the town council had agreed to erect a rotunda by the river, in honour of the war officially ending and of the local lads who'd served.

'We've got all the wood donated and tools, but we need man-power. And woman-power. Can I sign you up to help?' She waved a clipboard at them.

Albert got slowly to his feet. 'Count me in.' He signed his name.

Rosalie held out her hand and he helped her up. 'Of course.'

Bernie and Penelope signed on too. By the look of the sheet, nearly the whole town had.

'Brilliant. Thank you.' Mrs Donaldson hurried off again.

Albert steered Rosalie away from Penelope and Bernie.

'I miss you,' he whispered in her ear.

'You saw me two days ago,' Rosalie smiled.

'Still miss you.' He stole a quick kiss of her cheek.

'Well, we'll be working on the rotunda together, it seems, so we'll get to see a lot more of each other soon.'

He leaned in, his lips just an inch from hers. 'Still won't be enough.'

A cough made them jump.

'Let's go, lad.' Bernie put his hand on Albert's shoulder. 'We should let Rosalie get home.'

Albert caught up with his mother, who'd started to head off.

'Rosalie? A word?' Bernie said.

'Of course.' She frowned. There was a look in Bernie's eyes Rosalie hadn't seen in a while. Concern?

'I just wanted to say . . .' He watched Albert walking away, his arm over Penelope's shoulder. 'Life . . . People . . . We aren't always straightforward, are we? I mean to say . . .' Bernie trailed off.

'What *do* you mean, Uncle Bernie?' Rosalie asked, a little exasperated.

'I . . . I just don't want you to get hurt if things don't work out the way you hope.'

'Do you mean Mother and Father?' she asked and Bernie frowned.

'Are you coming with us, Bernie?' Albert called.

'Just be careful. I have to go.' Bernie squeezed her arm and ran off after Penelope and Albert.

Rosalie watched them till they were out of sight. She *was* being careful. Taking things slowly. Ensuring her parents knew nothing of her feelings for Albert. Not yet.

Two weeks later, as the sun began to rise, the riverbank was a hive of activity as the rotunda working bee got underway. Penelope, Millie and Dot had provided a delicious spread of sandwiches, slices and lemonade, which Mrs Donaldson helped them set up on a table she'd carried down from the store. Even Iris had come to help serve, though her eyes rarely strayed from Rosalie. Especially not after she'd caught Albert brush Rosalie's arm when they stood under the large gum tree, a sandwich each for lunch.

Rosalie would have to be more careful.

Young men went about lifting and cutting wood while some of the older men barked orders, and slowly the structure began to take shape. Neville Payne was there, too, lending a hand, his ability to cut a perfectly straight edge of wood with a saw coming in most useful.

'I didn't know you were good on the tools,' Rosalie said, handing him a glass of lemonade.

'I actually have many talents. A way with words is just one of them.' He downed the entire glass in one gulp.

Rosalie spent a good part of the day taking photos or entertaining the children, trying to keep them out of the way of the workers. She was successful, mostly, except for one moment when little Frederick ran after a ball that had got away, straight into the path of a man carrying a tin of white paint, the two of them colliding, paint splashing over them both. Instead of being useful helping them clean up, Rosalie simply pointed her camera and snapped.

At the end of the day, they all stood back in a semicircle. They'd done it. The white wooden rotunda, with fretwork balustrading, was complete. A cheer went up. Everyone wanted their photo taken in front of it, under it, alone holding a hammer up triumphantly, together as a group – every possible option. So many photos Rosalie had to put a couple of new rolls of film into her camera.

Eventually the crowd began to head home and there was only Rosalie and her family left. Iris had not left Rosalie's side all afternoon. It would have bothered her more, except it meant her mother and Bernie actually interacted with each other. Politely. General topics like the weather and the day's efforts only, but still. It was something.

Bernie cleared his throat. 'I'm glad we're the only ones left.' He seemed unsure of himself. 'I have something I'd like to share with you all.'

He bent down on one knee. Iris gasped. Rosalie grabbed Albert's hand. Penelope began to cry.

'Penny, these last few months you have filled a void in my life I never thought could be filled. I want to love you for the rest of my life. Protect you always.' He pulled a ring out of his pocket.

'Oh Bernie. Yes! Of course yes.' Penelope threw her arms around him.

Albert nudged Rosalie and pointed at her camera.

Right. Of course.

She took a number of photos before congratulating the couple. Hugs and kisses ensued, even Iris hugging her brother-in-law. As she pulled away from him, Albert put his arm around Rosalie. Right there in full view of her mother.

'When will the big day be?' Iris asked, her steely gaze leaving Albert's arm and turning to Penelope.

Penelope looked at Bernie and he nodded.

'When Edward comes home.'

That night, Iris came to Rosalie as she was getting ready for bed.

'Can we have a talk?'

Rosalie was expecting this and she was just grateful Frank was in Sydney. It would have been ten times worse if he were here.

Iris sat on the end of Rosalie's bed, smoothing the sky-blue quilt with her hands. 'That boy. Albert? Is there anything I need to know?'

Rosalie hadn't often lied to her mother. 'No. Nothing.'

'He isn't right for you, darling.'

'Why? Because he isn't from money? He's a good honourable man, Mother.'

Iris nodded tersely. 'That may be. But that doesn't mean he's right for you. You have a bright future ahead of you. Henry always speaks so highly of your talents. And so, he says, does that Reggie fellow.'

'Mother, I am very fond of Henry. I miss his friendship. But I don't love him.'

Irritation flitted across Iris's face. 'I think you're just too young to realise what's in front of you.' She raised her hand as Rosalie opened her mouth to protest. 'Don't be a fool and throw your life, your future, away, for a fleeting infatuation.'

Rosalie stared at her mother. 'That's not what this is.'

'I hope not.'

Iris left Rosalie standing in the middle of the room. If only her mother knew just how much she loved Albert. But she would never listen. Rosalie knew that now.

With her head heavy with memories, Rosalie left Albert and returned to the retreat. Sarah was sitting on the porch, a steaming cup of tea in her hand.

'You're back. Where did you get to?'

There was no point lying, Rosalie figured. Sarah had probably already guessed. 'To see them.'

'Right.'

Rosalie could see Sarah's chest rise and fall. She could see her frustration. But she had to ignore it for just a little longer. 'How's Melody?' she asked.

A lightness flashed across Sarah's face. 'She spoke!'

'*What?*'

'Today! To Albert when we were at the home. Just one word. But we all heard it.'

'Oh darling!' Rosalie threw her arms around her granddaughter. 'That's . . . that's amazing.' And it solidified her determination not to distract Sarah until this breakthrough became a corner turned. 'And that's what we focus on for now.'

'For now.'

Sarah held out her hand and Rosalie squeezed it tightly.

For now.

Twenty-nine

Off the coast of eastern Australia

Late October 1945

Edward shifted his body weight, trying not to disturb the men either side of him, as he adjusted the khaki shirt that was too big for him now. They were packed in tightly on the ship, but none of the soldiers minded. They were going home!

The demobilisation had been slow and gradual: men with families and soldiers who had served a long time were the first being demobbed. The rest would be sent in waves when operations allowed and space on a ship could be found. Edward, a relatively new recruit and without a wife or children, was lucky to be shipping home with this group.

As the days unfolded on the ship, small groups of men played cards, cigarettes hanging from their mouths; others stretched their legs with laps of the deck.

'Who are you going back to?' the soldier sitting opposite Edward asked, nodding to the book stuffed full of letters in Edward's lap.

'My mother and my brother. He served too, but was medically discharged a couple of months back. It will be good to see him again. He made that hellhole bearable.'

The man nodded.

'And have you got family at home?' Edward wondered if it was a silly question. Surely everyone had someone at home missing them.

He smiled. 'My wife. No kids. I can't wait to hold her in my arms again. And I'll be fixing that no kids thing.'

Edward laughed.

'No special sheila waiting for you?' the man asked Edward.

He sighed and pulled the photo of Rosalie out of his breast pocket.

'She's a beauty,' the man whistled. 'You're a lucky man.'

Edward nodded, put the photo back in his pocket and closed his eyes, imagining what it would be like to have Rosalie waiting for him.

On a bright spring day, Edward sat on the transport truck, three other lads beside him, keeping his eyes open for familiar landmarks. He could barely remember the area, but by his recollection they couldn't be far from Redgum River. Yet the next minutes seemed to take forever. Down a rough street they bounced and when the driver beeped his horn, Edward heard clapping, getting louder and louder. A band began to play, and a choir to sing.

As the truck came into view, cheers erupted, and people were waving flags.

The four men stood up on the back of the truck and waved back to the crowd. The man beside Edward, George, jumped from the truck before it stopped and ran towards a woman standing with three young girls next to her. He lifted all three in a large embrace. Young Ralphy jumped off next, a kelpie licking him all over his face.

Then Edward saw her. She was standing right there next to his mum, a vision in a blue and white shirtdress, camera around her neck.

He jumped off the truck and Penelope rushed forward and threw her arms around him. She was closely followed by Albert, and he wrapped them both in a tight hug.

'Oh, my.' Penelope laughed between sobs. 'Today my heart is healed.' She stepped out of the squash and held each of her sons.

'Did you miss me over there, grumble bum?' Albert play-punched Edward in the stomach.

Edward rubbed his fist over the top of Albert's head. 'Ha. You wish. The place was so much quieter after you left, cyclone.'

Edward wrapped his baby brother in a bear hug and whispered in his ear. 'How have you been?'

Albert leaned back but wouldn't let go of him. 'I have moments. But now you're home everything will be okay.'

There was a darkness in Albert's eyes that unnerved Edward. He looked to his mother and thought Penelope's smile was touched with sadness as she fiddled with the sleeve of her blouse. Albert detached himself from Edward's embrace and waved at Rosalie to come closer. 'Come meet Edward!'

Rosalie stepped forward, poised and confident, like he'd imagined her to be, and Edward extended his hand. 'We don't need an introduction.' He shook her hand – fire bursting up his arm. 'Rosalie, it's so wonderful to meet you finally. I feel like we are already good friends.'

'Edward.' She smiled. 'We are indeed. I have cherished every one of your letters.'

'And I yours. You brought much needed light into a dark world.'

'Even darker after I wasn't there to lift the mood of things.' Albert swung his banjo off his back and strummed a few chords.

'I can't believe of all the things that managed to survive the war, that bloody thing was one.' Edward laughed.

'Come on, you two.' Penelope said. 'There's plenty of time for you to carry on later. Right now, we've a celebration to enjoy, and Rosalie has work to do.'

'Your mother's right,' Rosalie said. 'Neville wants these pictures in tonight's edition. I'd better head to the Shack and get them developed. And I'm sure, Edward, you'll be wanting to get acquainted with Bernie.'

From behind Rosalie a thickset man stepped forward, his hand outstretched. Edward looked him up and down, this man who had intentions with his mother.

'Nice to meet you, son,' Bernie said and Edward simply nodded.

'Come for dinner tonight, Rosalie?' Penelope suggested. 'After you finish at the paper.'

Edward looked back to Rosalie, hoping she'd say yes.

'I'd love to join you.' Edward swelled with joy.

They were already playing music before Rosalie arrived. Albert on his banjo and Edward on the piano. Penelope and Bernie sat beside each other on the couch. It was a long time since Edward had seen his mother this happy and from what he could discern there was no reason he shouldn't be pleased about the match, although he wondered if there was something between Bernie and Albert – the man did seem a little frosty towards his brother.

Edward was grateful to be playing music, a distraction from the muddled haze he'd been in since arriving in Redgum River that morning, relieved to be back, to be safe, yet not feeling like he quite belonged. There was a comforting familiarity being with his brother and mother again, but it wasn't the same as he remembered. None of them was quite the same. He looked over to Penelope, her eyes darting between him and Albert, her smile nervous.

Rosalie let herself in, and Edward saw Albert look up, a smile spreading across his face when he saw her. Edward stopped playing and stood up.

'Rosalie.'

Bernie and Penelope turned around.

'I didn't mean to interrupt,' Rosalie said. 'Please don't stop on my account.'

'Join us.' Albert beckoned her over. 'Edward, she might even be better than you on that thing.' He nodded towards the piano.

'Please.' Edward offered her the stool. The exhaustion that had plagued him since arriving back on Australian soil dissolved as he watched her.

'No . . . I . . . but what will *you* play?' She looked up at him with her bright eyes and in that moment he felt for the first time he was home.

Albert hurried out of the room. 'I've got that covered.' He called over his shoulder. He returned moments later with a violin in his hand, a red bow tied to the neck of the instrument.

Edward frowned. 'Where did you get that?'

'I saved up. I thought you might like to play a welcome-home present.'

Edward shook his head and cleared his throat. 'Well, then, shall we see how she plays?'

Albert nodded and pulled the sheet music out of the trunk sitting beside the piano. The most complete scores they had, with parts for different instruments, were the Berlins. He pulled out 'Putting on the Ritz'.

'We shall.'

Albert leaned over and whispered in Rosalie's ear. His hand squeezed her shoulder and as he pulled it away, his fingers trailed across the back of her neck.

Edward blinked, not wanting to believe what he saw.

'Right then,' he said, straightening himself up. 'Cyclone, you count us in.'

An hour passed in a moment, and Rosalie prepared to leave.

'As much as I'd like to stay, I really must go.'

Albert joined her at the front door. 'I'll see you home safely.'

Edward saw the way they looked at each other and his heart splintered.

Sitting on the porch staring up at the night sky later that night, Edward rolled his shoulders in an attempt to loosen the tension he'd been holding on to all day. The homecoming so long desired. The anticipation of seeing Rosalie. The realisation she had fallen for his brother.

Albert and Rosalie.

He threw his head back and let a silent groan out into the night. It was foolish of him, he supposed, to think there could have been a future with a woman he'd never even met; to fall in love with a photo and a few words. But he had.

And now he'd have to put them aside. All his life he'd wanted to protect Albert, to give him a better life. He knew he mustn't stand in the way of his brother's happiness. Even if it meant losing his own.

A piercing scream rang through the midnight silence.

'Mum?' Edward jumped up and burst inside.

He flung the door to her bedroom open, but she wasn't there. He heard a muffled shuffling from the room he shared with Albert. He burst in and froze, just for a moment, before launching himself forwards.

Albert had Penelope by the throat. Squeezing. Her eyes bulged.

Edward grabbed Albert's hands and tore them off his mother's neck, pushing his brother on to his bed. The eyes staring back at him were dark, wild. Albert wasn't in there.

Behind him, Penelope slumped to the floor, panting, gasping.

Albert was up and off the bed and coming towards Edward. Edward slapped him across the face. Hard.

Albert blinked, the rage leaving his eyes. He looked at Edward, then at Penelope, crumpling to the floor.

Penelope rose gingerly. 'It's okay. I'm fine.'

Edward held her back from her younger son.

Neither of them moved, the air around them thick with fear, and their senses on high alert. Eventually Albert's jagged breathing calmed.

'What did I do?' Albert pleaded with Edward.

'You were *choking* her.' Edward tried to make sense of what had just happened.

Albert shook his head. 'I couldn't . . . I wouldn't . . .'

Penelope pushed past Edward and took Albert into her arms. '*Shh*. It's okay. I'm all right. Everything will be okay.'

He collapsed against her chest and sobbed as she stroked his head.

She looked at Edward. 'Thank you. It's okay now.'

Edward knew she was dismissing him, but there was no way he was leaving the room. He stood and took a few steps back, leaning against the door, not taking his eyes off them.

Penelope soothed Albert until his shaking body stilled. 'There we are,' she whispered. 'Close your eyes. I'm here.'

'I'm sorry, Mum. I'm sorry.' He repeated the words over and over again.

Edward helped Penelope get Albert into bed, then he guided her out of the room and onto the porch. They sat on the old wicker loveseat and he waited.

Eventually, Penelope spoke, her voice quivering.

'He's been disturbed since he came home.'

Edward moved to stand up, his fist clenched, but Penelope put a firm hand on his leg and sat him back down.

'Never this bad. He's never done . . . that . . . before. But the nightmares, yes. And lashing out. He'll wake up screaming, sweating, confused. I think, in his mind, he is back there.'

Edward rubbed his hands together, not knowing what to say or do.

'He doesn't mean to hurt me, and sometimes he goes out in the evenings. He says goodnight to me and heads to bed, but I've got into the habit of checking on him in the middle of the night, and often he's not there. I think it's his way of protecting me. He's always back by dawn though. He thinks I don't know.'

Edward stood up, pacing back and forth. 'Combat fatigue?' It was the only explanation he could think of.

'It must be.' She wrung her hands together.

'I've heard stories of other men come back from war with demons. But Albie? Oh, Mum. Sweet, happy, gentle Albie.'

'I know, Edward. But sometimes the lights that shine the brightest are the ones trying to find their way out of the dark.'

He shook his head.

'It's hard. But he's still the brother you love. He's just . . . unwell. And we have to help him any way we can.'

Edward squared his shoulders and wrapped his mum in his arms. 'Of course we will. It will be okay, Mum.' Her body shook against him as she cried silent tears.

Thirty

On Monday morning, Sarah was itching to get to Melody's session, and she was dressed and ready an hour early, 'The Winner Takes It All' on repeat through her headphones. Every time Agnetha sang that lyric, that one perfectly formed word that had come out of Melody's mouth, she smiled. *Ice.*

She'd spent the weekend messaging Joshua – what did this mean, how long until they'd know if it was just a one-off anomaly, what did they do if it was, what should she be doing to capitalise on the moment? He answered each question patiently, reassuring her that whatever happened next, they could handle it. And she believed him.

Everyone else, though, that morning, stumbled out of bed like it was any other day.

Doubt crept in. What if it was just any other day?

Her phone pinged.

'Remember to breathe.' The message from Joshua made her smile.

*

Inside the therapy room, it *was* just like a normal day. Joshua playing his guitar, Melody accompanying him on the bongos. Twenty minutes. Nothing different. No sound from Melody.

The hope Sarah had brought into the day started to fade. That's what you got for breaking your own rules. Never hope. It's too dangerous.

With ten minutes to go of the session, Joshua leaned forward. 'Would you like to play a game, Melody?'

She nodded, eyeing him suspiciously.

'It's called fast-slow. But I have to warn you, I'm pretty good at it.'

She raised her chin in defiance.

'I want you to play a beat, and I'm going to say a word, and you have to play that word and its opposite. So, if I say fast, you have to play fast, then slow.'

Melody saluted. *Got it.*

'It can be any word as long as it's a describing word.'

She blew out her cheeks and sucked them in again, raising her eyebrows at him.

'Fat and thin?'

She nodded.

'Yep. Fat might be . . .' he strummed a few slow deep notes. 'And thin might be . . .' sharp, quick plucking higher up the scale.

She gave him a thumbs up.

'All right. We'll start with something easy.' He scratched his head. 'What about sad?'

Sarah could see the overly dramatic eyeroll Melody shot him from where she sat. With far too much ease, Melody beat out a sad rhythm then a happy one.

'Great job. What about . . . winter?'

Melody paused for a moment. Then she beat out something that sounded like thunder rumbling, followed by a light tapping. Summer.

'Wow. I thought that one might trip you up. But perhaps I underestimated you.'

She gave him her *well-duh* look.

'Hmm. Maybe I've met my match. When we come back this afternoon, let's try this again, and I'll see if I can't stump you.'

Melody held out her hand and Joshua shook it. Challenge accepted.

Sarah swallowed her disappointment deep down inside, and took Melody's hand as they left. 'That looked fun.'

Melody nodded.

'Do you think he's as good as he says he is?'

A strong shake of the head.

'Maybe we test him this afternoon.'

A cheeky grin.

Rain pelted down, soaking Sarah and Melody as they raced into the Stave for their afternoon session.

'Did you two go for a swim?' Joshua laughed when he saw them.

Melody's shoulder shook, but instead of her silent giggle a quiet titter escaped her lips.

Sarah looked at Joshua, and he subtly raised his eyebrows.

'I've got the heater on in the room – Pineapple is loving it – and there are some towels just inside the door. Shall we?' He bowed in front of Melody and she bowed back.

Once they had dried off a little and settled into their spots, Joshua started. 'Are you ready to be defeated?'

Melody glared at him, smiling, and shook her head.

'I've had my thinking cap on, and I don't reckon you'll get these. Let's start with . . . tall.'

Melody didn't even hesitate. With exaggerated arm movements, her hands reaching high above the bongos, she beat out a long, slow rhythm, then, with her fingers close to the drumhead, a short, fast beat.

'I'm impressed. What about . . .'

Melody raised her hand and Joshua stopped. She pointed at him.

'You have one for me?'

She nodded.

'Okay. What have you got?'

She pressed her finger to her temple. 'Hot,' she said, the actual word coming out of her mouth.

Sarah leaned forward; Joshua carried on as if it were no big deal.

'Hmmm. Hot and cold.' He picked up his guitar. After a pause that Sarah was fairly certain was solely for dramatic effect, he strummed out two tunes that seemed, indeed, the embodiment of hot and cold.

Melody clapped his effort.

'Thank you. Next?'

Melody looked at Sarah.

'Me?'

Melody nodded and pointed to the cello over against the far wall.

Sarah looked at Joshua, afraid to speak, afraid to move. He leaned into Melody. 'Maybe she knows she can't beat us.'

The tiny titter again.

'Oh. You two think I'm not up to the challenge?' Inspired by the courage her daughter had just shown, Sarah stood. If Melody could speak, even just one whispered word, surely she could play. Even just one note. She walked over to the cello across the room, flexing her left hand as she did. *Be brave. Just like Melody.*

She sat back down with the instrument, and positioned herself at the front of the chair. She lengthened her spine. With her heart racing she positioned the cello correctly. Her whole body flooded with emotion. She hadn't allowed herself to realise just how much she'd missed her old friend.

'What's your word for Mama then?' Joshua asked.

'Silly.' It was barely above a whisper, but it was the sweetest sound Sarah had ever heard.

Sarah plucked at the strings in the silliest way she could.

Melody giggled. Actually giggled. Out loud.

Then Sarah slowed her fingers and plucked out a few serious notes.

'Bravo.' Joshua clapped, and Melody turned to him and put her hands on her hips, an exaggerated frown adorning her face.

'Right. Yes. We don't want her to win,' Joshua said. 'I forgot. What about . . .' he beckoned Melody over and whispered in her ear. She leaned back and nodded, a rather scheming look in her eye. Then she moved closer to Sarah and whispered, 'Sweet.'

With slightly rusty fingers, Sarah moved her fingers up and down the fingerboard while she plucked out a high, light tune.

'Hmm,' she mused when she'd finished sweet. 'Sour?' How would she do sour? If she had a bow, it would be easy to draw it across the strings and make the instrument groan in just the right way. But she couldn't risk it. Wouldn't dare introduce a bow into the mix when everything was going so perfectly.

Melody spun back round to Joshua and whispered something in his ear.

'I'll be right back,' he said.

Moments later he returned with a bow in his hands. 'Will this do the trick?'

Melody nodded, but without the confidence she'd shown just moments ago.

Panic rippled through Sarah. No. This was too much. Too quick. Melody wasn't ready. *She* wasn't ready.

'Would you like Mama to use the bow?' Joshua knelt beside Melody.

She cast her eyes down and shrugged.

'It's up to you, Melody.'

She grabbed his spare hand and moved her head up and down very slowly.

'Okay then.' He handed the bow to Sarah.

Don't shake. Don't shake.

Sarah looked at Melody, still holding Joshua's hand, and smiled.

Don't stuff this up.

She raised the bow slowly and drew it across the strings. The cello groaned and she moved her fingers, changing chords, drawing another creak out of the instrument's belly. The sound she created was most definitely sour. She looked at Melody, who was sitting a little taller, her eyes fixed on Sarah.

Be brave.

She kept playing.

Melody's frown morphed into a smile and in her eyes there was a twinkle.

'Did your mama just win?' Joshua asked her.

She smiled, and nodded and clapped loudly. 'Yes,' she whispered.

Joshua hissed and made a fist. And Melody obliged with a sparkle-finger fist bump.

Later that evening the retreat put on a barbecue for all the residents in the clearing behind the Stave. Trestle tables were scattered about, with families chatting quietly and the staff cooking up a spread of sausages, kebabs and steaks, far too much for them to consume in one evening.

Sarah sat under the shade of one of the large gum trees, looking at Melody and Ryan playing with Vinny over by the tree line. Rosalie had her old camera and started taking photos of the gathering. Sarah leaned forward and watched her work, catching glimpses of the woman she must have been back in the day. Her grandmother was clearly very comfortable behind the lens and Sarah felt a wave of affection seeing Rosalie in her element.

Joshua, paper plate in hand laden with sausages and sauce, came and sat beside her. 'How are you feeling after today?' he asked.

Sarah wasn't sure how to answer that. 'Excited. Scared. A little overwhelmed, to be honest.'

'All perfectly valid, I'd say.' He tilted his head. 'Melody is such a great kid. You've done a great job with her.'

Sarah shrugged. 'Except for when I didn't.'

'I know I can't erase your guilt just by telling you not to feel guilty, but I hope over time you can maybe tuck it away somewhere and not let it take up too much space in here.' He tapped her on the side of her head. 'You are an amazing mum and I'm professionally qualified to judge that, so you have to believe me.'

Sarah let out a small laugh, and, to her shock, a few tears that had snuck up on her.

Joshua put his plate on the table behind him and wiped the tears from her cheek. Her skin tingled and flushed with warmth. 'Thank you.' She pushed the croaky words out.

'You're welcome.' He cleared his throat.

Smoke billowed from the barbecue and Katie screamed.

'I'd better go see if they need help.' He gave her two thumbs up and then looked mortified. 'Not again.' He slapped his forehead.

'Go save the day, Mr Cool,' Sarah laughed.

Ryan sidled up to her a few seconds after Joshua had gone to attend to the barbecue. 'What's that all about?' He pointed to Joshua.

'What? Nothing.'

Ryan shot her a look. 'Don't you lie to me, Sar-bear. I know you, and I haven't seen that pathetic look on your face for a very long time. Spill.'

'There's nothing to spill. He's my daughter's therapist. That would be weird and unethical. Not that there is a *that*.'

Standing up, Ryan wrapped his arms around her. 'Well, therapy won't last forever.' He ruffled her hair and ran off back to Melody. 'Just saying,' he called over his shoulder.

Thirty-one

It was a long time since Rosalie had used her old camera, and she had to admit it felt good. She was glad Sarah had it refurbished before they came out here. While all the modern gadgets and what-nots and phones masquerading as cameras were perfectly adequate devices, nothing was quite as satisfying as taking photos the old-fashioned way. At least not for her.

This old camera had certainly seen a lot of the best and worst life had to offer. So had Rosalie. She'd seen beauty in war zones through its lens, and the horror Mother Nature, in her glory, could inflict. And it always surprised her that one moment in time could be both happy and sad, exquisite and excruciating, light and dark.

Redgum River
November 1945

Rosalie stood on the church steps dressed in her finest pink chiffon dress, her hair in a perfect victory roll. She adjusted the collar of Penelope's ivory blouse.

'You look stunning.' Penelope wore a simple ensemble of a satin blouse and a soft pink skirt.

'You look perfect, Mum.' Edward stepped up beside them and kissed Penelope on the cheek. 'Shall we?' He bent his arm and Penelope linked hers in his. Edward pushed open the church doors and led Penelope down the aisle. Rosalie followed, holding a bouquet of peonies from Penelope's garden.

Waiting for them at the altar, Bernie beamed with joy, his brown suit a little threadbare at the seams. Beside him, Albert stood tall, his dimples deep. He smiled at Rosalie and her cheeks warmed. As she took her place as bridesmaid, she looked around the small congregation – Dot and Millie and their families, Mrs Donaldson, Neville, and some other friends and acquaintances from the village – small, but bursting with love. Iris attended the wedding, but Frank didn't return from Sydney for the event.

Rosalie was pleased that Iris had, on the surface, forgiven Bernie for her sister's demise, but it seemed the rift between Bernie and Frank was so great that not even an occasion such as a wedding could mend it. Did Bernie still blame Frank for the death of his wife and child? Did Frank still carry the burden of guilt?

Edward placed Penelope's hand in Bernie's and gave him a nod, standing beside Albert, his hand at his brother's elbow.

As the vows were exchanged, Rosalie looked at Albert, his smile broad but his eyes dark. The organ started up as the ceremony ended and Iris shot Rosalie a disapproving look. Rosalie chose to ignore her.

After the ceremony, they had a picnic at the rotunda. Albert on his banjo and Edward on his violin played song after song as everyone danced and ate and talked and hugged, with the orange sun setting over the river. Iris stood chatting quietly to some of the guests, her eyes never wandering off her daughter for long. Rosalie had managed to secure a glass of champagne and after just a few sips she felt a little giddy.

Bernie clinked his glass and the brothers stopped their music. 'Thank you, everyone, for sharing our special day with us.' He wrapped his arm tightly around Penelope's shoulders. 'We know that with you in our lives, we are beyond rich.' He raised his glass. 'To love and peace.'

'To love and peace,' everyone repeated.

As the evening darkened, the party wound up with people bidding each other goodnight.

'We should be going too,' Iris said to Rosalie, with a gentle tug on her elbow.

'Of course, Mother.'

Rosalie hugged Penelope and Bernie, tears of joy in her eyes. Edward embraced her quickly and Albert whispered in her ear as she said goodnight, 'Meet me in the grove later?'

For the last few weeks they'd seen each other every day, stealing moments alone when they could, but it was never enough.

Just after midnight Rosalie snuck out of her house and rode to the grove. She pushed her way under the trees to find Albert sitting on a blanket, waiting for her.

'I'm glad you came.' He stood up and spun Rosalie around.

She giggled and he put her down gently.

'It was a magical day.'

'Do you ever think, Rosalie . . . ever think about us . . . like that?' Concern etched across his face.

Rosalie's heart beat faster. Yes. She did. All the time. But she was scared to say so out loud.

'Because I do.' He cupped her face in his gentle hands. 'I know I'm not worthy of you yet, Rosalie . . .'

'Of course you are.'

He shook his head. 'No, I'm not. But I promise you I will be. I'll be the man you deserve. If you'll just give me some time . . .'

She nodded. 'Of course. I love you. And that's all that matters to me.'

He kissed her, softly and her hands moved behind his back and she pulled him closer. It was the encouragement he needed and the heat in his kiss intensified. His hands slipped under her shirt and she let him. Gently he laid her back on the blanket and held his body above her.

'I love you too, Rosalie.' Albert lowered himself and kissed her lips, her neck, her collar bone. Rosalie closed her eyes and surrendered to him.

Rosalie's skin burned at the memory. How could something that had happened so long ago still feel so real?

The weight of that night had sat heavily on her for more than seven decades now. The joy of it was the one memory that she'd held on to the tightest all this time. The one she didn't want to let go of. The one she couldn't make sense of.

In her room she tucked the camera safely away back in her old hatbox.

From the living space muffled conversations reached her as Sarah and Ryan tried to wrangle Melody into bed. They would all be okay. She felt that deep down inside. Ryan had told her of a half-formed plan he was concocting with Herman, and she thought it was a cracker of an idea. So much so, she may have even offered some assistance of the financial kind. After being miserable in his job for so long, and seeing him so relaxed now, she would do anything to help him hang on to his new lease on life.

Sarah and Melody would also be all right. Sarah didn't think anyone noticed her doing her hand exercises. But Rosalie did.

There was a spark of light there now for Sarah, where once there had only been dark.

And she was sure Melody would also thrive. Not that Rosalie had ever had any doubts about that. It was the right thing to bring her here, and for that alone it was worth the anguish Rosalie had felt since they arrived. The anguish she knew was still to come.

She pulled out the photo album and flicked through the pages for the umpteenth time since she'd been back in Redgum River.

It was time.

Edward and Albert being here may well have forced the issue, but deep down she already knew.

It was time to let it go. To tell Sarah the truth. The beauty of it. The pain of it. The whole of it.

Thirty-two

It took Melody a while to wind down after the barbecue – four chapters of *The Magic Faraway Tree*, a game of snap with Ryan, which had the opposite effect of calming her down, and three games of I-spy.

Once Melody was soundly asleep and Ryan was in bed reading, Sarah took a mug of hot chocolate out onto the porch and sat with her legs up on the railing, looking out to the stars and dark silhouettes of the gums, a blanket tucked around her, shielding her from the chilly night air.

'May I join you?' Rosalie came up beside her.

Sarah scooched over and made room for her grandmother under the blanket.

'It was fun seeing you with your camera today.' Sarah leaned into her, their arms touching.

'It was fun taking photos again with that thing. It's been a while.'

Sarah took a sip of her hot chocolate. 'Such a big part of your life once, Granny Rose.'

'It was.' Rosalie sighed. 'Would you like to hear a little about it?'

With her pulse thrumming, Sarah fought to offer a nonchalant response. 'Sure. If you'd like to tell me.'

For a second Rosalie closed her eyes and when she opened them again she spoke of growing up in Redgum River and of heading to university in Sydney. Of coming home. Story after story of the Snapshots, of meeting Henry, of Albert and Edward returning to Redgum River. Every minute detail as if all of it had happened only yesterday.

Sarah hung on every word, desperate to pepper her grandmother with questions, not daring to interrupt. Working at the *River Times*, the gala ball, how she covered those last months of the war. Every word a window into the life Rosalie had never spoken of before.

'After Bernie and Penelope's wedding, Albert started to become distant, cancel plans, ensure we were never alone. He often disappeared for a few days at a time,' Rosalie said. 'At first, I thought it was just his determination to make a go of his life. Make good his promise to be worthy of me. Not that I ever thought he wasn't. He started to travel to neighbouring towns, Thompson's Ridge, Wombat Hollow, looking for work, and he found some, always tired when he got home. He never said much about what he did, and if I tried to ask about what our future might look like together, he would evade the question with a joke or a kiss. He often did that. I suppose that should have been a . . . what would your generation call it? A red flag. But I was young. In love.'

Sarah smiled at the thought of a young swooning Rosalie.

'And I didn't want to admit that I knew in my gut there was something else going on. I just wasn't sure what.'

'Do you think he had another woman in one of those towns?'

Rosalie shook her head. 'Not once did I think that. But . . .' she paused, and Sarah studied her – anguish and hurt and confusion playing across the lined markers of time on her face.

'I did wonder if he'd lost interest in me after that night. You know, why buy the cow when the milk is free?'

Sarah spat out the sip of hot chocolate she'd just taken. 'Granny Rose!'

'What? We're both adults.' She shook her head. 'Anyway, about a month after the wedding, I realised something else.'

Redgum River
December 1945

The first Snapshots picnic after the wedding took place on a warm summer day and it was going to be their best one yet. Millie's Freddy had returned on the latest ship to bring men home, and Rosalie was looking forward to meeting him. Dot was bringing her George, and even Ralphy and his family were going to come over to Redgum River for it. Rosalie strapped the basket of food to her bike, threw her leg over the crossbar and headed off into the morning.

When she arrived at the giant river gum, everyone was already there. Everyone except Albert. Rosalie placed her basket on the blanket spread over the grass and Millie and Mrs Donaldson greeted her with a hug. The kids were down by the riverbank with their fathers, dancing to a lively tune Bernie and Edward were playing together.

Rosalie smiled at the sight, though her heart ached. Where was Albert?

Penelope stepped up beside her. 'Albert wanted to come, but he's off working.' She played with the strands of hair falling over her shoulder.

Rosalie frowned.

Bernie caught her eye and left Edward with the children.

'Morning, Rose-petal.'

'He's avoiding me, isn't he?' Shame washed over her. Not that anyone here knew what had happened that night of the wedding. But she did. How could she have been so stupid? Her mother's warning raced through her mind. *Don't be a fool and throw your life, your future away, for a fleeting infatuation.*

'No. It's not like that. Really.' Penelope's expression was deadly serious.

'Then what is it?'

Their silence confirmed her suspicion that Albert had lost interest in her. Used her and was now discarding her. A wave of nausea washed over her.

Edward came over. 'Are you all right? You look very pale.'

She nodded. 'I guess I'm more tired than I realised.'

'Come and sit down.' He directed her to the blanket. 'Can I get you something to eat? There are fresh passionfruit from Ralphy's place, or I can get you one of Mum's scones?'

Rosalie's stomach churned at the thought. 'Perhaps just some lemonade?'

He got up and poured Rosalie a glass, returning to her side. 'There you go. Millie says it's her best batch yet.'

It tasted a little strange to Rosalie, but she said nothing.

Tess brought Edward's violin over and plucked the strings before holding it out to him.

'Can you teach me?' she asked.

'Oh, Rosalie isn't feeling too well . . .'

'No. I'm fine,' she insisted. 'Please do.'

Within minutes, Edward had Tess playing a simple tune.

'You're a natural teacher.' Rosalie forced a smile.

'Might be my new calling.' He gave her a weak smile back.

*

In the early hours of the following morning, Rosalie leaned over the toilet bowl, emptying her stomach for the third time since waking up an hour ago. Her tummy hurt, her breasts were tender. She'd known the last few days, she supposed, if she were being honest with herself, but now there was no denying it. She must be pregnant.

Excitement and fear swirled around inside her as she tried to come to grips with the realisation that she was carrying Albert's child. They'd only spent that one night together. That one perfect night, now tainted by Albert's discard of her. That one perfect night now a part of her forever. Perhaps he would be happy and come back to her. All she had to do was tell him.

Frank heard her vomiting and came to check on her.

'It must have been the sausage I ate at the picnic – it didn't agree with me.'

He nodded perfunctorily. 'Okay. Drink some water and go back to bed. I have to make an urgent house call. Let your mother know when she gets up.'

By mid-morning Rosalie was feeling better, and she took a late breakfast with Iris, picking at her food. By the afternoon she was feeling up to riding to work, but just as she was about to leave, her father returned home, looking positively exhausted. 'Where is your mother?' he asked Rosalie curtly.

'In the garden.'

'Fetch her for me, please.'

Rosalie and Iris sat at the dining table with Frank opposite them. His words came slowly, gentler, now, than Rosalie had heard him for ages.

'Bernie's had a heart attack. I tried everything I could, but there was nothing I could do.'

Iris burst into tears and Rosalie stood. She had to get to Penelope. To Albert and Edward.

Frank rested a hand on her shoulder. 'Not yet, Rosalie. Penelope is too distraught. She has her son with her. Leave it for now.'

———

'I didn't notice at the time my father had said son, not sons.' Rosalie shook her head and Sarah leaned forward.

'The next morning, I rode over to Bernie's cabin.' Rosalie continued her story and Sarah hung on every word. 'I'll never forget the sight of poor Penelope. Her ashen skin, her eyes rimmed red.'

Rosalie's breathing shallowed. 'Edward took me outside and sat me down with a cup of tea, and that's when he told me.' She looked up and Sarah could see the agony in her eyes.

'He was gone. Albert had left.'

Sarah gasped. 'What? Where? Why?'

'All very good questions, my darling. I'm still asking them myself. Edward said Albert had headed off the morning before Bernie's heart attack, chasing a job opportunity.'

Sarah frowned. 'You didn't believe him?'

Rosalie shook her head. 'He said Albert had gone to work on a ship. But that didn't make sense. Albert didn't like boats. Not after his evacuation from Tarakan. But I also knew he was trying to find better work. Nothing quite added up. Parts of it did, but I really didn't think he'd leave without saying goodbye.'

'Oh, Granny Rose.' Sarah sighed. 'What did you do?' She couldn't imagine how terrified Rosalie must have been. So young. Single. Pregnant. Abandoned. In 1945.

'I wrote Albert a letter telling him about the baby and asked Edward to get it to him.'

'And?'

'And I never saw Albert again. Until now.'

Sarah put her mug down on the ground and embraced her grandmother, realising how frail she looked and sounded.

'If you don't mind, my darling, we'll leave it there. That was more tiring than I was expecting. I'll finish the story tomorrow.' Her voice was soft, broken.

'Of course.'

Sarah didn't want to leave it there at all. She desperately wanted to know what happened next. But the sorrow in Rosalie's eyes, complete and utter sorrow, stopped her from asking more.

Rosalie shuffled back inside, and Sarah let out a long breath.

Thirty-three

The next morning was grey and miserable. Rosalie could hear the rain falling on their cabin as she woke.

She had resolved to visit Albert at the nursing home again. It had been taxing telling Sarah so much last night, and there was much more to say – the hardest part of the story was yet to come. She needed to see Albert first, though. Not that he could answer any of the questions she had, questions she had been wanting to ask for so long. Being near him would have to do – a way to connect to the past, for Rosalie to imagine the conversation *could* be had, if only they both tried.

Sitting beside him, her fingers danced across the black and white keys of the piano. Well, danced might have been an embellishment – her old, gnarled digits weren't as agile as they used to be. But still, for an old duck very much out of practice, they weren't doing too badly.

Albert played as he'd always done – with elegance and ease, having lost none of his skill to the ravages of time. Every now and then he gazed at Rosalie, and his green eyes seemed so full of love it made her heart ache.

Oh, how much they'd missed.

Redgum River
December 1945

A week after Bernie's death, Rosalie padded through the hallway to answer a knock on the door.

A familiar deep voice sounded her name as she opened it.

'Henry? What are you doing here?' She stepped back and in the space between he came inside.

'I heard about Bernie.' He fiddled with the hat in his hands that he'd removed when entering the house. 'I'm sorry.'

'Thank you for coming.' It had been months since they had spoken. She couldn't believe he'd come.

'Of course. Your father let me know. I . . . I wouldn't be anywhere else right now.' He shifted back and forth on his feet.

His nervous caring undid her and the tears she'd been holding back burst through. With a gentle touch he wiped them away.

'How long do we have?' Rosalie asked. 'I have no idea of the time.'

'The funeral is in an hour.'

'I should probably make myself presentable, then.'

Henry ran his finger down her cheek and frowned. A gesture so comforting, so disconcerting. Her hand moved to her stomach.

'Have you eaten? You look like you need a good feed.'

She managed to laugh. 'Thank you. Every girl needs to hear that.'

He smiled and put his arm around her shoulder, leading her into the kitchen. 'What shall I make you?'

Frank and Iris were with Penelope. Betty had been given the day off. Rosalie was all alone this morning.

Henry pulled some eggs out of the fridge. Oh no. Not eggs. The mere thought made Rosalie nauseated. She'd managed to avoid

Betty's omelettes in the mornings by heading to work before she started preparing breakfast.

But it was too late now. As soon as they hit the pan, the smell had her running to the bathroom.

When she returned, Henry looked concerned.

'Stress,' she said. 'I haven't slept much lately.'

'I can imagine.' He looked at her intently then went back to the frying pan.

With his back to her she placed her hand on her stomach, sending a silent message to her unborn child to not do that again.

He turned around and she removed her hands. 'Would you like ham?' His gaze roamed over her but he said nothing. 'There's some in the fridge.'

'Thank you. That would be nice.'

She stared at the plate, pushing the food around without taking a bite, before excusing herself to go and get changed. On the way to her bedroom, she vomited once more.

Inside the church, the whole town had gathered in uneasy silence. Mrs Donaldson, Dot and Millie and their husbands sat together dressed in black, their crying eyes lowered. Penelope and Edward were in the front pew, Edward's arm protectively draped around his mother's shoulder. Penelope sat dead still, her posture perfect, her eyes looking straight ahead. Albert wasn't there.

With the heavy notes of Mozart's 'Ave Verum Corpus' playing from the organ, Henry escorted Rosalie to the second front pew, where Frank and Iris sat behind Penelope and Edward, and he held her hand gently during the service.

Outside, the sun shone brighter than it should have been allowed to on such an occasion, and Rosalie and her family offered condolences to Penelope as they filed out of the church.

In the church hall next door, the ladies of the CWA, led by Mrs Donaldson, had put on a spread for the wake. Rosalie just wanted to go home, but she knew she had to stay for her mother, for Penelope.

She hid herself in the corner, away from the egg sandwiches, and watched the gathering. Every now and then she looked at the door, hoping, expecting to see Albert walk in. Come home for her. For Bernie, for his mother. But he never appeared.

Eventually Edward made it through the throng to her.

'Did you get my letter to him?' she asked.

He nodded.

So, Albert had her letter, yet there'd been no quickly fired-off telegram in response. No phone call.

'You got word to him about Bernie?'

'He knows.'

'And he didn't . . .' She let the words hang between them.

'He couldn't.' Edward frowned slightly.

Rosalie was filled with momentary fury. Even if he wanted nothing to do with her and their baby, surely he would have come today to support Penelope?

She went outside, desperate for air. In the garden behind the church hall she retched into the flower bed.

'Whoa there.' Henry was beside her in an instant and caught her. 'Let's get you home.'

In silence they drove through the streets of Redgum River and when they pulled up outside Rosalie's house, Henry asked, 'Would you like some fresh air, or to go inside?'

'Air.'

Together they sat under the jacaranda tree. 'How are you?' he asked.

Numb? Scared? Sad? Angry? 'To be honest I'm not sure.'

'I don't doubt that. How far along are you?'

She stared at him. 'How did you . . . ?'

'This morning there was something I couldn't quite read in your eyes. Then you were sick when I made your eggs, and I noticed you holding your stomach a few times today. Am I right?'

'Oh Henry.' She dropped her head and covered her face with her hands. 'What am I going to do?'

'Albert wasn't at the funeral, I noticed. Does he know?'

She nodded.

'And you haven't heard from him?'

'No.'

'Look at me.' He took her hands and raised her chin, looking her in the eye. 'What would you do if he did come back, tomorrow or next week?'

That was a question she'd been asking herself a lot over the past few days. And it was only today that she knew the answer. Albert had been so cavalier with her, had let her down so completely, that even if he did return, she wasn't sure she'd want him back.

'I think maybe he's not the man I thought he was.' The words shattered her heart into a million pieces as she spoke them.

'Come back to Sydney with me.' Henry's words were gentle. 'Reggie saw the photos you took of the townsfolk after the bombing of Nagasaki, of their reactions when the war came to end. He was impressed. He's told me he'd offer you a job in a heartbeat.'

'How?' Rosalie shook her head. 'How did he see the photos?'

'I showed him. I get a copy of every edition of the *River Times* sent to me,' Henry said.

'Every copy?'

He nodded. 'Yes.'

'Even after I hurt you so?'

'Yes.'

'Henry, it was generous of you to show him.' Her head was trying to form coherent thoughts. 'But have you already forgotten my minor predicament? Once he finds out I'm single and pregnant, there's no way he'll employ me.'

Henry slipped off the bench and knelt before her.

'Then marry me.'

Rosalie sat back. 'What? Have you gone mad? Why would you want to marry a woman who's carrying another man's child?'

'Because I love you. It's as simple as that. This isn't how I ever imagined this happening, but I love you. Your happiness means everything to me. I hope, over time, the friendship you feel for me will grow into something more. But I want to look after you. No matter what.'

Rosalie couldn't believe the words coming out of his mouth, and yet she knew them to be true. She knew, without any shadow of doubt, that Henry would love her, that he would care for her, protect her, that he would be by her side. Always.

She cast her eyes down. 'Henry Burton, I don't deserve you.'

Henry lifted her chin and smiled. 'Well, lucky for me, that's not how love works.' He placed a hand on his chest. 'It simply exists. In here. No rhyme or reason.'

Rosalie looked into his eyes.

'Yes,' she whispered.

Rosalie let the memory fade and focused on Albert's tune. He continued to play while the choir packed up and she basked in the moment for a little longer. When he stopped playing she took his hands.

'Why did you never come back?' she asked him. 'To me? To our baby? Why?'

He raised his hand and brushed a stray strand of hair from her cheek. His touch soft, full of love, just as she always remembered it.

'My Rosalie. Tonight. The grove.'

She held back her tears. He was trapped in a moment in time, and she couldn't escape the memory of it.

All that might have been. All that was instead.

Thirty-four

Rain fell as if it was never going to end. Sarah and Melody had finished their morning session with Joshua, and Melody was off with Ryan on a lunch date. With Rosalie gone to visit Albert at the nursing home, Sarah took the chance to practise the cello Phoebe had loaned her over the weekend. She was getting better, slowly, her left hand more agile every day, and she allowed buried hope to surface. Imagining for the first time since the accident a future for her and Melody, filled with music and laughter, and words spoken.

'You play very well.' Edward's voice startled her. He stood on the porch, his umbrella dripping water.

'Hello, Edward, to what do I owe this visit?'

'Well . . . May I sit?'

'Yes. Please.'

He sat next to her on the porch.

'Rosalie told me about your work with the museum and how you want to use her photos for an exhibit.'

'That's right.'

'I think that's rather swell.' He rubbed his chin. 'She was an extraordinary woman, your grandmother, and she did some extraordinary work. Even before she became a big shot journalist with *Life*.'

He pulled a scrapbook out of his bag. Inside were faded, yellowed articles from the *River Times* from 1945, all written by Rosalie. The glue that had held them in place had lost its stick in most places and many were loose between the pages.

'This is amazing.'

'Maybe the stories she filed about the local community during the war could be of interest to the museum. Or to you.'

Other than the one uploaded on the net, Sarah had never seen these early examples of Rosalie's work. 'Yes. To both.' She nodded emphatically. Originally, she and Herman had discussed using the Snapshot photos as a small exhibit to highlight this little-known part of the war. But with these articles, the scope was even broader. Together they painted a vivid picture of small-town life at the time and how a rural community coped with the war. 'This is wonderful, Edward. Would you mind if I took copies of these?'

'You can have them.'

'Oh no, I couldn't . . .' She tried to hand him back the scrapbook, but he refused to take it. 'My mother sent me these while Albert and I were serving, but they belong with you. They're a part of Rosalie.'

Sarah hugged the scrapbook to her chest. 'Thank you.'

'You're welcome.' He paused. 'I have . . . something else for you. They go somewhat with the Snapshot photos in Rosalie's albums, but . . . well, they're a little more personal. You won't be able to use all of them, but some might help flesh out the story, so to speak. Give insight into just what receiving the photos from home meant to us on the frontline.'

He pulled a small box out of his bag and handed it to Sarah. She opened the lid. Inside were letters from Rosalie to Edward.

Some of them stamped with the YMCA insignia, some of them with Rosalie's initials embossed on faded pink paper.

She looked up, the penny finally dropping. 'Edward, was something going on between you and Rosalie?'

'No.' He shook his head, then there was a long silence. 'I was in love with her,' he finally said. 'But she wasn't in love with me.'

Sarah tried to stay calm. Was this the missing piece of the puzzle Rosalie had yet to share?

'Have a look through these letters and anything you think you can use for the exhibit, please do take a copy of. You're here for another week, aren't you?'

Sarah stared at him.

'Don't worry.' The corners of his mouth turned up. 'There's nothing scandalous in there. As I said, she wasn't in love with me. But, as you can imagine, she wrote a bloody good letter, news from home, kind words of hope, that sort of thing. As I said, something to round out the story.'

'Oh Edward, you don't know what this means. To me. To the museum. Thank you for being so generous.' Even without opening a single letter, Sarah knew the exhibit would now be one that would garner great interest. The personal stories always did. Had he just handed her the key to saving the Forgotten Pasts Museum?

Rosalie returned to the cabin just before lunchtime.

'What have you got there?' She pointed to the box in Sarah's lap.

'Edward gave this to me. You just missed him. They're letters you wrote him during the war. He thought some of them might be good for the museum. I've been reading them.'

Rosalie sat down beside her. Sarah didn't dare look at her.

'He kept them?' Rosalie said. 'All these years?'

'Yes. They clearly meant a lot to him. Granny Rose, did you know he was in love with you?'

Another silence. Then Rosalie nodded.

'What happened, after Bernie's death?'

'Oh, my darling. I was scared. Alone. And Henry came back.'

Sarah listened intently as Rosalie told her of the proposal, everything she thought she knew about her grandparents' life together dissolving.

'Did you ever love Grandpa?' she asked.

Rosalie nodded. 'I grew to love him dearly. He was a bosom and loyal friend. From the very beginning until he left me too soon. Such a good man and so good to me. Far better than I deserved. And he was a wonderful father to your mother, Sarah.'

'But he wasn't the love of your life?'

'I'm not sure there's really such a thing. I loved Henry. I loved Albert in a different way. And I was very fond of Edward. I think someone can have many loves of their life.'

Sarah let the words sit there between them for a moment. *Albert* was her biological grandfather. He'd abandoned Rosalie and she'd kept this a secret all these years.

'Well, Granny Rose, I have to say, you've surprised me.'

'Good. It doesn't do to get too comfortable in this world. You know, people always say you're like me, but really, you're a lot like him.'

'I am?'

'Yes. And I don't just mean the musical talent. You have always reminded me so much of him, in every way.'

'How?'

'Your smile for starters. And that look you get in your eyes sometimes. Many times over the years when I've looked at you, I swear I've been looking at him.'

'Did you ever try to find out why Albert didn't want to know his child? That must have been terrible for you.'

Rosalie shook her head. 'I didn't want to know. Henry and I were happy. We made a family. Albert made his choice and I made mine. Certainly, it was painful. As you know, I never came back here.' She let out a long, deep breath. 'After I left, Mother and Father moved to Sydney. Frank was given his promotion at the hospital, and they were triumphantly happy I had finally chosen the "right" man. They were thrilled to be close to their grand-daughter when she was born. There was no reason for me to come back. Bernie was gone and I feared Penelope would realise the truth about my baby. And the rest . . . It was all far too painful to go back to.'

Sarah knew she would have more questions later. Knew that she would be turning over all of this new information in her mind for a very long time.

'Thank you, Granny Rose, for sharing this with me.'

'I have to say, it does feel better now it's all out in the open.'

'What do you say we head over to the Stave? I think there's hot chocolate on offer.'

Rosalie nodded. 'Fabulous idea.'

The rain had stopped, but a deep, damp cold had settled over the valley. The retreat guests had gathered in the Stave for some much-needed hot chocolate along with the afternoon tea on offer. Ryan and Melody were back, and Sarah and Rosalie joined the crowd.

In the foyer of the Stave, a soft murmur floated on the air as people talked, and in the corner where Joshua had laid out a number of instruments, Melody and three other children – ranging in age from six to thirteen – were beating, strumming and blowing in complete disharmony.

In the corner of the room, Sarah spotted Edward. He strode towards her and Rosalie.

'Thank you for giving Sarah the articles,' Rosalie said. 'I never kept any of them.'

'My pleasure. I suppose you two have had a lot to talk about.'

Sarah smiled. 'We have just had a long chat, actually.'

Edward looked to Rosalie. 'What did you tell her?'

'Everything.' Rosalie shrugged.

Pain danced across Edward's face. 'Not . . . everything.' He shook his head.

'What do you mean?' Sarah shot Rosalie a look, but she appeared as confused as Sarah.

Edward looked around. 'Let's find somewhere where we can talk privately.'

He led them into one of the therapy rooms and there he started to pace back and forth, wringing his sun-spotted hands in front of his chest. Then he stopped dead and looked at Rosalie directly. 'I never thought I'd see you again, Rosalie, yet here you are and truths have been laid bare. But not all the truths. I've carried another with me for so long. And now you're here, it's time I laid it down. I hope you can forgive me.' Edward looked tortured, almost close to tears.

Sarah watched Rosalie for any reaction, but her grandmother stood tall and straight, no emotions showing.

'I think you should sit. Maybe *I* should sit.'

'Edward Dawson.' Rosalie's voice was firm. 'Stop faffing about and get to it. Neither one of us is getting younger.'

Edward nodded and he stood perfectly still. 'When Albie returned from the Pacific, he brought with him some demons. Shellshock, they used to call it. Or combat fatigue in our day. Now we'd call it PTSD. I believe today he would be diagnosed with intrusive memories. But back then we didn't have names for such things.

'He'd have these god-awful nightmares. And he'd lash out.'

Sarah could see the colour draining from Rosalie's face and she moved closer to her.

'What happened, Edward?' Rosalie's voice was soft and measured.

'He'd been violent a few times, but after Mum and Bernie's wedding, it seemed to get worse. He'd lose control. Then feel dreadful shame. I think he was terrified these episodes would happen with you, too, while you were with him. He started distancing himself from you, to protect you. He didn't want to hurt you.'

Rosalie made a strange sort of squeaking sound. 'He'd never hurt me.' She took a step forward.

'He hurt Mum, more than once. When she married Bernie and moved in with him, I thought she was safe.'

Rosalie began to shake. 'What are you saying?'

Sarah wanted to stop the conversation. There was no way this was going to end well, no matter which way it went. But she couldn't. She had to know. Rosalie had to know.

Thirty-five

Redgum River
December 1945

A month after the wedding, some of Penelope's belongings still needed to be moved from her old worker's cottage into Bernie's cabin. Early one Friday morning Bernie and Penelope arrived to get the last load – Penelope's gardening equipment.

'Hello, you two love birds,' Edward called from the porch as they approached. 'How's married life?'

'Perfectly blissful,' Penelope answered with her sweet smile that always melted Edward's heart.

'How are things here?' Bernie asked pointedly.

'He's had another bad night.' Edward said.

'I'll go check on him.' Penelope stepped forward.

'He's very agitated, Mum,' Edward warned her, and she dismissed him with a wave of her hand.

Bernie and Edward got started on packing up Penelope's shovels and the hoe and random pots she always seemed to have, when there was a high-pitched scream from inside the cottage.

Edward ran towards the door, but Bernie was faster.

Inside, Penelope was sprawled on the floor. Bernie was tackling Albert as he thrashed about, punching, kicking.

Edward leaped across the room and separated them, heaving his brother away from Bernie.

'Albie. Look at me! Come back to me.' Edward tried to keep his voice calm.

Behind him, Bernie groaned, his face red, sweat pouring from him.

Edward turned around to see him struggling for air, his right hand clutching his left arm. Penelope screamed.

Oh, god, no.

Edward stared at Frank Reynolds across the kitchen table. Edward hadn't known who else to call but by the time Frank had got there, it was too late. Bernie could not be revived, and Penelope was so hysterical that Frank had sedated her and told Edward to put her to bed. On the floor in the corner of the kitchen Albert rocked back and forth.

Frank quickly arranged for the undertaker in Thompson's Ridge to take care of Bernie's body.

Now they had to decide what to do with Albert.

Frank's expression was hard. 'I should have you locked up for this.' The doctor looked down on Albert, whose sobs were subsiding.

Edward stepped forward. 'He's sick, Dr Reynolds. Isn't there something we can do to help him?' How could sweet gentle Albert have done this? How could his baby brother have been so violent? Edward's whole body was suffused by panic. *Oh god, Bernie.*

Frank was pacing, muttering to himself. Finally, he shook his head. 'I don't know. There are some newfangled treatment ideas out of the States around this . . .' he waved his hands in the air, '. . . combat trauma idea.' He stopped pacing.

'Please,' Edward begged. He had to help his brother.

Albert looked up at him, unbridled fear in his eyes, his knuckles turning white with the grip he had around his legs, which he'd pulled into his chest.

Frank rubbed his chin. 'It *was* a heart attack. It may have been brought on by the stress of the event, but it was, at the end of the day, a heart attack. That's what will be in my medical report. So, I suppose . . .'

Edward stepped forward.

'There is a hospital,' Frank continued. 'In Victoria. Heidelberg. I think they deal with cases like this. I could put in a call.'

'No!' Albert called out. 'You can't send me away.'

Frank stood over him and pulled himself to his full height. 'You're in no position to make demands, young man. If it weren't for my daughter's fondness of you, and what it would do to her if she knew what you did here, we would be having a very different conversation. To think she's spent so much time with you. What could have happened to her . . .'

Frank turned his back and headed to the phone in the living room.

'Eddy, Eddy, please. Don't let him send me away.' Albert stood on shaking legs. 'I can't leave Rosalie.'

Edward grabbed Albert's shoulders and pushed him against the wall, anger coursing through him at the mention of her name. 'Don't you see? Don't you see that she is the reason you have to go? Do you realise what you've done? You've killed her uncle. Maybe next time it will be her.'

Albert shook his head wildly. 'But I'd never . . .'

'How could you trust yourself around her now? Gentle, beautiful, gifted Rosalie, who is nothing but love. Do you really want to put her in danger?'

'No, no, no.' Albert's words tumbled into each other.

'And what about Mum?' Edward had to make him see this was for the best.

As Albert sobbed, Edward sighed heavily and softened his voice. 'I don't see that we have any other choice, cyclone.'

Slowly, his brother's eyes focused and he nodded. Just the once.

An hour later, they stood outside as Walter pulled the car up.

'I don't want to go.' Albert's eyes brimmed with shame and guilt.

'You have to,' Frank snapped. 'It will be better for everyone.' He opened the door.

Albert turned to Edward. 'What will she think of me? Going off to a loony farm?'

'It's not a loony farm. It's a medical facility.'

'It's a loony farm.'

Edward couldn't help but grimace at Albert's sardonic tone. 'We'll tell her you've gone off for work. She never needs to know about what happened today. Or any of your other . . . episodes.'

Tears ran down Albert's cheeks. 'What if they can't fix me?'

'We have to have faith they will.' Edward put his hands on Albert's shoulders. 'I'll go wake Mum so she can say goodbye.'

'No. I don't want her to see this.' Albert's voice dripped with disgrace. 'Just promise me you'll look after her.'

Edward nodded. 'Of course. I'll move in with her.'

'And Rosalie?'

'I'll take care of it.'

'Make sure you tell her that I didn't want to go. But I had to. And that I'll write as soon as I get the chance.'

'I will.'

'Tell her . . . tell her I've gone to make my fortune so I can give her the life she deserves. And that I'll be back for her when I can.'

Edward watched the car take his brother away.

*

Rosalie came by the following morning and it broke Edward's heart to tell her Albert had gone. She hadn't understood. How could she? But it was for the best. He told himself that over and over again.

In the evening light Edward opened the letter she had given him to pass on to Albert. He read it. Folded it back up. He got up and walked into the kitchen, lit the stove and burned it, watching it until it was nothing but ash.

Rosalie was perfectly still as Edward finished his story, but Sarah's hands were shaking.

'You have to know, Rosalie, that's all any of us wanted – to protect you. I needed to protect you and your baby.'

'How could you?' The words whispered slowly. 'Play with my future?' A little louder. 'With Albert's?' Louder still. 'With our daughter's?' The words exploded from her mouth.

Tears ran down Edward's cheeks. 'To keep you safe.'

'Did you ever tell him? About the baby?'

He shook his head. 'It was two years before he came home. The drugs, the shock therapy; Heidelberg possibly made him worse. He was never stable again. Never safe. I looked after him as best I could, but I couldn't tell him, Rosalie. I could never tell how he'd react. I had to protect you and your baby.'

'That wasn't your decision to make.' Her words soft once more. 'I'd like you to leave now.'

'But . . .'

She shot him a look of pure anger.

Edward left the room, his shoulders slumped, his head low as he headed into the foyer.

Sarah rubbed her grandmother's back. 'Are you okay, Granny Rose?' she asked tentatively.

'No. I should think not.' Her whole body began to shake and Sarah guided her to the closest arm chair.

'I never knew he was ill.' Her voice was a distant echo. 'And he never knew about our baby. All these years I thought he didn't want me. Didn't want us. But he never knew.'

Sarah patted her knee, a futile attempt to make her feel better.

'He was sick.' Rosalie shook her head. 'It wasn't his fault. Bernie's death wasn't his fault.'

'I'm not sure anyone's to blame here, except circumstance. And those times. That terrible war.' Sarah whispered croakily.

'I need a few minutes.' Rosalie looked at Sarah with watery eyes.

Sarah nodded. 'I'll get you some tea.'

Thirty-six

Voices rose in the foyer as Sarah walked in, a hint of agitation in the higher than usual lilts.

'What's happening?' she asked Joshua.

'The river.' He shook his head. 'All this rain. The run-off from up north. The south bank has burst. I'm going to have to let everyone know.'

A ripple went through the gathered guests as he cleared his throat and spoke above the din. 'Thanks, everyone,' he said, raising his hands in the air to get their attention. Gradually the hubbub died down. 'As some of you have heard by now, the river is flooding. It seems that the south of town is under threat from the rising waters, but we're fine here. We're quite high up and are in no danger.'

A few sighs and murmurs.

'As I say, the south part of town isn't so lucky. They're sandbagging, but it's coming up fast and they need help. I'm going to go lend a hand, and I could do with an extra body or two.'

Ryan stepped forward, and some other guests.

'Thanks, all of you,' Joshua said. 'Let's nip this in the bud before it becomes a problem.'

Sarah fell into step behind them as the group hurried towards the door. 'Are you sure it's safe?'

Joshua nodded. 'Every couple of years this happens. It never gets past the bakery. They just need a few more bodies on the ground to make easier work of it.'

Sarah looked between Joshua and her cousin.

'Really,' Joshua assured her. 'We'll be fine, and you guys are perfectly safe here.' He squeezed her arm and when he let go, she felt its absence keenly.

'Be careful.' She threw her arms around Ryan.

After the volunteers left, most of the guests stayed in the Stave chatting quietly, no one wanting to head back to their cabins. Sarah sat in silence with Melody, who was playing a quiet tune on the bongos. She saw Edward hovering at the edge of the group looking drained, watching on quietly. She couldn't bring herself to talk to him – she had enough to process right now.

Phoebe came running over to them a few moments later, a mobile phone outstretched in her hands. 'It's for you, Eddy.' She handed him the phone.

Edward took it and listened intently to whoever was on the other end. He walked over to Sarah. 'Yes. Right. No,' he was saying. 'I don't know. I'll . . . figure something out. Will call you back.' He hung up and handed the mobile back to Phoebe, who'd followed behind him.

'What's wrong?' Sarah asked.

'That was the nursing home. It would appear Albert has taken himself on an unauthorised excursion.'

'He's what?' Sarah's voice was louder than she'd meant it to be. Beside her, Melody stopped playing her bongos. 'Where?' Sarah lowered her voice.

'That's why they've rung. They can't find him.'

'Well, he can't have gone far.' She shook her head.

'No,' said Edward. 'Unless . . .' His eyes widened.

'What?'

'Oh no.' He closed his eyes.

'What! Edward, I need you to tell me what you think has happened.'

'All week, Albert's been mumbling about the grove.'

'Rosalie and Albert's grove?' Sarah asked.

'Yes.'

'You think he could be there?'

Edward nodded. 'And it's right by the river.'

'Oh shit.' Sarah stared at him, unable to move.

'We need to get there. Now,' Edward said, sounding panicked. 'Do you have a car? It'll be much quicker. I can show you the way.'

'Ryan's van is out the front. But . . .'

Edward grabbed her hand. 'Then let's go.'

'If the grove is already flooded, what good will us getting stuck there do?'

He shook his head. 'It won't be flooded. It's on a rise. But with all the rain we've had lately, the path there is slippery.'

'What's slippery?' Rosalie's voice cut through.

'Oh, Granny Rose.' Sarah hugged her.

'What's going on?'

'We had a call from the nursing home. Albert is missing.'

'What?'

Sarah filled her in.

The phone Phoebe was carrying rang again. 'Oh god,' she said when she'd hung up. 'They've realised there's a scooter missing.'

All eyes fell on Rosalie. 'No. He wouldn't have . . . He told me to meet him, but it was just a fragment of something from the past. He didn't know what he was saying, surely?' She looked at Edward, fear in her eyes. 'You don't think he *actually* went there?'

'I do. This is the first time he's spoken in a while. Because you're here. Back before we lost him to the dementia, he was stuck in the past. I *know* that's where he's gone.'

'But he's in no state to drive a scooter. And with all this rain.' Rosalie grabbed Sarah's hands and gripped them tightly. 'You have to go find him. Bring him back. Sarah. You have to.'

'I can't . . . you know . . .'

Melody took her hand. 'You can,' she whispered.

'I'll come with you, Sarah,' Phoebe offered. 'I don't have my licence, but maybe I can be of help if he's confused. We can do this together.'

'Yes. Take Phoebe,' Rosalie pleaded. 'Bring him back.'

Sarah looked around the room. She could feel Melody squeezing her hand. She lowered her eyes and looked at her daughter.

'Go,' Melody whispered.

Sitting in the driver's seat of Gertie, Edward next to her, Sarah counted her breathing in and out. *You can do this, one, two. You can do this, three, four.* She turned the ignition and got into reverse, then she pulled ever so slowly out of the car park, her hands shaking, her heart racing.

'Are you okay?' Phoebe asked from the back seat.

'Well, no, actually. But we don't have time to worry about that, do we?'

'Probably not.'

Sarah appreciated the woman's honesty.

'I feel like I need to give full disclosure to you both before we go any further.' Sarah slammed on the brakes and the van jolted forward. 'The accident we had last year, the one that injured Melody: I was driving. I haven't been able to drive since.'

There. She'd said it.

Edward checked his seatbelt. 'Right. Well, thank you for the information. I'm good to go.'

In the rear-view mirror, Sarah could see Phoebe nodding. 'Me too.'

'Okay. Let's go, then.' Thank goodness they couldn't see how fast her heart was beating.

Following Edward's instructions, Sarah manoeuvred the van through the back streets of Redgum River, heading north out of town until they came to a clearing. She slowed the van right down and peered out the window but the rain was getting heavier, making visibility poor. 'I don't see him.'

Edward shook his head. 'It's a little further up. I know the road has ended, but this clearing goes for a bit before we come to the hill. Maybe we could get closer.'

It might have been a while since Sarah had driven, but she still knew Gertie's – and her – limits. And she knew how heavy the rain had been lately. 'No. I think we'll stop here. That ground's going to be very soft and I don't want to get us bogged.'

'Good point,' Phoebe said from behind. 'We'll have to go on foot from here. Can you manage, Edward? We'll help you along.'

He simply nodded.

They piled out of the van, driving rain hitting their faces. *Poor Albert, was he really out here on his own?* Sarah's stomach was tight, her head pounding.

Edward took the lead, with Phoebe and Sarah flanking him in case he lost his footing. He was far too old to be doing this safely, but Sarah knew there was no stopping him from getting to his brother.

Slipping and sliding more frequently than any of them were comfortable with, they came across the scooter, abandoned in the mud.

Edward pointed. 'Up there.'

Sarah wasn't sure where 'there' was. All she could see in front of her were trees. They took a couple more steps forward, and then she saw it. A gap.

All three of them stumbled forward, and a few metres on, standing perfectly still at the edge of what was a clearing surrounded by a circle of gums, was Albert, his hands pressed against the trunk of a large tree.

Phoebe stepped forward. 'Albert?' she said gently. He didn't move. 'It's me, Phoebe. We've come to take you home.'

Albert shook his head.

Edward followed Phoebe and put his arm around Albert's shoulder. 'She's back at home, cyclone, waiting for you.'

Albert turned, looked at Edward, and nodded. They started walking but after a few metres Albert faltered on the slippery ground. Sarah jumped forward and helped Edward steady him. The tree he had been leaning on was engraved with jagged letters. R.R. and A.D. inside a heart.

Edward took most of Albert's weight as they left the clearing and headed back down the path. Then, without warning, Albert twisted, turned, broke free from their hold and staggered down the slope to the river.

Just at its edge, he slipped and fell on his back.

'Albert!' screamed Edward, and he flung himself after him, careening down the steep decline. As he reached his brother, he grabbed him and pushed him away from the edge. Then, he teetered for a moment, looked up with wide eyes, and in an instant he was in the water as the ground beneath him slipped away.

Thirty-seven

Sitting in one of the lounges in the middle of the foyer, Rosalie couldn't take her eyes off the door to the Stave. Why had they been gone so long? Had they not found Albert? Had Sarah crashed the van? Oh, she shouldn't have let her drive.

Melody put something in her lap and she looked down. A ukulele. 'Play?' her great-granddaughter whispered.

It was the last thing Rosalie wanted to do at the moment, but she couldn't very well explain that to Melody. The poor child was probably just as worried as she was. Perhaps even reliving her accident. Yes. Good point. She'd better help keep her distracted.

Rosalie started playing the ukulele – 'Somewhere Over the Rainbow', the medley version by Hawaiian musician IZ – and Melody looked at her in shock.

Rosalie leaned in to her great-grandbaby. 'Yes, your granny can play.' She winked.

Melody picked up the bongos and after listening to just one more bar, she joined in with a beat that complemented the tune perfectly.

The people around them began to sway and hum. Someone at the back of the room started to sing. Rosalie couldn't remember the lyrics, but her talents were never her singing voice anyway. As they came to the last verse the whole room was in concert – some people singing, some humming, others had picked up instruments, others simply moving in time.

The sliding doors opened as the last note played and Rosalie looked up. Soaking wet, Sarah stood in the doorway, Joshua's arm around her waist. Was he holding her up? Had she gone to help him at the sandbagging? Where was Albert? Edward?

Ryan walked in behind them, looking thoroughly exhausted, and Phoebe then slipped into the foyer, her face ashen.

Melody raced forwards and threw her arms around Sarah's legs. Sarah crumbled into her embrace. 'Hey, minim.' She brushed the girl's hair from her forehead. Melody mimicked her mother's action, pushing Sarah's wet strands aside.

Rosalie could see Sarah's brave veneer shatter at the touch, tears falling down her cheeks. No. No. Rosalie simply wouldn't have it.

Sarah said something to Melody and made her way over to Rosalie.

'Albert is fine,' Sarah began. 'He's in the hospital, just to be safe. He was out in that wind and rain for a while.'

Rosalie exhaled. Well, that was a nasty thing to do, scare her like that. That explained where Edward was too, then. Always looking out for his little brother, no doubt by his bedside now.

Then why was Sarah crying?

'Granny Rose.' Sarah took her hands, but Rosalie snatched them back. Nothing good ever happened when someone took your hands like that. 'Granny. Albert slipped. On the path. There was so much mud. Edward went after him. But . . .'

No. No buts. Rosalie wouldn't have a but.

She turned her back on her granddaughter. She couldn't *but* her if her back was turned.

Sarah moved and stood in front of her.

No. No.

'Granny Rose. Edward . . . fell. Into the river. He . . .'

The room went black. Silent.

Rosalie could hear light murmurs beside her, but she refused to open her eyes. Opening her eyes would make it real. And it couldn't be real. It had to be a dream. Some horrible, cruel dream.

Except she knew it wasn't.

And lying here wouldn't change that.

'Hey, Granny Rose,' Sarah said as she opened her eyes. 'You gave us such a scare. How are you feeling?'

'Is it still real? Is Edward gone?'

Sarah nodded.

'Then I'd rather not say how I feel. Does Albert know?'

'He's been told, but I don't think he understands.'

If there were any infinitesimal blessing in any of this horrible situation, that was it. Albert would be spared that pain, at least.

Not that any of this was fair. Not what had happened in the past. Not today. None of it.

The truth was now out, all their secrets revealed, but for what? It didn't change anything. All these years were still wasted. Albert was still lost. And now Edward was dead.

Rosalie would never be able to tell him she'd forgiven him. And she had. The moment he'd left the room.

Because when everything else was lost, what else did anyone have but forgiveness?

Thirty-eight

Edward's funeral was held the following Wednesday.

The Vital Voices choir sang beautifully, Albert leading them perfectly on the piano. Many of Edward's former students came and they formed an ensemble, led by Joshua, and played a piece Edward had composed sometime in his fifties. As they finished, Sarah looked over to Albert, and she saw a tear fall down his cheek.

The next day after breakfast, Ryan and Sarah sat on the porch of their cabin, each with a steaming hot cup of tea in their hands. Rosalie was still asleep; Melody was at her session with Joshua – without Sarah there. Only three more until their time at the retreat was over. She was still only whispering the odd word or two here and there, but Sarah was content with that. For now.

Katie strode towards the cabin, her pink ponytail swinging behind her, a grey-haired woman in a suit beside her.

'Morning, Sarah, Ryan,' she said.

'Hey, Katie.' Sarah smiled.

'This,' Katie indicated the woman with her, 'is Ms Christine Sturdy. She's Edward's lawyer. She's keen to speak to you.'

The lawyer sat at the table and pulled out a file.

'I wanted to talk to you about Mr Edward Dawson's will. I'm not sure whether you know this, but you are his sole beneficiary, Ms Blakely.'

'What?' Sarah frowned. 'I'm sorry, I don't think that can be right. Edward, Mr Dawson, only met me a couple of weeks ago.'

Ms Sturdy shook her head. 'I've been Mr Dawson's attorney for quite a while and I can assure you there is no mistake.'

Sarah sat frozen, confused.

'Maybe this will help explain the matter to you.' She handed Sarah a letter. 'Mr Dawson wrote this two years ago, after he'd had a health scare.'

'Well, open it!' Ryan nudged her.

'Give me a second.' She tore open the envelope and unfolded the thick paper. Penned in terribly neat script was a note from Edward.

'Out loud.' Ryan nudged her again and she swatted him away.

> Dear Sarah,
> We are yet to meet, and perhaps we never will. My name is Edward Dawson and I'm the owner of the Redgum River Retreat. I knew your grandmother, Rosalie, when we were both much younger. She was a very good friend of mine and my brother, Albert.
>
> Neither Albert nor I have been blessed to be called father . . .

Sarah stumbled over the choice of wording.

> . . . and I find myself in a position, as my years advance, to contemplate my own mortality and what legacy I'd like to leave behind. And to whom.

While I did not keep in contact with Rosalie, I watched her career from afar. And every now and then I checked in on her and her family. On your mother, Lynne, and your father. On you. A talented family of musicians indeed.

The pieces of puzzle were now coming into sharp focus.

Your grandmother and I parted with much unsaid, unresolved, and I'm sorry to say that my actions years ago altered the course of her life significantly. It is a guilt I have always carried. And I'd like to make up for it somehow. To that end, I have decided to leave you, Sarah Blakely, the Redgum River Retreat in my last will and testament.

Yours truly,
Edward

'Well, bugger me.' Ryan blew out a whistle.

Ms Sturdy cleared her throat. 'Shall we continue?'

'Sorry. Yes,' Sarah stuttered.

When Edward's solicitor left forty minutes later, Sarah's head was spinning. Yet she knew exactly what she was going to do.

At lunchtime, Joshua and Melody made their way along the path back to the cabin.

'How was today's session?' Sarah hugged her daughter.

'Good,' the whispered answer.

'She's done brilliantly well, in her time here,' Joshua said. 'There's still a way to go, obviously, and to that end I can recommend a few therapists in Sydney who aren't too shabby. I would suggest you continue with them to capitalise on the progress we've made here. Guide Melody to her best recovery.'

'Thank you. For everything you've done for her, for us.'

Melody turned to him. 'Thank you,' she whispered and then wheeled inside.

'It's been my absolute pleasure.' Joshua smiled at Sarah. 'I hope maybe you'll keep in touch.' He cleared his throat. 'Keep me posted on Melody's progress.'

'Actually . . .' A smile spread across Sarah's face. 'I'd like to discuss something with you.'

Epilogue

January 2019

'Hurry up, minim. We're going to be late,' Sarah called down the hall, which was still lined with unpacked boxes. She knew they hadn't got rid of enough of their junk and bits and bobs when Rosalie had sold the house in Sydney. Their new home in Redgum River was nowhere near as big, and three months after moving in they were still trying to find places for everything. The two-bedroom house was a single-storey bungalow with spacious open-plan living spaces, but they would still have to cull their things to fit into it comfortably. The biggest drawcard of the property was the second cottage at the end of the large garden, just perfect for Granny Rose.

'Coming, Mama,' Melody called back, a sound as sweet as any song. There was still a long way to go, but Melody was in group sessions with Katie, thriving at the local school and had even joined the school band. Her instrument of choice – the cello. Sarah knew it was only a matter of time before her daughter was fully vocal and for that she couldn't wait. Melody hadn't yet sung again, but Sarah was full of unchecked hope that she would.

The last six months had passed in a blur. After leaving the retreat, Melody had continued with therapy in Sydney and in the July school holidays Rosalie had paid for all of them to visit Pierre in France. When they'd returned, Rosalie had put her house on the market and by the beginning of October they had moved to Redgum River. Sarah was relieved things had finally settled into some sort of routine and rhythm. Not that today was going to be anything routine.

'Let's go.' Sarah ushered Melody out of the door and to their car, where Granny Rose was ready for them.

'Big day, ladies.' Rosalie slipped into the passenger seat. 'Best not keep anyone waiting.'

They pulled up at the retreat and parked in Sarah's reserved spot. There in the car park, Ryan and Herman stood beside Gertie, waiting for their arrival.

Sarah hugged Ryan and Melody gave Herman a high five. Inside, Joshua and Albert would be with the choir, and Sarah was looking forward to the performance. But first, she had to admire Gertie's makeover.

'This looks amazing!' Sarah squeezed Ryan tightly. 'You've done an incredible job.'

Ryan had converted the van himself, pouring all of his creative juices into the project since their stay at the retreat. Gertie's once patchy hodgepodge of grey, yellow and blue had been derusted, buffed, polished and painted over in sage and tan. The van glistened under the morning sun, in perfect harmony with her bush surroundings. Her new skin was overlaid with hand-painted pictures of memorabilia from past eras – a nineteenth-century typewriter, an eighteenth-century bicycle, aerograms from the First World War, a 1940s Kodak camera – so many different images of relics that wrapped right the way around Gertie.

Ryan had engineered the sides of the van to open like wings, revealing, inside, shelves and pull-out display panels full of artefacts from Herman's former building at the Rocks, which he had sold a few months before; it was now being refurbished as a fancy new café.

'This is where we'll display the general museum items that show the breadth of our collections at Forgotten Pasts.' Herman stood at the back of the van, pointing to a glass-fronted cabinet. 'Ryan suggested it would be a good way to attract patrons. He says it's our version of a mobile Instagram feed, though I still say social media is the downfall of society,' Herman grumbled.

'But I'll drag him into the twenty-first century,' Ryan laughed. 'With every tour,' he continued, 'we'll rent a community space for the "one-week-only" special exhibit, which we can transport in these specially crafted hidden storage areas.' He tapped the floor of the van with his heel.

A crowd of people had gathered behind a blue velvet rope that had been set up at the entrance to the Redgum River Retreat car park, and with a dramatic swish of his hand Herman threw the rope aside and officially opened the Forgotten Pasts Travelling Museum.

Ryan popped the cork of a champagne bottle and started pouring drinks for the very first patrons. The Redgum River locals had turned out in droves, excited to take in the first exhibition, especially as it featured their own history so heavily. From the open doors of the Stave, a medley of 1940s music spilled out over the clearing – Berlin, Porter, Crosby – aiding the illusion they had stepped back in time.

People mingled around the van and admired the nostalgic pieces before wandering over to the Stave, where Ryan and Herman had spent the night setting up the main exhibit, titled 'Snapshots'.

Sarah, Melody and Rosalie moved around inside the Stave, where the walls of the foyer were adorned with hundreds of Rosalie's articles and photos – a collection that spanned fifty years, and all seven continents. Photos from the Korean and Vietnam wars, from

Woodstock, copies of her articles in *Life* magazine covering Queen Elizabeth II's coronation, Martin Luther King's speech, the 1964 Olympics, Roe *v.* Wade marches, right through to her final professional photos of the fall of the Berlin Wall. And in pride of place, in the middle of the room, were Rosalie's images for the Snapshots From Home League.

The original album was in a cabinet behind glass. But copies of the photos, which had been blown up into large prints, hung in frames from the ceiling. Next to each print were replicas of the request cards. Some of Edward's letters were also on show, and photos of Edward and Albert. Over the past few months Sarah had been recording Rosalie's recollections of the people and places in the Snapshots photos, stories of Penelope, Millie and Dot, and Ralphy's dog, and she'd then had them engraved in black ink onto thin Perspex blocks. These hung by invisible wire from the ceiling between the enlarged photos.

'Are you okay, Granny Rose?' Sarah touched Rosalie's arm. Beside her, Rosalie was standing very quiet, her eyes roaming the room. She shook her head. 'This is . . . I can't . . . For the first time in my life I have no words, Sarah.' She didn't even try to hide the tears falling down her cheeks. 'It is a wonderful tribute to Edward and Albert. To all the men and families of the river of that time.'

'And to *you*,' Sarah said.

Rosalie cleared her throat and in the performance space, the Vital Voices choir moved into position.

'I'd better take my place.' Rosalie walked forward, flicking the choir's signature teal scarf over her shoulders. She sat next to Albert, who was sitting tall in front of the piano. Melody joined them and placed herself beside Katie, ready to help her conduct.

'This is amazing!' Joshua stepped up beside Sarah, his hand brushing hers.

'Thank you for letting us use the space.' She smiled at him.

'Boss's orders.' He leaned into her, bumping her gently with his shoulder.

'I hear she's a bit of a tyrant, your new boss,' Sarah smiled.

'She's the worst. But she is paying for more extensions, and has great plans for this place.' He turned to face her. 'We're so glad to have you on board, *boss*.' His smile was full of warmth.

'None of this boss stuff. I'm just a silent partner.'

'Okay, silent partner. Now that you've settled into life here in Redgum River, do you think maybe it would be okay if I asked you out for dinner?'

Sarah raised her eyebrows. 'As in on a date?'

Joshua nodded and gave her a thumbs up.

'How can I resist, Mr Cool?' She laughed. 'But for now, should we go enjoy the music?'

'We should.' He put his hand on the small of her back and they made their way towards the choir.

Melody beckoned Sarah over and pointed to her cello leaning up against the wall behind her. Sarah nodded and set up at the edge of the group, bow in hand, the neck of the cello resting on her shoulder. Melody counted her in, her beaming smile lighting up the whole room.

As Sarah drew her bow across the strings, she knew they were all where they belonged.

Acknowledgements

Writing during the pandemic certainly had its challenges and if it weren't for the daily Zoom writing sprints (and counselling sessions) with the wonderful Claudine Tinellis every morning, and Tabitha Bird in the afternoons, *The Redgum River Retreat* might never have got written. Thank you both for being there for me and spurring me on. Simply, your presence is inspirational.

Thank you, Sarah Mercer, for shedding light on selective mutism, the various forms and nuances of PTSD, and helping me craft Melody's and Albert's journeys. Scott Greenaway, thank you for all your insight into music therapy and how it could be used to help with Melody's selective mutism – your information was vital to bringing the story together. And thank you to Kaneana May, who answered my call on Facebook and put me in touch with Scott. Understanding in each of these areas of mental health is always evolving and new treatment methods are always emerging, so any errors or artistic licence in portraying Melody's and Albert's conditions are entirely my own.

Speaking of artistic licence, while researching how long mail took during the Second World War, I found it could be anywhere from two weeks to more than two months, depending on many variables, so I often went with the shorter timeframe in the story, even if, strictly speaking, this may not have always happened. A book which really helped me bring Edward's pages to life was *Tarakan: An Australian Tragedy* by Peter Stanley. Again, any errors or artistic licence portraying Edward's time at war are entirely my own.

Seok Walker, thank you for straightening out my Chinese proverbs. Thank you Maya Linnell for always answering my random questions, usually about plants and gardens. You are one of the most generous writers in our community.

Penelope Janu, you have no idea how much your kindness and understanding has meant to me this last year when certain areas of my life went belly up, and I thank you from the bottom of my heart. I hope you are okay with me naming a character after you to show my gratitude!

To the wonderful ladies of the Not So Solitary Scribes Facebook group, thank you for the support, for being sounding boards, for the information sharing, for the friendship and camaraderie; and to those of you who join in our Scribblers Ink Zoom sessions, thank you for being a joyful and generous constant in my writing life.

Mishell Currie, as always, deserves a special mention, not just for plying me with chocolatey care packages from Bowral Sweets & Treats when deadlines are looming, but also for being the fastest reader in the west (west of me, anyway), often turning around my awful drafts with superhuman speed and thoughtful, insightful feedback. Thank you also Jennifer Johnson for casting your eagle eye over the proof pages.

Cassie Hamer, Anna Loder, Michelle Parsons, Rosemary Puddy and Claudine Tinellis, thank you for being the best posse a woman could ask for! We write, we read, we create festivals, we support each other like nothing else – you ladies are the true embodiment of the beauty of female friendship, and what you can achieve when you surround yourself with the right people.

I am blessed to work with the most amazing team at Penguin Random House – Ali Watts, my publisher extraordinaire; Catherine Hill, my super editor; Lily Crozier, my fabulous publicist; Tanaya Lowden, marketing guru; and Laura Thomas, my amazing cover designer – thank you for shaping, cajoling and polishing my manuscript (and me) and helping me get my stories out into the world. I cannot believe how lucky I am to work with you all!

As always to my family, the biggest thank you for your ongoing support and love. Especially to my daughter, Emily, who was my music consultant on this novel, as I am tone deaf with very little knowledge of anything musical. You are my motivation every day; you keep me on my toes; your bravery in the face of life's challenges is my inspiration. Being your mum is the best gig in the world, with all its ups and downs, heartaches and joys. This one is for you, baby girl.

And finally, to the booksellers, bookstagrammers, reviewers, podcasters and librarians who support the Australian writing community and help get our books into the hands of readers – thank you. And to my readers – without you, the voices inside my head would stay there and not end up on the page; without you authors don't exist. Thank you for embracing my stories.

Book Club Questions

1. The author has described *The Redgum River Retreat* as her love letter to motherhood. How is motherhood explored in the novel? How does this resemble your own experience, either as a mother, or as a child?

2. Sarah carries a lot of guilt over the accident. Do you think she has come to terms with this by the end of the novel? What evidence is there that she has/hasn't?

3. Were you aware of the 'Snapshots From Home League' before reading this novel? If you were sent off to a foreign place, what type of photo would you request?

4. Music is a strong thread running through the novel. Have you ever felt healed or comforted by music and why do you think that is?

5. Ryan makes the seemingly rash decision to throw away his very successful career. Do you think he did the right thing? Have you ever wanted to start over like this?

6. Do you think Henry was driven by love, or duty, or some other force?

7. Was Edward justified in keeping the truth from Rosalie and Albert? Have you ever had to keep something significant from someone, and if so why did you choose to do so?

8. Edward says to Sarah, 'Sometimes when we go looking for the truth, what we find isn't what we expect. What we find is pain.' Were Sarah and Rosalie better off knowing the truth?

9. How do you think Rosalie's life would have been different if she and Albert had remained a couple?

10. Rosalie says, 'How could you make peace with a past whose pieces could never be put back together?' Do you think by the end of the novel she has made peace with her past? How did she? Or why couldn't she?

11. Sandie Docker is known for her bittersweet endings. How is *The Redgum River Retreat* like her other novels in this regard? Do you like a bittersweet ending, or do you prefer your endings tied up in a neat pink bow?